The GODS OF AMYRANTHA

Tor Books by Jennifer Fallon

THE HYTHRUN CHRONICLES

THE DEMON CHILD TRILOGY
Medalon (Book One)
Treason Keep (Book Two)
Harshini (Book Three)

THE WOLFBLADE TRILOGY
Wolfblade (Book One)
Warrior (Book Two)
Warlord (Book Three)

THE TIDE LORDS

The Immortal Prince (Book One)
The Gods of Amyrantha (Book Two)

The GODS OF AMYRANTHA

The Tide Lords:
Book Two

JENNIFER FALLON

TOR®

A Tom Doherty Associates Book

New York

This is a work of fiction. All of the characters, organizations, and events portrayed in this novel are either products of the author's imagination or are used fictitiously.

THE GODS OF AMYRANTHA

Originally published in 2007 by Voyager, an imprint of HarperCollins*Publishers*, Australia.

Maps by Russell Kirkpatrick

A Tor Book
Published by Tom Doherty Associates, LLC
175 Fifth Avenue
New York, NY 10010

www.tor-forge.com

Tor® is a registered trademark of Tom Doherty Associates, LLC.

Library of Congress Cataloging-in-Publication Data

Fallon, Jennifer.
  The gods of Amyrantha / Jennifer Fallon.—1st U.S. ed.
      p.   cm.
  "A Tom Doherty Associates book."
  ISBN-13: 978-0-7653-1683-7
  ISBN-10: 0-7653-1683-8
  I. Title.

  PR9619.4.F35 G63 2009
  823'.92—dc22

                                                      2009001509

First U.S. Edition: July 2009

Printed in the United States of America

0 9 8 7 6 5 4 3 2 1

For Susie, Edwina, Ashley, John and
all the wonderful people at Oscars—best restaurant in the galaxy

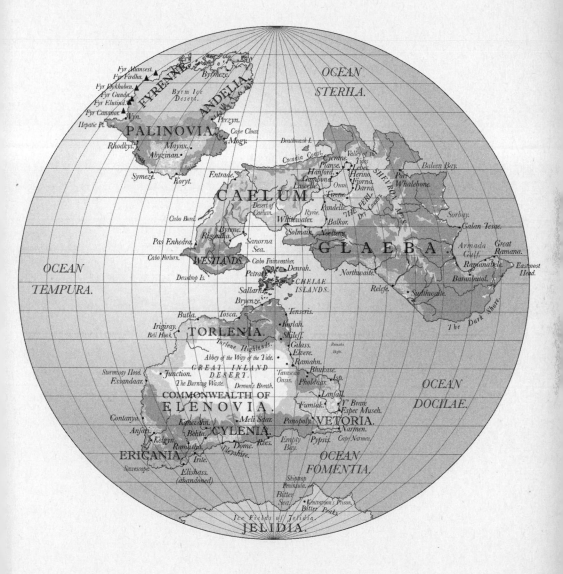

Fyr Mumsest.
Fyr Vadha.
Fyr Dykhoben.
Fyr Gunda.
Fyr Eluind.
Fyr Canghor.
Hepatic Pt.

FYRENNE
ANDELIA
Byrmeze.
Byrm Ice
Desert.
Perzyn.
Cape Cloax.
Mogy.

Wyn.

PALINOVIA

Rhodkyl.
Maynx.
Abyzinan.

Symeze.
Koryt.
Entrade.

OCEAN
STERHA.

Denthmask I.

Cycadia Coast.
Cyerane.
Planse.
Hebet.
Hanford.
Gambona.
Lasette.
Oran.
Valley of the
Tides.
Herrno.
Darra.
Port
Whalebone.
Baleen Bay.

Tirene.

SHEVRON MTS.

CAELUM
Desert of
Caelum.
Ryrie.
Randello.
Whitewater.
Balkor.

THE PERI

Dry Canyon

Sorbuy.
Galan Tesae.

Crbo Bora.
Byrne.
Rigontha.
Sanorna
Sea.
Solmain.
Noeltens.

GLAEBA.

Armada
Gulf.
Great
Ramana.

Pas Enhedra.
Raynanalele.
Eastmost
Head.

Cabo Forlorn.
WESTLANDS.
Cabo Fairweather.
Denrah.
Northwaite.
Barunhuiol.

OCEAN
Devdrop Is.
Petra.
CHELAE
ISLANDS.
Relefe.
Sulthwaite.

TEMPURA.
Sallarn.
Bryenze.

The Dark Shore.

Butta.
Tosca.
Tenseris.

Irigiray.
Bell Husk.
TORLENIA.
Kaylah.
Shileff.
Gilass.
Elvere.
Ramahn.
Ramaha
Bight.

Torlene Highlands.
Abbey of the Way of the Tide.

Stormway Head.
Essandaar.
Junction.
GREAT INLAND
DESERT.
Bhukase.
Ist.
OCEAN

The Burning Waste.
Demon's Breath.
Tanascan
Oasis.
Pholdaar.
DOCILAE.

COMMONWEALTH OF
ELENOVIA
Lansall.
Fumiak.
Y' Brave
Espec Museh.

Contanya.
Meli Sdar.
Panopoly.
VETORIA.
Narmen.

Anfari.
Kanevdin.
Belitu.
CYLENIA.
Pypsis.
Cape Narmen.

Kelgyn.
Rees.
Empty
Bay.

Ramusha.
Dome.
Ilevshire.
OCEAN

ERICANIA
Irite.
FOMENTIA.

Siavescape.
Elishass.
(abandoned)
Shiphap
Peninsula.

Bitter
Sea.
Kentrazyon's Prison.
Bitter Peaks.

Ice Fields of Jelidia.

JELIDIA.

The
GODS OF
AMYRANTHA

LOW TIDE

PROLOGUE

Three thousand years ago. Prior to the Fourth Cataclysm . . .

The hardest thing about torturing someone, Balen decided, was trying not to empathise with your victim's pain. You had to distance yourself from it. Detach that part of you which was human and make sure it stayed detached.

Most of all, you had to remind yourself the creature you were torturing wasn't really human.

The latter wasn't easy. Lyna looked human. With her long dark hair and her soulful dark eyes, she looked more like Balen's married daughter than a monster.

Balen closed his eyes for a moment, trying to shut out her screaming. *I'm doing this because I have to,* he reminded himself, tossing the severed hand on the forge's glowing coals. *There must be a way to kill these creatures.*

The disembodied hand browned and burned, the leaking blood hissing and spitting. It smelt horribly reminiscent of last night's roast.

It's not logical to think something cannot die.

Logical or not, they'd had no luck killing their captive immortal so far.

Perhaps they'd used up all their luck just finding her. But with the Tide on the rise, and the immortals with it, they were much less careful, these days, about hiding their identities. Balen and his compatriots would never have had a chance of capturing a true Tide Lord. Lyna, fortunately, was one of the lesser immortals. She didn't have the power to do the sort of damage someone like Cayal or Pellys or Tryan could do. She could touch the Tide, sure enough—all the immortals could—but she didn't seem to be able to do much with it.

That was fortunate. If she'd been a Tide Lord . . . if the Tide had peaked . . . well, given what they'd done to her these past few weeks, if she'd been able to wreak any sort of vengeance on them, they'd all be dead.

And probably everyone within a hundred-mile radius, as well.

Bracing himself, Balen turned to look at her. Naked and filthy, Lyna lay on the floor of her cell, curled into a foetal position, weeping with the pain of her amputation. Despite the burns, the stab wounds, even the hand he'd just amputated to see if she would bleed to death, the rest of her body was whole and unmarked. Everything he'd done to her had healed, and the more traumatic the injury, the faster she seemed to recover from it.

Tides, what's it going to take?

Perhaps these unnatural creatures truly *were* immortal. Perhaps there *was* no end for them. Ever. Perhaps, some unimaginable time in the future when the universe grew cold, they would still be here, alone and alive, with nothing but their endless existence to sustain them . . .

It's not possible, Balen assured himself. *Besides, until we reach the end of time, how will we* know *if they can survive that long?*

"Has she recovered again?"

Balen looked up to find his son standing at the entrance to the smithy. The boy was morbidly fascinated by what his father was doing. A little *too* fascinated, perhaps. He feared the young man didn't see the monster lying in the cage regrowing a hand his father had just hacked off, he only saw the tormented young woman. At seventeen, Minark was too young to appreciate the danger immortality presented to the mortals of this world.

"It would appear so."

"Can I see her?"

Balen frowned. "Why?"

"I . . . I just can't believe she's not hurt."

Balen glanced over his shoulder at the pathetic, weeping young woman. He didn't know how old she was exactly—five thousand . . . ten thousand years old? She looked little more than twenty-five, more than young enough for an impressionable youth to find her appealing. Already the bleeding had stopped and there was new bone and flesh taking shape. "She's hurting, sure enough, Minark. But she just keeps healing up."

"Can I see . . . ?"

"No," he said, concerned Minark was taking far too much interest in the tortured immortal's plight. The last thing he needed was the lad sneaking back here in the dead of night to offer her sympathy. Or worse. Lyna had been a whore, after all, before she was made immortal. She'd not hesitate to use her wiles on someone as wide-eyed and credulous as his son. "What are you doing here, anyway, boy? I thought I told you to stay away from this place."

Minark ventured a few steps further into the smithy, straining to see past his father. "Vorak sent me."

Balen took a step sideways to block his son's view of the naked young woman with her regrowing hand. "What does he want, Minark?"

"He's just got back from the markets in L'bekken. He said there was someone asking around in the village. About her," he added, pointing to the immortal.

"Did he say who it was?"

Minark shook his head. "Just that he was asking. And he was heading this way when he left."

Balen cursed silently. *Surely they hadn't come for her yet?* And if they had, was it one of the other lesser immortals, which would be bad enough? Or was it one of the Tide Lords themselves? He shuddered at the thought. If someone like Cayal or Tryan or Kentravyon discovered Lyna caged and tortured like this, everyone in this village and the neighbouring village of L'bekken would, in all probability, soon be dead.

"This man was a stranger, yes?"

"That's what I said, wasn't it?" Minark leaned a little to the left so he could catch sight of the immortal. "Did you try cutting her into smaller pieces? Vorak thought that if you fed the meat to the dogs . . ."

"She heals too quickly," he said, wishing Vorak would stop discussing his wild theories with Minark. "And the faster you cut, the faster she heals. Did Vorak think this stranger was an immortal?"

Minark shrugged. "He didn't say. Just to tell you someone was asking about Lyna."

Balen glanced over his shoulder at his prisoner, wondering if he should just let her go. She'd been blindfolded when she was overpowered in the streets of L'bekken and brought here in chains. If they took her far away from their village before they dumped her, it was unlikely she would know how to find this place again.

But how often did one get a chance like this? How often did one capture an immortal? How often had they been able to put their theories on how to put an end to them to the test?

The opportunity against the risk . . . that was Balen's problem.

"I warned you," the young woman said, pushing herself up on her elbows.

He looked over his shoulder. Lyna's face was tear-streaked and filthy. On hearing the news someone was asking after her, she rallied her strength. A fresh stump had already formed on the end of her arm, even though it had only been minutes since he'd cut off her hand. "You'll die for what you've done to me, you pathetic mortal *pig*."

"It was probably just one of your regular customers," Balen said, hoping he sounded unafraid. "Good whores have repeat customers, I'm told, and I hear you were a *very* good whore."

She smiled, which Balen found disturbing. Three days ago, he'd beaten her so badly, most of her teeth had broken. Yet her smile now was white and even, mocking him with its unnatural perfection.

"My brothers will level this place," she warned, pushing herself to her feet. "They will take apart your pitiful village, kill you, your son, your wife, your grandchildren and everyone else in this valley."

"They have to find you first, you immortal whore!" Minark retorted gamely.

Lyna smiled through the pain of her regenerating hand. "*Find* me? Tides, boy, that's the easy part."

"What do you mean?"

"I mean we can sense each other on the Tide, you fool. If there's another immortal around, he'll feel my presence and there's nothing you can do to stop him finding me, short of killing me. But you've tried that, haven't you? I'll bet you're sorry now, that none of your brilliant little plans worked."

Balen had no reason to doubt her. If anything, he began to get nervous. Her growing defiance was at such odds with the lack of resistance she'd shown thus far, he had to wonder at the cause of it.

Was her confidence brought on by the news that one of her immortal brethren was nearby?

We can sense each other on the Tide, she'd said, which meant if another immortal could feel her presence, then she would be able to . . . *Tides*!

"Get to the house, now!" he ordered Minark. "Tell your mother and your sister to take only what they can carry. We must flee. *Now!*"

"Flee?" Minark asked in confusion. "Why must we flee? Vorak said the stranger asked about her and then moved on. Nobody told him anything."

"Nobody had to, Minark," Balen said, shoving him toward the entrance to the smithy. "Didn't you hear what she said? They can sense each other on the Tide. He'll know she's here. Which means he's probably on his way. And if he finds us with her . . ."

"But it might only be one of the lesser immortals, like Taryx or Rance . . ."

"Are you willing to risk your mother's life on that, son?"

The boy hesitated for a moment longer, staring at the immortal woman, and then he turned and fled. Balen grabbed one of the hammers from his forge, shoved it into his belt in case he needed a weapon, and then turned to face Lyna. She was standing at the bars of the cage they'd fashioned to contain her. Already, short stubby fingers were protruding from the stump. Although still in pain, he guessed she was improving by the minute, her recovery accelerated, no doubt, by the sense that there was another of her kind nearby.

"It wasn't anything personal," he said, as if an explanation or an apology was going to make the slightest difference at this point.

She glared at him and held up her mangled wrist. "Trust me, Balen. You *made* it personal."

He shook his head, wondering what he hoped to achieve by lingering here, trying to explain himself. He had tortured this creature relentlessly for weeks. It was too late now to ask for forgiveness. "You must tell them . . . I am the one at fault here. Not my family."

"I'm sure that will be a great comfort to them as they're dying."

Balen stared at her, only now, perhaps, realising the enormity of what he'd done. "Is there no chance of mercy?"

Lyna studied him for a moment and then nodded. "Despite what you think, we're not monsters, Balen. You want mercy for you and your family?" The immortal smiled coldly, showing her perfect teeth. "Then I shall see you get it."

"Really?"

"*Really*," she said. "It will be my pleasure, in fact when my friends arrive to free me, to recommend they show you all the *mercy* you showed me."

"*If* your friends arrive," he replied gamely.

"Oh, I think you can be sure they will," a deep voice behind him announced.

Startled, Balen turned to discover a stranger standing in the entrance to the forge. He was a big man, wearing leather armour, a dark crimson cloak caught up in a jewelled brooch on his right shoulder.

"Kentravyon!" Lyna called as soon as she saw him, although Balen needed no introduction.

He backed up against the forge. There was no hope he could defeat an immortal, certainly not a Tide Lord as powerful as Kentravyon, but he might be able to distract him long enough for the others to get away.

"You have hurt my friend," the immortal said, walking toward him.

"It was . . . We only meant . . ."

"I know what you meant to do," Kentravyon said. He didn't sound angry. He sounded calm. Almost disinterested. "You were trying to find a way to kill us, weren't you?"

Balen nodded as he felt the warm stone of the forge against his back. It was too late to run now. He had nowhere else to go.

"It must be hard for you to deal with the notion of immortality," the Tide Lord said as he moved closer. "I can appreciate that."

His tone was far more reasonable than Balen might have expected. He allowed a glimmer of hope to flicker in his soul. Perhaps the rumours he'd heard about Kentravyon were just that. Rumours . . . nothing else . . .

The Tide Lord stopped before him. He smiled, and reached up with both hands. Balen leaned back from him, but the immortal didn't try to strike him. He took Balen's face between his hands with a gentleness that shocked him, smiling beatifically.

"Poor, poor mortals," he whispered softly, seductively. "You so badly want what we have, don't you?"

Balen couldn't answer. Kentravyon's gloved hand caressed his face. The world seemed to retreat. Even Lyna's whimpering faded into the background . . .

Kentravyon leaned forward and kissed him on the mouth and then he pulled back and smiled at Balen. "I forgive you."

Balen sagged with relief. "My lord . . ."

"And because I forgive you, I will save you from witnessing what I'm going to do to your family. And your village. And anybody else who thinks they can torment their gods."

It was the look deep in the immortal's eyes as much as his words that panicked Balen. There was forgiveness, sure enough, but it was for-giveness without reason. Balen struggled to break free, but the Tide Lord held him fast, moving his hands until his thumbs pressed against his eyelids.

Slowly, Kentravyon pushed down against Balen's eyes, until the pres-sure was unbearable. Balen heard someone screaming and realised it was his own voice. The pressure grew worse until he could stand it no more. The left eye collapsed a moment after the right, blood streaming from his eye sockets, his screams tasting salty as the blood mixed with his tears.

Kentravyon let him go and he collapsed to the floor, sobbing not only for his own torment, but the pain of impending death.

This was just a precursor, he knew. He did not have much longer to live.

In the distance he heard a lock rattle and realised Kentravyon must have released Lyna from her cage. A moment later a foot slammed into his ribs. He grunted with the force of it, rolling onto his side to avoid a second blow. The world remained black, his ruined eyes nothing more than a gelatinous goo leaking out of his bloody eye sockets.

"Bastard!"

"Now, now, Lyna . . . that wasn't very nice." Kentravyon's voice was still calm . . . soothing even . . .

"I'm going to kill the sadistic little prick."

"No, my dear, you're not."

"He cut off my hand!"

"And you *will* be avenged," the Tide Lord promised. "But your tor-menter must *know* you are being avenged, my dear, or he cannot achieve redemption."

"How's he going to know anything?" she demanded of her saviour impatiently. "You put out his eyes."

"But he can still hear us," Kentravyon said.

Balen whimpered in fear, but not for himself.

Tides, please let my family be safely away from here . . .

The Tide ignored his plea. His family were still in the house, he soon discovered; the villagers asleep in their homes, unaware of the danger he had brought down upon them in his arrogance.

He couldn't see them, of course.

But as he lay by the forge, feeling it grow cold, he discovered Kentravyon was right.

He could—and did—hear their screams as they died.

PART I

'Twixt tide and tide's returning
Great store of newly dead,—
The bones of those that faced us,
And the hearts of those that fled.
                    —"White Horses,"
            RUDYARD KIPLING (1865–1936)

Chapter 1

Only someone looking very closely would have noticed the chameleon Crasii standing against the elaborately detailed mural. The stylised hunting scene lined the west side of the Ladies Walking Room and ran the length of the vast Caelum Royal Palace's third floor. The room was a long narrow promenade, built to afford the ladies of the court a place to exercise during the long Caelish winters, when the palace was snowbound for months at a time. Fortunately it was summer now; otherwise Tiji would have risked hypothermia standing naked as she was, blending in with the mural so she could listen in on the conversations of those who chose this favourite concourse to discuss affairs of the court.

Tiji resisted the urge to scratch an itch on the side of her nose, falling into the unnatural stillness unique to her kind as the door opened at the end of the hall. As she'd hoped, the Queen of Caelum's guests had arrived. The Grand Duchess of Torfail and her children let themselves into the room, checked the door was firmly closed and then walked further along the hall until they were closer to where Tiji was, blending with the wall so completely she had ceased to exist as a separate entity.

"The queen has given us an answer," the grand duchess announced, as they approached.

"And?" her daughter prompted. Although she was dressed in a hooped gown similar to her mother's, made from heavily brocaded silk, even Tiji considered the daughter plain. She had pale eyes and dark hair braided in the elaborate fashion currently in favour in Caelum. Being completely hairless herself, Tiji often wondered how humans coped with all that grooming and washing and tying it out of the way every day, certain even a small amount of hair would have driven her mad.

"And she said yes," the duchess announced. She glanced at her son and smiled. "Looks like you're getting married, dear."

The young man was unfairly pretty, dark haired and perfectly formed, with eyes the colour of twilight framed by long dark lashes. He seemed to be about twenty or so, his beauty marred, however, by the scowl he wore. "Tides! Do I have to?"

"It's the quickest way to secure the throne." His mother shrugged.

"She's a wretched *child*, mother."

"That wretched child becomes queen as soon as she marries," his sister reminded him. "That makes you king if you're her husband, you know." She added the last bit, no doubt, to aggravate her sibling.

The young man seemed quite annoyed. "They'll expect me to sleep with her."

As they talked, the group neared Tiji. The sister smiled nastily. "Surely you're not objecting on *moral* grounds, Try?"

This was the closest Tiji had been able to get to the grand duchess and her family in the month since she'd been sent to infiltrate the Caelum Palace. It was rumours of their arrival that had brought Tiji to Caelum in the first place. Declan Hawkes had learned that after Glaeba's potentially disastrous refusal to unite their crown prince with Princess Nyah, the heir to the Caelish throne, another contender had appeared on the scene. Declan had wanted to know who it was, so Tiji was dispatched from Herino and sent north to discover the truth behind this new offer.

The truth was before her now. Tiji was glad of it, too. Caelum was a cold, miserable place and when she was using her chameleonic abilities, she couldn't wear clothes to protect her body from the elements. The sooner she learned what this lot of grasping foreigners were up to, the sooner she could head home.

"I'm objecting on the grounds that the Tide is on the turn and I don't see why we need to keep up this ridiculous charade."

Almost at the same time the young man spoke, Tiji's skin began to prickle. A feeling akin to nausea washed over her, threatening her concentration, and with it her camouflage. The trio drew closer, the danger with them. The sensation was sickening, and familiar, although she was a child when she'd felt it last. That was back in Senestra, before she'd met Declan Hawkes.

This feeling was the reason she *worked* for Declan Hawkes.

Suzerain.

That this trio were not who they claimed was no surprise to Tiji. When Declan heard the Grand Duchess of Torfail had made an offer for her son to wed Princess Nyah, he'd been instantly suspicious, certain there was no such place as Torfail—in Caelum or anywhere else on Amyrantha—let alone a grand duchy attached to it. But Declan had been expecting at best some ambitious grifters, at worst agents of a neighbouring country trying to mess with the Caelish succession by providing a contender of their own.

He wouldn't be expecting three immortals seeking to take the throne of Glaeba's closest neighbour, any more than Tiji was.

Quashing the fear and nausea all Scards felt in the presence of the immortals, Tiji forced herself to concentrate.

"It's easier this way," the older woman was saying. "And faster. You marry the child, she takes the throne, you become king, then I can call the others back, and we're set for the next three hundred years. Why go to the effort of trying to achieve the same thing by force, when the only work you have to do is smile nicely and not terrify the little brat until after the wedding?"

"It's humiliating," her son complained. "I command the Tide, for pity's sake. I shouldn't have to work for anything."

"One whisper of the Tide returning and all of a sudden ordinary work is humiliating?" The plain young woman laughed. "Tides, Tryan, a century ago you were hiding out in Parve, pretending to be a cobbler."

Tryan? Tides, it's the Empress of the Five Realms!

Tiji forced her racing pulse to slow, afraid if she let her dread get the better of her, she'd let her camouflage drop, a mistake that might result in her instant annihilation. She had to remain a part of the wall for as long as this took. It was critical she survive to take this news back to Glaeba.

"I've no time for your bickering," Syrolee snapped, before Tryan could respond. "You'll both do what you have to, and that's an end to it. Have either of you had word from your brothers?"

Elyssa nodded, but she was smirking at Tryan. "A messenger arrived this morning while you and the queen were negotiating. Krydence has heard a rumour that Cayal might be in Glaeba."

Tryan rolled his eyes in disgust. "Tides, that's all we need."

"It's just a rumour, Tryan."

The young man eyed his sister speculatively. "One you'd like confirmed, I don't doubt."

"What's that supposed to mean?" Elyssa demanded.

"As if you didn't know."

"Tryan, leave your sister alone. Has there been no word from Rance or Engarhod?"

"Last I heard Rance was so far south he was almost in Jelidia," Tryan reminded them. "He could be anywhere. As for Engarhod, he's more likely to contact you than either one of us."

Syrolee nodded in agreement. "As soon as he gets word the wedding is going ahead, I'm sure he'll be here."

"But I'll be king," Tryan pointed out.

Syrolee's eyes narrowed. "What do you mean?"

"I mean, mother dear, I'll be King of Caelum. Not you. And certainly not Engarhod. If I have to take this child to my bed to stake a claim on this wretched throne, I'm not giving it away. I'll have earned the damn thing and you're not bringing Engarhod here and unseating me just because you like being empress."

Syrolee scowled at her son for a moment and then forced a smile. "Let's take this throne first, dearest, before we start arguing about who's going to sit on it. You both know what you have to do. I expect you to do it."

With that, the Empress of the Five Realms turned on her heel and strode the long length of the Ladies Walking Room, slamming the door behind her.

Tiji held her breath, waiting for the others to follow, but it seemed the siblings weren't done squabbling yet.

"Look on the bright side, Try," Elyssa suggested. "Nyah's only ten years old. She's too young to notice what a lousy lover you are."

"At least I've *got* a lover."

Elyssa's eyes narrowed. "Don't you dare . . ."

"Or you'll what?" Tryan asked. When Elyssa didn't seem to have an answer, he smiled. "Maybe Cayal *is* in Glaeba, Lyss. Maybe he'll finally come looking for you. I mean . . . Tides, it's been how long since you saw him last? He must have screwed everything else that walks on Amyrantha, by now. I'm sure he'll get around to you eventually."

The sharp crack of Elyssa's hand striking her brother's face almost startled Tiji into revealing herself.

"Bastard."

Her brother smiled, sending a chill down Tiji's spine. Such malice, such inhuman malevolence, was more than she'd bargained for. Tryan the Devil, the Tarot called him. Tiji began to understand why. She felt her camouflage slipping, but forced it under control. With their attention fixed on each other, neither Tryan nor Elyssa seemed to notice.

"Bastard I may be, Elyssa, but soon I'll be king. And this time, I'm not planning to share it with anyone."

"Syrolee might have something to say about that."

"Let her say whatever she wants. Let her find somewhere else to play Empress of the Five Realms, if it comes to it. I'm a Tide Lord. I'm fed up with being a minion."

"Maybe that's all you're good for, Tryan."

"We'll find out soon enough, Elyssa."

His sister didn't seem to have an answer to that. Tossing her head, Elyssa swept up her skirts and headed for the door. Tiji closed her eyes in relief, expecting Tryan to follow, but the booted footsteps she heard didn't dwindle into the distance.

They seemed to be getting closer . . .

A strong hand closed around her throat before she had time to register what that meant. Tiji's eyes flew open. Her camouflage vanished in her fright, leaving her naked and vulnerable, dressed in nothing but her silver-scaled skin. She couldn't breathe. Tryan's face was only inches away, his eyes boring into hers.

"What are you doing here, you Crasii scum?"

"To serve you is the reason I breathe, my lord," Tiji gasped. Scard she may be, but she knew the forms. If she remained a quivering mass of terror—which required no acting on her part at all—he would have no reason to suspect she was anything but just another Crasii, probably a spy set on the Grand Duchess of Torfail by the Queen of Caelum.

"Why were you spying on us?"

Tiji didn't answer. All her breath had been spent swearing allegiance to him.

It seemed Tryan wasn't interested in an explanation anyway. He shoved her away as he let her go, turning his back on her. "It doesn't matter why. You will repeat nothing of what you heard today."

"To serve you is the reason I breathe," she managed to wheeze, as she fell.

Heading for the door, Tryan didn't even acknowledge her reply.

But then, why would he? The Crasii were slaves, bred with unquestioning obedience to the orders of their masters. Tryan had no reason to doubt her, believing, as did all the Tide Lords, that the reptilian Crasii had been purged of any rebellious tendencies several thousand years ago. He had no reason to assume every word he and his conspirators uttered would not remain secret because the Crasii were incapable of doing anything else.

Unless the Crasii was a Scard.

Unless the compulsion wasn't as assured as Tryan assumed. And if the Tide Lords had a weakness, it was their inability to tell a Scard from a loyal Crasii until the Scard disobeyed a direct order.

And Tiji *was* a Scard, recruited, trained and loyal to the enemies of the Tide Lords. And if it killed her, she would get word to Declan Hawkes and the Cabal of the Tarot, that Tryan the Devil was planning to take the reins of power in Caelum, and that Engarhod, Krydence and Rance probably weren't far behind them.

The Empress of the Five Realms was among them once again.

Chapter 2

Declan Hawkes flexed his fingers, hoping to ease the sting, while silently cursing his own stupidity for hitting any man on the jaw with a closed fist. His men had been at this prisoner for several hours, down here in the gloomy basement cells of Herino Prison, where the screams of prisoners under interrogation were unlikely to disturb the good citizens of the capital. Declan knew he was wasting his time. It was optimistic beyond imagining to risk breaking the fragile bones in his hand on the off-chance a single frustrated blow from the King's Spymaster would be the defining moment in this man's interrogation.

Battered and bruised, but still defiant, the prisoner's head had snapped back with the force of Declan's punch. His eyes watering with the pain, he slowly turned back to stare at his tormentors. "I won't betray my country."

Declan exchanged a glance with Rye Barnes, the man who had—up until now—been unsuccessfully trying to beat a confession out of this suspected Caelish spy. They'd found him in the sewers beneath the palace, claiming to be one of the workers employed to keep them free of debris. It was a foolish claim. No human worked the sewers of Herino. That was a job reserved exclusively for amphibious Crasii slaves. The only plausible reason any human would be lurking around the palace sewers was that he was up to no good.

This defiant declaration was a breakthrough. It was the first time he'd even hinted his loyalties lay somewhere other than Glaeba.

Maybe several hours of relentless beatings *had* softened him up. Of course, the man's rebelliousness could have been for himself as much as his tormenters—a last-ditch effort to remind himself of his purpose. Declan consciously fostered a reputation of a ruthless and fearsome spymaster, after all, a piece of advice he'd taken from his predecessor and applied to great effect. He forgot, sometimes, how successful he'd been at that and had to fight the urge to smile.

"You keep telling yourself that, friend," Declan said. "I'll make sure Ricard Li knows what a trouper you were." He turned to Rye Barnes and added in an uninterested voice, "Kill him."

Declan turned for the cell door, as Rye pulled a wicked-looking knife from his belt. It was nearly a foot long, curved and serrated along one edge. As a killing tool, it was fairly inefficient. You couldn't fault the psychological effect of it, though.

"No! Wait!" the man cried.

Declan smiled, forced it away and then turned back to look at the prisoner. "Wait? For what? You've made your position clear. You're never going to betray your country. I respect that. But I've got other places to be, you know. If you're not going to tell us anything, I'm not going to waste any more time beating a confession out of you that you've made it quite clear you're never going to give." He nodded to Rye Barnes. "Try not to make too much mess, Rye. You know how hard it is to get blood off these walls."

Again, Declan turned away. He made it all the way to the door, this time, before the prisoner was convinced they weren't bluffing.

"I was looking for something!"

"Looking for what?" Rye asked, pushing the wickedly serrated blade against the prisoner's neck.

"I don't know!"

Declan waved Rye's blade away and studied the battered prisoner hanging from the chains. "If you don't know what you were looking for, how did you expect to find it?"

The man met Declan's eye for a moment, the last glimmer of defiance fading from his eyes. "They said I'd know when I found it."

"And what exactly is *it* supposed to be?"

The prisoner shrugged. "An artefact. Something really old. Left over from the last Cataclysm. It's supposed to hold the key to ultimate power."

Declan smiled openly this time. "I see. You were searching the Herino palace sewers for the secret to ultimate power." He turned to

Rye Barnes. "Because that's where we'd keep the secret to ultimate power, isn't it? In the sewers?"

Rye smiled crookedly. "Aye. Along with the crown jewels."

"It's the truth," the Caelishman said. "I swear it."

Oddly, Declan believed him. His story made no sense, but there was a ring of truth about his words. More than that, the man looked defeated. It was that lack of defiance that told him when the fight had gone out of a man.

He wished he had the time to investigate this further, but he was already late for a meeting that—in the grand scheme of things—was far more important to the future of the entire world than what some misguided Caelishman was up to in the sewers beneath Herino Palace.

"Let him rest," Declan ordered, deciding to reward the man's cooperation. Torture was, in many ways, like training a dog. You rewarded the behaviour you wanted to encourage and punished what you wanted to *dis*courage. He'd told them something useful and it would result in food, water and a cessation of pain. The prisoner would learn very quickly, from this point on, what it took to stay in Rye Barnes's favour. "We'll talk to him again tomorrow."

"Yes, sir."

He turned to the prisoner. "You'll tell us more tomorrow." It wasn't a question.

The prisoner looked at him bleakly and then looked away. However much he might despise himself, Declan could see the surrender in his dull eyes and knew he was right.

"Sorry I'm late."

"That's all right, Declan. We were just wondering how another immortal could be under our nose all this time and we not know about it," Tilly Ponting said as she took her seat at the table, glaring at the small group of men gathered in the parlour of her Herino townhouse. A savage summer thunderstorm rattled the windows as it hammered down outside, lighting the room with occasional flashes, visible even around the edge of the heavy drapes.

Although elegantly furnished, the room was small and felt unbearably close. So close, the bloodstained cells beneath the prison, from which he'd just departed, seemed almost airy by comparison. It was crammed with generations of clutter and keepsakes belonging to the Ponting family; the lamp in the centre of the table cast ominous shadows across the faces of the conspirators.

Between the thunderstorm and the secret nature of this meeting, there was no question of opening the windows or the heavy curtains covering them. It had been a hot day building up to the storm, and the low cloud had trapped the day's heat so effectively it felt hotter now, close to midnight, than it had at midday, despite the rain.

Declan loosened his collar before he spoke, certain Tilly's statement was directed at him, although the Guardian of the Lore seemed to be addressing all of them.

"Kylia was in Lebec until the wedding," he explained. "The only Scard we had in place at the Lebec Palace was a feline and she never came into contact with the family. We might have had a chance if we'd known about Boots, but she'd already had her run-in with Jaxyn by then and escaped by the time the girl posing as the Duke of Lebec's niece became a fixture."

"It wouldn't have made any difference," Aleki said. "We didn't know about Boots being a Scard back then, either."

A tall, dark-haired man a few years older than Declan, Lord Aleki Ponting, the Earl of Summerton, was Tilly's only son. He was in town ostensibly for the royal wedding and the start of the court season, but more importantly, he was here to attend this meeting of the Glaeban-based members of the Cabal of the Tarot.

Just as Declan's assigned role was to serve the Cabal as the King's Spymaster, Aleki's was to protect and train the Scards living in Hidden Valley, a place that existed not in Caelum to the west of the Great Lakes, as popular Crasii legend held, but barely fifty miles from the Glaeban capital, tucked away in the heavily forested slopes of the Shevron Mountains, in a remote part of the Summerton Earldom, halfway between Herino and Lebec.

"*You* were in Lebec Palace," Lord Deryon reminded Declan. "Several times. You met Kylia, didn't you? Did *you* notice anything amiss?"

"I'm not a Scard, my lord. I wouldn't know an immortal if he came up and pinched me on the backside. Would *you*?" Declan was more than a little peeved to think he was being blamed for this.

Tilly seemed to agree with him. She placed a comforting hand over

Lord Deryon's arm. "There's nothing to be gained by trying to appor-tion blame, Karyl. We'll do the immortals' job for them if we start tearing ourselves apart with recrimination. What we should be doing is finding out exactly what we're dealing with. Are we *sure* about this girl being an immortal?" She shook her head in disbelief. "It seems too incredible to be true."

"I've had two Scards confirm it now," Declan assured her. "They both agree the new Crown Princess of Glaeba is a suzerain."

"Do we know which one?" Aleki asked.

"It's unlikely she's a Tide Lord," Shalimar remarked.

Declan's grandfather was sitting in the armchair near the unlit fire-place, settled in as comfortably as if this was his parlour, not Lady Ponting's. It was rare for him to leave his attic in the Lebec slums and he appeared to be making the most of this opportunity to enjoy Tilly's hospitality and the comforts of great wealth for a few days.

"How do you figure that?" Declan asked.

"Jaxyn's not the sort to share power and he was here long before Kylia appeared on the scene. Given there's been no sign of the Em-press of the Five Realms, or any of her kin, we can probably discount it being Elyssa."

"Kylia's too pretty," Declan said. "It's definitely not Elyssa."

Lord Deryon nodded in agreement. "She's more likely one of the lesser immortals looking for a comfy berth to await the returning Tide."

"But *which* lesser immortal?" Tilly looked at the four men, expect-ing one of them to answer.

"I'd take odds on Medwen or Diala," Aleki suggested after thinking about it for a moment.

Declan glanced at Aleki and then nodded, realising what he was get-ting at. "Because Kylia Debrell is . . . what . . . only seventeen? This immortal's been passing herself off as that age without raising any sus-picions at all." He nodded in agreement. "All the others would be too old to get away with it."

"If we're sure it's not Elyssa, then Medwen and Diala were the youngest when they were immortalised," Aleki agreed, "so you're prob-ably right. It's likely to be one of them."

Tilly turned to Shalimar. "I thought you said Medwen was in Senes-tra?"

"And so she was," he agreed. "We've had an unconfirmed rumour Arryl was hiding out there, too. At least that's the last word I had from Markun." Markun Far Jisa was one of the two missing members of the Pentangle. The fifth member's identity was so secret, even as highly placed as he was in the Cabal of the Tarot, Declan wasn't privy to his name. "He'd have sent word by now if she'd moved on."

"That just leaves us with the Minion Maker," Tilly said. "Tides, that's a depressing thought. Still, it's odd to find her in company with Jaxyn. She's not traditionally an ally of the Lord of Temperance."

"Maybe she's *not* his ally," Lord Deryon suggested. "Could it be chance has brought them both to Glaeba at the same time?"

"There's no way of knowing what brought them here," Shalimar said. "And not much point speculating. The real question is: are they allies now?"

All eyes turned to Lord Deryon, who as the King's Private Secretary was in the best position to witness the daily movements of the crown prince's bride.

"I would have to say it's likely," the old man confirmed. "Her relationship with Jaxyn Aranville seems very cordial."

"I'm curious," Shalimar said. "What does Mathu think of his wife's friendship with a known womaniser like Jaxyn?"

"He's probably still in the first flush of love," Tilly said. "Whichever immortal she is, she's had plenty of time to work on her seduction techniques. And Mathu is only young. I'm guessing he's too blinded by his infatuation with Kylia—or whatever her name is—to think it's a problem."

"Perhaps the first thing to do would be to draw the young man's attention to it?" the old man suggested, stretching his feet out in front of him. "Whose idea was it to bring Jaxyn here to Herino, anyway?"

"Yours," Declan reminded his grandfather before he could be blamed for that fiasco, too. "You were worried about him training Lebec's Crasii army."

"Ah, yes . . . I remember that. Seems a bit ridiculous in hindsight."

Tilly smiled faintly. "Most disastrous decisions do. Any suggestions about how we should proceed?"

"Are we so sure chopping an immortal into little pieces and feeding him to the hounds won't get rid of him?" Declan enquired as the thunder rattled the windows once more. The lightning and thunder seemed much further apart now. Perhaps the storm was moving away.

Somewhat to his surprise, Tilly took his question seriously. "I believe it's been tried. The immortal healed too quickly. According to the Lore the assassins never got a chance to cut the body into small enough pieces to feed it to anything."

"Just a thought," he said. "Which immortal was it?"

"The Lore says it was Lyna. It happened before the Third Cataclysm, I believe. Kentravyon's wrath was something to behold when he learned of the attack on his compatriot. The death toll was horrendous."

"It just occurred to me, Tilly," he said, looking at the widow in a new light. "You must have a head full of the most appalling murders. It's a wonder it doesn't drive you mad."

"*Attempted* murders," she corrected. "And since the Pentangle convened the first Cabal of the Tarot five thousand years ago, in the hope of finding a way to defeat the immortals, the idea that one of them might work someday is all that keeps the Guardian of the Lore sane."

"And this particular Guardian of the Lore's not shy about sharing the details, either," Aleki remarked with a sour smile. "She used to threaten me with the most dreadful fates when I was a child."

"What makes you so sure they were only threats?" Tilly grumbled. "I can assure you, my boy, if you and Davista don't set a date soon, so I can actually see a grandchild before I die, I'll start rifling through the Lore for the most painful way to get my point across."

"Ah, family," Shalimar sighed. "Who'd be without them?"

"I've often thought it might be interesting to find out," Aleki replied with a perfectly straight face.

Declan smiled at Aleki's dry humour, but they were getting off the point. "What do you want me to do about Diala . . . assuming it is Diala we're dealing with?"

"Confirm her identity first," Lord Deryon suggested. "In the meantime, I'll see if I can determine the exact nature of the relationship between her and Jaxyn. We need to know that before we decide how to proceed. Do you think I should warn the king?"

"And tell him what?" Shalimar asked. "That his daughter-in-law is an evil immortal bent on stealing his throne? There's a conversation I'd like to sit in on."

Karyl Deryon sighed. "It would be so much easier if more people knew the truth about the immortals, and didn't consider them just myths."

"You may get your wish sooner than you imagine," Tilly predicted with a grim look. She turned to Shalimar. "How long do we have before the Tide peaks?"

The old man shrugged. "Predicting the moods of the Tide is an inexact science at best, Tilly. I can't tell you exactly. I'm guessing a few months at worst, a few years if we're lucky."

"Then we don't have time to muck about." Decisively, Tilly turned to Declan. "Do as Karyl advises, Declan. Find out if we really do have the High Priestess living in our midst. In the meantime, I'll contact Markun Far Jisa and see if Medwen is still in Senestra."

"I'll check with the Scards up in the Valley," Aleki offered. "One of them may have encountered Diala before and can identify her."

"That reminds me," Declan said. "Pop's got a couple more recruits for you to take back with you when you return."

"More Scards?" Aleki asked with interest, looking at Shalimar. "Felines?"

The old man shook his head. "Canines. One's quite young. A female. The other, the male, shared a cell block with the Immortal Prince."

Aleki's eyebrows shot up in surprise. "Well, he'll have us all entranced with his fireside tales, I don't doubt."

"He's been very well house-trained," Declan said. "You'll find him useful for more than storytelling, I warrant."

"Then I'll send word when I'm ready to leave for Summerton. I can pick them up on my way through Lebec."

"And on that note," Lord Deryon announced, rising to his feet, "I should take my leave. The gossips will start to talk if I spend too much longer under your roof, Lady Ponting."

Tilly smiled. "Ah, to be the subject of such gossip at our age, Karyl."

"I can give you a lift back to the palace if you want," Declan said. "That rain's still pretty heavy by the sound of it."

"Thank you, Declan, but I have my own carriage outside, hence the reason I fear the wagging tongues of Herino. Shall we meet again before you return to Lebec, Shalimar?"

"I'm heading back tomorrow."

"Then I wish you well until we meet again, old friend, and trust our next meeting brings happier tidings."

Shalimar shook his head. "The Tide is on the turn and we've already got two immortals making themselves at home in the Glaeban palace, Karyl. I fear the days of happy tidings, not just for us, but for all of humankind, are far, far behind us."

Chapter 3

"Sooner or later, we all try our hand at ruling the world."

The barman glanced across at Cayal and nodded with practised sincerity. It was quiet in the dingy Torlenian taproom so he was probably prepared to indulge a customer, Cayal guessed, even a drunken one. The man picked up another amber glass tumbler from the dripping tray standing on the tiled countertop and began polishing it. "That a fact?"

Cayal took another swig of the rich dark Torlenian ale, but it did nothing to take the edge off his awareness. The returning Tide ebbed and flowed around him constantly now, tantalisingly close at times, at others so far out of reach that Cayal feared it was slipping away from him forever. It tormented and enticed him, daring him to embrace it fully.

It was the returning Tide that had brought him here to Ramahn ahead of the new Glaeban ambassador.

It was the returning Tide that made him drink himself into oblivion.

At least that's what he told himself. It sounded better in his head than the other excuse . . . that he'd come here in pursuit of a woman he was afraid to think about, in case he discovered a reason to live.

Despite his vow never to undertake such a sea voyage again, a berth on an oared galley proved the most expeditious way to reach Torlenia. The Tide was back sufficiently for him to ensure their ship enjoyed fair winds all the way and when the breeze faltered his accelerated healing ability meant he no longer suffered the pain of blistered hands or burning muscles. He no longer got fatigued the way a mortal man did, either, so he rarely even caught the attention of the oar-master. The journey had taken Cayal a little over ten days—something of a record the captain claimed—and here he was in Ramahn, the capital of Torlenia, getting drunk, wondering about his own foolishness, feeling the madness creep up on him, wishing the rising Tide didn't feel so seductive and lamenting the venality of his kind.

"S'right, you know . . . Even the goody-goody types who swear they'll never succumb to the lure of ultimate power. Even they've tried it, too. The hunger . . . the curiosity . . . it gets you in the end . . . every time." He was slurring his words and knew he sounded like a fool, but Cayal didn't care. It took a monumental quantity of alcohol to make an immortal drunk, and he was more than a little proud of himself for achieving the feat. In fact, it was a reflection of this impressive achievement that had set him thinking about many of the other things he'd accomplished in his impossibly long lifetime, and it was that which prompted his announcement about ruling the world.

"S'pose it does," the barman agreed in a tone that was hard-pressed to disguise his lack of interest.

"Funny thing is, the more they reckon they don't want it, the worse they are when they get it."

"Mmmm . . ." the barman replied, putting the now-sparkling glass on the shelf above the bar and picking up another to polish. "I've heard that can be the case."

Cayal drained his glass and thrust it toward the barman. "Kentravyon was a right little prick when he was in charge."

The barman took the glass and refilled it from the barrel sitting to the end of the bar. "I've no doubt he was."

"Course . . . I probably wasn't much better, truth be told."

He handed Cayal the refilled glass. "Of course."

Cayal accepted the drink and smiled crookedly. "You don't have any idea who I am, do you?"

The barman shrugged his broad shoulders. "Not sure who you are in your own country, sir, but here in Torlenia you're just a paying customer. Least you will be when you settle up your tab." He frowned at Cayal. "You *will* be settling your tab soon, won't you, sir?"

"Afraid I'm not good for it?"

"You have run up quite a bill, sir."

"Not long now, and you'll be bragging that I was drinking in your grubby little flophouse," Cayal predicted. "Couple of months . . . a year or two from now maybe, you'll be getting rich off me."

"I'd rather be getting rich off you now, sir, if you don't mind."

"Do you believe in the immortals?"

The barman eyed him warily. "Don't see how that makes that much difference to whether or not you can pay your bill, my friend. And your stalling ain't making me feel any better about your ability to come up with the cash, neither."

"You didn't answer my question."

He shrugged. "I know there's them what still prays to the Tide Lords, but I ain't ever seen the point of 'em, really. I mean, it's not like they ever did anything 'sides bugger things up for the rest of us."

"Your inn is named Cayal's Rest," Cayal pointed out. It was the reason he'd chosen this inn to get drunk in, over the many other worthy establishments in Ramahn.

"Only 'cause them interfering sods at the palace wouldn't let me name it Cayal's a Bastard," the barman grumbled.

That announcement amused Cayal no end. Interesting that his name had not been forgotten here. Or that it was still so universally despised. "Perhaps you'd have been better off naming your establishment after a more worthy Tide Lord."

"Like who?" the man asked. "Ain't none of 'em worth spitting on."

"Then why name your place after an immortal at all?"

"Seemed like a good idea at the time."

Cayal laughed. "Tides, I've used that excuse myself. In fact—"

"In fact *what*?" the barman prompted when Cayal stopped midsentence, interested now the discussion had moved to his client's line of credit.

The Tide tickled the edge of Cayal's awareness. Splashing his ale on the counter as he slammed his glass down, he staggered to the window, staring out into the shimmering heat. The marketplace was dusty and deserted—market day wasn't until tomorrow—the midday sun having driven most of the residents of Ramahn inside until the witching hour.

"Sir?" the barman called after him, perhaps concerned that his only customer—and the cash he owed—were heading for the door.

Cayal ignored him, trying to concentrate, cursing the impulse that had driven him to drown his sorrows with the Tide on the turn. His mind was befuddled, his senses dulled, but even through that, he could feel the presence of another immortal. He could sense it within the very marrow of his bones.

The ripples in the Tide grew stronger, getting closer with each passing moment.

Cayal held his breath.

Waiting.

But the street remained empty. There was nobody out there.

Disappointed, Cayal returned to the bar, tossing a few coins on the counter to keep the barman happy. He wasn't feeling nearly so garrulous anymore. That ripple on the Tide reminded him he was not alone. Close by, there were others of his kind. Given this was Torlenia, it might be Kinta or Brynden he'd felt. Neither of them ever ventured far from this land they had adopted as their own. Or it might have been one of the others, perhaps, on the move now the Tide was turning . . .

Cayal stared into the bottom of his ale, trying to muster some enthusiasm for the prospect of another High Tide.

"Oh come on! It can't be that bad, can it?" a wry voice remarked behind him. "You look like the world's about to come crashing down on top of you."

Cayal's slumped shoulders straightened at the voice. He spun around, shocked to discover someone could sneak up on him like that.

"Tides," the newcomer exclaimed, eyeing Cayal up and down with despair. "You haven't spent the last thousand years sitting here crying into your ale, I hope?"

"How did you . . . ?"

"Sneak up on you? You weren't paying attention. You gonna buy an old friend a drink, or what?"

"Um . . . of course . . ." Cayal signalled the bartender for two more ales and then studied his companion for a moment. As expected, his appearance hadn't changed. His skin was still the same dusky brown, no more wrinkled or weather-beaten than it had been a hundred or a thousand years ago. His white-blond hair was trimmed neatly, although it still struck Cayal as being an unusual colour in one so dark. His eyes were just as blue, his smile just as world-weary. There was no sign of the tame rat, Coron, however. Perhaps he'd left him outside, fearful of what the bartender's reaction might be to such an unwanted guest. "What are you doing in Torlenia, Lukys?"

"Looking for you."

"Why?"

"Do I need a reason?"

"Never known you to do anything without one."

Lukys smiled. "Fair enough." He waited until the barman had delivered his drink with a speculative look, and then took a long swig before adding, "I think I have something you want."

"I want nothing," Cayal said miserably, downing the last ale so he could tackle the fresh one. "Where have you been?"

"Here and there. You know me."

"And your little furry friend?"

"Who? Coron? He's dead."

Cayal let out a short, unsympathetic laugh and then froze as the full meaning of what Lukys was implying dawned on him. He stared at Lukys. "*Dead?*"

"As a doorpost."

"But . . . how . . . how can that be? He was immortal . . ."

Lukys nodded. "Not as immortal as we assumed, it would seem."

Cayal was stunned. "Do you know *how* he died?"

"Of course."

"Then that would mean . . ." Cayal was almost afraid to say it aloud in case this proved to be nothing more than a drunken hallucination.

"That I know the secret to killing an immortal," Lukys finished for him. "Yes, it would mean that, wouldn't it?"

Cayal was too staggered to speak. Lukys raised his glass in Cayal's direction, took another swig of his ale and then smiled at the younger man. "So it seems, my jaded and melancholic old friend, I do have something you want, after all."

Chapter 4

The heat of Torlenia was the first thing that hit Stellan as their ship sailed toward the crowded docks. For days now it had been building up but this morning it was relentless; like taking deep heaving breaths too close to a furnace. The sun seemed closer, the view sharper . . . even the very air seemed to burn. Before he'd reached the railing to witness the sunrise, sweat stained his shirt in unsightly dark patches under his arms and in a "V" down his back.

Much wiser than their passengers, the sailors manning the ropes had long ago shed any clothing other than their thin linen trousers, their tanned bodies glistening with sweat in the bright sunlight. The few amphibious Crasii left on board dived over the edge as often as they could manage, returning via the ropes hanging on the side of the ship for that purpose only long enough to perform the duties required of them before returning to the water as soon as they were able. They were uniformly miserable. The amphibious Crasii were freshwater creatures. The salt water burned their eyes and accelerated the drying of their skin so they were forced to remain in the water. Staying wet was marginally less painful than drying out.

Stellan watched the city approach, fascinated by it. Ramahn's unofficial name was the Crystal City and it was easy to see why. Built on the edge of the sea, eons of crashing waves had encrusted the chalky cliffs and the city walls above them with layer upon layer of salt, which the harsh sun had baked into a glistening wall of crystal. The rising sun illuminated the salts as if they were gemstones, setting the whole city alight and making it almost too bright to look upon. They were arriving just in time to witness the full effect. Their timing was so perfect, in fact, Stellan wondered if it hadn't been a deliberate ploy on the captain's part, to make sure the new Glaeban ambassador was suitably impressed by the magnificence of the Torlenian capital.

Regardless of the circumstances that had brought him here, or the suspiciously perfect timing, Stellan was glad he had witnessed dawn over Ramahn. It truly was a sight to behold.

At the muttered greeting of a sailor behind him, he turned to find the man bowing respectfully as Arkady headed toward her husband. She was covered, head-to-toe, in a white cotton sheath that allowed only a small, square cut-out around her eyes so she could see where she was going.

"Come to view the Crystal City in all its glory?"

"I'm assured it's a sight not to be missed."

He offered her his hand and smiled apologetically. "I am so sorry you have to get about in that ridiculous thing."

"No apology necessary," she assured him. "I'm actually stark naked under here and quite cool as a consequence, thank you. I think I'm going to quite like Torlenian fashion."

He eyed her askance. "*Really*?"

She shrugged. "What do you think?"

Stellan frowned. "You sounded so . . . sincere."

"Just being a good diplomat's wife, dear. Truth is, I feel like a small child who's stolen the sheets from her parents' bed so she can run around scaring people by pretending she's a ghost."

He smiled. "You rather look like you have, too."

Although he couldn't see anything but her eyes, he could tell she didn't think it was all that amusing.

"You only have to wear it in public, you know. In the privacy of our own home, you're free to dress as you please."

"In the privacy of the seraglium, you mean," she corrected. "Those three small rooms where I can do as I please, provided it doesn't involve me being seen, or having my opinion heard."

"You know I would never confine you against your will, Arkady."

She sighed, clearly doubting his ability to keep such a promise. "This is Torlenia, Stellan. You may not have a choice."

"Your grace?"

"Yes?" Although they both turned to the Torlenian sailor addressing them, it was Stellan who answered him. There was no question of another man speaking to Arkady on board the ship. Not here. Not in Torlenia.

"The captain asked me to inform you we'll be disembarking within the hour, your grace. And to tell you the Imperator has sent an envoy to meet you." The man spoke haltingly, as if trying to find the right words. Stellan was impressed. Although Glaeban clearly wasn't the sailor's native tongue, he spoke it very well.

Squinting against the glare of the sunlight on the salt crystals, he looked back toward the city. They were past the rocks guarding the harbour, heading for the bustling port of Ramahn itself. The amphibians were all in the harness now, towing the ship toward the city. Stellan scanned the approaching dock and spied several gilded litters accompanied by a squad of Imperial Guards forming up on the wharf by the empty berth toward which the amphibians were pulling their ship.

"Thank the captain for me," Stellan told the sailor, addressing him in Glaeban. No need yet to let the Torlenians know he had more than a passing acquaintance with their language. "And tell him we await his pleasure."

The sailor sketched a quick bow and hurried away.

"Do you suppose it's really just an escort?" Stellan asked, turning back to lean on the railing. The harbour was crowded and even from here the noise of the busy docks reached them.

"I doubt they're waiting to arrest us," Arkady replied. "After all, the Imperator sent his own flagship to meet us."

"Only because he didn't want any Royal Glaeban ships in Torlenian waters," he reminded her. "I'm still wondering if I shouldn't have insisted we arrive in our own ship."

They had planned to. It was only when the Glaeban delegation arrived in the Chelae Islands to restock their dwindling freshwater supplies that they discovered the Imperator of Torlenia was refusing to allow the King of Glaeba's ship into Torlenian waters. He wasn't refusing his ambassador entry—they were fulsomely assured—just his ship.

The envoy sent to inform them of the Imperator's decision had waxed lyrical for some time on the treacherous entrance to the Crystal City's harbour and how no Glaeban seaman, no matter how experienced, could possibly assure the protection of the new ambassador and his lovely wife. Stellan had debated arguing the point. The bone of contention between Torlenia and Glaeba was all about where exactly the line between Glaeban and Torlenian waters lay. The Chelae Islands, which sat squarely in the middle of the disputed line, were the reason the two nations had been at odds for so long, and much of the reason Stellan was here now.

In the end, he decided to acquiesce to the Torlenian ruler's wishes. It was still unclear how much damage Lord Jorgan had done when he lost his temper with the Imperator and got himself expelled. If there was a chance to smooth things over, better to try it first.

Stellan was a diplomat, after all. Pouring oil on troubled waters was his job.

"You did the right thing," Arkady assured him, putting a comforting hand on his shoulder. "You couldn't have done anything to fix this mess stranded on Chelae."

He turned to look at her. "Can I apologise now? In advance? For all the indignities I fear you'll be forced to suffer while we're here?"

Her eyes narrowed in annoyance. "If you think it will help."

"I'll make it up to you, Arkady."

"How?"

"Name your price," he declared. "Whatever your little heart desires, if it's in my power, I'll grant it."

Arkady was silent for a moment and then she turned to look at the approaching city. "What my heart desires is not in your power to grant me, Stellan."

There was a note of yearning in her voice that surprised him. Although it was more than two months since her ordeal as a hostage of the escaped convict Kyle Lakesh, she clearly hadn't forgotten him. Stellan wished he could read her expression, but the wretched shroud she wore prevented him from reading anything but her eyes and she kept them determinedly averted to prevent him doing just that.

He forced a smile, hoping to make light of the awkward silence that followed her statement. "Then suppose I promise to look the other way?"

This time she did look at him. And he was fairly certain she was amused. "Look the other *way*?"

"I'm a very tolerant sort of fellow, you know."

"You're a romantic fool, actually," she corrected. "But I do appreciate the offer, no matter how impractical or unlikely it might be."

"And I appreciate the fact that you're standing here with me in that ridiculous outfit, prepared to suffer all manner of inconvenience for the sake of an ungrateful king."

"We're both going to suffer all manner of inconvenience for the sake of an ungrateful king," she pointed out, clearly not pleased to be reminded of the fact that it was Stellan's offer to help the Crown Prince of Glaeba that had landed them in this mess.

Stellan smiled thinly. "I wonder if that means we're patriots or fools."

"The latter, I suspect," Arkady replied.

Afraid his wife had the right of it, Stellan turned in time to see the amphibians edging their ship into its berth while the human sailors on board threw ropes to the stevedores waiting on the dock to secure the vessel. As it bumped gently against the wharf, the Imperial Guard moved into position to provide an honour guard either side of the gangway. It thumped down onto the dock with a loud crash. A thin man in a long, embroidered red silk coat stepped forward to await their arrival.

"I suspect that's our cue," Stellan remarked, offering Arkady his arm.

She said nothing, but took his arm and let him lead her across the deck and down the treacherously bouncy gangway. As they stepped onto the salt-encrusted wharf, the thin man stepped forward and bowed, his left fist clasped in his right hand in the traditional Torlenian greeting gesture.

"Your grace," the man announced in flawless Glaeban, to Stellan significantly, as if Arkady wasn't standing right beside him, "welcome to Torlenia."

Chapter 5

Shalimar led Warlock and Boots out of Lebec City on horseback early one morning. It was a little over a month after the canine Crasii had met with Declan Hawkes for the first time and been invited to join his secret Scard army in Hidden Valley. Warlock still wasn't sure he believed such an opportunity existed, particularly as further investigation had revealed some interesting information about Hawkes. The alarming news that Declan Hawkes was the King's Spymaster had only been slightly offset by the news that he was also their friend Shalimar's grandson.

Warlock had been even more disturbed to discover that while their relationship seemed to be common knowledge in the slums, rumour also had it the two men hadn't exchanged a civil word in years. Shalimar, according to the gossips, wasn't at all pleased that his grandson had chosen a life which put him at odds with most of the people he'd grown up with and once thought of as his friends.

Warlock was fairly certain that was not the case, given Shalimar was the one who'd brought them to this ramshackle inn. It was here, on the orders of Declan Hawkes, they were waiting to meet the next—and as yet unknown—person in the unexpected chain of humans who seemed to be a part of this secret underground movement set up to help Lebec's dispossessed Crasii.

"Stop pacing."

His tail lashing impatiently, Warlock turned to look at Boots, who was sitting opposite Shalimar at the rough table set under the eaves of Clyden's Inn. She was finishing off her second bowl of the inn's surprisingly tasty stew, enjoying the bright summer sunshine. Shalimar sat opposite her, leaning back against the wall, his hat pulled down over his eyes, apparently asleep.

"I can't help it," he told her.

"Try," she suggested. "You're driving me crazy."

"I don't know how you can sit there stuffing your face as if there's nothing going on."

"You're too used to knowing where your next meal is coming from, Farm Dog," she replied through a mouthful of half-chewed meat. "Otherwise you wouldn't need an explanation."

"I wish you'd stop calling me Farm Dog."

"Then stop acting like one."

Warlock stared at her, trying to recall what he'd seen in this young female that had resulted in their savage mating in the alley outside the Kennel. He'd not been able to get enough of her back then. Deep down, he understood it was instinct. He knew when the heat was on her, there was nothing he or any other male could do to resist it. The Boots he'd come to know since then, however, was prickly, impatient and dismissive of many of the customs and traditions that, for Warlock, defined their very natures as Crasii. The timing of their mating made him wonder about something else, too. Although she showed no signs of being with pup yet, it might be too early to tell. She was certainly eating as if she had more than one belly to fill. Would she still treat him so impatiently if he'd fathered a litter on her?

"Someone's coming."

It was Shalimar who spoke, although he hadn't moved or even raised his head.

"How can you tell?" Boots asked.

The old man sat up stiffly and pushed back his wide-brimmed, woven hat. "I can feel it in the wall."

As he was speaking, Warlock's sharp canine hearing picked up the sound of cantering hooves. They slowed before they became audible to less-gifted ears and by the time the newcomers came into sight along the western arm of the narrow crossroads, Boots, Shalimar and Warlock were on their feet and the horsemen were approaching at a steady trot.

A few moments later the three human riders reined in and dismounted. The man in the lead was a dark-haired, not unpleasant looking man in his mid-thirties. His cloak was expensive, his riding gloves made of the finest kid, and he wore the kind of arrogant look Warlock had long ago learned to associate with Glaeba's ruling class.

The man stepped forward, his gaze sending a shiver of apprehension down Warlock's spine. Had they been betrayed, after all? Was this man here not to help them, but enslave them again? Warlock glanced around, wondering if he could outrun the henchmen accompanying this arrogant-looking nobleman, who were, he was sure, here only to make certain the Crasii didn't cause trouble.

Shalimar stepped up to greet the nobleman. His expression softened and he smiled, transforming his whole countenance. "You beat me here, old man. What did you do? Fly?"

Shalimar shook the younger man's hand warmly. "No, we just left half a day before you and didn't founder anything getting here, that's all. This is Warlock, by the way. And his friend, Boots."

The man handed his reins to one of his companions, who led the horses off around the yard to walk them a little while they cooled down. He then turned to the two Crasii and, to Warlock's astonishment, offered him his hand. "I'm Aleki Ponting. Shalimar speaks highly of you both."

"*Lord* Ponting?" Boots asked, as shocked as Warlock at the man's lack of artifice. "Of Summerton?"

"You've heard of me?"

"I grew up at Lebec Palace."

"Ah! Then you probably know my mother, yes?" Lord Ponting didn't seem particularly worried by the notion. "She's a frequent guest at the palace."

Boots shook her head. "No, my lord, I never met her. I mean . . . I know of her."

Warlock thought it interesting Boots had automatically granted Aleki Ponting his title. She wasn't usually so accommodating.

"I can imagine you do," Aleki agreed with a smile. "She's fairly notorious. Have you eaten?"

"Yes," Warlock informed him. "Shalimar arranged—"

"A snack," Boots interjected. "So if you want to stop for lunch, we don't mind staying for seconds."

"Thirds," Warlock corrected under his breath.

Boots grinned, wagging her tail. "The stew here is pretty good."

"I know. Clyden is quite famous for his stew," Aleki agreed. "And we have the time, I suppose. Did you arrange horses for them, Shalimar?"

The old man nodded. "In the stable. And if you're happy to take care of these two now, I'd like to get going."

"Of course," Lord Ponting agreed, and then he turned and indicated his two companions. "Lon and Tenry will escort you."

"We've talked about this, Aleki," Shalimar reminded him.

"You're a lone old man on a road notorious for its highwaymen, Shalimar, heading into a potentially dangerous situation. Take the damned escort and be thankful."

The old man frowned. "Declan put you up to this, didn't he?"

Lord Ponting smiled. "And what loyal servant of the king would dare defy the King's Spymaster?"

"This one, for starters."

"You know I'll only make them follow you if you refuse," the younger man warned, making Warlock wonder where the old man was heading. The road from Lebec was well travelled and the city was a mere hour or two away, even on foot.

Surely he's just going to turn around and go home?

Aleki sighed. "You might as well just accept them and enjoy their company."

Shalimar muttered something rude under his breath and then nodded with ill grace. "It's not nice to bully an old man."

"I'll be sure to mention your displeasure to your grandson, when next I see him."

"I'm sure he already knows," Shalimar grumbled.

The old man turned to the bodyguard who was standing behind Lord Ponting, fixing his displeased gaze on him. "Well, don't just stand there, man! Fetch my horse from the stable. It's the piebald. And you," he called to the other man walking the horses. "Try to look a bit more intimidating, would you. If we *are* set upon by bandits, you'll be the first one they kill, just because you look so damned pathetic."

Aleki smiled even wider, shaking his head, and then issued his own instructions to his men, which were to not let Shalimar Hawkes out of their sight. As he spoke, the first guard returned from the inn's stables with Shalimar's piebald pony. The old man shucked off any attempt at assistance and swung into the saddle with surprising agility.

When he was mounted, he turned the horse until he was facing

Warlock and Boots. "You can trust Aleki. He'll see you come to no harm."

"Thanks for the help, Shalimar," Boots replied. "And the food."

"Thanks for the company," the old man replied. He looked at Warlock and then bent down to offer him his handshake. "It's been good knowing you, Warlock."

"And you, too, Shalimar," the Crasii agreed, out of politeness more than genuine appreciation for the old man's help. He still wasn't entirely convinced this wasn't an elaborate trap, although why any human would go to such trouble just to ensnare a couple of unindentured slaves was a question to which he had no answer.

"We'll meet again, perhaps," the old man said, as his guards mounted, after handing Lord Ponting's mount back to him. "Or maybe not. I suspect Aleki has great things planned for you."

Warlock looked to the earl for some indication Shalimar spoke the truth, but the nobleman's expression revealed nothing.

Shalimar tugged on his reins and turned his horse out of the yard and onto the eastern road—away from the city—with Lon and Tenry close on his heels. Boots stepped up close to Warlock as he watched him leave. "You know, I think I'm going to miss that old man."

"You'll miss the food, you mean."

"That too." She turned to look at Aleki Ponting. "Will you feed us as well as Shalimar did, my lord?"

The earl seemed amused. "I doubt there's another soul on Amyrantha who'll feed you as well as Shalimar did." He began to pull off his gloves and cloak. It was warm standing here in the sun, and although Shalimar had provided the Crasii with warmer clothes packed into their saddlebags, they were both still wearing the thin cotton shifts common to all city-dwelling Crasii. The human, with his fine wool cloak, would be sweltering. "You won't starve, however. Did he tell you where we're going?"

"Hidden Valley," Warlock answered for her.

"Did he tell you anything else?"

"Not really."

"Then we have quite a lot to discuss along the way." Leading his horse, Aleki turned for the stables, as if that was the end of the discussion.

"Are we free to leave?"

The earl stopped and turned to look at them. "Are you *planning* to?"

"That's not an answer."

Lord Ponting stepped a little closer, and while he seemed pleasant enough, there was an undercurrent of threat in his bearing that, strangely, Warlock found reassuring. If these people were planning to lull him and Boots into believing they were being escorted to paradise, only to enslave them again, Aleki should be bending over backward to convince them they had nothing to fear. But the Earl of Summerton was acting like a man with something to protect. Just as Declan Hawkes had made the consequences of their refusal clear, Aleki wasn't trying to paint a rosy picture, either.

"You and your friend are here on trust," Lord Ponting told him, looking up at the big Crasii. "And while ever you demonstrate yourself worthy of that trust, Warlock, you'll be treated accordingly. The Tide Lords are returning and that means every man, woman and child in this world is in danger, not to mention the Crasii. You've been offered a chance to do something to protect the Crasii from being abused the way they were the last time the immortals controlled Amyrantha. You should know enough of your own history to know what that means."

"He only meant . . ." Boots began, her tail wagging slightly, a little alarmed at the seriousness of the nobleman's tone.

"I know what he meant, Boots. He wants to know if you're prisoners. So let me put your mind at ease. Both of you. You want to leave? Fine. Go now, and good luck to you both. But know this: the closer we get to Hidden Valley, the more we have to protect, and I promise you, we're prepared to do whatever it takes to protect our people. If that means hunting you down and killing you before you can betray our secrets, so be it."

Chapter 6

The seraglium attached to the Glaeban embassy in Ramahn turned out to be much less depressing than Arkady was expecting. Rather than the three rooms she feared, the women's quarters took up most of the north wing of the embassy and included a small lawn and a water garden, an extravagance of the most amazing kind in Ramahn's hot and arid climate.

The embassy itself was an impressive building, even for someone who had grown accustomed to the opulent wealth of Lebec. Two storeys high, flat-roofed and covering almost an entire city block, it was a palace in its own right. The building was covered with millions of tiny ceramic tiles, both inside and out, some done in geometric patterns, others worked into delightful murals depicting all manner of imaginary creatures, and more than a few scenes Arkady recognised from the Tide Lord Tarot.

It also boasted extensive (not to mention expensive-to-maintain) stables almost as impressive as the royal stables. The Torlenians were mad for horseracing, she soon discovered, and expected every man of substance to keep a number of thoroughbreds for just that purpose. They'd inherited, along with the vast ambassadorial palace, the Glaeban racing stables and Stellan was already receiving polite challenges on a daily basis to race his horses against other noble houses in the capital.

There were several other wives living in the seraglium, but few of them struck Arkady as being the sort of women she might befriend. They were either privately scornful of her common-born origins, or scandalised by her much-talked-about independence. They had their own lives and concerns and weren't all that interested in welcoming a newcomer into their midst, which really didn't bother Arkady, because there wasn't one of them capable of holding an intelligent conversation in the first place.

The palace staff numbered over a hundred and was made up of a mixture of Torlenian and Glaeban Crasii and a number of human servants. Before they'd left Glaeba, Declan Hawkes, the King's Spymaster, had provided Arkady and Stellan with a comprehensive list of who, among their vast staff, was thought to be a spy, not only of Torlenia but of Caelum, Senestra, Tenacia, the Commonwealth of Elenovia, Stevania and half a dozen other countries who considered it prudent to know what was happening in the Glaeban embassy. Stellan had dismissed a dozen of the suspected spies on his arrival, but kept on the ones Declan was certain of. The dismissals were for show, of course. Everyone would think the new ambassador had cleaned out his palace, unaware of the other spies in his midst. It meant Stellan was now free to spread a great deal of disinformation among the remaining spies who believed they had escaped detection.

This whole business of spies and disinformation made Arkady's head ache. She had two known spies in her service: her hairdresser, a canine Crasii named Peppi, who spied for the Elenovians and a Glaeban wardrobe mistress named Natalay Wren, who was, according to Declan's report, in the pay of the Torlenians. Arkady couldn't understand why they put up with her. The woman was selling out her own country for a tidy monthly stipend. She should be beheaded for treason, in Arkady's opinion, not indulged or ignored. Arkady had made a point of telling Declan that, too, for all the good it did.

She was thinking it still, as Natalay put the finishing touches on her hair and the palace seamstress, Linnie Kirell, adjusted the hem of her gown. Arkady was being very careful of her appearance this morning. The Imperator's Consort had issued an invitation to the Glaeban ambassador's wife to visit her in the royal seraglium.

Although hidden away by their men like valuable treasures one feared the neighbours might steal, in their own way, the women of Torlenia had power. Of a sort. It was subtle and it was usually hidden and the pinnacle of that power was the Imperator's Consort.

Arkady couldn't afford to offend her.

"Have you ever met the consort?" Arkady asked her seamstress, as the woman bit off a loose thread and then smoothed down the hem of the gown. It was made from embroidered gold cloth, exquisite in its detail and completely wasted, given that over the top of all this finery would have to go that wretched shroud.

"No, your grace," the woman replied, standing back to admire her handiwork. "Lady Jorgan met her, though."

"And how did they get along—Lady Jorgan and the Imperator's Consort?"

"Not very well," Linnie admitted. And then she smiled. "But I'd not place too much store in that, your grace. Nobody got on very well with Lady Jorgan. Not even *Lord* Jorgan."

Arkady frowned at the seamstress. "I'm not sure how things were run here in the past, Linnie, but I've no wish to hear you repeating gossip." Even as she said it, she knew she was probably making a mistake. Gossip was the lifeblood of this place. "Unless you're certain there's some truth in it," she amended, thinking she must sound like a flanking fool. "Can you tell me anything *useful* about the consort?"

"She's very beautiful."

"Has anybody actually seen her, or is that just another rumour?"

"Lady Jorgan told us as much after she first met her," Natalay said, no doubt trying to appear more reliable than her companion. "She also said she was foreign."

"What nationality is she?"

"Lady Jorgan didn't say," Natalay replied. "Just that she was foreign."

Arkady glanced at Linnie for confirmation but the seamstress just shrugged. "Lady Jorgan wasn't the type to share her observations with the help, your grace."

Get to know the servants. They'll be your greatest source of intelligence, Declan had advised her before they left Glaeba.

What did he know?

Taking one last look in the tall polished mirror in her dressing room, Arkady decided she'd probably do. She swept up her layered skirts and turned to Natalay. "Would you let the guards know I'm ready to leave, please?"

"Of course, your grace."

The wardrobe mistress hurried away to do as Arkady ordered, leaving her alone with Linnie. "Did Lady Jorgan tell you *anything* useful, Linnie?"

The seamstress pursed her lips for a moment and then nodded. "The only other thing I remember her saying was that the Lady Chintara seemed bored."

"Bored? By Lady Jorgan?"

"By everything," Linnie corrected. "Lady Jorgan was quite put out by her, I gather. They only met a couple of times, and after that she wasn't invited back to the palace. Before she could get too upset about it, though, Lord Jorgan and the Imperator had that awful row over the Chelae Islands and they were ordered out of Ramahn." She shrugged apologetically. "There's not much more than that I can tell you, your grace."

"You *know* the reason our ambassador was expelled?" Arkady asked, a little concerned to think something like that was common knowledge among the servants.

Linnie smiled, leaning forward to brush a speck from the shoulder of Arkady's exquisite golden gown. "Everybody in Ramahn knows the reason, your grace. There aren't a lot of secrets in this city." With that warning issued, the seamstress gathered up the ubiquitous shroud to help Arkady into it.

"I'll have to remember that," Arkady replied, thinking of how many dangerous secrets she was already privy to as she helped Linnie lift the shroud over her head. Careful not to catch it in the pins holding her hair in place, the two women managed to get it on without doing any damage to their hours of hard work.

"Well, if you forget, your grace," Linnie assured her, as she smoothed down the folds, "someone will remind you soon enough. I can *promise* you that."

Lady Chintara sent a carriage to collect Arkady. It was an exquisitely lacquered closed-in phaeton, drawn by two matched greys and perforated across the front of the cabin for ventilation and to allow the occupants to see out. It did neither job very well and the shroud just made it worse. Although it was still quite early in the day, encased in a full-length mantle and crammed into a closed box, Arkady was feeling quite faint by the time the carriage pulled up inside the entrance to the royal seraglium.

The door opened to a welcome gust of cooler air. By the time a step had been placed at the door of the phaeton for her to alight safely, the male coach driver had been hurried from the enclosed entrance so only the palace's female staff were on hand to greet the Glaeban ambassador's wife. Much to Arkady's delight, not one of the women was covered and as soon as the phaeton was led away, the women swarmed around her and lifted her shroud away. Then a tall, thin woman with greying hair stepped forward and curtseyed graciously.

"Welcome, your grace," she said in near flawless Glaeban. "If you will follow me, please? The Lady Chintara is expecting you."

Arkady inclined her head and followed the older woman, looking around with open curiosity as she walked through the palace seraglium. Although similar in its construction and decor, the royal seraglium was much larger and emptier than Arkady's quarters at the ambassador's palace and seemed much quieter as a result. It was also staffed— somewhat to her surprise—with the occasional male servant.

"There are men here," she couldn't help remarking, after walking past one room where a tall and quite pleasant-looking young man was holding forth to a group of young women seated on the floor around him, on a topic Arkady could only guess at, given they were speaking Torlenian.

"The men are blinded before being allowed to take up service in the seraglium," the woman informed her, as if such a thing was an everyday occurrence. "And castrated."

"A man has to be a blind eunuch to work here?" Arkady smiled. "I'm guessing you don't have too many volunteers."

Her escort was not amused. "On the contrary, your grace. To serve in the royal seraglium is an honour without peer. We select only the most worthy applicants."

"Forgive me," she said, wishing she'd kept her opinion to herself. *Some diplomat's wife you'll make, Arkady.* "I did not mean to give offence."

"I am but a slave, your grace. It is not possible to offend me."

Arkady was quite sure that wasn't the case, but she was more interested in the woman's status as a slave. Human slavery in Glaeba was rare. "Are there many human slaves in Torlenia?"

"Quite a number," the woman replied, looking at Arkady curiously. "Why?"

"In Glaeba, only the Crasii are permitted to be enslaved. We count human life to be more valuable than that of an animal and believe freedom is an inherent right of all men."

The Torlenian woman frowned as she walked. "As do we, your grace, but neither do we have slums where the dispossessed and homeless gather for cold comfort while they slowly starve to death on the streets of our wealthiest cities."

The woman's hostility was astonishing, all the more surprising given she was a slave. "What are you implying?" Arkady asked. "That slavery is your idea of a *welfare* system?"

"Only the poor, the disenfranchised, those with a debt they cannot meet or a debt to society they must repay are enslaved, your grace," the woman said as they reached the end of a long tiled hall and stepped into another vast chamber. "Slavery in Torlenia means these people are cared for, fed, and given an opportunity to redeem themselves through honest hard work. If you wish to call that a welfare system, then I suppose you're right. It may not suit your delicate Glaeban sensibilities, but at least we *have* a system, which is more than you can say for your country."

Arkady stopped and stared at the woman, a little appalled at her outburst. Such outspokenness was completely unexpected. Obviously the Torlenian definition of slavery varied a great deal from the Glaeban idea of the practice. Why hadn't Declan warned her about *that*?

"You'll have to forgive Nitta's passion on the subject of slavery, your grace," a voice said from behind Arkady. "She fancies herself something of a champion of injustice and doesn't get nearly enough opportunities to vent her spleen."

Arkady spun around to find a woman who could only be the Imperator's Consort standing behind her.

"My lady!" she said, bending in a deep curtsey.

As she rose, her first thought was that Lady Jorgan had been right. The Imperator's Consort *was* foreign. In this land of delicate women, dusky skin and dark eyes she was as tall as Arkady, blue-eyed, blonde and statuesque. She seemed to be about thirty, but her skin was so flawless, it was hard to pinpoint her exact age. Her Glaeban was perfect, her bearing effortlessly elegant, her white, sleeveless gown stylish but simple. Arkady felt overdressed and ungainly beside her.

"I heard rumours you were quite the Glaeban beauty, Lady Desean," the consort remarked. "I see they were not exaggerated."

"You flatter me, my lady."

"Such was not my intention. Leave us, Nitta." With a final glare at

Arkady, the slave bowed silently and withdrew, leaving the women alone. "I also hear you're very well educated," Lady Chintara added, indicating with her arm that Arkady should accompany her to the couches on the other side of the vast room. Through the open doors on the other side of the hall she could see part of a lush garden, and the hall had a fountain trickling down from an outlet near the garden doors. "Perhaps that's why Nitta felt the urge to berate you. Such a tongue-lashing would have been wasted on your predecessor."

Arkady wasn't sure how to answer that. "Yes . . . she's very outspoken for a . . ."

"Slave?" the consort finished for her with a faint smile.

"Actually, I was going to say for a woman," Arkady corrected, falling into step beside the consort, a little surprised by how pleasantly the woman was behaving. She'd heard Lady Chintara could be a terror. "I was under the impression education was something denied the women of Torlenia."

"Then you are as sadly misinformed about our country as Nitta is about yours. What exactly is it that you are educated in, your grace?"

"I have a doctorate in history from the University of Lebec."

Chintara seemed amused. "History? You have no history beyond the last Cataclysm, have you? Why would you want to study such a thing?"

"In truth? I had no desire to be a historian at the outset. I wanted to study medicine, and become a physician like my father, but I'm a woman so that meant they wouldn't accept me into any other faculty."

The Imperator's Consort smiled. "So we're not that different, Torlenians and Glaebans, after all. Please, be seated. I took the liberty of ordering breakfast. Have you eaten?"

Arkady had been too tense to eat this morning. She wondered if Chintara suspected as much. The table between the couches was laid out with a selection of chilled fruits and pastries, and there seemed to be enough food to feed a score of women, but there were only the two of them present and Chintara gave no indication they were expecting anyone else.

"Thank you," she said, taking a seat on the reclining couch opposite Chintara's. "I admit to being rather too busy to eat this morning."

"Too busy or too nervous?" the consort asked. When she saw Arkady's expression, she smiled. "It's all right, your grace. I do know my reputation. I've no doubt your servants have you believing I eat raw babies for breakfast."

Taking a huge gamble, Arkady smiled. "Well, they got that wrong, didn't they, my lady?" she said, casting her gaze over the heavily laden table. "Or is this just the first course?"

Chintara laughed. "Thank the Tides! Finally, a Glaeban with a sense of humour. I'm delighted you've come to Ramahn, my dear. Your predecessor was a sour old hag."

"So I've been told," Arkady agreed, a little warily. This pleasant, disarming young woman was the last thing she'd expected and with all the lectures she'd been given before coming here about what a monster the Imperator's Consort was, she was starting to worry that they'd taken a wrong turn and finished up at the wrong royal palace with the wrong royal consort.

"Don't look so alarmed, Arkady," Chintara said, reaching for the crystal wine jug that was beaded with condensation. "May I call you Arkady?"

"Of course."

"You may call me Chintara."

"I'm honoured, my lady."

"Because I permit you to use my first name? My, you are starved for entertainment, aren't you?"

Arkady leaned forward, accepting the wine Chintara poured with her own hand and smiled. "I admit, after having the freedom to do as I please in Glaeba, I find Torlenia's rules about women rather . . . limiting."

"But you just said you're a historian because they wouldn't let you be a physician, so you weren't actually free to do as you pleased in Glaeba, at all."

Arkady frowned. "I suppose, but I could walk down the street unescorted."

"There are some women who find that prospect quite daunting."

"Not in Glaeba," Arkady countered, and then she smiled, hoping she hadn't overstepped the mark. "I'm sorry. It's rude of me to question your religious practices."

"Religious practices?" Chintara scoffed. "The Torlenian rule about women not showing their faces in public isn't about religion, Arkady, it's about men being jealous and possessive."

"But I thought . . ."

Chintara smiled and leaned back on her couch. "I think we shall have to educate each other, you and I, Arkady. I will tell you of Torlenia's more idiotic customs and you can tell me of Glaeba's."

"I'd be delighted to learn more of Torlenia's history," Arkady agreed, not sure exactly what came under the heading of "Glaeban Idiotic Customs." And then before she could stop herself, she added, "Particularly the myths and legends you have of the Tide Lords."

Chintara eyed Arkady curiously. "Why do you want to know about the Tide Lords?"

"I've been studying them recently," she replied.

"And what did you learn about them?"

Arkady's brow furrowed at the question. "I'm not sure what you mean."

"I'm curious," Chintara said. "Did you learn anything interesting? Is the Tide returning? Do you know where they are?"

"*You* believe in the Tide Lords?" Arkady asked, mentally kicking herself for not assuming as much. Torlenians were quite passionate about their Tide Lords.

"Of course I do. Don't you?"

She hesitated before answering. "I'm starting to think there may be some merit in the notion they exist."

That reply made Chintara laugh out loud. "Then we have our work cut out for us, Arkady. I am clearly going to have to convince you the Tide Lords are real."

Arkady smiled and sipped her wine, thinking she didn't need any convincing at all, but she wasn't sure—for the sake of diplomatic relations between Glaeba and Torlenia—if she should inform the Imperator's Consort that not only did she know the Tide Lords were real, but she'd met two of them, and even slept with one of them.

She thought it prudent not to mention, either, that she had quite possibly fallen in love with the Immortal Prince and since leaving him buried alive in a mine collapse in the middle of the Shevron Mountains, had been recruited into the secret organisation whose sole function was to find a way to destroy them.

Chapter 7

Arkady was gone for an alarmingly long time; so long, Stellan began to wonder if she had somehow inadvertently offended the Imperator's Consort and been thrown into a dungeon to await execution. It wouldn't be the first time the consort had done something like that, and given the fragile relations between Glaeba and Torlenia at present, Stellan didn't think his fears unfounded. He was pacing his office, trying to come up with a reason to visit the royal palace that wouldn't look like he was worried for the safety of his wife, when the door opened and a shrouded figure stepped into the room.

"Tides, would you get me out of this wretched thing?" the spectre asked impatiently.

Almost faint with relief, Stellan hurried to her side and helped her lift off the shroud. Underneath she was wearing a gorgeous, multi-layered, embroidered gold dress. By the look of her, she'd pulled out all the stops to impress the Imperator's Consort.

"Thank the Tides you're safe," he told her, tossing the shroud over a nearby chair. "I was starting to panic about what might have happened to you. It's almost dark. Did something go wrong?"

"On the contrary," Arkady assured him, collapsing with a sigh onto the couch facing the marble-topped wrought-iron table that served as his desk. "The Lady Chintara and I got along famously. Apparently, I'm the first Glaeban she's ever met with a sense of humour."

"So it went well, then?"

Arkady eyed him oddly. "Isn't that what I just said?"

"I'm sorry, it just seems so unlikely. The woman is reputed to be a terror."

"Well, she's nobody's fool, I'll grant you that, but she hardly struck me as being terrible," Arkady assured him. "Were you really so worried about me?"

Stellan nodded and moved to the sideboard to pour them both a drink. "She imprisoned the Senestran ambassador's wife a few months ago, apparently for wearing the wrong colour. It was only for a couple of days, but it almost caused Torlenia and Senestra to go to war."

"That doesn't sound like the woman I met today."

"Perhaps she was on her best behaviour for the Glaeban ambassador's wife."

Arkady shrugged and accepted the wine he poured for her. "Actually, we spent much of the day discussing various customs unique to our homelands. She's a very knowledgeable woman."

Stellan took a seat beside her on the couch. "That could be why she liked you. Women of your talents are rare in this country."

"Women of my *talents*?" she repeated with a raised brow. "I'm not sure I like the sound of that. You make me sound like the prize exhibit in a particularly expensive brothel."

He smiled. "Trust me, it was meant as a compliment. Did you learn anything useful?"

"You mean other than the fact she's definitely not Torlenian and doesn't eat raw babies for breakfast? Not really." Arkady sipped her wine and smiled at his expression. "She was the one who brought up the topic of raw babies for breakfast, by the way, not me, so you can stop looking so worried."

Stellan shook his head, not sure he wanted to know the details of such a potentially offensive and diplomatically disastrous conversation. "Do you think she'll invite you back?"

It was more than an idle question. If Arkady could gain favour with the Imperator's Consort, the Imperator himself would be that much easier to deal with. It was no secret in diplomatic circles that Lady Chintara stood close behind the Torlenian throne and had a hand in most of the decisions her husband made.

"She already has," Arkady told him. "Tomorrow. She's invited me to join her for a bath."

Stellan was flabbergasted. Such an honour was almost unheard of for a foreigner, particularly one who'd been in the country barely a week. The Torlenians treated bathing the way Glaebans treated intimate dinner parties. They were reserved for close friends, meant for relaxing among one's peers and a sign of great favour. Although public baths were quite common in the city, only the wealthiest of men could afford private baths in their seraglium.

Only a most favoured courtier would be invited to share the palace baths with the Imperator's Consort.

"Tides, Arkady! What did you say to her? There are diplomats' wives all over Ramahn who'd kill for such an opportunity and they can't even get in to see her."

"I have no idea," his wife said with a shrug. "I don't recall doing or saying anything special, although—"

"What?" he asked, when she stopped mid-sentence.

She pursed her lips thoughtfully. "On the way to meet her I was subjected to something of a tirade by one of her slaves. I'm wondering now, if it wasn't some sort of test."

"What do you mean by a tirade?"

"The slave took me to task about the condition of our Glaeban slums."

"How did you respond?"

She thought for a moment before replying. "I'm not sure I did respond, come to think of it. I was too surprised by her telling me off to say anything and in the middle of it, Lady Chintara appeared."

Stellan tried to puzzle out what such a thing might mean. "Perhaps it was your lack of a response that pleased her?"

"I wish I knew. Whatever it was, we spent a very pleasant day together and she wants me to come back tomorrow."

"You'll go, of course."

Arkady smiled. "As I've not much else to do here, lazing around the royal seraglium all day while being massaged, oiled, perfumed and generally waited on hand and foot is one way to kill the time, I suppose. Did you know they blind and castrate the males who work in the seraglium?"

"I'd heard rumours," Stellan replied, wincing at the very thought of it. "What about his other wives?"

"If the Imperator has any other wives stashed about, Stellan, I saw no sign of them. And Chintara didn't strike me as the type to bother with the politics of a cage full of ambitious women, no matter how pleasantly gilded. There were other women there, but they seemed to be servants, or the wives of other palace staff. My guess is, if the Imperator had any other wives before Chintara came along, she's gotten rid of them. I doubt she'd tolerate the competition."

"Perhaps that's why she likes you," Stellan suggested.

"Because I'm no competition?"

He nodded, sipping his wine, wishing it was chilled. "You're foreign and married. Better yet, you're married to someone over whom the Imperator has no direct control. Even if he took a fancy to you, he couldn't order me to hand you over as he could one of his own subjects."

"Would he though?" Arkady asked. "Adultery is a capital crime here, isn't it?"

"The Imperator is above the law."

"It's a moot question anyway, dear," Arkady pointed out. "When is the Imperator ever likely to see me for long enough to take a fancy to me when I'm required to walk around wearing a bedsheet with eye-holes in it whenever I'm in his presence? Which begs another question—how does anybody manage to meet and fall in love in this country, anyway? Do the young men here swoon over a particularly well-worn sheet?"

Stellan smiled. "Tides, I hope you weren't making comments like that to Lady Chintara."

"No, Stellan," she promised, sipping her wine. "I behaved myself. You'd have been most impressed by my tact and forbearance."

He was relieved to hear it, although not really surprised. Arkady was a smart woman; too smart to endanger either herself or their position here in Ramahn with a frivolous remark to the wrong person. "I don't think falling in love is an issue here. Arranged marriages are the norm, I gather."

"Speaking of marriages, have you heard from Kylia or Mathu since we arrived?"

Stellan frowned and shook his head. "Not a word. I'm starting to worry a little, actually."

"They're probably too busy having a good time in Herino to think about writing to anybody," Arkady suggested. "It's only been a couple of months since the wedding. I'd not read too much into their silence, if I were you. Lord Deryon hasn't said anything in his dispatches that gives you cause for concern, has he?"

"No," he replied with a shake of his head. "But I still worry about my niece."

She smiled reassuringly. "I think this is one of those no-news-is-good-news situations, Stellan. If there was anything really going on with the crown prince or his wife, we'd have heard about it by now, I'm quite certain."

"You're probably right. Will you join me for dinner this evening?"

Arkady nodded. "Provided there's no law in this Tide-forsaken country against a husband and wife sharing a meal in their own home."

"Well, technically here in the embassy we're on Glaeban soil, anyway. I guess that means we can do as we please."

"In that case, I'd be delighted to join you for dinner, minus that miserable shroud, of course."

He reached across and took her hand, squeezing it affectionately. "I'll find a way to repay your forbearance someday, Arkady."

"We've only been here a short time, Stellan," she informed him with a wry expression. "You may want to reserve judgement on my wonderful levels of patience or the remarkable strength of my character until we've been here a while longer." She downed the rest of her wine in an unladylike gulp and added, "If I haven't choked anybody by ramming that wretched shroud down their throat in the next year or so, you can thank me then."

Chapter 8

In the normal course of events, Declan Hawkes had no mandate to keep tabs on the affairs of the royal family. His job was to keep Glaeba safe from outside threats. The implicit understanding was if Glaeba were under threat, that threat would not come from a member of its ruling family.

Lord Deryon, the King's Private Secretary, was responsible for security in the palace and except on the rare occasion when a fractious nobleman needed reminding he was a guest in the palace and was expected to behave accordingly, the King's Spymaster had little reason to interfere. All this had changed, of course, with the arrival of Kylia Debrell, the new wife of Glaeba's crown prince, and Jaxyn Aranville, the Lebec Ambassador to Court.

Were either of them the real Kylia or the real Jaxyn, Declan wouldn't have had a problem, but the fate of the Duke of Lebec's niece and the real Lord Aranville was anybody's guess. The impostors who had stolen their names and their lives were immortals with their eye on a much bigger prize than the Crown Prince of Glaeba or an ambassadorial appointment.

It might not have been so bad, Declan mused, as he strode the long tiled halls of the Herino Royal Palace toward his meeting with Lord Deryon, if it were only Kylia he had to deal with. Even if she was Diala—"The High Priestess" the Tarot named her—she was relatively powerless. She could heal—which meant she could probably kill just as effectively—using the Tide, and create localised disturbances that were unlikely to wreak the same sort of global devastation someone like Cayal or Jaxyn was capable of. Her accomplice, however, was a different problem entirely. Jaxyn, the Lord of Temperance (although he was anything but temperate), was one of the nine immortal Lords of the Tide—a creature capable of destroying Glaeba if the mood took him.

And well it might.

The Tide Lords had destroyed whole civilisations in the past, often over nothing more than an insult.

So lost in this morose line of thought was he, Declan was quite surprised to find he had reached the end of the long corridor of the east wing where Lord Deryon's private rooms were located. The King's Spymaster was recognised by the soldiers outside the door and admitted without question, the guards seeing nothing odd in a meeting so late between two officials who arguably were the two most powerful men in Glaeba after the king. Declan nodded a greeting to the guards and closed the door behind him. Glancing around, he found the King's Private Secretary seated at his writing table, muttering to himself as he signed his way through a pile of official-looking documents. The old man glanced over each one briefly before adding his name to it and then placed it aside on a pile that seemed about the same size as the one he was working on.

He glanced up at the sound of the door closing, and tossed his quill down on the desk with relief. "Tides, but I'm glad to see you, Declan."

"Is something wrong?"

"Not especially," the old man replied. "I'm just glad of the excuse to take a break. Do you have news on the whereabouts of the Immortal Prince?"

Declan shook his head, crossing the beautifully worked rug so he could take a seat beside the writing table. It was a warm evening, but Lord Deryon had a fire going, anyway, his age making him more sensitive to the cold than most.

Flopping into the chair, he shook his head. "Not a sign of him. He could be still trying to dig his way out of that cave-in up in the Shevron Mountains, you know." In truth, Declan would be quite happy if they never heard from the Immortal Prince again, although he knew how unlikely that was, given the Tide was on the turn.

Although Arkady had never admitted to it, Declan worried about what might have happened between Cayal and the Duchess of Lebec while she was his prisoner. Thank the Tides she was safely tucked away in Ramahn, at present. If the Immortal Prince did return, at least Arkady was out of harm's way for the time being.

Stretching his long legs out in front of him, Declan folded his arms with a glum expression. "Actually, I was hoping you'd have some good news for me."

"I'm no closer to learning the true identity of our new crown princess, if that's what you're asking," Lord Deryon told him. He sounded tired, the lines on his face reflecting every one of his seventy-odd years. "It's hard to get anyone close to her. All her slaves are Crasii, which means none of them is going to betray her confidence, even if they wanted to."

"Have you spoken to Mathu?"

The old man's brows knitted together. "And tell him what exactly, Declan? That we suspect his seventeen-year-old bride—with whom he is completely besotted—is actually a ten-thousand-year-old immortal with designs on his father's throne?"

Declan allowed himself a small smile. "It does sound a trifle peculiar, doesn't it? What about Jaxyn?"

"Lord Aranville is making himself right at home," the secretary assured him. "He's becoming a permanent fixture at Princess Kylia's side. And he's getting far too friendly with Prince Mathu, too."

"That could be a problem, you know," Declan mused.

"Yes, well I hardly thought it was going to help matters," Deryon snapped. Then he sighed, shaking his head. "I'm sorry, Declan. I don't mean to bite your head off. I'm just at my wits' end. Every time I see the two of them together it makes my blood run cold."

"I know what you mean."

"All my life I've protected the Lore and striven to keep humanity free of the meddling of immortals and yet here we are, with two of them living under our very noses, the Tide returning, and I find myself helpless to do anything about it."

"Not quite helpless," Declan assured him. "We have the Scards on our side this time."

"And how many Scards can we count on, eh? A few thousand at most? That's not going to bring down the Tide Lords."

"We need to get a Scard on Kylia's staff."

"I would have thought that was obvious. The question is: who?"

Declan frowned, trying to think of a suitable candidate. "None of the Scards I can think of that we've got stashed up in the Valley has the skill to carry off being a ladies maid. Most of them would try biting her soon as look at her, anyway."

Lord Deryon smiled grimly. "I fear you're right about that. What about your chameleon Crasii? What's her name? Tiji, isn't it? Couldn't she do the job?"

Declan shook his head. "Her skill is her ability to get into places where she doesn't belong and stay there long enough to find out something useful. She's not trained as a servant and even if I wanted to, I couldn't let you have her. She's in Caelum."

Lord Deryon frowned. "What is she doing in Caelum?"

Declan smiled at such a silly question. "I'm the spymaster and I sent her there. What do you *think* she's doing, Karyl?"

"Caelum is a Glaeban ally," the old man pointed out, looking a little concerned. "Why are we spying on them?"

"Two reasons. Firstly, because despite what she says in public, Queen Jilna of Caelum is furious over our refusal of her daughter, Nyah, as a bride for Mathu. Secondly, because someone called the Duchess of Torfail has offered her son as an alternative husband."

"And why do we care if the Caelish have managed to find some fool willing to marry a ten-year-old girl?"

"Because once she weds him, Nyah can take the throne, and this unknown fool becomes king of our closest neighbour."

Lord Deryon looked quite puzzled. "Then we'll deal with him if that happens. I'm surprised you're wasting a resource like Tiji on something like this when we have Tide Lords piling up all over the palace."

"I probably wouldn't be," Declan replied, "if there was actually such a place as Torfail."

Now the old man looked really confused. "You mean there's *not*?"

"Not on any map I can find."

He looked quite stunned. "Then it's a good chance this man is . . . or rather this duchess . . . is running some sort of scam?"

Declan smiled at the old man's gift for understatement. "I'd say so."

"Have we alerted Queen Jilna to the possibility this man is an impostor?" he asked with alarm.

Declan shook his head. "I'm more concerned about who this duchess and her son really are, than warning Jilna about them. She has her own spymaster and if she's stupid enough to accept this suit for her daughter's hand without getting Ricard Li to check out the suitor, then more fool her. I'm worried about something else. The Tide is turning, Karyl, and all of a sudden there seem to be impostors popping up all over the place. Given who we've got skulking around our own royal palace these days, I thought it prudent to discover if our neighbours are suffering from the same malady."

The old man visibly paled at what Declan was implying. "Tides! You're not suggesting this duchess is another immortal, are you?"

"Who knows?" he replied with a shrug. "What's worrying me more than the notion she's immortal, though, is the prospect of *which* immortal. A mother and son act? There's only one lot of Tide Lords I can think of who can carry that off with any hope of success."

Lord Deryon slumped in his chair. "Syrolee and Engarhod. Or Syrolee and her son, to be more accurate."

"If the Empress of the Five Realms is back, then you're right. But worse, it means so are Tryan and Elyssa. They're the ones we really have to worry about, because they're the ones who can manipulate the Tide. Syrolee and Engarhod are just the puppet-masters; the real show is their children."

"You may be wrong, Declan."

"And I'll never be happier to admit it, if it turns out I am. I won't know for certain until Tiji gets back from Caelum, however."

"Did you warn her of your suspicions?"

Declan shook his head. "I didn't want to prejudice her opinion. If she comes back and says she's seen a suzerain, then we can rely on her information."

"Can't she send word? Surely that would be quicker?"

"I told her to report back to me in person and not risk sending a message. We can't afford this news to fall into the wrong hands."

Lord Deryon nodded in reluctant agreement. "You mean another Crasii's hands, I suppose?"

He shrugged. "Any one of them could have been suborned by a Tide Lord, by now. The Scards are the only Crasii we can trust. That includes every Crasii in the palace, I hope you realise."

Lord Deryon closed his eyes for a moment, as if he hoped all these problems might be gone by the time he opened them again. Declan waited without saying a word, understanding how he felt, wishing he could offer the old man a solution, or even some comfort. Unfortunately, he could offer neither.

"That limits the people in the palace I can trust to the king, the queen, Prince Mathu and a handful of aides I've known since they were children," the secretary concluded with a heavy sigh. "Everyone else surrounding the royal family is suspect . . . Tides, Declan, that's over a hundred people. And then there's the Royal Guard to consider. How many of those felines will Jaxyn or this other immortal we have posing as Kylia get to? How many of their officers are human and how many are immortals in disguise . . . ? The more I think about it, the more I think it'll be less painful if I just fall on my sword now and be done with it."

"That does seem to be the easiest solution," Declan agreed with a thin smile. "Probably try it myself, only I can't stand the sight of blood."

Lord Deryon took a deep breath. "Ah . . . If only it was that simple, eh?"

"If only," Declan agreed. To Declan, Lord Deryon looked like an old man trying to brace himself against the force of an incoming tide, a depressing analogy fairly close to the reality of their situation. "Did you want me to see if I can find you some more Scards to work in the palace? It'd be useful to get a few Crasii we can trust surrounding the king and queen, at least."

Lord Deryon nodded. "If you could. In the meantime, I shall start quizzing every palace staff member I encounter to see if I can trip one of them up in a lie."

"That's going to make you popular."

"Nobody becomes the King's Private Secretary if they want to be popular, Declan," the old man assured him with a heavy sigh. "Nor the King's Spymaster, for that matter. When do you expect to hear from Tiji?"

"Any day now," he replied.

"And if our worst fears are realised?"

Declan shrugged, certain there was only one course of action open to him.

"Then I guess I'm going to Caelum," he said.

Chapter 9

It took Arkady quite a few visits to the royal baths to get used to being naked in front of complete strangers and she was convinced she was never going to be comfortable being touched by them, either. Although the masseurs working in the royal seraglium—blind eunuchs, one and all—were very professional and completely impersonal as they pounded and oiled her body into submission, Arkady came from a culture where nudity was frowned upon and physical contact between men and women that involved anything more than a handshake or a peck on the cheek held sexual connotations for everyone involved.

In Ramahn, however, bathing was a ritual in its own right. Full-body massages were considered a necessity, rather than an extravagance, and in a climate where more often than not clothing just made you sweat, it was—in the privacy of one's own baths—considered optional.

Arkady found this casual attitude toward the human body more than a little disturbing. Glaebans were much more conservative than Torlenians, she'd discovered, in addition to which, Arkady had plenty of her own reasons to be wary of exposing herself. She thought she'd concealed her discomfort well, until Lady Chintara, who was lying facedown on the massage table with her eyes closed, opened them abruptly and fixed her imperious gaze on Arkady.

"You need to learn how to relax, my girl."

"I beg your pardon?"

"I said you must learn to relax. You flinch every time someone touches you."

Arkady lifted her head, trying to remember if she had flinched or not. She hadn't done it consciously, but she also knew she was a long way from being able to lounge around wearing nothing but her bare skin and the family jewels in the presence of strangers—even if they *were* blind. And she certainly didn't want to give this woman any cause for concern. Although this was her tenth visit to the royal seraglium in as many days, Stellan still hadn't been able to get an appointment with the Imperator to discuss the Chelae Islands. As Stellan was keen for Arkady to ask Chintara to intercede on his behalf, she could do nothing that might offend her hostess. "I wasn't aware of flinching, my lady."

The Imperator's Consort pushed away the probing hands of the masseur who'd been working on her back and sat up, swinging her legs around so she was sitting on the edge of the table staring at Arkady. "You don't like to be touched, do you?"

"I don't believe I said anything to indicate—"

"It's not what you say," Chintara cut in. "It's the look on your face. You're not relaxing. You look as if you're in pain. Is that ham-fisted fool hurting you?"

"Of course not!" she hurried to assure her hostess, fearful for the man's fate should she complain about his work. "Your people are very good at their jobs. I was just . . ." Arkady's voice trailed off, as she re-alised there was no excuse she could offer. Better to just be sorry about it and move the discussion on to something less personal. "I apologise if I have somehow offended you or your generous hospitality, my lady, by giving the impression I don't appreciate the honour you have be-stowed on me by—"

"Oh, for the Tide's sake, Arkady, you don't need to apologise. There are plenty of other women in Ramahn I could invite here if I wanted a sycophant. I'm curious, that's all. Is your aversion to intimate physical contact common to all Glaebans or is it something unique to Arkady Desean?"

Arkady hesitated, not sure how to reply.

"It's not that hard a question, is it?"

"I'm not sure I'm in a position to speak for all Glaebans," Arkady replied, finally. "Particularly when it comes to where or how they like being touched. That's not something we discuss in polite society."

Chintara laughed and stood up from the bench. She was a truly ex-traordinary creature, her physique sculpted like a warrior's rather than an idle woman's body. The consort regularly shaved every hair from her body, with the exception of her eyebrows and her head of stunning blonde hair that cascaded in natural waves to below her waist. She had introduced Arkady to the custom, which seemed both decadent and delightful all at once. Torlenians considered unshaven women little better than Crasii, the consort had explained the first time they bathed together and she'd spied Arkady's natural body hair. Chintara had insisted Arkady follow suit, assuring her that unless she wished to become a social pariah among the women of Ramahn, she would be well advised to continue the practice on a regular basis. Arkady—once she got over the strangeness of the notion—discovered she quite liked the smooth feel of her skin after the shaving was done.

Chintara must have mistaken her silence for reticence in the presence of the masseurs. "Leave us," she ordered the young men, and then waited until they had departed and the women were alone before fixing her gaze on Arkady. "You are uncomfortable when undressed in the presence of slaves. I find that odd. You're used to being waited on, are you not?"

"I've become used to it, yes."

"But your Glaeban slaves do not deal so intimately with their masters as ours, do they?"

Arkady shook her head. "Not at all. And they're usually Crasii, rather than human, which makes their attention seem much less personal. We are much more . . . reserved. In private, at least, although in public we're quite wanton and liberal by Torlenian standards."

Chintara smiled. "There was a time we were just as wanton and liberal."

"What happened to change things?"

"A Tide Lord became jealous that another immortal was lusting after his lover."

Arkady sat up a little straighter, fascinated to hear Chintara admit such a thing. "Then it *is* a religious custom, wearing the shroud?"

"To be a religious custom, belief in the Tide Lords would have to be our religion," Chintara pointed out.

"But *you* believe in them."

"I believe the sun will come up tomorrow, too, but that doesn't mean I worship it, or that it's my religion."

"But you have monasteries and temples devoted to studying the Tide—"

"We have people who choose a life of seclusion to contemplate the various ways in which the Tide affects us. Others study the teachings of the Lord of Reckoning, who has left us with much to contemplate. That doesn't make it a religion, Arkady."

"So the Way of the Tide is a way of life, not a creed?" Arkady asked.

Chintara smiled. "Tides, but you're a pleasant change from the usual ambassadorial trophy wife I have to tolerate, Arkady. Shall we spend the afternoon discussing more of the differences between our religions, or the lack of them? You, who claim your women are better off than ours, but who flinches when a stranger touches her body?"

Arkady was quite sure there was nothing down that road she wanted to discuss with the Imperator's Consort. "I think, my lady, it's not a matter of *where* one is touched, but by *whom*."

Chintara seemed amused by her reply. "A fair comment, albeit an evasive one."

"I'm curious as to why you refer to Torlenian customs and the Way of the Tide as your own," she asked, hoping to move the topic away from herself and the reasons for her own particular inhibitions. "Torlenia is clearly not the country of your birth. Have you embraced their way of life so completely because of your husband, or because it appeals to you personally?"

"You see, that's why I like you, Arkady," Chintara announced, slipping a light silken robe over her statuesque body and then shaking her magnificent hair free from the knot that had been holding it clear of the oil. "Nobody else in Torlenia would dare ask me a question like that. Come to think of it, few of them would have the wit to think of it in the first place. Why don't you stop sitting there clutching that wretched sheet like your virginity's at stake and put a robe on? We'll have some lunch."

A little embarrassed at how transparent her inhibitions were to this perceptive woman, Arkady hopped off the bench and slipped on the silken bathrobe left for her by the slaves, tying it closed with relief. Chintara watched her dressing, a wry smile on her face.

"You can't help it, can you?"

"Can't help what, my lady?"

"Acting as if you have something no other woman has ever seen. Do you not bathe communally in Glaeba?"

"Tides no!" Arkady exclaimed. "At least not in any decent establishment."

"It's all the fault of the weather," Chintara concluded, as Arkady fell into step beside her. The women padded barefoot across the tiled floor of the anteroom to the main chamber where the slaves had already laid out lunch. "Once you start having to cover your body to stop yourself from freezing to death, you're doomed."

"I'm not sure I follow your reasoning, my lady."

Chintara shrugged, as if the answer was self-evident, and indicated that Arkady should take a seat. "After a while, people forget *why* they're dressed from head to toe in furs. The clothes take on other purposes. They become less and less about protection from the elements and more about assuming false identities, boasting of rank, displaying wealth . . . or any number of other human foibles. Once you conceal it, flesh becomes a currency, Arkady, remember that. We should make everyone on Amyrantha move to the equatorial zones where clothing is an adornment, rather than a crutch."

"Even if such a thing were possible, my lady," Arkady said, taking a seat opposite the consort on the couches facing the low table where lunch awaited them, "your argument is flawed. Despite the temperature, your women cover their bodies from head to toe here in Torlenia, with a shroud that is mandated by law."

"In public, yes," the consort conceded, helping herself to a platter which she began to pile with sliced fruit. "But we don't have the same constraints in the privacy of our own homes. And if you think about it, the shroud serves the same purpose as being naked."

Arkady shook her head. There was a piece of logic begging an explanation if ever she'd heard one. "I would have said the two were diametrically opposed."

"They equalise us, Arkady," Chintara replied. "Under the shroud, all women are beautiful; all women carry the promise of something exquisite. Stripped of clothing, in the eyes of men, we are the same, too, believe it or not. It is not our appearance that attracts men. If men only cared about physical perfection, the handful of perfect women in this world would have all the men chasing them and the rest of womankind would be ignored."

Arkady smiled. "According to my father, that's the main function of alcohol. *Everyone is beautiful through the bottom of a glass*, he used to say."

Chintara laughed. "Perhaps he has a point, but I fear you're missing mine. It is the promise of the pleasure we offer them, that makes a man foolish over the butcher's fat daughter as easily as someone as lovely as you. The lure of immortality is more than most men can resist."

"*Immortality?*"

Chintara nodded, apparently seeing nothing peculiar in the reference. "Since the Immortal Prince extinguished the Eternal Flame, Arkady, the only hope for any man on this world to achieve immortality is to do it the old-fashioned way—through his descendants."

"You *know* the story of how the Immortal Prince extinguished the Eternal Flame?" Arkady asked, fascinated to realise here was an opportunity to hear the legend from someone who believed in the Tide Lords as real beings, rather than mythical figures on a painted set of Tarot cards.

And to hear something other than Cayal's version of events.

"Of course. I'm surprised you know anything of it, though. I thought you Glaebans considered anything to do with the Tide Lords to be superstitious nonsense."

"I have a . . . friend," she replied. "She is something of an expert on the Tarot. She used to tell fortunes at our dinner parties."

"And what did your friend tell you about the destruction of the Eternal Flame?"

"That Cayal . . . the Immortal Prince . . . was so angered by the death of his daughter, he emptied the Great Inland Sea of Torlenia, making it rain down on Glaeba in an effort to douse the Eternal Flame, creating the Great Lakes in the process."

"Ah yes," Chintara agreed, picking through the fruit bowl until she found a small bunch of grapes she considered pleasing. "The Tears of the Immortal Prince. I've heard that version."

"Is there another?"

"Several."

"I've not heard of them."

"That's hardly surprising, given you're a Glaeban sceptic."

"Will you tell me about them?"

Chintara studied Arkady for a moment, her expression intrigued. "I'm surprised you want to know."

"I'm a historian, my lady. I collect legends the way others collect shells or porcelain figurines."

That answer seemed to satisfy the consort. She leaned forward and picked up her glass. "Well, everyone agrees the Immortal Prince was driven by rage when he destroyed the Flame," she said, taking a sip of chilled wine. "But not all of us share the Tarot's romantic notion of his motives. In fact, there are many who believe it was his anger at Diala and Arryl for thwarting his plans, not his grief over a child—who may or may not have been his—that drove Cayal to destroy Amyrantha's climate so comprehensively it took the world the better part of a millennium to recover from it."

"Plans for what?"

The consort shrugged, her attention once more fixed on the buffet. "That we'll never know, I suppose. Some think he was planning to challenge Syrolee and Engarhod. Others thought he was still looking for a way to get even with Tryan for destroying his homeland and planned to use Fliss to do it. Then there's the chance Lukys had something to do with it. He always seems to be lurking in the background whenever something catastrophic happens."

As she listened to Chintara, Arkady was struck by an odd feeling that she'd heard all this before. It wasn't so much *what* Chintara was telling her, but the *way* in which she told it. The familiarity, the assurance with which she spoke, was hauntingly reminiscent of the way Cayal spoke when he was telling his story . . .

In fact, not since the Immortal Prince had Arkady met anyone who spoke with such confidence about the Tide Lords and their motives.

And then something else occurred to her that left Arkady breathless. "My lady, you talk of Cayal flooding Glaeba's Great Rift Valley over the death of a child named Fliss."

The consort leaned back against her couch, tucking her legs underneath her. "So?"

"The Tarot mentions nothing about a child. According to the Tarot, the Immortal Prince flooded Glaeba with his tears over the death of his one true love, Amaleta."

The Imperator's Consort barely even hesitated before offering an explanation. "We are much better educated, here in Torlenia, than those in other countries who rely on a charlatan's tool for their information, Arkady. As a historian, surely you understand that."

"Yes, my lady, of course I do. It's just you seem so . . ." Arkady hesitated, searching for the right words. "So . . . well informed . . ."

Chintara smiled. "Do you think Glaeba is the only place where a woman might gain an education?"

"Of course not."

"Then don't look so surprised, Arkady. Some of us know the history of the Tide Lords quite intimately."

"You must have studied them extensively, my lady," she said, wondering if this woman could be recruited to Declan's Cabal. Someone with such in-depth knowledge would be a great asset to those looking to find a way to protect Amyrantha from the Tide Lords' return.

"You have no idea," the consort agreed with a smile. "More wine?"

"Thank you," Arkady replied, wishing she was brave enough to pursue the matter further. But Stellan's position in Ramahn was still too tenuous and for all her outward appearance of friendliness, Arkady didn't know Chintara well enough to know if she could risk mentioning the Cabal of the Tarot.

One thing was certain, though, she decided as Chintara rang the bell for a slave. As soon as she returned to the embassy, Arkady was going to send a message to Declan Hawkes in Glaeba.

Perhaps the King's Spymaster knew whether or not the Torlenian Imperator's Consort could be trusted.

Chapter 10

Hidden Valley proved to be everything Warlock had hoped for, while being nothing like he expected. Nestled in a small valley some eight miles from the main manor house of the Summerton estate, it was a place of fertile soil, abundant game and several hundred Crasii of every species Warlock had ever heard of.

Aleki Ponting had delivered Warlock and Boots into the care of a large canine named William Phydeau. He ran the camp and was responsible for training the Scards who'd found a home there, not as fighters, as Warlock had assumed, but as spies. The Cabal of the Tarot needed Crasii who could slip in and out of the halls of power for one very simple reason—if you were looking for a Tide Lord, once the Tide was on the turn, the halls of power were the best places to look for them.

Warlock had few complaints about the camp. He and Boots were allocated a bunk in a small hut on the canine side of the valley and welcomed with surprisingly little fuss by the other occupants. The food was plain but plentiful and there was always something new to learn, either about the Tide Lords or ways to deal with them. They were instructed on the secrets to appearing servile when you were anything but, how to get messages out secretly, how to write and read simple codes and phrases that would identify other Scards, trained by and working for the Cabal.

The weather was warm, the other Crasii didn't care that he was an ex-convict and Boots treated him like a friend, which—given their previous intimacy—was more than he expected. Female canines were notorious for their fickle natures, and he wasn't sure what had brought about this change in her until she'd informed him, quite matter-of-factly over dinner one evening, that she was pregnant.

Since then, despite the fact she acted more as if she was resigned to the idea of impending motherhood, rather than excited by it, she had been not just friendly, but almost affectionate. Like it or not, she was his mate now. Warlock was still adjusting to the notion that he had one, let alone the news that in a few months' time, he was going to be a father.

Warlock had only one complaint, really. On his arrival in Hidden Valley, Phydeau announced that he would have to change his name.

"I am Warlock," he'd announced. "Out of Bella, by Segura. I have no need of another name."

"Your name brands you as less than human," Phydeau had said. He was a large, shaggy canine with a dark-brown pelt covered in nicks and scars indicating he'd not found Hidden Valley without a fight. He'd been a tracker once—according to the other Scards in their hut—who'd murdered his master when ordered to tear apart another Crasii who'd displeased the man by letting their quarry get away from them on a weekend hunt. Whether he was a true Scard—one who could defy an immortal—was unknown. Like many of the creatures here in Hidden Valley, their rebellious natures had brought them to the Cabal's attention, but until they'd confronted and defied an immortal, as both Warlock and Boots had done, nobody was really sure who were the true Scards and who were the hopefuls. It was a sobering thought, and made their predicament all the more dangerous. The Cabal was building up a secret army of Scards with no guarantee they wouldn't change sides and betray them all, the first time an immortal commanded them to do so.

"But I'm *not* human," Warlock replied. "I am Crasii."

"And an animal, according to the vast majority of humans," Phydeau reminded him.

"My master always treated me with respect."

"*Respect*? Tides, lad! Why do you think they name us like household pets? Out of consideration for our feelings?"

"I never really gave the issue any thought."

"Well, you should," Phydeau suggested. "Have you ever heard a human announce their pedigree the way you so proudly announce yours?"

"Warlock is who I am," he maintained stubbornly. "I cannot change that. Nor do I wish to change it."

Phydeau shook his head. "You are no longer called Warlock. Warlock is a name one gives a pet dog. You are Cecil Segura. Cecil will be your first name, and Segura, because that's your father's name. From now on, that's how you'll be called."

"I wish to be called Warlock."

The old Crasii had smiled, clapping Warlock on the shoulder. "It's a good name, Cecil. You'll get used to it."

"I am Warlock," he insisted.

"Your mate didn't have a problem with her new name."

For a moment, he didn't understand who Phydeau was referring to, the idea of having a mate was still so new to him. When he did, Warlock was shocked. "You gave Boots another name, too?"

The camp commander nodded. "From now on, she will be known as Tabitha Belle."

Warlock had frowned, trying to imagine calling Boots by anything but her given name, but he couldn't do it. Boots was tough and cheeky and resilient. The dam of his cubs wasn't a *Tabitha Belle*.

"She didn't object?"

Phydeau shook his large, shaggy head. "Why would she object, Cecil? She was named after a type of human footwear. What dignity is there in that?"

What dignity indeed, Warlock thought, as he helped carry water back to their hut on the slope, overlooking the thatched common-house where the Scards gathered for meetings and any business that involved all of them. It was cleaning day in Hidden Valley. William Phydeau ran a tight camp and every Crasii in it was expected to pull their weight and help maintain the camp in good order.

Dignity, be damned. There wasn't a lot of dignity in being named Cecil that Warlock could see.

"Hey! Farm Dog! Wait up!"

Warlock stopped and turned to find Boots hurrying up the path behind him, rather disturbed to realise that he actually preferred "Farm Dog" to "Cecil." She had shed her linen shift now she was living among her own kind with no humans to please or offend. Her pelt was brushed to a shine, her bushy tail pert and enticing. She looked fabulous, Warlock thought, eyeing her swelling belly. It was almost three months since their mating and there was no longer any chance of hiding her pregnancy. Now he'd gotten used to the idea, Warlock was secretly bursting with delight that he was to become a father, although Boots seemed a little more pragmatic about impending motherhood.

"Hello, Boots."

"My name is Tabitha," she reminded him, falling into step beside him. Then she grinned and nudged him with her elbow. "*Cecil.*"

Warlock was not amused. "I am Warlock."

"You're an obstinate fool," she corrected as they resumed walking up the steep path to the hut. "Why don't you just give in and accept it? Everyone else here has a proper name."

"Giving us human names doesn't make us human. We are Crasii."

"Actually, we're Scards," she pointed out. "Even the Crasii don't accept us."

"Then I am a Scard and proud of it. I don't need a different name to remind me of the fact."

Boots shook her head at his stubbornness, but said nothing further on the matter and they walked the rest of the way up to the hut in silence, squinting into the rising sun. Warlock wished he knew how to explain what he felt; how much a part of his identity his pedigree was. He wanted Boots to understand.

Tides, he wanted Phydeau and every Scard in Hidden Valley to understand.

I am Warlock. It's who I am.

"Cecil! Cecil!"

Boots turned before Warlock at the cry. When it did register that he was the one being hailed, he looked over his shoulder to find a young feline named Marianne running up the path behind them.

It was rare to see a feline on this side of the valley, so Marianne's visit could only mean something out of the ordinary. Phydeau preferred the two most populous subspecies to stay apart. Although they shared a common purpose, and trained together during the day, it was hard to overcome their natural instincts regarding the other Crasii species, and their commander preferred to avoid incidents rather than deal with them after the fact. Life was peaceful, here in Hidden Valley, but it was an enforced peace and one endangered it at their peril.

Marianne was a kitten bred here in the valley, the offspring of two known Scards and therefore guaranteed a Scard herself. She had an older sister, she'd told Boots, who was already off working for the Cabal and she couldn't wait to be old enough to do the same. Warlock was fairly certain her enthusiasm was only because she had never known slavery or even human company that wasn't friendly to her kind. He wondered how she would fare in the world outside Hidden Valley when it came time for her to leave.

"What's wrong?"

"Captain Phydeau wants you."

"Did he say why?"

The young feline nodded. "Tiji's back."

"Who's Tiji?" Boots asked.

"She's one of us," Marianne explained unhelpfully. "You'd best hurry. The captain wasn't actually asking, you know."

Boots took the water bucket from Warlock before he could respond. "You'd better get down there. I'll finish off your chores."

"Are you sure you should be carrying anything heavy?"

"Don't be ridiculous," she replied. "Anyway, I'd rather do your chores than have Phydeau growling at me."

Warlock nodded, and turned to the feline. "Take me to him."

Warlock had never seen a chameleon Crasii before. Apparently they were common once, bred by the immortals primarily to spy on each other. But they were difficult to breed and because of their ability to blend with their surroundings, they became as much a nuisance to their creators as an asset. The Tide Lords had obliterated most of them before the last Cataclysm. The few who'd escaped the purge were the descendants of the Scards who'd run away in the years before the immortals had determined to be rid of their reptilian creations. As a consequence, there were few chameleons who weren't genuine Scards, although that was something not generally known among humans, or even most ordinary Crasii.

The silver-skinned female was sitting cross-legged on the end of the long wooden table in the room they used as a communal meeting hall on the few occasions all the residents of Hidden Valley were required to gather en masse. The chameleon was dressed in a plain linen shift, speaking in a low voice to Phydeau and Aleki Ponting. Warlock was surprised to see the Lord of Summerton here. In the month he'd been in Hidden Valley, this was the first time he'd laid eyes on their human benefactor.

Lord Ponting looked up when he heard the door of the hall closing, beckoning Warlock forward.

The big canine bowed politely to the nobleman. "My lord."

"Phydeau tells me your new name is Cecil."

"I prefer to keep the name Warlock, my lord."

Aleki smiled humourlessly. "You may yet have your wish granted, my friend. You've not met Tiji before, I take it?"

Warlock turned his attention to the Crasii who was watching him with large, dark, unblinking eyes. She sat unnaturally still; at rest, but somehow poised for flight at the same time. It was unnerving.

"No, my lord."

"Then allow me to introduce you," Phydeau said. "Tiji, this is Cecil Segura."

"Hello," she said, staring at him warily.

"Hello," he replied, trying to imagine what circumstance involving this Crasii might also involve him.

Before he had a chance to ask, however, Phydeau offered an explanation. "Tiji's just got back from Caelum."

"I see."

The big, shaggy Crasii smiled. "I doubt that, old son. Tell Cecil what you saw, Tiji."

"Syrolee, Tryan and Elyssa," the chameleon replied without emotion.

"You saw the Empress of the Five Realms?" Warlock gasped, staring at her in open disbelief.

"Yes, I did."

"Are you certain?"

"No," the chameleon replied. "I mistake ordinary humans for the suzerain all the time."

"Settle down, Tiji," Phydeau advised. "He doesn't mean to question your ability."

Actually, that's exactly what Warlock was doing, but he chose not to argue the point. "What is the Empress of the Five Realms doing in Caelum?"

"Positioning herself to take control of the country when her son marries Princess Nyah," Aleki explained.

"But . . . they must be stopped!" he declared, looking at the three of them standing around so calmly, realising, even as he uttered the words, how futile they were.

Stopping the Tide Lords was no more possible than stopping the Tide.

Somewhat to his surprise, however, nobody laughed at his hopeless show of bravado.

"I'm not sure if that's possible," Aleki said. "But it *is* vital that Declan Hawkes knows of this. He'll be able to advise the rest of the Pentangle and they can decide how to deal with the news."

"What do you want of me?"

"Tiji is exhausted," Phydeau explained. "She's just crossed over from Caelum through the mountains and she still needs to get to Herino. If this wasn't so critical, she could get there on her own and nobody would even know she'd passed by, but this is too important to leave her unescorted and dependent on her own devices, and a lone female of any species is in danger on the Herino road."

"You want *me* to take her to the capital?" He stared at them in surprise. "Why?"

"Firstly, because you're big and scary enough to protect her," Aleki told him with an encouraging smile. "Secondly, because Declan needs you. He's looking for Scards he can place in the palace to keep an eye on Jaxyn and the other immortal."

"There is *another* immortal in Glaeba?"

"We think so," Aleki confirmed. "Which is why we need you in Herino. You're trained as an estate steward. In fact you're probably better trained than half the staff in the Herino Palace."

"Can Boots come with me?" he asked.

Aleki shook his head. "Jaxyn knows her. Worse, he knows she's a Scard. Your mate will have to stay here, I'm afraid."

This was happening far too quickly for Warlock. "But Boots is with pup. I'd rather stay here."

"Then you'll be killed," Tiji announced, before either of the others could reply. She was looking at Warlock with that disconcerting, unblinking stare. "You are either with us, or against us, dog-boy. And the Cabal has only one way of dealing with Scards who are against us."

He glared at the reptilian Crasii, but before he could retort, Phydeau intervened with a conciliatory smile. "Tiji's tired, Cecil. She's not thinking about what she's saying."

"But I'm right," the chameleon insisted.

Oddly, Tiji's frankness was comforting. Warlock had no time for subterfuge. He wanted to know exactly where he stood.

"Is she speaking the truth?" he asked, his gaze swinging between the canine and human. "If I choose to stay here with my mate, you'll have me killed?"

After an awkward few moments of silence, it was Aleki Ponting who answered him. "If you refuse, I admit, we will be forced to examine your commitment to our cause."

"Do you think me disloyal?"

"I think you sat opposite the Immortal Prince in a Lebec gaol cell for several months," Phydeau reminded him. "It wouldn't be the first time a Tide Lord has sent a loyal Crasii among us, posing as a Scard."

Warlock was shocked at what they were suggesting. "You mean, this is some kind of *test*?"

"If that's how you want to view it." Aleki shrugged.

"And suppose I *am* a spy; a Tide Lord plant, sent among you by the Immortal Prince? What happens to me when I get to Herino?"

"If you turn out to be a Tide Lord spy," Tiji replied in a tone that matched her flat, unblinking stare, "you won't *make* it to Herino, dog-boy."

"Stop calling me that!!"

"He's right, Tiji," Phydeau scolded. "You're not helping."

"Hey, you're giving me over to the care of a canine who's spent the last few months keeping an immortal entertained," she pointed out. "I'll be as unhelpful as I want, Phydeau."

"I am not a Tide Lord spy. I want to be free of them as much as any other Scard in Hidden Valley," Warlock announced tightly. "I just want to stay with my mate and be here when my pups are born. And the Tide take you all if my word on that isn't good enough for you."

In the nervous silence that followed, Warlock could feel them weighing up the risk he might pose to the Cabal against the value of his word.

The tension was so thick he could almost touch it.

"What if we try to arrange it so you're back in time for the birth?" Phydeau asked.

"Can you do that?"

He glanced at Aleki and then shrugged. "We can try."

"Will that prove my loyalty? Will you be satisfied then? Will my pups be permitted to be born here in Hidden Valley, safe and free?"

It was Aleki—the only human present—who stepped forward, in the end, offering Warlock his hand. "Whatever you think of the suzerain, Warlock, I don't doubt your intentions as a father. Do this for us, and I'll ask Declan to arrange to have you home before Tabitha whelps."

"Thank you, my lord," he said, not convinced agreeing to this was a good idea, but certain refusing was a bad one.

The human glanced at the other two and then smiled at the big canine. "Just don't make me regret it, eh?"

"He'll be fine," Tiji shocked Warlock by announcing. "If he was spying for the Tide Lords, he'd be tripping over himself to be of assistance, not complaining about us doubting his honour or begging to stay here so he can be with his mate."

"But you just said . . ."

She shrugged. "I was just wondering what you'd do." The chameleon eyed him up and down. "Are you really as tough as you look?"

More than a little disoriented by Tiji's complete turnabout, he shook his head. "I don't know."

"Well, hurry up and make up your mind, Cesspool," she said, gracefully unwrapping her long, silver-scaled legs. She jumped to the floor without a sound. "We're on the road first thing in the morning. It'll be better if you've got it figured out before then."

Chapter 11

Dawn was a stark, brutal affair in Torlenia. The sun didn't tenderly warm the land as it spread gentle fingers across the sky. It strode over the horizon, searing the landscape as it went. The chill of the desert nights buckled under the relentless onslaught of the rising heat, wilting all but the sturdiest of creatures.

The immortals, being the sturdiest of all creatures, still felt the heat, but other than vague discomfort, it had little effect on them. Immortal skin didn't burn, their bodies refused to dehydrate. It irritated rather than debilitated them, and—as it turned out—tested their ingenuity. Cayal was admiring one such example of Tide Lord ingenuity as dawn burned away the night, revealing the desert in all its stark and barren splendour.

To Cayal's surprise, Lukys lived permanently in Torlenia, these days. They'd travelled here in leisurely style, a journey that had taken almost a month. When he got here, he discovered the Tide Lord had built himself a villa carved out of the sandstone in the low hills on the very edge of the Great Inland Desert near the city of Elvere. Even more impressive, he'd designed a way to cool his palatial home by forcing what little breeze there was out here in the desert through narrow vents tunnelled through the walls of the house that were hung with gauze soaked in water from the natural spring underneath the house, which he also channelled through the same vents. With the Tide on the way back, there was no need to rely on the vagaries of the wind any longer. A steady breeze blew through the vents, cooling the house as the sun clawed its way across the sky, immolating any promise of relief.

Cayal studied the vent high on the wall of the atrium, appreciating the cool air tumbling from it, wondering when Lukys had mastered the finer points of architecture and engineering. The house was large and well furnished, showing signs of long habitation. It seemed odd to find Lukys so domesticated, particularly as he'd apparently acquired—along with all these other worldly possessions—a rather attractive young wife.

"I'm rather proud of my cooling system. It's ingenious, don't you think?"

Cayal turned to find Lukys walking into the atrium, dressed in a loose wrap, similar to those the natives wore in Magreth before it was destroyed. His feet were bare on the cool, blue tiles, and he was carrying two glasses full of juice, beaded with condensation.

"I'm surprised by it, actually," Cayal replied, accepting the juice. It was thick and pulpy, pale green and delicious. Cayal wasn't sure what fruits it was made from, but apparently Lukys had chosen his wife for more than her spectacular body. He'd also dispensed with the rule about women wearing a shroud in the presence of any man not a member of their family, which Cayal was grateful for. He found speaking to any woman concealed from head to toe by those wretched shrouds a disturbing proposition.

"Why are you surprised, Cayal?"

"You never struck me as the sort to put down roots, Lukys," Cayal said. "And yet here you are, as settled as any mortal. A house, a wife . . . Tides, you haven't got a couple brats hiding out the back, have you?"

Lukys smiled. "I'm not all that fond of children. But don't tell Oritha that. She thinks I can't wait to start a family. She believes I just have . . . emotional issues to deal with first."

"Does she know you're immortal?" he asked as he followed Lukys to the terrace, wondering how the young woman might have reacted to the news.

"Of course not. She thinks I'm a gem merchant from Stevania."

He sat down next to his old companion on the elegantly wrought marble bench, already warmed by the rising sun. "You haven't been married that long, I take it?"

"A couple of years. I found her in Ramahn. She's the youngest of five daughters. Her father couldn't wait to be rid of her."

"You don't love her?"

Lukys laughed at the very idea. "Tides, Cayal! Surely you've learnt better than that by now? When was the last time you were stupid enough to fall in love? *She* loves *me*, that's what's important."

Cayal took a long drink from his glass to avoid answering the question, certain any discussion about his love life would attract nothing but the older man's derision. "What made you decide to take a wife again after all this time?"

"I'm studying something important."

"What are you studying that requires a wife? Marital bliss?"

The older man seemed amused. "I just decided if I was going to take time to work on this thing, I might as well be comfortable. Oritha is very pleasant to look at, runs my household efficiently and keeps me company when I'm in the mood."

"You could get all that from a Crasii."

"Only if bestiality was my particular hobby, which it's not. Besides, with a Crasii I could never be sure I haven't got a Scard lurking around, waiting to slit my throat while I'm asleep one night in a futile attempt to rid the world of an evil Tide Lord." He leaned back and took a sip of his juice. "No thanks, Oritha is everything I need in the way of companionship at the moment."

"So she's really a replacement for your pet rat," Cayal concluded.

Lukys smiled. "Do me a favour, would you, and don't repeat that in front of my wife. She was actually quite glad to see the end of Coron and it was hard to explain to her how long we'd been together."

"What happened to Coron, anyway?"

"I told you," Lukys reminded him. "He died."

Cayal leaned forward and placed his glass on the low railing on the edge of the terrace. "You haven't told me how."

Ignoring his guest's impatience, Lukys finished off his drink before answering. "Has it never occurred to you, Sparky, in the depths of your relentless, self-obsessed depression, that your futile quest for a way to end your own life is a dire threat to the rest of us?"

"It's *my* existence I want to end," he said. "It's not a threat to anyone else."

"But if you succeed in dying, then the rest of the immortals can be killed, too. Effectively, we'll cease to be immortal."

Cayal remained unmoved. "I really don't care, Lukys."

"*You* might not care, Sunshine, but you need to be aware that others do. Hard as I know you find this to grasp, some of us don't mind the idea of living forever. If our immortal brethren thought you might actually succeed in your insane desire to commit suicide, they'd go to a great deal of trouble to stop you."

"But if what you're telling me about Coron is right, you *have* succeeded, Lukys. Why aren't *you* battening down the hatches and preparing for the siege?"

He shrugged. "Because nobody knows about it, yet. And I'm counting on the fact that you don't plan to spread the news." Lukys rose to his feet, looked out over the desert for a time and then turned to look at Cayal. "In fact, I'm willing to wager anything you name that you'll keep it quiet."

"You seem very certain of that," Cayal replied with a frown. Since he'd first confided his desire to put an end to his insanely long life to Lukys, more than a thousand years ago, the older man had taken to teasing him about his morose outlook, "Sparky" and "Sunshine" being some of the least offensive names he had for the Immortal Prince.

"I am," Lukys told him confidently.

Cayal gave an exasperated sigh. "You're going to make me ask why, aren't you?"

"Oh, yes, I most certainly am."

"Very well, Lukys. Why are you so certain I won't shout how to kill an immortal from the rooftops to anybody who'll listen, as soon as you tell me what it is?"

"Because we'll need quite a few of the others to do it," Lukys replied. "And if they knew what you were up to, none of the others would help. You're not going to say a word."

"Then how do I get them to help me die?"

"By doing the thing we do best, old son. Lying about it."

Cayal shook his head doubtfully. "So you intend to share this news with me, only provided I agree to lie, cheat and manipulate several other Tide Lords into helping us do me in?"

"You always were a sharp lad," Lukys remarked. "A bit unstable, perhaps, but you never lacked for intelligence."

"What's in it for you?"

Lukys looked wounded. "My desire to help an old friend isn't enough, Cayal? Nothing more. I swear."

"Bullshit," Cayal retorted pleasantly.

He treated Cayal to an ingenuous smile. "Would you believe I'm motivated by idle curiosity?"

"Not for a moment. What do you intend to get out of this, Lukys, other than my death?"

"Very well," the older man replied after a moment. "I want to be God."

"I thought we'd decided immortals who want to be God were a really bad idea, Lukys."

"Did we?"

Cayal nodded. "The name Kentravyon leaps to mind."

"Ah, but there's a difference between me and that lunatic," Lukys said, sitting on the edge of the railing. "I want to *be* God, Kentravyon thought he *was* God."

"There's a difference?"

"Absolutely! I *know* I'm not God, Cayal. I'd just like everyone *else* to think I am. Kentravyon, now . . . he believed he really was God. That's what made him so unstable."

"And you think killing me will somehow prove to everyone that you're a god?"

"Better than that," Lukys said, shaking his head. "By killing all the other immortals, I'll prove I'm *the* God."

Cayal stared at him for a moment, remembering Medwen's warning thousands of years ago in the chilly darkness of Brynden's castle that Lukys had his own agenda and it probably included ruling the entire galaxy.

"Let me get this straight. You want *my* help to kill me *and* all the other immortals?"

"In a nutshell," Lukys agreed.

"You're a maniac."

"Only from a certain perspective."

"What makes you think I'd have anything to do with such an idiotic plan?"

"Why do you care, Sparky? If you're dead, what matter is it to you what happens to the others?"

"They'll try to stop us."

"Only if we tell them what we're doing."

"Suppose they realise you're trying to kill them?"

"I was planning on keeping that small but pertinent detail a secret, you know."

Cayal studied Lukys for a moment and then shrugged. Lukys was right. What did he care? "Why not?"

Lukys smiled. "I had a feeling you'd say that, Sparky."

"Hence the reason you came looking for me," Cayal concluded, Lukys's sudden desire to seek him out after all these years starting to make sense. "How do we do it?"

"You don't need the details just yet. First we need at least another three immortals. And they have to be of the nine. A lesser mortal hasn't got the power to get the job done. This will require the power of a Tide Lord."

"Any ideas?"

"I thought I'd ask Maralyce first. She's always been fond of you."

Cayal frowned, unable to imagine Maralyce agreeing to anything that involved working in concert with another Tide Lord. She didn't care enough for the others, one way or the other, to do anything about removing them, either.

"What if she says no? Who does that leave? Brynden? He and I haven't been on speaking terms since Kinta and I . . . well, she's not speaking to me, either, for the same reason. Pellys is too unreliable. Kentravyon's still doing his icicle impression in Jelidia. That just leaves Tryan and Elyssa. I can't imagine any circumstance where Tryan would lift a finger to help me. As for Elyssa, she's—"

"Had a crush on you for eight thousand years," Lukys finished for him.

Cayal gave Lukys a baleful glare. "You *cannot* be serious."

The older Tide Lord looked at Cayal for a moment and then raised a questioning brow. "How badly do you want to die, Cayal?" Lukys asked.

Chapter 12

The canine Lord Ponting assigned to guard Tiji on her way back to Herino to report the whereabouts of the Emperor and Empress of the Five Realms and their vicious Tide Lord offspring proved to be an intimidating, yet taciturn sort of creature. He was easily the largest canine she'd ever met, with a pelt of red-brown fur, liquid brown eyes and a tail that gave away a lot more than he intended about his mood. He was efficient, admittedly, and civilised enough if you could get him talking, but he was a hard nut to crack.

And he wouldn't even acknowledge that Tiji had spoken to him if she called him Cecil.

The journey from Hidden Valley took more than a week on foot. Tiji was glad of the change of pace, not to mention the warmer weather, although this being Glaeba, even in summer it rained incessantly. Caelum was a mountainous, chilly place, and her month-long journey home had been a tense and harrowing affair.

Tiji looked outwardly human from a distance, but her silver-scaled skin always attracted attention. Not only was she a lone female travelling along notoriously dangerous roads, she was a member of a race usually enslaved, and as such, rarely travelled without a master somewhere close by. To further complicate matters, chameleon Crasii were rare enough to cause comment wherever they went.

Nobody cared about, or paid much attention to, a canine or a feline passing by, but a chameleon would be the talk of a small Caelish village for months. Even more worrying, if word got back to Tryan that a reptilian Crasii was seen heading toward Glaeba, Tiji didn't think it would take him long to realise that given their rarity, it was probably the same chameleon he'd caught lurking in the Ladies Walking Room in the Caelish Royal Palace.

To stay hidden on the way back from Caelum, she'd had to shed her clothes and use her natural camouflage ability to slip past danger, sneaking a ride on one of the many ferries that plied the well-worn trade route across the lake between Cycrane on the western shore and Lebec on the eastern side of the Lower Oran. But it had meant being cold, travelling with next to nothing in the way of supplies, and spending an awful lot of time standing still as a post, pretending she wasn't there.

With Cecil as her escort—or Warlock as he preferred to be called—Tiji didn't have to worry about any of that. They carried papers marking them the property of the Earl of Summerton, travelling to Herino to report to his mother, the dowager Baroness, Lady Tilly Ponting. Warlock's size meant nobody bothered them along the road, and because Aleki had made sure they had plenty of coin, they were able to stay at inns along the way instead of camping in the open, a rare luxury Tiji was relishing, all the more because of the wet weather.

After two days on the road, however, Tiji grew annoyed with Cecil's long bouts of silence. It was rare for her to have a travelling companion and it irritated her to think she got just as much conversation with this big brute who was supposed to be protecting her, as she did when she was on the road alone.

"Why don't you like being called Cecil?" she asked on the third morning of their journey as they trudged south toward the capital. They'd spent a comfortable night at a place near Lebec called Clyden's Inn and the owner had surprised them both by allowing them rooms with proper—albeit dangerously rickety—beds, rather than insisting they sleep in the stables, which was the common reaction to any Crasii looking for a room at a Glaeban inn.

As she suspected, Tiji's question got an immediate response from her large, canine companion. "My name is Warlock."

"But that's your kennel name. Your slave name. Don't you want a name that proclaims you're free to be who you want to be?"

"I am who I want to be. I am Warlock."

She stared up at him for a moment, amazed at his stubbornness. "I couldn't wait to change my name."

"Isn't Tiji your kennel name?"

She shook her head, shouldering her pack a little higher. "Tides, no!"

"You didn't mind that Captain Phydeau forced you to change your name?"

"I wasn't forced, I was delighted," she said, as they walked along the road. Traffic was light so far. Anybody heading out of Lebec for Herino wouldn't catch up or pass them for a few hours yet. "Tiji means 'strikes in darkness.' It's from one of the ancient languages. I'm not sure which one. It seemed appropriate, though. And it was a damn sight better than being called *Slinky*."

The big canine glanced down at her, a rare smile on his face. Even his tail wagged for a moment. "Slinky, eh? Yes . . . now I look at you . . . I can imagine you being called Slinky. In fact, it suits you."

Tiji glared at him. "I'm glad you find it amusing."

"May I call you Slinky?"

"Not if you expect me to answer you."

The canine's smile faded and his tail drooped a little. "That is how I feel about being addressed as Cecil."

She smiled up at him. "If I promise to call you Warlock from now on, do you think you could utter more than one word a mile?"

He seemed quite surprised by her request. "I wasn't aware you wanted to talk."

"You never asked."

Warlock shrugged, wagging his tail just enough to make Tiji believe he was probably not as unfriendly as she'd assumed. "What would you like me to speak of?"

"Tell me about the Immortal Prince," she said.

They reached Herino three days later, making their way straight to the townhouse belonging to Lady Ponting. The capital was set on an island that jutted into the Lower Oran, the largest of the Great Lakes that divided Glaeba from Caelum. Joined to the mainland by three wide, majestic bridges carved of the local dark granite and dominated by the royal palace—located in the peak of the only real hill on the island— the city had grown so much it had started to spill onto the shores of the lake surrounding the island. Many of the city's elite, in fact, had opted to build lake-shore villas, rather than live in the cramped and crowded houses they were forced to put up with in the city. Lady Ponting's townhouse proved to be one of the latter.

Although small and cluttered, her house was only four streets from the palace in a quiet but expensive street where most of the houses had high walls surrounding the perimeter to ensure the privacy of the occupants. It took Tiji and Warlock most of a wet and miserable day to find it, and when they did, it was to discover the lady of the house wasn't even in residence. Tilly Ponting had returned to her home in Lebec, the housekeeper informed them, and wasn't expected back until the Autumn Ball, some nine weeks from now. The new slaves were expected, however, and the Crasii steward welcomed them into the house, gave them towels to dry off, organised a hearty meal, and sent a messenger to the palace to fetch Declan Hawkes.

The King's Spymaster was a tall man, almost as tall as Warlock, and he walked like a fighter, or as if he expected to get into a fight at any moment. He was—in Tiji's opinion—symmetrical, the highest compliment she was willing to pay any creature suffering the indignity of hair, or who lacked scales or the ability to change their skin tone at will. She knew human women probably found him attractive, but had always suspected it had as much to do with his job as it did his physical appearance. Human women in particular were attracted to men of power. And human females, Tiji had observed, seemed to like a bit of mystery and danger, as well.

Declan Hawkes reeked of both.

Tiji had first met him in Senestra when she was barely more than a hatchling, a prisoner in a travelling carnival where her freakish gift for camouflage was worth five coppers a peek. Of course, Declan wasn't the Glaeban King's Spymaster back then, but with the help of Markun Far Jisa, he'd managed to cajole or intimidate her owner (Tiji was never sure which) into selling her to them. Although she remained a slave on paper, since being purchased by the Glaeban human she'd never felt like one. Starved, beaten and treated worse than an animal in the carnival, her change of fortune still felt a little surreal, at times.

It was more than six years since Declan—taking a chance on the likelihood that being a chameleon also meant she was a Scard—had recruited her into both the king's service and, secretly, into the Cabal of the Tarot. On the day she met Declan Hawkes, Tiji had gone from a circus freak to a noble warrior in the war to save Amyrantha from the Tide Lords.

She had a purpose in life now. A reason to live.

For that alone, Tiji would have willingly taken a sword in the belly for him.

When he arrived later that night he smiled when he saw her, obviously relieved she was unharmed. To her surprise, however, he didn't seem in a hurry to question her. He seemed more interested in Warlock's arrival than her own, which struck her as a little odd. Admittedly, he'd been sent here to work in the palace, but Tiji was certain the information she carried outweighed the employment prospects of some big, dumb canine. She made herself comfortable on the scrubbed wooden table, crossing her legs beneath her in the position she favoured, listening to the conversation with interest. For Declan to want to speak to Warlock before he grilled her on the news she carried from Caelum meant this was likely to be very interesting indeed.

"I'm very glad you're here, Warlock," Declan said, once they'd exchanged greetings. They met in Lady Ponting's kitchen, the room illuminated by several lamps on the walls and the red glow of the banked cooking fires. "I've got a job for you."

"So Lord Ponting informed me," the big canine agreed, although to Tiji, he sounded a little uncertain.

"How do you feel about being a slave again?"

Warlock shrugged. "I'm not at all certain I've gotten used to being free, Master Hawkes. But provided I'm back in Hidden Valley in time for the birth of my pups, I suppose I can handle it."

Declan nodded. "I'll see what I can arrange. In the meantime, I want to give you away as a belated wedding present. To the Crown Princess Kylia from Lady Tilly Ponting."

"I am trained for such a role."

The spymaster shook his head. "Nobody is trained for this role, Warlock. We're pretty sure Princess Kylia is actually the immortal Diala."

Tiji stared up at Declan in shock. "You're kidding!"

Declan glanced at Tiji. "She popped up a few months ago in Lebec

posing as the Duke of Lebec's long-lost niece. The crown prince arrived for a visit a few weeks later, and the rest—as they say—is history.
Poor Mathu didn't stand a chance."

"Tides, Declan! Who else knows about this?"

"Only the Cabal, at present," Declan replied. "But given the Tide is
on the turn, I don't imagine we've got long before either Diala or
Jaxyn makes their move and the whole world discovers the Tide Lords
aren't a myth."

"I saw Syrolee in Caelum," she reminded him. Aleki had sent word
on ahead about the news she carried. Not the details, of course, but
enough to make certain Declan was here in Herino when she arrived.
Given this news, however, Tiji thought it unlikely he was planning to
go anywhere for a time.

"You want me to spy for you in the palace," Warlock concluded. "In
the service of the High Priestess."

Tiji was impressed. He might look dumb as an ox, but when it came
down to it, this canine didn't lack for intelligence.

"Didn't you say Cayal told you her own kind call her the Minion
Maker?" Tiji reminded him.

Warlock nodded. "Cayal also called her a slut. She was the one who
made him immortal."

Tiji grinned. "You know, for an immortal, Cayal does seem to be an
excellent judge of character, doesn't he?"

Declan didn't seem nearly as amused as she was. He looked at Warlock, frowning. "What I'm asking of you isn't going to be easy," he
warned.

"I *am* trained to serve in a high-born household, Master Hawkes."

"That's not what I mean. Jaxyn and Diala are both understandably
wary of Scards and with the Tide on the turn they're in no mood to
tolerate them. To ensure all the slaves they've surrounded themselves
with are loyal, they've taken to randomly testing any Crasii they've got
in service."

Warlock's tail dipped a little. "Testing them *how*, exactly?"

"The last one I heard of, Jaxyn had one Crasii kill another member
of Princess Kylia's staff who'd misbehaved."

Tiji shook her head in disgust. "Bastards."

"I know," Declan agreed, "but they're smart bastards, and you
both need to remember that. And you," he added, fixing his gaze on

Warlock, "are going to have to do whatever they ask. You *must* pass their test, or we're all done for."

"I'm not sure I understand what you're getting at."

"Do you remember the Duchess of Lebec?"

The question puzzled Tiji because she couldn't see what Arkady Desean had to do with the matter at hand. *Unless Declan is just so obsessed with his legendary duchess he's managed to find a way to work her into every single conversation.* Tiji smiled to herself, wondering if she should suggest such a thing, then decided against it. Declan didn't seem to be in a very jokey mood.

"Of course I remember Lady Desean," Warlock replied, glaring at Declan as if he was offended the spymaster thought he might *not* remember her.

Declan crossed his arms, leaning against the edge of the counter opposite the table. "Jaxyn had a canine from Lebec slit his own throat in front of her to prove how loyal the Crasii are, Warlock. I can't impress upon you enough the danger you'll be in until the immortals are convinced you're loyal."

Warlock was silent for a time, digesting that information.

"You do understand what Declan's telling you, don't you?" Tiji asked, not at all certain that even with Declan's dire warning, Warlock fully appreciated the threat he faced once he reached the palace. He may have spent a couple of months across the hall from the Immortal Prince, but, by all accounts, Cayal had been on his best behaviour during his incarceration. Besides, Cayal wasn't known for his wanton cruelty. Except in Torlenia where he was universally reviled, the Immortal Prince was mostly famous for his exploits with the opposite sex, and the dire consequences of his various dalliances. Although as ruthless and self-obsessed as any other immortal when he had to be, it seemed the Immortal Prince just wanted to die. He didn't care enough about lording it over humanity, as a rule, to cause the sort of trouble the Tide Lords like Jaxyn and Diala did.

"I understand," Warlock said, nodding his head. "You want me to behave like a Crasii. To obey the orders of the immortals, even if it means killing an innocent Crasii."

"Even if it means killing ten of them," Declan corrected, the firelight from the stoves adding a demonic cast to his features that Tiji suspected would do little to reassure Warlock. "We must find out what they're planning. That's only going to happen if we have someone in the palace who can get close enough to Jaxyn and Diala to find out what's going on. *That* won't happen unless you pass Jaxyn's test."

Tiji guessed he was trying to give the impression it didn't bother him, but Warlock couldn't completely hide his horrified expression. "You expect me to accede to such a request? Without objecting?"

"Worse. If you take on this job, I expect you to do it without so much as blinking," the spymaster told him. "The slightest hesitation and you're blown, my friend. The Tide Lords will know you're a Scard, and they'll kill you. Then they'll wonder why Lady Ponting sent them a Scard as a wedding present and they'll kill her. Then they'll trace your movements back to Aleki and the rest of your brethren in Hidden Valley and kill all of them, too, including your mate and your unborn pups. Do you get the picture?"

Warlock nodded, looking decidedly unhappy.

"I need to be very sure you can do this, Warlock," Declan added, eyeing the big canine warily. Tiji could tell Declan was doubtful. Nor was she surprised by his doubts. What the spymaster was asking of this Scard was no easy thing.

"If you don't think you can do this, we won't hold it against you," she said, hoping to reassure him. "This is a dreadful thing to ask of any creature, human or Crasii. Declan will understand if you're not sure you can handle killing in cold blood just to satisfy a wretched Tide Lord that you really are totally subservient to his will, *won't* you, Declan?"

The spymaster nodded, a little miffed, perhaps, at her implication that he was forcing Warlock into something against his will. "Of course, I'll understand. And Tiji's right. Nobody will think any less of you for not wanting to kill your own kind."

Warlock's gaze swivelled between them. "Is there nobody else who can do this thing for you? No other way?"

"Qualified Scards are pretty thin on the ground, Warlock. Tides, *Scards* are pretty thin on the ground, for that matter." Declan shook his head apologetically. "You're it, I'm afraid."

"Not that he's trying to *pressure* you, or anything," Tiji added, giving Declan a look that spoke volumes. She was beginning to think this was a very bad idea. Warlock was big and scary to look at, sure enough, but after a week on the road with him, she'd begun to realise he was quite a gentle creature at heart. She wasn't sure the canine possessed the ruthlessness required to be a really effective spy.

"May I think about it?"

"If you want," Declan agreed. "I'd like a decision soon, though. Every day the Tide comes back a little stronger. We don't have long."

"And you'll make sure I'm back in Hidden Valley in time for the birth of my pups?"

"I'll certainly try," Declan agreed.

Warlock nodded, his expression grim. "Then I'll let you know my decision tomorrow. May I be excused?"

"You're free, Warlock," Tiji reminded him. "You don't need his permission to leave the room."

"Old habits are hard to break, Tiji," the canine replied. "Will you excuse me, Master Hawkes? I have a lot to consider."

"By all means. I'll speak to you tomorrow."

The canine bowed with court-bred grace and turned away. Neither Declan nor Tiji spoke until he'd closed the kitchen door behind him.

"Well, you were a big help. Thanks," the spymaster said, once they were alone.

She smiled at him brightly. "Any time."

"What do you think?"

"About Warlock? I think you're nuts, Declan. He'll get himself killed the first time someone looks at him sideways. He's no spy."

"Which is why he should do well, I think."

She cocked her head at him, amazed at the ability of humans to justify anything unpalatable with such ridiculous logic. "There's an interesting rationalisation. And you appear to have thought it up on the spot. I'm impressed."

Declan shrugged. "I mean he's the real thing. He'll not be trying to pretend to be a steward whilst really being a spy."

"No, he'll be pretending to be a spy whilst really being a steward. That's *so* much safer."

Declan smiled at her. "Think you'd make a better spymaster than me, Slinky? Be my guest."

"No, thanks." Tiji didn't react to being called by her slave name. This man had saved her from a lifetime of pain and humiliation, and even when he was teasing her, she never felt belittled. In fact, Declan Hawkes was probably the only living creature on Amyrantha who could call her "Slinky" and get away with it. "The King's Spymaster has to work for that pompous idiot, King Enteny, the pay stinks, and the hours are terrible . . ."

"But you do get to send innocent people to their deaths, on occasion," Declan reminded her. "Not to mention the opportunity to torture enemies of the state all you want, and the odd invitation to a ball at the palace."

"Well . . . if it includes balls at the palace," Tiji mused, rubbing her chin as she feigned deep thought on the matter. "That's a different story. I might have to consider deposing you, after all."

Declan's good humour faded as he asked his next question. "Well, while you're thinking about it, tell me what happened in Cycrane."

She smiled. "Well, the *good* news is that having been confronted by a Tide Lord and walked away from him without doing a single thing he ordered me to do, I know for certain now that I'm a Scard."

"And the *bad* news?"

"The Empress of the Five Realms is back, Declan," she said, all trace of amusement evaporating with her announcement. "And you can bet she's planning to bring the rest of her Tide-forsaken family with her."

Chapter 13

It was several weeks before the Imperator of Torlenia agreed to receive the Glaeban ambassador. Arkady wasn't permitted to attend the meeting, of course, so she had to settle for pacing the seraglium for half the morning until Stellan returned from the royal palace to tell her what had happened.

The importance of this meeting could not be underestimated. If it went well, then Stellan had some hope of resolving the issue of who owned the Chelae Islands, which meant they could return home sometime before they both died of old age. On the other hand, if it went badly, it might set their cause back years. The Imperator was a fickle and difficult young man, by all accounts. Although Chintara only rarely mentioned her husband, when she did speak of her lord and master, it was in glowing terms of his strength and honour.

At the sound of the outer door of the seraglium opening, Arkady turned in time to see Stellan stepping into the hall. He was still dressed in his court finery. He'd obviously come straight from his audience with the Imperator.

"How did it go?" she asked without preamble.

"All right, I suppose," he said, shrugging off his formal velvet Glaeban-styled coat with its fine, embroidered cuffs and lapels, tossing it aside with relief. He looked ready to wilt. It must have been awful for him, sitting through an entire audience with the Imperator in such cumbersome attire.

"Did you get around to mentioning the Chelae Islands?"

Stellan shook his head and sat on the couch, loosening the high collar of his shirt. "Tides, no! That would have been far too easy. We spoke of the weather. And horseracing. Lots and *lots* of horseracing. Have you noticed these people are obsessed with horseracing?"

Arkady forced a smile and took a seat opposite her husband, pouring him a drink from the wine jug on the low enamelled table between them. "Yes, I've noticed that. Will he agree to meet again to discuss Chelae, do you think?"

Stellan nodded. "I imagine so. It was a pleasant enough audience, so he may not mind seeing me a second time. You're disappointed, aren't you?"

"A little," she admitted. "Although, I don't know why. It's a miracle you got in to see him at all after your predecessor's less-than-diplomatic tantrum. I never expected the Imperator to invite you over for tea and resolve an issue on your first meeting that's been a bone of contention for two hundred years."

"The wheels of diplomacy turn very, very slowly, I'm afraid," he agreed, studying her closely for a moment. "Are you so desperately unhappy here, Arkady?"

"I'm not sure I'm unhappy," she replied with a shrug. "I'm bored, I'm homesick, I'm fed up with going out in public wearing a sheet and I'm certain I'll never be truly cool again as long as I live, but unhappy? No, I don't think so."

Stellan smiled. "I'm glad to see you still have your sense of humour."

"They haven't actually outlawed laughter here yet, but let's not say it too loud, dear, someone might overhear us."

Stellan shook his head with a rueful smile. "It is a bit like that, isn't it? But at least you have Lady Chintara for company. Even the Imperator mentioned how much his wife enjoys your visits."

"Visits?" she asked with a raised brow. "More like royal command performances. I keep wondering what she'd do if I tell her I've made other plans the next time she tells me she'll 'see me tomorrow' as if I had a choice in the matter."

Stellan's smile faded. "I thought you liked her?"

"I do," she assured him. "She's just a bit . . . imperious . . . at times."

"Well, imperious or not, she obviously has her husband's ear. I got the impression I was only permitted to visit the Imperator because Chintara suggested it."

"Does he have a name?"

"Who?" Stellan asked, taking a sip from his wine and then replacing it on the table.

"The Imperator? That's all you ever hear him called. Doesn't he have real a name, like Henri or Jorge, or something?"

"Of course he does, but only his closest family are permitted to speak it."

"So how does the population keep track?"

"Keep track of what?"

"Of who's in charge? Do Torlenians just number the Imperators so people can tell which one it is? I mean, we have 'King Enteny the Fourth,' and Mathu will be 'Mathu the Second' when he takes the throne. What do they call their king here? Imperator Number Sixty-Four?"

Stellan smiled. "Why don't you ask Lady Chintara?"

"I might. What's he like anyway, Imperator Number Sixty-four?"

Stellan thought for a moment before answering. "Truly? If I had to describe him briefly, I'd say a callow boy."

The description shocked Arkady. The last impression she would have formed from the way Chintara spoke of him was of a callow boy.

"A callow *boy*? Are you certain you were talking to the right Imperator?"

"Oh, yes, he was the right one. But he's very young. Eighteen, perhaps, maybe nineteen—certainly no older than Mathu. His skin is still pimpled. He's indecisive, insecure and struck me as being more than a little nervous, although that could be Jorgan's fault. After our last ambassador lost his temper with him, the boy probably has reason to fear unpredictable Glaebans."

She shook her head, unable to picture Chintara married to anyone as vacillating and unappealing as the young man Stellan described. "That doesn't sound like the man Chintara calls her lord and master."

"She calls her husband her 'lord and *master*'?"

"What of it?"

He smiled. "Do you call *me* your 'lord and master'?"

Arkady wasn't nearly so amused as her husband. "Only when I'm forced to, Stellan, so don't let it go to your head."

"I wouldn't dream of it," he assured her, rising to his feet. "Are you visiting with Chintara again today?"

"Oh, yes," she told him with a sigh. "I've been commanded to appear for lunch."

"Well, let me know if she says anything about the meeting, would you?" Stellan said, picking up his coat. "I'd like to meet with her husband again as soon as I can, and if you're able to speed up the timing of our next meeting even by a few days, I'd be very grateful. You're not the only one who's feeling homesick."

"Have you heard from Jaxyn?" Arkady asked, guessing that was the reason behind Stellan's comment.

"No. He's probably having too much fun at court to think of writing me."

"He's supposed to be looking after your *interests* at court," she reminded her husband. "That should warrant the odd letter now and then, don't you think?"

He shook his head, sighing. "You still don't like him, do you? Even when he's on another continent?"

Arkady wished she could tell Stellan why she despised his lover so vehemently. But how do you describe colour to a blind man? Stellan didn't even believe the Tide Lords existed. There simply weren't the words to tell him he'd been callously used by an immortal as he clawed his way up the ladder to the Glaeban throne.

And even if she could convince Stellan that Jaxyn had used him; even if she could somehow make him realise Jaxyn was an immortal and no more loved him than he loved the Crasii he'd ordered to commit suicide just to convince Arkady he could, what was the point? Her husband would never accept he might have endangered—however unwittingly—his king or the Glaeban throne.

"I think he's . . . unreliable," she conceded, unable to think of a better word.

"You were the one who convinced me to send him to court in the first place," he said. "Now you're claiming he can't be trusted? What's happened in the last few weeks to make you change your mind?"

There was no answer to that so Arkady said nothing.

Stellan waited for a moment but when she remained silent, he shook his head. The mood had changed in the last few seconds, the mere mention of Jaxyn Aranville's name enough to set them at each other's throats. "While we're on the topic of lovers," Stellan said, all trace of his former humour gone. "I don't suppose you're pregnant, are you?"

His question cut her to the quick, but she knew the reason he asked it. "No."

"Pity," he remarked. "I suppose I'll have to write to Enteny and tell him the bad news."

"*Bad* news? I thought you'd be delighted to discover I wasn't carrying a convicted murderer's bastard."

Stellan hesitated before he answered, perhaps realising that he, of all people, had no claim on the moral high ground. "I'm sorry, Arkady. It just would have been easier, that's all, if you were with child, regardless who fathered it."

"It would be easier if you hadn't caused the problem by lying to the king and telling him I was pregnant."

Stellan frowned. "As it would have been, had you not forged my signature on Kyle Lakesh's release papers so your murderer lover could go free," he retorted. "Let's not get into a game of who did what, Arkady. Neither of us is on very solid ground."

She nodded, conceding he was right, smarting nonetheless over the realisation he was still peeved with her. After she'd kept the secret of all his lovers—and specifically their gender—without complaint for so long, she felt she deserved a little more consideration.

"I wasn't trying to pick a fight, Stellan. It's just . . ."

To her astonishment, Stellan's expression softened. He actually looked as if he sympathised with her dilemma. "I understand, Arkady. Really, I do. Do you miss him much?"

She shrugged. "More than I should. Less than I thought I would."

"Perhaps you're not as in love with this man as you imagined," he suggested gently.

"I'm not sure I ever *was* in love with Cayal, Stellan."

"You still refer to him as if he's an immortal," he noted, as if it were a curiosity, rather than a fact.

Arkady was long past trying to convince her husband of it, however. The truth would come out soon enough. Declan had pointedly assured her of that. In the meantime, it was easier not to argue about it.

"Perhaps it's easier for me to believe he was."

Stellan nodded with a wan smile. "Oddly, Arkady, that actually makes sense."

A few minutes before the appointed time, Arkady was led into the consort's chambers as usual by Nitta, who was quite pleasant these days, apparently under orders not to offend the Glaeban ambassador's wife any more than she already had. When they reached the entrance to the main hall, however, Nitta held her arm out to block Arkady's way.

She stopped as low voices reached them. Across the chamber by the couches, a saffron-robed monk knelt at Chintara's feet.

". . . and tell my lord I anxiously await his arrival," Chintara was instructing the monk, who seemed afraid to look the consort in the eye.

Arkady smothered a smile. Poor man. He'd probably have to do penance for a month after being admitted into the presence of an unshrouded woman, let alone one as enticing as the Imperator's Consort.

The monk lowered his head, but spoke clearly, as if reciting something learned by rote. "My lord also said to tell you that he, too, anxiously awaits the return of his queen to his side, his companion to his table and his lover to his bed."

Chintara rolled her eyes. "He's not the only one anxiously awaiting the latter, I can promise him that." She glanced across the room and spied Arkady. A momentary frown flickered over her lovely face—almost too quick to register—and then she smiled at her guest. "Ah, Arkady! You're early! Come! Brother Ostin was just leaving us."

Nitta lowered her arm and allowed Arkady to enter the hall. She crossed the tiles to where the monk had risen to his feet, although he kept his eyes averted.

"Arkady, Duchess of Lebec and wife of our Glaeban ambassador, this is Brother Ostin," she said, when Arkady reached them. "He's a follower of the Way of the Tide."

"Yes," Arkady agreed. "I recognise his yellow robes. I did not expect to meet a male in the royal seraglium, Brother Ostin. Are you not bound by the same rules as other men regarding unshrouded females?"

He shook his head, surprising Arkady by answering in Glaeban. "I have been granted a dispensation, my lady."

"Really? A dispensation? By whom?"

"The head of his order," Chintara told Arkady before the monk could answer. "You may go, Brother Ostin."

The monk took the hint and, after bowing quickly to both Chintara and Arkady, hurried from the hall, followed by Nitta. Arkady watched him leave and then turned to Chintara. "Do you often use a third party to communicate with your husband?"

"I beg your pardon?" the consort asked with a blank look.

"I'm sorry, I couldn't help but overhear Brother Ostin's rather lyrical declaration about your lord anxiously awaiting . . . how did he put it? The return of his queen to his side, his companion to his table and his lover to his bed? I wish my husband was as poetic."

Chintara studied her with an odd look for a moment and then smiled. "I'm blessed," she agreed, not completely able to hide the irony in her voice. "Truly, I am."

"I wasn't aware that you were such a devout follower of the Way of the Tide, either, my lady."

"Which just shows how little you know me, Arkady. Shall we bathe first before we eat? This wretched heat is driving me mad this morning."

"As you wish," Arkady agreed, thinking nobody she'd met in Torlenia seemed less bothered by the heat than Chintara, and unable to avoid the niggling feeling that she'd just witnessed something very important and she couldn't, for the life of her, figure out what it was.

Chapter 14

The office assigned to the King's Spymaster was located in the Herino Palace only two doors down from the King's Private Secretary. Not many people knew this. Most believed his headquarters were located several blocks away behind the forbidding walls of Herino Prison. It was Lord Deryon's idea, for him to work out of the palace. The King's Private Secretary didn't like the inconvenience of having to send a message to the prison every time he wanted the spymaster to do something for the king. He found it easier, and far less public, to simply take a walk down the hall.

Although it was a nuisance sometimes, Declan didn't really mind. He liked that people didn't always know where to find him. It helped keep up the mystery, and for Declan Hawkes, the air of mystery he'd somehow acquired since taking up this thankless post at the behest of the powerbrokers who ran the Cabal of the Tarot was one of the few things that was even remotely fun about being spymaster.

When he opened the door to his office at first glance it appeared unoccupied. The room was lit by the overcast morning light coming in from the windows behind the desk and seemed undisturbed from how he'd left it the previous evening. Although only a quarter the size of the Private Secretary's office down the hall, it was furnished in the same style as the rest of the palace with over-done gilt furniture, priceless artworks hanging on the walls and a beautifully worked Tenacian rug on the floor. He glanced at his chair and smiled. It appeared to be empty but if one knew what to look for, the faint warping of a humanoid form could be seen.

"Took my suggestion about becoming spymaster seriously, did you, Slinky?"

The slight warping around his chair began to change, the colour of his leather chair taking on a silver tone. Within a few moments, Tiji's silver-scaled skin had returned to its normal hue and she appeared, sitting comfortably in his chair with her feet on his desk, wearing not a stitch of clothing.

"How come you always know where I am?"

"Because I'm smarter than you," he told her. "Making yourself at home, I see."

"You've got a very nice chair."

"I'll make sure the king knows you approve."

"You get interesting mail, too."

Declan closed the door and crossed the rug to the desk. He picked up the letter sitting on his desk that Tiji had obviously opened in his absence and frowned. The broken seal was that of Lebec.

"It's from your girlfriend," Tiji offered helpfully.

"First, the Duchess of Lebec is *not* my girlfriend. Second, get out of my chair. And third, put some clothes on. You can't wander around the palace dressed in nothing but your shiny silver scales."

Tiji grinned and did as he ordered, stepping aside to allow him to take a seat behind the desk. She picked her shift up off the floor—where she'd no doubt dropped it when she heard him coming down the hall—and slipped it over her head. Then she pushed aside a pile of requisitions waiting to be signed, so she could sit cross-legged on the edge of his desk.

"Do you want to know what it says?" she asked.

"I can read, you know."

"Yes, but sometimes it's better to have someone tell you bad news, rather than read it for yourself."

Declan looked up at her, frowning. He'd been expecting to hear from Arkady for weeks, but couldn't imagine what news this letter might contain that required a third party to break it to him. "Exactly what bad news are you talking about?"

"Well, nothing really," she said. "I just meant that sometimes it's better to have someone tell you bad news, rather than read it, that's all."

He glared at her, in no mood for Tiji's jokes. "Haven't you got something you should be doing?"

"Not a thing," the chameleon assured him, shaking her head. "I am here awaiting your orders, O great and terrible spymaster. Bid me to do something spy-ish!"

"How about you get off my desk?"

"I actually had something a bit more heroic in mind."

"Life is full of disappointment, Slinky."

She sighed and uncurled her long silver legs, hopped off his desk and walked around it, taking a seat in the straight-backed wooden chair on the other side. Declan began to read Arkady's letter. Tiji fidgeted for a moment, sitting like a normal human for all of thirty seconds before she crossed her legs underneath herself again.

"Your girlfriend says it's hot in Torlenia."

"Arkady is not my girlfriend," he repeated, without looking up from the letter.

"Aren't you two childhood sweethearts, or something?"

"No."

"But you both grew up in Lebec, together, didn't you?"

"That's common knowledge."

"So how come she married the richest duke in Glaeba and you wound up doing the king's dirty work for a pittance?"

Declan glanced up from the letter in annoyance. "Do you mind? I'm busy."

"Not as busy as you're going to be," the little Crasii predicted.

Declan glared at her. "What are you talking about?"

"Get to the bit where your lady friend talks about the Imperator's Consort," Tiji advised.

Declan flicked the page over. The first few paragraphs had been filled with benign, unimportant matters. There had been no real point in teaching Arkady how to send a coded letter in the short time they'd had before she sailed for Torlenia with her husband, but he had advised her to couch any information she wished to pass on in the most banal terms she could manage. To alert him that the information was relevant to their search for the remaining unaccounted-for Tide Lords, she had promised to start the paragraph with: *Please tell Uncle Lukys . . .*

Sure enough, on the second page was a paragraph that began with their pre-arranged phrase.

"Please tell Uncle Lukys," Declan read aloud, "that I have met the

Imperator's Consort. Although clearly not from Torlenia (I'm not sure where she's from), Lady Chintara is a delightful and well-educated woman with an interest in the Tarot that rivals Lady Ponting's knowledge." Declan sat a little straighter in his chair, a sick feeling settling in the centre of his stomach. "Her knowledge of the Tide Lords seems encyclopedic. I believe she and Tilly should correspond. I am sure there are things about the Tarot that Lady Chintara knows which Tilly would be most interested in . . ." Declan's voice trailed off and he looked at Tiji in despair. "Tides . . . this can't be happening . . . not now . . ."

"Why not?" Tiji asked. She'd already read the letter, so she'd had time to get over the initial shock of Arkady's news. "Chinta is the Torlenian way of pronouncing Kinta. She probably added the 'ra' on the end because in Torlenia, a chinta is a small smelly rodent."

"I don't mean the name," Declan said, although Tiji was probably right about that. "If this is right, what's Kinta doing married to the Imperator of Torlenia?"

"Same as all the rest of them, probably—waiting for the Tide to turn so she can take over the world." Tiji shrugged, as if she couldn't understand his question. "Tides, Declan, why are you so surprised? We've got an immortal married to the Crown Prince of Glaeba. As we speak there's a Tide Lord roaming our own palace halls pretending to be her best friend, and the Empress of the Five Realms is ready to move on the throne of Caelum as soon as her son marries Princess Nyah. Why are you so astounded by the idea the Charioteer isn't above doing the same thing in Torlenia? It's no more than the rest of her wretched brethren are doing elsewhere."

Declan frowned, not convinced it was that simple. "It's not Kinta's style."

"Maybe she's setting things up for Brynden, then? He's up for ruling the world any chance he gets. Tides, if you look at how Torlenia is these days, you could argue he's never really let it go."

Declan shook his head. "By all accounts Kinta and Brynden are enemies now. In fact, it was more than likely their break-up that caused the last Cataclysm."

"I thought the Immortal Prince caused the last Cataclysm?"

"Well, he did, indirectly. According to the Lore, that's who Kinta left Brynden for."

"Maybe her love affair with Cayal didn't last," Tiji suggested. "Maybe this is her way of patching things up with Brynden. I mean . . . delivering a whole *country*? That's a fairly impressive way of saying you're sorry."

For a moment, Declan was swamped with a rare sensation of being overwhelmed. And it was only going to get worse. The Tide was on the turn and the immortals were on the move. Every day was likely to bring word of another one popping up somewhere they least expected it.

What disturbed Declan most was their consistency. With the exception of Maralyce, who never moved from her mine in the Shevron Mountains, and the Immortal Prince, who was last heard of buried under half a mountain inside it, every Tide Lord who'd reappeared so far had done so awfully close to a seat of power, poised to strike the moment their magical powers returned. And there was no telling where the rest of them would pop up. Or when.

"What are you going to do?" Tiji asked. "Tell the Guardian of the Lore your girlfriend wants to invite a Tide Lord to join her secret organisation dedicated to destroying them?"

"Tides! Will you stop that!" he snapped. "There is nothing going on between me and Arkady! Now, if you don't mind, I have work to do."

"Did you want my help?"

"No!"

"Touchy, touchy!" she scolded. "Don't take your frustration out on me."

"Just go, Tiji," he ordered.

"I suppose I could sneak into Kylia's apartments and find out if Cecil's still alive, if you like."

"By all means," he agreed, focusing on the letter to avoid looking at her. "Go find out if Cecil is still alive."

Tiji rose to her feet with the fluid grace that betrayed her reptilian ancestry. "Is there anything *useful* I can do?"

He shook his head, recognising the apology in her tone, if not in her actual words. "Not at the moment. I'm going to have to get word to Tilly about this, but first, I need to take a walk down the hall and break the news to Lord Deryon that we've found the Empress *and* the Charioteer and then figure out how I'm going to be in two places at once."

"Why two places at once?"

"I was planning to go to Caelum and check on the Empress and her gang." He leaned back in his chair, still holding Arkady's letter with a frown. "Now I'm starting to think I should be in Torlenia."

Tiji eyed him speculatively. "Why?"

"Because Kinta has reappeared," he reminded her.

"You don't actually know that, Declan."

"No, I don't," he agreed. "It's nothing but a baseless fear I have that the Imperator of Torlenia's consort, who apparently has an encyclopedic knowledge of the Tide Lords, just happens to share the name of the woman who was, until the last Cataclysm, the eternal partner of the Lord of Reckoning. Tides, what *could* I be thinking?"

She eyed him suspiciously. "Is it really that? Or because you think Arkady Desean might be in danger?"

Declan shrugged, wishing Tiji wasn't so obsessed by his relationship with his childhood friend. "Arkady can handle herself. She's already faced down at least four Tide Lords."

"Yeah . . . funny about that," Tiji mused, turning for the door.

He didn't like what Tiji's tone seemed to imply. "What's that supposed to mean?"

Tiji stopped with her hand on the door, where it began to turn an interesting coppery shade as it rested on the knob. "It's just that your girlfriend had Jaxyn, the Lord of Temperance, living under her roof for a year or more, Declan. Then she welcomed Diala, the High Priestess, into her home with open arms, and then . . . oh, that's right, she ran off into the mountains with the Immortal Prince, and if you think all they did up there was talk about nature, you truly are an idiot. And while they were up in the mountains, they just happened to drop in on Maralyce, the Seeker, didn't they? And now, all of a sudden, she stumbles over Kinta, the Charioteer? You're the spymaster, Declan. You tell me. Are we starting to see a pattern emerge here?"

He smiled at the ridiculousness of what she was suggesting. "You think *Arkady* is in league with the immortals?"

"If she isn't, then she attracts them like a magnet attracts iron filings," Tiji warned, her expression grim. "Maybe if you want to trap the Tide Lords, Declan, you don't need a great master plan. You just need Arkady Desean as bait."

Chapter 15

Despite Declan Hawkes's dire warnings of what might happen when he entered the service of the Crown Princess Kylia, nothing terrible happened to Warlock when he joined the palace staff. Jaxyn didn't order him to murder another Crasii, or carve a baby into bite-size pieces, or any of the other dire fates Tiji and the spymaster had warned him about. The crown princess had smiled and clapped her hands delightedly when Lord Deryon announced that Lady Ponting had sent her and her husband, Prince Mathu, a wedding present in the shape of this exceptionally well-trained canine Crasii slave. She sent him along with a note saying she hoped he would serve them well, and how she was sure he would be an excellent addition to their staff.

For the most part, Diala paid little attention to her new slave. She was too busy playing the ingenue princess for her new in-laws, the King and Queen of Glaeba, to be bothered tormenting a mere canine. Of course, none of the humans surrounding her—with the exception of the spymaster and the King's Private Secretary—knew the seventeen-year-old Princess Kylia was in fact a ten-thousand-year-old immortal, known to the Cabal as the High Priestess and to her fellow immortals as Diala, the Minion Maker. King Enteny and Queen Inala had no reason to suspect their son's wife was anything but what she appeared—young, in love, and excited to be living in the royal palace with her new husband.

It astounded Warlock that nobody saw through her.

To the Crasii—whose race was created by the immortals, consequently they could smell one across a room—every word she uttered seemed false, every smile cynical, every action contrived. When she clung to Prince Mathu's arm, laughing at his jokes, staring up at him with wide, adoring eyes, Warlock didn't see a young woman in love. He saw an evil, manipulative bitch, using an essentially decent young man for her own amusement.

The presence of the Tide Lord Jaxyn was even harder to stomach. Posing as the Duke of Lebec's envoy to the royal court, he'd made a point of becoming Prince Mathu's newest best friend, which kept him close to Diala, as well as the young and credulous prince. When Jaxyn wasn't playing cards with the other courtiers or malletball on the lawns with the court ladies, he was sneaking Mathu out of the palace to visit a bear baiting, or a cockfight, and probably the odd brothel or two into the bargain. The king didn't know anything about Mathu's extracurricular activities, of course, and wasn't likely to, unless Mathu got into trouble.

Far from complaining about it, Kylia actually encouraged him, making noises about how a good wife would never stand in the way of her husband enjoying time out with his friends. Warlock suspected her tolerance was inspired by impatience with her immature young husband, rather than any desire to be an understanding wife. For a woman as old as Diala, with her tastes and experience, Mathu must have seemed a trying prospect, indeed.

Not quite as cavalier as Diala regarding the dedication of all Crasii slaves, Jaxyn had made himself known to Warlock within days of his arrival, to ensure the Crasii would do what his companion had not bothered to ask. As Warlock was taking a tray back to the kitchens from the royal apartments one evening, about three days after he'd joined the royal household, the Tide Lord had cornered him in a quiet hallway.

He'd glanced up and down the hall to be sure they were alone and then stepped so close to Warlock the big Crasii was forced back against the wall.

"Do you know what . . . and who . . . I am, Cecil?" Fearful Jaxyn might remember the name Warlock from Arkady Desean's anecdotes around the dining room table in Lebec Palace while she'd been interrogating Cayal, he'd agreed to be known as Cecil while spying for the Cabal. Hearing Jaxyn call him by that name just made Warlock hate it even more.

The question was asked with quiet menace, Jaxyn's eyes boring into

Warlock's as though *they*, and not the returning Tide, were the source of his power. Although he was taller than the Tide Lord, at that moment, Warlock didn't feel like it.

"To serve you is the reason I breathe," Warlock had replied. Then he'd added for good measure: "My lord."

He didn't try to hide his terror. Jaxyn not only sensed it, he probably expected it.

"Then you understand my presence here is a secret until I choose to make it otherwise?"

"I assumed as much, my lord," he agreed, "when I noticed nobody showing you or your companion the respect you truly deserve."

Warlock had no idea why he'd tempted fate so blatantly with that reply. When he thought about it afterward, he realised he'd been behaving as if he wanted the immortals to know they had no power over this particular Crasii, even though he knew the knowledge would kill him.

Fortunately, Jaxyn seemed oblivious to the irony in Warlock's tone. "You will say nothing until I command it," he'd ordered. "About me or the Lady Diala."

"To serve you both is the reason I breathe, my lord," Warlock assured him solemnly, while noting that Jaxyn had, in his arrogance, given away the identity of his immortal companion. "I will await your command."

Jaxyn had studied him closely for a few moments longer, as if trying to decide how genuine Warlock's subservience was, before stepping back to let the slave continue on his way.

With admirable calm, his heart pounding in his chest so loudly it was a wonder Jaxyn couldn't hear it thumping, Warlock had walked back along the hall, only just beginning to realise how dangerous a game he had been coopted into.

The immortals were biding their time—even without Jaxyn admitting as much to him, Warlock knew that—waiting for the Tide to return sufficiently so their powers were unassailable. They were old hands at this. The immortals knew the perils of making their move too soon. It might take the Tide years to return fully. In the meantime, they were prepared to play a waiting game.

Jaxyn and Diala had designs on the Glaeban throne. That was a given. All that remained was to discover exactly how they intended to go about taking it and then he could go home to Boots and be there when his pups were born.

Warlock agonised over the Tide Lords' intentions every time he was forced to spend time in their company, fearing it would take too long to discover their plans, or that they were so complex and devious, Declan Hawkes would keep finding reasons to delay his return to Hidden Valley. This morning was particularly trying and a complete waste of time. He wasn't learning anything useful. He was playing fetch for Diala—or rather Princess Kylia, he reminded himself—in the gardens below the palace bordering the lake, during her game of malletball with Jaxyn and Queen Inala.

Malletball involved players trying to hit a wooden ball through a series of wooden arches set into the lawn in a very specific sequence. The player who managed to get their balls through the course in the fewest number of hits was the winner, but one could score extra points by knocking an opponent's ball out of the way. This was Kylia's favoured tactic, and one she frequently misjudged, which meant the ball often went wildly off course. Every time it happened she would laugh delightedly, turn to Warlock, point in the direction of the ball and say, "Fetch, Cecil, fetch!"

As Crasii were supposed to consider it an honour to be singled out by a suzerain, rather than an insult, Warlock had no choice but to hurry eagerly after the ball and retrieve it for his mistress, placing in on the ground by her feet, his tail wagging, all but panting for her approval, giving the impression he hungered for nothing more than a pat or a kind word from her.

In truth, Warlock wanted to tear her throat out with his teeth.

It wouldn't have killed her, he knew that, but it certainly would have made him feel better in the thirty or so seconds he'd have to live after attacking a member of the royal family before the felines of the royal guard cut him down.

Warlock lost count of how many times he'd played "fetch" by the time Prince Mathu arrived. The young man was looking bleary-eyed and more than a little worse for wear, squinting in the bright summer sunlight reflecting off the raindrops glistening on the grass from an earlier rain shower. Kylia thrust her mallet at Warlock and ran to him, the moment she spied her husband, leaving the Crasii standing there fantasising about how it would feel to crush a suzerain's skull with it.

"Mathu! You're up!" She stood on her toes, kissed his check and beamed at him. "Good morning, my love."

"And about time, I would have said," Queen Inala remarked with a disapproving frown. The king might not be aware of Mathu's night-time forays into the city, but it seemed Queen Inala wasn't so ill-informed.

"Good morning, Mother," Mathu replied over the top of Kylia's head. He kissed his wife on the mouth and then turned to Jaxyn. "I see you're out and about early, Lord Aranville. I'm impressed."

"Never was one for lying in late," Jaxyn said with a laugh. "Life's too short to waste it sleeping."

Life's too short, Warlock echoed silently, trusting in the human inability to read Crasii facial expression to hide his scorn. By all accounts, Jaxyn was the better part of nine thousand years old. To hear him mocking mortality so openly made Warlock grip the handle of the mallet tighter. The urge to hit something immortal with it was proving almost too hard to resist.

"Pity my son doesn't seem to share your enthusiasm for life, Lord Aranville," the queen remarked with a frown. "How late were you out last night, Mathu?"

"Don't know." The prince shrugged.

"Oh, Mother!" Kylia said with a laugh. "Don't pick on him! Mathu's allowed a little fun, isn't he? Once he's a father, he'll have to be quite boringly responsible."

"She has a point, your majesty," Jaxyn added. "You shouldn't blame him for wanting a little freedom now."

"Once he's a *father*?" the queen repeated with a raised brow. "Is there an announcement you're planning to make, Mathu?"

Mathu looked down at Kylia in surprise. "I don't know, is there?"

"Not yet," the young princess replied with a coy smile. "But we've been practising a lot, so maybe soon . . ."

As Warlock watched the humans talking among themselves as if the Crasii wasn't even there, he was struck by how easily the immortals lied, how easily they were able to slip into the skins of their stolen identities. They never once hesitated, never once faltered. Had Warlock not known every word coming out of Jaxyn's and Diala's mouths was false, he would have been just as fooled as were the queen and Prince Mathu.

I have to get a message to Declan Hawkes, he reminded himself, as Kylia flirted with Mathu and Jaxyn needled the queen for entertainment.

Since Jaxyn had confirmed the identity of the female immortal impersonating Princess Kylia, Warlock had not had an opportunity to pass the message along. He'd barely stopped working, in fact, and time off was not something one bothered to award their slaves unless they were sick.

Warlock gripped the mallet handle wistfully, wondering if he could arrange to get a message to the spymaster the next time he was sent to the kitchens. Or maybe he'd run into Tiji. There were no other Scards he knew of in the palace, and he was fairly certain it was because there weren't any other Scards, not that he was being kept ignorant of their identities. Scards were rare; that's what made him and Boots so valuable to the Cabal.

If Declan Hawkes had access to more Scards, Warlock reasoned, *he'd have the palace riddled with them.*

And maybe I'd be allowed to go home to Boots.

It was all just speculation, though, so Warlock stood there on the damp grass, waiting for the humans to resume their game, imagining he had some power to save the world from the devastation these Tide Lords would bring down upon his world once their powers returned.

And trying to convince himself that even if he couldn't stop them, perhaps the Cabal of the Tarot had something up their sleeve; some way of preventing these amoral, unfeeling monsters from once again destroying Amyrantha.

When that proved to be too depressing, he tried to cheer himself up by imagining what his pups might look like when they were born.

Chapter 16

It wasn't often that Tilly Ponting came to Herino to visit Declan. Although she kept a house in the capital, it was used mostly by her son, Aleki, when he was in town for various business reasons relating to his estate.

The wedding of the Duke of Lebec's niece to the Crown Prince of Glaeba had been sufficient incentive to bring her south from her home in Lebec, but as a rule, if one wanted to see Lady Ponting, one expected to visit her, not the other way around.

When Declan received her summons—as any request to visit the Guardian of the Lore invariably was—he was still debating which was more important: Visiting Caelum in the north to see for himself if the Empress of the Five Realms and her dangerous Tide Lord offspring were making themselves at home there. Or dropping everything to travel south to Torlenia to warn Arkady that in all likelihood her new best friend, the Imperator's Consort, was the immortal Kinta in disguise.

Despite how often he denied it to Tiji, the chameleon Crasii had read him far too well. No matter how logical it might be to head north to Caelum, he desperately wanted to go to Arkady. Declan had let her down once before, when they were children. He didn't intend to let it happen a second time.

Tilly's unexpected arrival, he hoped, would make his decision easier. She was the Guardian of the Lore, the Head of the Pentangle and therefore the head of the Cabal of the Tarot. There was nobody better placed to advise him about the wisest course of action, and Declan knew he needed her counsel.

"I need you to find your grandfather for me," Tilly told him, once the pleasantries were dispensed with. It was very late—the same day of her summons—but that had more to do with Declan's schedule as spymaster than any deliberate attempt on his part to act in a clandestine manner. He'd arrived by an anonymous hired cab which waited out front, even now. The driver didn't mind the wait. He didn't know who Declan was but he knew the sound of a heavy purse when he heard one and in this quiet, exclusive neighbourhood, he was safe enough dozing in his seat, waiting for his customer. Declan had smiled as the cabbie settled down to wait, obviously convinced his passenger had an amorous assignation planned with the lady of the house.

All thoughts of what his driver might be imagining fled at Tilly's announcement, which she made as she led her late-night guest into the parlour, where the fitful light of a single candelabrum on the table cast dancing shadows over the room, shrouding the detail of the furnishings in darkness and making the old lady appear quite sinister.

Declan gazed at her in confusion. "I wasn't aware he was lost."

Expecting a smile, he was more than a little alarmed when Tilly nodded, her expression grim, indicating he should take a seat at the table.

"I don't suppose he's lost in the truest sense of the word," Tilly replied as she took the seat opposite. "But I haven't heard from Shalimar in almost two months, Declan. I'm starting to get worried."

"Send someone around to check on him, then," Declan suggested, wondering why such an easily solved problem would bring her to Herino. "He's probably engrossed in something he's working on and lost track of time. You know how he can be."

"He's not in Lebec, Declan," Tilly informed him. She hesitated, and then added, "I sent him to look for Maralyce."

Declan stared at the old lady for a moment, not sure what shocked him most—that she would attempt such a foolish thing, or that she might send his aging grandfather into the mountains to attempt it for her.

"*What*, in the name of the *Tide*, possessed you to . . ." he began, too angry to finish the sentence. Tilly was the leader of the Cabal and deserved his respect, but right now Declan's fists clenched so tight they whitened with the effort of remaining still.

"We've always known the rough area where Maralyce's mine is," Tilly explained with an apologetic shrug. "After Arkady described the terrain to you following her kidnapping, we were able to narrow it down even further. In fact, we were able to provide Shalimar with almost the exact location."

"And then you sent him into the mountains, alone and unprotected, to face down a Tide Lord with the Tide on the turn?"

Tilly shook her head. "It wasn't like that, Declan. He wasn't alone. Aleki saw to that. He had two bodyguards and plenty of supplies. And Maralyce isn't dangerous."

"She's an immortal, Tilly," he reminded her, too angry to award her the title she deserved. "And a Tide Lord. You can't use the words *Tide Lord* and *not dangerous* in the same breath. You taught me that before I could walk."

"Maralyce has tried to help us in the past."

"Not killing us with quite the same enthusiasm as her immortal cronies doesn't actually qualify as helping, you know."

The old lady smiled. "You see the world so clearly, Declan. Are there no grey areas for you?"

"Not when it comes to the Tide Lords," he said, fear for his grandfather making him reckless. "What were you *thinking*, Tilly? My *grandfather*? And a Tide Lord? Is there some secret suicide pact you members of the Pentangle have sworn that I don't know about?"

"No," she said, more than a little defensively. "But there is an expectation in the Cabal that one will do whatever is asked of them without complaining about it, young man. A lesson you seem not to have learned yet."

"I pull my weight," he reminded her. "And I've never done anything other than what was asked of me. But that doesn't mean you can toss away the life of the only family I own for the good of the cause."

Tilly threw her hands up impatiently. "Oh, do stop being such an idiot, Declan. Shalimar chose to do this, and to be honest, I don't blame him. Do you know how much we would gain if Maralyce was willing to champion our cause once more?"

"She didn't champion it the last time, as I recall."

"That's your trouble, Declan, you *don't* recall."

"But the Tarot says—"

"Whatever we need it to say," Tilly cut in. "If we'd recorded Maralyce's efforts to help humanity, it would bring the wrath of her immortal brethren down upon her like a firestorm."

Declan smiled then, deliberately goading her. "So now you're telling me this wretched cause to which I've dedicated my whole life is a lie?"

Tilly wasn't amused. "Everything is a lie, Declan. Every one of us is steeped in them. The truth—the only truth—is that which we choose to reveal. There's a reason there's the Lore *and* a Tarot, you know."

Declan nodded. He did know. "The Tarot is for the Tide Lords so they think we've got it wrong, and the Lore for the future, for the day we finally find a way to defeat them."

"Ah, then you did listen to the odd thing your grandfather tried to teach you?"

"I listened, my lady. I just wasn't prepared for there to be quite so much difference between them. I was always under the impression the Tarot was deliberately based on loose fact to give it a ring of authenticity."

"And so it is," she agreed. "But there are some things that are too inflammatory to be recorded at all."

"Maralyce helping humanity being one of them, I suppose?"

She nodded. "Truly, Declan, I'm not afraid Maralyce has hurt your grandfather. I'm more afraid he's come to harm in the mountains."

"Then can't you send someone else after him? There's any number of Scards sitting in Hidden Valley twiddling their thumbs. You could send some of them, couldn't you?"

"I can't risk sending any Crasii, Scard or otherwise, after him, Declan," she said, shaking her head. "If he has found Maralyce's mine, and there's even the remotest chance she might help us, I don't want to ruin our chances by making her deal with the Crasii. She despises them; thinks they're abominations. And that's a rumour Arkady was able to confirm without a doubt. No, whoever I send after Shalimar has to be human and in a position to negotiate if your grandfather can't."

"I'm the King's Spymaster, Tilly. I can't just drop everything to go charging off into the mountains after my grandfather. And it's not that I don't want to, you know that. But since we've had Cecil working in the palace, we know for certain that it's Diala posing as Kylia here in Glaeba, which means any day this whole city might go up in flames. Tiji had a run-in with the Empress and her lot in Caelum and now it looks as if Kinta may be posing as the Imperator's Consort in Torlenia."

Tilly's eyes widened in shock. "Does Arkady know about this?"

"It was Arkady who sent us word. But no, as far as I know, she's not aware who the Lady Chintara is."

"Chintara, eh? She's modified her name then, for the benefit of her Torlenian subjects." Tilly smiled. "Not that I blame her. Isn't a chinta a smelly little Torlenian rodent?"

"The point, my lady, is that I need to go south—"

"To save Arkady?" Tilly said with disturbing insight before he could present his elegant argument defending his decision. "Does she *need* saving?"

"Tides, Tilly! She's meeting with Kinta on an almost daily basis . . ."

"And probably being treated like a queen, Declan. Kinta's done nothing to harm her, has she, or even threaten Glaeba's interests? In fact, I hear on the grapevine Stellan actually got an audience with the Imperator that didn't end in bloodshed thanks to Arkady's friendship with the consort. Exactly what is the threat here?"

"If Kinta is back then it's likely Brynden is nearby. Or worse, the Immortal Prince."

Tilly's eyes narrowed. "That what's really bothering you, isn't it? You fear Arkady may run into Cayal again."

Declan took a deep breath, at pains to appear unemotional about this. "Brynden all but destroyed Amyrantha during the last Cataclysm because the Immortal Prince stole his lover. You can't tell me that everything has been forgiven and they're all back to being friends again. Kinta has married the Imperator of Torlenia and the only reason she'll have done that is so she can hand the prize of the Torlenian throne over to her lover when he returns. And we don't know which lover that might be. Given what happened the last time there was a battle for her affections, I don't think it's unreasonable that we do something to ensure the same thing doesn't happen again."

"I'll bet you practised that little speech all the way here."

"That doesn't make it wrong."

She smiled sympathetically. "Nor does it make it compelling. If Kinta is back and preparing to take Torlenia, it will be for Brynden. Cayal's death wish will have put paid to any future he might once have wanted with Kinta, and besides, why else would she be interested in securing Torlenia? It's traditionally Brynden's stomping ground. She'll be getting ready to offer it to him. If she was looking for something to give Cayal, she'd more likely be here in Glaeba. This is his territory, not the continent where people curse his very name."

"I can't just up and leave Herino. There's too much happening at the moment . . ."

"Ask Daly to help."

Declan looked at her in surprise. "He's retired."

"And dying of terminal boredom," Tilly added with a smile. "Bring Daly out of retirement to keep an eye on things in Caelum. He was the King's Spymaster longer than you've been alive and he's still a member of the Cabal. There's nobody better qualified for the job and five years of fishing is driving him to distraction. He'd welcome the chance to do something useful. You've got Cecil in the palace now, so we'll know what Jaxyn and Diala are up to. He can report to Lord Deryon just as easily—probably more easily—than he can get word to you, anyway. So send someone you trust to Torlenia to warn Arkady she might be dealing with Kinta and do what I require of you, young man. Go into the mountains, find your grandfather, speak to Maralyce if he hasn't already done it, and convince her that the humans of Amyrantha are going to need her help."

"*That's* the plan?" he asked, making no attempt to hide his irritation at the way she was trampling all over his wishes to suit the Cabal's agenda. "Ten thousand years of sacrifice, ten thousand years of hoarding every scrap of knowledge we could get our hands on and the best the Cabal can come up with is: *let's ask one of the nice Tide Lords to be on our side?*"

The old lady frowned. "You have your grandfather's gift for vast oversimplification, I see."

"I'm a regular chip off the old block. Is there any point trying to argue about this?"

Tilly smiled and leaned forward to pat his hand. "We can fight about this for a bit longer if it will make you feel better, dear. But in the end, you'll do as I say. We both know that."

He snatched his hand away, in no mood to play her games. This woman might have everybody in Glaeba convinced she was an eccentric fool, but Declan knew better. "You know, someday, I'm going to tell the king who really rules Glaeba."

"Well, while you're waiting for your opportunity, do as I command, Declan Hawkes. Find Maralyce. And your grandfather."

"Even if I have to turn my back on more immediate dangers?"

"Declan, if we don't find a way to counter the rising power of the Tide Lords, it won't matter what you do to help your friends."

"You're assuming I meant Arkady."

"She's my friend too, you know. Nobody wishes her harm less than I do."

"But you're prepared to leave her in the power of a Tide Lord."

Tilly shrugged. "Arkady has already proved she can hold her own against a Tide Lord, Declan," she pointed out, rising to her feet. "Now it's time for you to do the same."

Chapter 17

Declan Hawkes liked to keep his private life and his working life strictly separate, so when Tiji received a summons to meet Declan at his home, rather than either of the offices he kept, she knew something important was afoot.

It was late in the afternoon when she arrived. He lived in a small apartment above an apothecary several blocks from the palace in an area of Herino that was as quiet as it was unremarkable. Being close to the lake's edge, the street was paved, but the houses were elevated to about waist height on thick wooden stumps and connected by a series of wooden pathways to allow the frequent spring floods a clear path through the streets. More than one house had a small boat propped up against the wall, waiting for the next flood, which Tiji had to skirt around as she made her way to Declan's house. The remains of the last inundation were long gone, she noted, although the street was damp from the most recent shower of rain. The streets of Herino, particularly this close to the palace, were designed to drain quickly and it hadn't flooded since early spring.

The people who lived in this part of the city were fishermen, shopkeepers and tradesmen for the most part, people who kept to themselves while quietly looking out for their neighbours. Tiji wasn't sure if Declan's neighbours knew who he was—she suspected they didn't—but they seemed to have no complaint about the nice young man living over the apothecary. One woman across the street, who was sweeping the wooden walkway in front of her house, even nodded a greeting as the Crasii approached.

Tiji smiled, acknowledging the greeting with a wave as she slipped through the doorway to the narrow stairs. With her gloved hands, her long, hooded cloak concealing her silver skin and scaly features, the woman probably thought Declan was entertaining a lady friend for dinner. Her arrival might be the talk of the street for days.

She was still smiling at the notion when Declan opened the door for her after she knocked. He stood back to let her enter. The apartment surprised Tiji. There was little here that gave any hint of the personality of its owner. There were no pictures on the roughly plastered walls, no trinkets or keepsakes on the wooden mantel over the soot-stained fireplace, or anything else in the sparsely furnished apartment that might indicate who lived here.

Maybe he doesn't live here at all, Tiji thought, glancing at the neatly made bed and the washed dishes lined up in a rack on a bench by the window. *Maybe Declan lives somewhere else and this place is just another front, just another lie, just another face on a man who has scores of them . . .*

"Did anybody see you coming here?" he asked, closing the door behind her.

"Only the woman across the street," she told him, turning to face the spymaster. She couldn't tell what mood he was in, but that didn't bother her. Very few people could read Declan Hawkes when he was in the mood to be enigmatic. "Is that a problem? You never told me I had to sneak in."

"It's not a problem if Maisie spotted you," the spymaster assured her, as he walked across the threadbare rug to the scrubbed wooden table that took up much of the northern corner of the small two-roomed apartment. "She's one of us."

"How come I never met her before?" she asked, following him with her eyes.

"You didn't need to."

"Fair enough," Tiji agreed, her gaze locking onto the partially filled pack sitting on the table, surrounded by a pile of gear—the sort of supplies one might need if they were planning an extended trip away from civilisation. "Going somewhere?"

"We both are," Declan informed her, tossing her a small, leather-wrapped packet he picked up from the table.

Tiji caught the package, undid the cord holding the satchel closed and then peered inside. "What's this?"

"Travel papers."

"I'm going somewhere?"

"Torlenia."

She looked up in surprise. "And I don't have to swim there because you've actually sprung for a ticket on a sailing ship? I'm shocked, Declan. You must be getting sentimental in your old age."

He smiled humourlessly, turning his attention to the gear on the table, which he began to stuff into the half-filled pack. "Resourceful as I know you are, Tiji, even you might struggle if you had to swim all the way across the straits to Torlenia."

"That's very thoughtful of you, Declan. And *why*, exactly, am I going to Torlenia?"

"To find out if Lady Chintara really is an immortal," he informed her as he stuffed a small wheel of cheese down the side of his pack.

"And when I find this out, what do I do then?"

"I want you to warn Arkady."

"I see."

He glanced at her. "What's that supposed to mean?"

"Nothing," she assured him. "I am curious, though. How come you're sending me? I thought once you suspected Kinta the Charioteer was the Imperator's Consort you'd be off like a firecracker to warn your little girlfriend of the danger she might be in."

"She's not my girlfriend," Declan replied automatically as he resumed his packing.

Tiji smiled. She liked needling Declan about the Duchess of Lebec, mostly because she'd never found anything else about him that even remotely hinted at a chink in his armour.

For all that, Tiji wasn't even sure Arkady Desean *was* a chink in his armour.

She did know, however, that in the past, the little Crasii had helped Declan—on at least three separate occasions—take care of a potentially embarrassing problem for Arkady's husband, the Duke of Lebec. Each incident had involved a young man. They were all visitors to Lebec Palace for one reason or another. And she'd helped ensure the silence of every one of them at Declan's command. As there was no logical reason for Declan to protect Stellan Desean from a scandal—as King's Spymaster his job was quite the opposite—Tiji had long ago concluded that it wasn't Stellan Declan was protecting.

He was protecting his childhood friend, Arkady.

Of course, their friendship might well be as innocent as Declan always insisted it was, and she'd certainly never seen anything that might lead her to believe otherwise, but still . . . there was a wistfulness about Declan when he spoke of Arkady. A slight softening in his demeanour that no other living creature on Amyrantha was able to evoke in him. If Declan Hawkes wasn't in love with Arkady Desean, Tiji reasoned, then he probably wasn't capable of loving anyone.

How it must irk him to see the woman he loves married to another man. Particularly a man incapable of loving her the way Tiji was certain Declan loved—or wanted to love—Arkady.

Tiji sometimes thought that's what she and Declan had in common; the reason they were friends as much as master and servant. They both knew the pain of incurable loneliness. Declan, because he could never have the woman he loved, and Tiji, because she had never even heard of another member of her species. Although she knew she must come from somewhere, Tiji had no idea if there were any other chameleon Crasii left alive on Amyrantha.

For all she knew, she was the last of her breed.

Like her master, Tiji might be destined to live and die without the comfort of someone to love her and only her . . . *Tides, but we're pitiable creatures, you and I, Declan Hawkes . . .*

Watching him stuff his pack with a force the job truly didn't deserve, Tiji knew Declan didn't wish to discuss the matter further, so she took a closer look at the papers he'd given her, shocked to see the seal of the King's Private Secretary on the letter of introduction.

"You've arranged *diplomatic* papers for me?"

"Time is of the essence," he told her, without looking up. "For the purpose of this journey, you're a courier on business for the King of Glaeba. Those letters give you the power to commandeer a ship, if need be."

"*Really?*"

He stared at her with a stern look. "I'd better not hear you *have* commandeered a ship, Slinky, unless the world's about to come to an end, or trust me, there'll be hell to pay."

She grinned at him, unable to hide her excitement. She'd never travelled as a diplomat before. That was something usually reserved for humans, not Crasii slaves. And these papers meant more than the ability to travel quickly. They meant respect, the best ships, the finest cabins, real sheets, edible food . . . "As if I'd abuse my power like that."

"You've never *had* any power before, Slinky."

She thought on that for a moment and then brightened as another thought occurred to her. "Can I throw my weight around once I get to Torlenia?"

He shook his head, but he seemed amused by her eagerness. "If anyone will listen to you, be my guest."

"Do I have to wear one of those silly shrouds?"

The question gave him pause. "You know, in a shroud, nobody would even notice you're not human."

" 'Cept for not having any eyelashes," she reminded him. "And then there's that whole 'silver scales instead of skin' problem . . ."

He studied her thoughtfully for a moment. "Do people look that closely at shrouded females?" Then Declan shook his head. "Better not risk it. Wear your shift as you would here, and don't try to pretend to be anything other than a slave on business for the Glaeban king. Given you *are* a slave, they'll not assume you're carrying anything too important."

"And when I get to Torlenia? How do I get in to see the Imperator's Consort so I can tell if she's really Kinta?"

"Tell Arkady I sent you. She'll arrange it and once we know for certain, she can help you get word back to the Cabal."

Tiji was a little surprised Declan had told Arkady even that much about the Cabal. Theirs was not an organisation that trusted strangers easily. Still, given Declan had known Arkady since they were small children, she probably didn't qualify as a stranger. "Did you want me to tell her anything else?"

"Such as?"

She shrugged. "That you send your love, perhaps?"

He stood the now-filled pack on its base and began to tie it closed, his expression determinedly neutral. "You really think you're funny, don't you, Slinky?"

"You know how I can tell you're in love with her?" she insisted, closing up her own precious pouch full of documents. "It's because you have no sense of humour at all, when it comes to the lovely Duchess of Lebec. It's a dead giveaway, Declan. I don't know why you keep denying it."

"I keep denying it, Tiji, because the love affair between me and Arkady Desean exists only in your sorry imagination."

"And yours," she retorted with a grin.

Declan sighed, lifting the pack onto his back, checking the weight distribution. He bounced up and down on the balls of his feet for a moment, testing the pack's stability, and then lifted it off with an effort. Wherever he was going, it was obvious Declan planned to be away for some time. "Give it up, Slinky. This joke of yours is getting very old and tiresome."

"Keeps *me* amused."

"Then I'm very happy for you."

"I can tell," she replied, smiling at his pained expression. "Where are you going?"

"None of your business."

"So it's important then?"

"Why do you assume it's important?"

"Because if it wasn't important, you'd probably tell me where you're off to. Or you'd be sending me in your stead and *you'd* be commandeering the next ship for Torlenia."

"Then, yes," he agreed, placing the pack on the floor beside the table where he rested it against the turned wooden leg. He turned to face her, his expression, as usual, betraying nothing. "It's important. Everything I do is important. I'm a very important fellow."

Her eyes narrowed suspiciously. "Must be *really* important if you're going somewhere other than Torlenia."

"You know, I could *write* Arkady a message and have you deliver it with your tongue cut out," he suggested.

"Will I still be able to commandeer a ship?" she asked with a hopeful grin.

Declan shook his head, but he relented a little and allowed himself a small smile. "I should have left you rotting in that wretched freak show, Slinky."

Tiji smiled at him. "You don't mean that."

"Yes, I do."

"You'd have nobody to boss around, if you did."

"I'm the King's Spymaster," he reminded her. "I've got plenty of people I can boss around."

"That's why you're taking off for parts unknown and leaving me to do the job you'd rather be doing yourself, I suppose?" she asked. "Because nobody gets to boss the fearsome Declan Hawkes around?"

Declan began patting his pockets, as if he was looking for something. "Tides! Where *did* I put that knife I keep for tongue extractions."

Tiji smiled. "You don't scare me, Declan Hawkes."

He glared at her. "All the more reason to silence you before you can spread your pernicious rumours, you miserable lizard."

Not fooled for a moment by his snarling threats or insults, Tiji crossed the rug, stood on tiptoe and kissed his cheek. "I'll always keep your secrets, Declan, you know that. Just be careful."

"Of what?"

"Of *whoever* it is you're going to confront," she corrected.

"I never said . . ."

"You don't have to," she replied, her smile fading. "If you're sending me to warn Arkady because you think she's in danger, the only reason is because the Cabal has other plans for you. The Pentangle of the Cabal of the Tarot is far too cautious to waste the likes of Declan Hawkes on trivial matters that can be taken care of by lesser men. So whoever you're going to see, or *whatever* it is you're going to do for the Cabal, Declan, be careful. I don't have that many friends, you know. I can't really afford to lose any of the few I do have."

Declan studied her for a moment and then he shook his head, looking more irritated than touched by her warning. "Tides, I really should cut out your tongue, you stupid, sentimental reptile. Get out of here. And I mean it about not commandeering a ship unless the world's coming to an end."

"Yes, sir!" she replied, standing dutifully to attention, offering a mocking salute. "Anything you say, sir!"

"You're pushing it, Slinky."

Tiji laughed at his frown and, clutching the precious diplomatic pouch to her breast, turned for the door, knowing how much Declan hated goodbyes, particularly when he was sending somebody off to do something dangerous. She hesitated with her hand on the door, and smiled back at him. "Did you want a souvenir of Torlenia?"

"Hang around here much longer and I won't need any souvenirs. I'll have you skinned and made into a belt."

Without answering such a preposterous threat, Tiji opened the door and slipped into the narrow stairwell, leaving Declan standing by the table next to his pack with its cold-weather gear that gave away far more than the spymaster imagined.

There was only one place Declan can be heading, she reasoned, hesitating at the foot of the stairs to check if the coast was clear. Maisie had finished her sweeping and now the street was empty, filled only with the aromas of half-cooked meat and any number of spices that didn't really complement each other as the residents of Apothecary Row prepared their many different dinners.

Waiting out of habit, as much as anything, to ensure the street was really deserted, Tiji's thoughts returned to Declan's pack. It had been filled with warm clothes, wet-weather gear and trail rations, which might mean he was heading to Caelum, but if that was the case, Declan would simply have packed a trunk and taken a boat across the lake. He'd need little else and certainly not the food he was packing if he was going to check on the Empress of the Five Realms.

No, Declan was packing for something rougher and far more primitive.

Which means he's heading for the mountains, she decided with a chill of fear, pulling the cloak around her as she stepped out onto the street. *To hunt down either Maralyce or the Immortal Prince.*

The wheel was turning. The game was being played once more.

The Cabal was getting ready to make contact with the Tide Lords.

PART II

The tide rises, the tide falls,
The twilight darkens, the curlew calls.
—"The Tide Rises, the Tide Falls,"
HENRY WADSWORTH LONGFELLOW
(1807–1882)

Chapter 18

Given how long the Cabal had been trying to locate Maralyce's mine, it proved disturbingly easy to locate the path, once they had the last few details to fill in the blanks in their knowledge. The vital pieces of missing information were provided by Arkady in the days leading up to the wedding of her husband's niece to the Crown Prince of Glaeba, during which time both Tilly and Declan had questioned her closely and at length about what really happened in the time she was Cayal's prisoner.

Her kidnapping by the Immortal Prince might have given Declan nightmares, he mused, but it had proved a boon for the Cabal of the Tarot in other things. She'd been able to confirm things they'd only suspected up until now, fill in details lost to antiquity or during the cataclysmic natural disasters so frequently caused by the Tide Lords that—time and again—almost wiped humanity off the face of Amyrantha.

The depth of Arkady's knowledge disturbed Declan more than he was willing to admit. For her to have learned such things from the Immortal Prince, he'd obviously confided in her—at length—sharing details Cayal had probably not shared with another living soul in centuries. Immortal or not, men didn't pour their hearts out to any woman on a whim. No . . . Declan decided as he trudged steadily upward through the rain, Cayal had told his tale to Arkady because he was looking for sympathy and that meant he wanted her to look favourably upon him.

Declan knew what *he* was after when he found himself trying to impress a girl.

He didn't kid himself for a moment that the Immortal Prince wasn't after exactly the same thing.

Still, it was his own fault Arkady and Cayal had become so close. Declan knew that and cursed his own stupidity. He was the one, after all, who'd sent her to interview the Immortal Prince after his hanging failed. He had nobody to blame but himself . . .

Which begged another question. What would have happened if the headsman had been on duty in Lebec Prison that chilly spring day a few months ago when they'd tried to execute the Immortal Prince? If Cayal's plan to destroy his memories by having himself decapitated had succeeded, would they even still be here worrying about it? Or would his beheading have unleashed the power of the Tide and destroyed Glaeba in a single, unsuspecting blow?

When you think about it like that, is there really anything for which to blame myself? he wondered, the solitude of the mountains giving him far too much time to dwell on such thoughts. *We were a heartbeat away from destroying the continent by accident, anyway.*

And, when all was said and done, Arkady had done nothing more than he'd asked of her. She'd simply learned all she could about the Immortal Prince and shared everything she knew with the Cabal.

Or did her relationship with that wretched immortal go further? Does she feel something for him? Has she fallen victim to his legendary charms?

Declan didn't like to think about it. And he was exceptionally good at not thinking about Arkady, a skill he'd been forced to master many years ago. It had been hard enough learning to deal with the notion of Arkady married to Stellan Desean. For seven years he'd tried not to think about that, too; the only thing making it bearable was the knowledge Stellan Desean—although he seemed a decent enough man—had little or no interest in Arkady physically, and that situation wasn't likely to change. Arkady had no idea Declan knew the truth about Stellan . . . at least, she acted as if she didn't. Perhaps she suspected the truth. Arkady wasn't stupid. She must know Stellan's secret was something not easily kept, particularly from the King's Spymaster.

Whatever the case, Stellan's secret and the sham of Arkady's marriage remained unspoken between them.

Declan could live with that. He had no *choice* but to live with it.

But it was the nature of the Cabal to demand a sacrifice of its members. For the sake of the Cabal of the Tarot—and the greater good of humanity, Declan liked to kid himself—he may well have pushed the woman he loved into the arms of an immortal, and there wasn't a damned thing he could do about it.

The worst of it was, as far as the Pentangle was concerned, the sacrifice was probably worth it. For the first time in several thousand years, the Cabal was able to pinpoint the Seeker's exact location. And they were able to confirm that Maralyce remained aloof and at odds with the majority of her immortal brethren. That was something they'd always suspected, but had never been able to confirm. The cost of such intelligence was not something the Cabal was too concerned about, particularly as no lives had been lost gaining the information and the only casualty was likely to be the tender feelings of a woman who existed on the very periphery of the Cabal's awareness. People had given their lives for information a lot less important in the past. Arkady's effort would barely rate a mention in the annals of the Cabal.

For the Cabal of the Tarot, the search for an answer was never ending. Now they knew for certain where Maralyce was hiding, Shalimar had come into these mountains to find the immortal miner, Maralyce the Seeker, to beg her aid.

Strangely enough, Declan's journey into the mountains was expedited by his missing grandfather. Perhaps fearing his fate when he confronted the immortal, Shalimar had marked the trail, either assuming he wasn't coming back, or in the belief he would be able to use the route again. The marks weren't obvious; a broken twig here, a small length of coloured twine tied to a bush there. Declan knew his grandfather well. He had no trouble finding the subtle signs Shalimar Hawkes left— which also explained why Tilly had sent Declan in pursuit of his grandfather, at a time when it could be argued he was badly needed elsewhere.

Declan had no trouble following in Shalimar's footsteps, all the way to the three unmarked graves he found just off the road where it widened for a short time and then narrowed once more, leading into the dark trees curving away to the left, disappearing amid the dense foliage ahead of him.

It was raining, as it had been most of the night. Declan was wet, miserable and too drained to feel much of anything when he spied the fresh graves.

Pushing away his increasingly morose thoughts about Arkady and his part in pushing her into the arms of the Immortal Prince, he fell to his knees against the muddy ground, weariness weighing him down more than his pack ever had.

"Tides," he muttered, staring at the three mounds.

He stared at the graves for a long time. Whoever had died here, they had been treated with respect. They'd not been killed and left to rot by bandits.

But there were three of them. And it was three men not heard of for months that Declan was in pursuit of. He hesitated, wondering if he should disturb the dead.

Was he looking at the last resting place of three loggers or hunters come to grief in the mountains?

Or was he kneeling at the side of Shalimar's final resting place?

Squinting in the rain that beat a steady, depressing tattoo on his oil-skin cape, Declan stood up. If these graves belonged to men he didn't know, they deserved to be left in peace.

He glanced up the path, knowing he was less than an hour from Maralyce's mine, and then looked down at the runnels of water cutting through the loose topsoil covering the bodies. If these graves contained the bodies of his grandfather and the two men Aleki Ponting had sent to watch over him, Declan didn't really want to know.

He needed a clear head, a mind not warped with grief or anger, if he was going to confront an immortal.

Forcing himself to move, Declan shouldered his pack a little higher and stepped back onto the faint trail leading further up the mountain. Without looking back he headed into the trees, hoping against all reasonable hope that his grandfather was still alive and waiting for him at Maralyce's mine.

The mine, when Declan finally reached it, proved to be something of a let-down. It was smaller than he'd imagined; the muddy clearing cluttered with numerous bits of discarded or broken mining equipment and the detritus of many lifetimes of habitation. On the far side the mountain loomed over the clearing, sheltering it in winter from the worst storms, but doing nothing to halt the steady downpour that had dogged Declan's heels all morning.

He looked around with interest, not really surprised to find—built into the lee of the cliff wall just as Arkady had described it—a cottage with two shuttered windows and a silent forge beside it. On his right were an outhouse and a rickety shaft that could only be the mine entrance, shored up by wooden planking that looked set to topple at any moment.

The rain beat down steadily, the camp showing no signs of life.

Tides, he thought. *Isn't that just typical? Come all this way and there's nobody home.*

Declan was still debating what to do next when, out of the corner of his eye, he caught the faintest wisp of smoke escaping the cabin's chimney pot.

It seemed he wasn't alone, after all.

He'd barely taken three steps across the yard before the cabin door opened and Declan found himself facing Maralyce. She was also exactly as Arkady had described her—wearing men's clothing, of middling height, slender, dark-haired, with unlined skin and an unwelcoming expression on her face.

"Are you Maralyce?" he asked, while thinking: *Tides, you moron, could you have thought up a more idiotic question?*

She glowered at him. "Reckon you know the answer to that without my help."

Declan nodded. "Reckon I do."

She folded her arms, glaring at him through the persistent rain. "Then I reckon you know the next thing I'm gonna do is tell you to piss off."

He smiled humourlessly. "Just as I'm quite sure you know, my lady, that I haven't come all this way just to turn around and go home again."

"Suit yourself," she said. Shrugging, she stepped back into the house and slammed the door on him.

Deftly handled, old boy, Declan told himself, as the rain drizzled down his neck. He glanced around the yard, spying the forge off to the right. Shouldering his pack a little higher, Declan headed for it, hoping there was a fire going in there. The rain had chilled him to the bone and who knew how long it would be before Maralyce emerged from her cabin once more.

The wish for a fire proved an idle hope, Declan discovered, when he stepped out of the downpour into the shelter of the forge, the rain beating down on the shingles so loudly he could barely hear himself think. The huge stone fire-pit was warm—it took a long time for a decent forge to cool down, even in these unpleasant conditions—but there were no welcoming flames waiting for him.

Shrugging off his pack, he walked to the huge stone rectangle in the centre of the cluttered lean-to, placing his hands on the rock for a moment, letting his frozen fingers soak up the little remaining warmth. As he did, he glanced around, discovering a pile of chopped wood in the corner. Declan looked around some more until he spied an iron poker. He picked it up and turned back to the forge, plunging it into the ashes in the fire-pit. He stirred them up until he exposed the last remnants of the fire's glowing coals at the bottom of the pit. Declan blew gently on the coals, raising a fine cloud of ash, but the coals responded by glowing a little brighter.

A bit of kindling and some tender loving care, he thought, glancing around the tattered lean-to with its split planking walls and leaking roof, *and it'll be quite toasty in here.*

Getting the fire going again gave him something to do. He was sure Maralyce would emerge eventually, if only to tell him to leave again. In the meantime, there was no reason why he shouldn't be warm.

Or as warm as I'm likely to get in this pitiful excuse for shelter.

The simple task also kept Declan's mind off another much more disturbing train of thought. The spectre of those three unmarked graves further down the trail still haunted him, and all the denials in the world couldn't hold back the creeping suspicion that he knew who must be buried in them.

It took a while to coax the fire back to life, but once he had, Declan opened his pack, took out the last of the cheese and jerky he'd brought with him, and with his back to the warm stone of the fire-pit in Maralyce's forge, he settled down to wait, trying not to dwell on the one question that refused to go away.

If Shalimar and his escort had made it here to Maralyce's mine without mishap, where are they?

Chapter 19

While it wasn't unheard of for a slave to act as a diplomat, it was rare enough that Tiji intended to make the most of her status as an official envoy of the Glaeban king. She travelled from Herino in style in a Crasii-guided ship—with her own cabin, no less—all the way to White-water, where she changed to a smaller, and therefore safer, vessel for the journey through the Whitewater Narrows to the coast. After several nights as a guest at an inn normally reserved for human patrons, she boarded a sleek ocean-going sloop for the crossing to the Chelae Islands and then south on to Ramahn, the fabled Crystal City of Torlenia.

The Crystal City didn't let her down. Approaching the city on the morning tide, the chalky, salt-encrusted cliffs glittered like gemstones. Tiji leaned on the railing, covered by a simple long white linen coat and broad straw hat, watching the city grow larger in the distance, trying to appear unimpressed. Secretly, her heart was pounding. She was enjoying this opportunity to stand on deck and watch the city approaching with-out feeling guilty or nervous. She'd not ventured out of her adopted country openly since Declan brought her back from Senestra when she was fifteen years old. Usually she was on missions that required much hiding, lurking in dark, dank holds and remaining hidden.

Tiji's life before Declan found her was more a montage of isolated incidents, rather than a coherent memory. She remembered random, disconnected faces. Odd, seemingly trivial incidents and a few bitter, tormented nightmares of beatings and lingering pain she had gone to a great deal of trouble to put out of her mind. It left her with nothing she could cling to. There was nothing in Tiji's past she could look back on and call childhood. It was almost as if she didn't *have* a past. As if she was born, fully grown, the day Declan traded a purse of gold for her freedom.

Tiji wondered if she'd simply blocked the past out of her mind, or if Declan's assertion she'd been drugged to keep her docile was actually the case. It may have been a little bit of both. Whatever the case, stepping into a foreign country with a diplomatic pouch—offering a level of protection few humans enjoyed, let alone other Crasii—filled the young chameleon with a sense of anticipation and delight she'd rarely experienced before, despite the gravity of the news she carried.

There was no need to sneak around in Ramahn, something Tiji was forced to do more often than not, when on a mission for Declan Hawkes. This time, when the ship docked, she asked the captain to arrange a litter for her, which he did without so much as a questioning look. Her small amount of baggage was unloaded first and carried off the ship for her by one of the crew. The customs man on the dock changed his manner from disdain to obsequiousness as soon as she showed him her papers and within minutes she was on her way to the Glaeban embassy compound while the second-class passengers were still getting off the boat.

Although her arrival was unexpected, to her intense relief Lady Desean was home when she arrived, saving Tiji the necessity of having to explain why she was here to the Duke of Lebec, who—according to Declan—had no idea the Tide Lords were even real, let alone any idea of the threat they posed to the mortal inhabitants of Amyrantha.

Arkady Desean at least knew the truth about the Tide Lords and would understand the importance of an envoy's arrival bearing news about them. Sure enough, once Tiji explained her status as a royal envoy to the steward who answered the door and showed him her commission, a few moments later, upon announcement that a courier had arrived with a message from the King's Spymaster, Tiji was led straight into the seraglium and the presence of the Duchess of Lebec.

Arkady Desean was a beautiful woman. Tiji had heard others say it, and knew it on an intellectual level, although her attractions were lost on the chameleon. Declan thought her beautiful, at any rate—Tiji knew that—so she supposed Arkady must be. She was tall for a woman, much taller than Tiji, and had obviously been relaxing in the afternoon heat.

Her long dark hair was let down and she wore a loose, red-silk shift, made of a fabric so fine the mere breeze created by her passing was enough to stir it into motion. Looking around with interest, Tiji followed the female servant who had admitted her to the seraglium. The main room reminded Tiji of the atriums sometimes featured in the larger houses of Glaeba, but this was roofed and although a fountain trickled musically into a tiled pool in the centre of the room, it did nothing to relieve the relentless heat.

Arkady rose to her feet, making no effort to hide her surprise as Tiji made her way to the couches on the other side of the fountain where the lady waited.

"You're Declan's chameleon," the duchess exclaimed.

"Yes, your grace," she agreed, snatching her wide-brimmed hat from her head, thinking the expression *Declan's chameleon* made her sound like somebody's pet lizard. "Master Hawkes sends his . . . regards."

"You must be tired after your journey," the duchess said, indicating Tiji should take a seat. "Would you like something to drink?"

Tiji nodded, and sat down opposite the small table between them, placing the hat on the seat beside her. "What's the water like here?"

Arkady Desean grimaced. "Not fit for human—or Crasii—consumption, I fear. Will wine do? Or we might have some ale in the kitchen if you'd prefer it."

"Wine would be fine, thank you, your grace."

Arkady sent the human woman who had led Tiji into the seraglium to fetch wine for her guest and resumed her own seat. "Your name is Tiji, isn't it?"

"Yes, your grace," she replied, a little surprised the duchess had known that. She'd never met her officially before. For Arkady to know her name, Declan must have said something about his chameleon Crasii to her in the past.

I wonder what else they talk about when they're alone.

"And Declan? Is he well?" the duchess asked, in a casual tone that made Tiji smile.

Tides, you're as bad as he is.

"Very well," Tiji assured her. "He regrets that the business of state prevents him from visiting you . . . and your honoured husband . . . himself."

Arkady smiled, which made her seem much less imperious. "Yes, I suppose it would raise the odd eyebrow, wouldn't it? Have you been to Torlenia before, Tiji?"

"A number of times, your grace."

"Then you must be fully informed about the unique, wearying and endless number of customs our hosts have regarding the females of *all* species. Did you come through the city dressed like that?"

Tiji nodded.

"I'm surprised you weren't stopped."

"I was in a covered litter, your grace," she explained. "And people tend to think I'm a boy, anyway. It's not having any hair, I think."

"A lucky misconception," Arkady said, and then she stopped as the servant sent to fetch the wine returned. She waited while the wine was poured, dismissed the woman with a distant smile and turned her attention back to Tiji. "You have news for me, I assume?"

Tiji glanced around the large atrium before fixing her eyes on the duchess. "Is it safe to talk here, my lady?"

"The garden might be safer."

"Then we should take a turn around it, your grace. What I have to tell you is for your ears only."

"Declan thinks your Lady Chintara is actually Kinta the Charioteer," Tiji blurted out as soon as they were alone amidst the riotous tropical gardens of the women's quarters.

The duchess was silent for a long time before she finally spoke, and when she did, she didn't sound in the least bit surprised.

"That would explain a great deal."

"You don't seem shocked by the news," Tiji remarked. She'd never pegged the duchess for such a cool head. Perhaps she didn't grasp what it meant. "If it's really Kinta . . ."

"Then we're facing a very serious problem," Arkady finished for her. "Or at least the Torlenians are. Has our Jaxyn made his move yet?"

Tiji shook her head. "Declan seems to think they're biding their time until the Tide returns enough to be certain that when they announce themselves, they'll be unassailable."

"They?" Arkady asked, glancing down at the chameleon. "When did Jaxyn become a *they*?"

"Tides, you wouldn't have heard," Tiji said apologetically. "Your husband's niece, your grace, the one who married Prince Mathu—"

"Yes, I know who she is," the duchess cut in. "What about her?"

"She's not who you think she is either, your grace. She's actually Diala the High Priestess."

"Kylia is the *Minion* Maker?" Arkady asked in surprise.

Tiji was shocked by the question. Very few people knew Diala's nickname was the Minion Maker. Most people referred to her as the High Priestess, the name the Tarot gave her. "So it seems."

"Tides, this is turning into a nightmare!"

Tiji nodded. "That's the general feeling all round, your grace."

"Well . . . what's Declan doing about it? What's the *Cabal* doing about it? And where is the real Kylia? Is she a prisoner somewhere? Or *dead*? Tides! What do I tell Stellan about his niece?"

Tiji stopped walking and placed her hand on Arkady's arm. "You'll tell him nothing, your grace," she informed the duchess in a tone that left no room for argument. "What you *will* do, however, is find a way to get me in to see Chintara so I can confirm her identity, one way or another."

"And then what?" Arkady asked, her expression grim.

"We get word to the Cabal," Tiji said with a shrug, as they resumed their walk through the gardens. "And hope *they've* got some idea on the subject of what we're supposed to do next, because the Tides know there's not a whole lot you and I can do about it, your grace."

Chapter 20

"You'll be replacing that wood you've burned before you leave."

Declan snapped out of his doze at the sound of Maralyce's voice, cracking his head on the side of the forge as he sat up. It was very dark and very cold in the lean-to, except for the small patch of warmth around the fire-pit. The wind had picked up and as he scrambled to his feet, he discovered his fingers were numb and he couldn't feel the end of his nose.

The immortal stood over him, hands on her hips, her expression as unwelcoming as it had been earlier in the day.

"You come here uninvited. You steal my firewood. Who the Tides do you think you are, boy?"

Declan rubbed his eyes, pushing the fugue of sleep away, cursing his foolishness in allowing himself to doze off. It was hours since he'd spoken to Maralyce the first time, so long that he'd almost made up his mind to try again in the morning, and if he still had no luck, return down the trail to those three graves and realise his worst fears by discovering who was buried in them.

He hadn't expected the immortal to seek him out. He certainly hadn't planned his first conversation of substance with her to start like this.

"My name is Declan Hawkes—"

"Shalimar's grandson?"

Declan looked at her in shock. "You *know* my grandfather?"

"Is your grandfather the Tidewatcher?"

"Yes."

"Then I know him. What are you doing here?"

"I came looking for him."

"Why?"

"Because he's missing, and he was last seen coming up here to visit you."

Maralyce stared at him for a long moment and then turned her back on him. "S'pose you'd better come into the house before you die of exposure then," she grumbled with ill grace, stalking out of the lean-to.

Not at all sure he wasn't still dreaming, Declan grabbed his pack and scurried after her. It had stopped raining but the wind had picked up and the clear sky meant it was icy at this altitude, even though it was still officially summer. Worried the immortal might change her mind about the invitation, he stuck close behind her as she stepped into the warm toasty glow of her tiny cabin. As he followed her inside, Declan received his second shock in as many minutes.

The cabin was small, no more than two rooms, with a fireplace stained black by eons of soot and a scrubbed wooden table with a couple of stools either side of it. Every flat surface was cluttered with random bits of mining equipment, clay canisters for storing food, and the odd mouldy book lying about on the shelves.

The most astonishing thing about Maralyce's cabin wasn't the decor, however. It was the company she kept. Because sitting at the table nursing a mug of tea was Shalimar Hawkes, large as life, hale and hearty as Declan had ever seen him.

"See," his grandfather said, addressing his remark to Maralyce. "I told you he wouldn't go away."

"Stubbornness always was a family trait," Maralyce complained. And then she turned on Declan, who was standing by the open door, stunned into immobility by the sight of his grandfather. "Don't just stand there gawking like a fool, boy. Shut that wretched door. You're letting all the warmth out, and you already owe me one load of firewood before you leave. 'Less you're particularly fond of chopping wood, you'd better not make it two."

"You're alive!"

"Sharp as a tack he is, too," Maralyce remarked.

Shivering, Declan slammed the door shut, still staring with awestruck disbelief at his grandfather. He'd been so certain one of the graves by the trail had been the old man's final resting place. It was the reason he'd decided not to uncover the bodies and find out for certain.

"I . . . I saw the graves . . . I thought . . ."

"That I was dead?" Shalimar laughed. "Tides, Declan, didn't you bother to check? What sort of spymaster *are* you?"

Declan chose to ignore that. "Who *is* buried down there, then?"

"Gang of hoodlums who found their way up here last spring," Maralyce said, walking to the fire. She picked up the poker and began to stoke the coals into life.

"And you *killed* them?" If this was the Cabal's definition of a Tide Lord who looked favourably upon mortals, he was glad they hadn't sent him to deal with one who *didn't* like them.

"Killed themselves," Maralyce said with a shrug. "Damn fools should have known these mountains can turn on you when you least expect it. Found 'em after a storm. All lying about like they was asleep around a fire that was dead as a doorpost. Frozen solid, they were."

"Where are the guards Aleki sent with you?" Declan asked his grandfather. "Tilly claimed nobody had heard from you for months so we thought . . . what do you mean *stubbornness always was a family trait*?" he demanded of Maralyce as it struck him, mid-sentence, that such a comment betrayed a familiarity with his family that was both disturbing as well as downright impossible.

"You mean it's *not* a family trait?" Maralyce asked with a raised eyebrow.

Declan turned to his grandfather. "What is going on here, Pop?"

"Nothing's going on." Shalimar shrugged. "The Cabal asked me to find Maralyce and I did."

"You've known all along where she was," he accused. Declan was tired, cold and hungry and this was simply too much to take in.

"Actually, I didn't," Shalimar told him. "I mean I always knew *roughly* where the mine was but we needed the details Arkady was able to provide before I could find it exactly."

"Then how do you know Maralyce?" Declan demanded. "She never leaves this place."

"I *rarely* leave it, son," the old woman corrected, lifting the hot kettle from the fire with her bare hands. "But even I hunger for a bit of human company, every now and then, and these supplies don't appear by magic, you know."

Declan's head swivelled between the pair of them for a moment as so many questions crowded his mind, clamouring for attention, he could barely think.

"How long have you known my grandfather?"

"All his life."

Shalimar seemed amused by Declan's bewilderment. "Tides, lad, think about it. How do you suppose I knew I was a Tidewatcher? I didn't just wake up one morning and decide I could feel the Tide returning."

"Someone had to tell you what it was you could sense," Declan concluded, cursing his own foolishness for not asking such a question sooner. He couldn't remember a time when he didn't know Shalimar was a Tidewatcher. It had never occurred to him to ask *how* Shalimar had learned about his gift. "Tides . . . this is unbelievable. How long have you been visiting Lebec?"

"Longer than your grandfather's been alive," Maralyce replied. "Longer than his grandfather's grandfather, I'd say. You want some tea or are your lips normally that shade of blue?"

"I think I'd prefer something stronger."

"I'm sure you would, but I ain't decided if I like you enough to offer it."

"Then I'll take the tea."

Maralyce topped up the pot on the table beside Shalimar, put the kettle back over the fire, and then took another chipped cup from the mantel, which she filled to the brim and pushed across the table.

"Sit down," she commanded in a voice that brooked no argument.

Declan did as she ordered, taking a grateful sip of the tea. The warmth from the cup seeped through his frozen fingers. "Are you going to tell me what's going on?" he asked his grandfather, as Maralyce sat herself down opposite him on the stool next to Shalimar.

His grandfather glanced at the immortal, almost as if he was seeking her permission to answer. Maralyce shrugged, as if it made no difference to her, which was enough, it seemed, for the old man. "I first met Maralyce in Lebec when I was a child. She sought me out and warned me I was probably a Tidewatcher."

"How did you know where to find him?" Declan asked the immortal.

"That's another story," she replied. "It'll do for you to know I knew what he was. It's irrelevant, for the purpose of this discussion, how I knew."

"Anyway . . ." Shalimar continued, clearly annoyed Declan had interrupted. "On the odd occasion, over the years, Maralyce would stop by to check on me, although she never let on how I could find her if I needed to."

"What need *was* there?" Maralyce grumbled. "It was Low Tide."

"It might have been nice to visit you once in a while," Shalimar said.

"And have you bring the rest of the family along for the vacation? I don't think so."

Shalimar smiled faintly, turning his attention back to Declan. "As you can see, she's not the most sociable of creatures. Anyway, when the Cabal asked me to come here, Aleki insisted on sending along a couple of roughs, as if that made the slightest difference. I knew Maralyce wouldn't want them around and that Aleki would panic if I sent them home, so I concocted a rather elaborate tale about needing information on the goings on in Caelum and sent them packing about a month ago, with strict instructions to report back to me—and only me—at the end of summer with what they'd learned. We've arranged to meet at The Lone Traveller's Inn just outside of Cycrane a few weeks from now."

"And that's why nobody's heard anything from any of you. Tilly is going out of her mind with worry, Pop."

He shrugged. "She should know better than to worry about me."

"Who's Tilly?" Maralyce asked.

"The Guardian of the Lore," Shalimar told her.

Declan put down his tea cup, staring at his grandfather in shock.

"*What?*" the old man demanded, when he saw the look on Declan's face. "Tides, boy, she's over ten thousand years old! You think she doesn't know about the Cabal?"

"You seem awfully keen to give up the identities of the Pentangle," Declan accused.

"Maralyce is on our side."

He glanced at the immortal warily, wishing he could talk to Shalimar alone. Everything about this was wrong. He wondered, for a moment, if the Tide was back sufficiently for Maralyce to warp his grandfather's mind. It didn't seem possible that Shalimar Hawkes, whose hatred of the immortals poisoned everything he touched, should be sitting here sharing tea with a Tide Lord, like they were lifelong friends.

"I only have *your* word for that."

Shalimar sighed heavily and then turned to Maralyce. "Maybe you should tell him."

"Why should I? He's your problem, old man, not mine."

"Things will be easier if he knows the whole story."

"You haven't told him already?"

"You asked me not to."

"Told me what?" Declan asked, glaring at the two of them across the table.

She shook her head. "I don't need to justify myself to some young stud who just happened to stumble onto my claim. You want him to know what happened? You tell him."

"It'll sound better coming from you."

"You spin a yarn better than anybody I know, Shalimar."

"But I wasn't there," the old man reminded her.

"You weren't *where*?" Declan demanded impatiently.

"At the death of Amyrantha's one true God," Maralyce replied.

Chapter 21

Was a time we thought immortality was a gift. Some of us still do. Others . . . well, some people just can't deal with forever. Makes 'em crazy.

Some, it makes crazier than others.

The first among us to lose his mind completely was Kentravyon. Your wretched Tarot calls him the Sleeper, doesn't it? Tides, you've no idea how true that is. Or the effort it took to make him that way.

I'll tell you this much, though—when a Tide Lord becomes completely detached from reality, nobody is safe, not even the immortals.

Kentravyon started out innocently enough. I'm not sure how he became immortal. Not all of us were made by that little bitch Diala and not all of us feel the need to make our origins known, either. The when doesn't matter anyway. Not now. Immortal is immortal.

He seemed a nice enough lad at the outset, as I recall. Quiet. Studious, even.

Course he was common-born like the rest of us, and plain to look at. His features were too rough to be handsome, but he wasn't particularly unattractive. Nondescript is the best way to describe him, I suppose. He never cut the dashing figure Cayal or Jaxyn or Tryan did, with their pretty-boy looks or their highborn manners and their unshakeable belief in the value of their own opinions. Of the three, I've always thought Jaxyn is the worst offender, but then, I suspect he was an arrogant ass *before* he was made immortal. Tryan's a petulant fool who's never been able to wander far from his wretched mother. And Cayal . . . well, he was well-intentioned enough in the beginning. Still is, on occasion, which is most of his problem and could account for why he wants to die.

But I'm getting off the topic. I know you think we're all evil monsters and I suppose, from where you sit, we are. But it's not that simple. Truth is, until we run afoul of each other, we're a fairly benign bunch.

Oh, I know you'll disagree. You'll start reminding me about how as soon as the Tide turns one or another of the immortals always ends up trying to rule the world—or a fair portion of it—but that's just because when you've lived as long as we have, you've seen it all before. You've not the energy left to watch some power-hungry, ambitious human megalomaniac scrabble for power, in the mistaken belief that only he can make a better world.

It's quicker, easier and less trouble, sometimes, just to do it yourself.

Kentravyon, now . . . he just went a little too far. So far, in fact, that the rest of us felt compelled to put an end to him. Permanently. Or at least as permanently as you can stop a Tide Lord.

The trouble started, as it usually does, with the turning of the Tide.

We didn't always hide out during Low Tides. Was a time we used to brag about our immortality. Course, it didn't pay to perform too many miracles—as Kentravyon discovered—even when the Tide was up, because people started to expect them and then it got a bit sticky during Low Tide, when you couldn't produce the goods.

Anyway, it all began innocently enough. Kentravyon and Lyna were a couple in those days. Lyna's a nice girl, although I'm not sure what she ever saw in Kentravyon. She used to be a whore, you know, back before she was immortal. Worked in the same brothel as Syrolee. I always thought him a bit dull for her tastes. A bit too intense, too serious, to warrant her attention.

Maybe the rumour about him saving her from a mob of crazy mortals bent on putting every plausible method of disposing of us to the test was true. I heard a story that Lyna was captured by the Holy Warriors once and they'd used her to test their theories. I don't know for certain, but they always seemed an odd couple to me.

They set themselves up in the northern hemisphere. The place is split into two nations now, you call them Caelum and Glaeba. Back then everyone just called the land Corcora.

Kentravyon's reign began as a religion, naturally. It's the best way to bend any population to your will. You can conquer a country if you have the mind to. But that takes an army and it takes money, resources and a great deal of energy, and even when you've won, you have to fight to hang on to it. Empires are such hard work. Religions are far more efficient. You own more than a man's body when he believes you're divine. You own his heart and soul, and that'll win out over brute force, any day.

The trouble with Kentravyon's religion is that he got a bit carried away with it. A few thousand years of immortality and the fool starts to think he's invincible as well as immortal.

Trust me, the two are nowhere near the same. Unfortunately, he didn't get that.

Anyway, Kentravyon started to believe in his own propaganda. Started to think he was God. And then he got this thing in his head about the racial purity of the Corcorans. He began by banning foreigners from owning anything in Corcora. Then he banned marriages between Corcorans and outsiders. Then he started deporting all the foreigners, and finally he started killing them.

I'm not sure how many of the other immortals knew what he was up to. Not sure any of us would have cared, even if we had known—there were none of us with much humanity left by then—although we'd come to seriously regret *not* paying attention.

But even if you ignored the atrocities, which got progressively worse as the years rolled by, Kentravyon's big mistake, really, was the miracles. Once a year, sure as sunrise, all the faithful would gather at the foot of the mountain where he'd built his temple and he'd stage a miracle for his disciples to witness. It might be a lightning bolt smiting some hapless foreigner or sending a tornado to strike down some distant village foolish enough to question the will of their god . . . it didn't really matter, although I always wondered if Lyna had a hand in the whole miracle business. She doesn't have the power to perform that sort of thing herself, but I wouldn't have put it past her to give Kentravyon the idea. It always seemed far too theatrical to be something he thought up on his own.

Anyway, it must have gone on like that for three or four hundred years. It was a long High Tide, I remember that, and by the time the Tide turned, Kentravyon's religion had spread beyond Corcora's borders.

It's not surprising, really. Humans are tribal by nature and territorial along with it. Fear is the most basic human emotion and xenophobia is ridiculously easy to encourage. It's not hard to convince them someone who looks different or sounds different is a threat to all they hold near and dear. Give them a religion that makes hating anyone who looks different a virtue and you're on to a real winner.

By the time we realised the Tide was waning, half the world worshipped the god Kentravyon and the killing was getting out of hand.

And then the miracles stopped.

It was his own stupid fault, you know. I mean, he must have felt the Tide retreating. He must have known his power was fading. Or maybe he didn't. Lyna told us later that she'd tried to talk him out of doing anything so foolish, but like I say, he'd lost touch with reality by then. Mind you, it could have been Lyna's way of distancing herself from what happened afterward, but I'm inclined to believe she had the right of it. Kentravyon didn't know what he was doing by then.

Anyway, Kentravyon's last few miracles had been less than spectacular. With the Tide on the way out, each year he had less and less power to call on. He certainly knew his grip was waning. After years of progressively less spectacular events, the natives were getting a bit restless, so he must have decided to go for broke. To quell the disappointed mutterings following a fairly pitiful thunderstorm, he announced at his annual festival that the next time he'd make the very world shake.

Lyna says she warned him he didn't have the power for it, but nothing would deter him, and by announcing it at the festival, he'd made sure the whole damned world knew about it, too. They reckon there were nigh on a half a million turned up the following year to witness the next miracle.

Course, it never happened. Oh sure, he made a few mountains smoke a bit and the ground rumbled for a day or so, but that was about the strength of it. The Tide was too far out to do much of anything else.

The reaction of the faithful was hard to judge at the outset. I mean, faith is all about believing in something, even *without* proof. And for a lot of people, that was enough.

But the seeds of discontent had been sown. The Tide was retreating. And Kentravyon was losing his ability to put down the opposition.

It started small. At first nobody paid the dissenters much attention. Frankly, I'm a little surprised it took people as long as it did to start complaining about some of the things Kentravyon had them doing in the name of their god. But his people believed he was the One God. He'd even convinced them that all the other immortals drew their power from him, that his existence was essential to the rest of us; even that *he* could destroy any immortal he chose. Problem with that logic is that once you believe an immortal can be killed, they ain't immortal any longer, just hard to kill.

So that's what they decided to do. Kentravyon's opposition—and they were an organised force by then—figured if Kentravyon could kill the immortals there must be a way for them to kill us too, and trust me, even if the story about Lyna wasn't true, the many and varied ways you might think of killing us were all put to the test in the next few score years.

We were hunted down like animals. The smart ones went to ground; actually, the smart ones always did. It was the fools like me who hung around wearing their immortality like a badge of honour who suffered most. Until then, I'd honestly never given it much thought, reasoning nobody cared that much about me one way or the other.

But I was wrong, and eventually, they found me.

It wasn't here in Glaeba. I had another claim then, further south in what you call the Commonwealth of Elenovia these days. The locals knew I was an immortal, but it didn't bother them and generally they left me alone.

At least, I *thought* it didn't bother them.

Turns out that even the nicest people can turn on you when they're all liquored up.

A bunch of Holy Warriors—Tides, can you believe that's what the movement to rid the world of immortals were calling themselves—came to town, looking for the immortal they'd heard about living in the mountains. With the Tide on the way out, I guess the townsfolk figured the Holy Warriors a bigger threat than me. Handed me over with barely a twinge of guilt, they did.

And then they tried to burn me at the stake.

It's a hideous way to die, being burnt alive. Even less fun when you're on fire and there's no end in sight. It's hard for a mortal to grasp, but the more dire the threat, the harder we are to maim. Chuck an immortal into a volcano or toss them in a pot of boiling acid, and they'll walk out—extremely pissed off with you, but unscathed, because our bodies seem to understand the need to heal something like that so rapidly that it becomes almost instantaneous. It's as if the magic that made us immortal understands the danger. Our bodies react to the immediacy of the threat. But try to kill an immortal slowly, do it so it takes time, and you won't kill us, but Tides, you can make us suffer. I stood there screaming, tied to that stake, wishing they had chucked me off the lip of a volcano.

I can't begin to describe what it felt like, being burned alive. Tides, it was agonising and the *smell* . . . indescribable. It still makes me shudder, just thinking about it. I didn't even lose consciousness, and the bastards kept stoking the fire, and drinking and chanting and cursing me like I'd done something personal to each and every one of them. I could call in the Tide to blow the fires out, and I did a few times, but remember, the Tide was waning, and they'd been at me for days. I was exhausted, in agony and losing my power.

If you were wondering how I escaped, it wasn't anything I did. Got saved by something far more mundane than that . . . Cayal and Lukys turned up.

Those two had been paying far more attention to the goings-on in the world than I was. And they were smart enough to hide who they were as soon as they realised the danger. Very smart in fact.

Tides, the cheeky bastards had actually *joined* the Holy Warriors.

Lukys had attained the rank of colonel, can you believe the *gall* of the man? Cayal—who for a time there was Lukys's willing accomplice in pretty much anything he dabbled in—was acting as his aide, or something like that. I never did really work it out, exactly.

Whatever . . . they were having a high old time strutting around in those ridiculous red cloaks, hunting down the other immortals. I think they even found a few they didn't like, and set the Holy Warriors on to them. I'm fairly certain Tryan was tossed off a cliff near Port Gallow by a raging mob because Cayal tipped off the Tenacian chapter of the Holy Warrior Order as to his whereabouts.

Anyway, there I was, smoking and crisping like an overdone roast, when this pompous Holy Warrior colonel and his arrogant aide turn up and order the mob to put out the fire because they want to interrogate me themselves. Took me a few moments to realise who my saviours were . . . as you can imagine, I was a trifle preoccupied at the time. They dragged me off the pyre, tied me across the saddle of a packhorse, and carted me off, while I was still crisping around my extremities.

They took me far enough away that I could heal in peace before they told me why I'd been the recipient of their heroic rescue and it had little to do with altruism.

Still, I've always had a soft spot for those two troublemakers since then, despite some of the things they've done. You can't help but feel warmly toward the men who save you from being burned at the stake.

"We think we've figured out a way to put an end to this persecution of immortals," Lukys informed me once I'd recovered.

A few days previously, I might have commented "who cares" but that bonfire party thrown for me by my former mortal friends put paid to that idea.

"How?"

"By putting an end to Kentravyon," Cayal said. It was late and we were sitting around a cheery campfire, safe for the time being from the hounding of the Holy Warriors.

"How do you figure that'll work?"

"He started it all," Lukys pointed out. "If we take him out, God will be dead, the mortals will settle down, eventually they'll forget there were ever any other immortals and they'll leave us alone." He grinned mischievously. "Cayal and I have taken some pains to put ourselves in a position where this idea might be encouraged to take hold, you know."

"How did you two wind up as Holy Warriors, anyway?" The absurdity of having this conversation with those two reprobates dressed in the uniform of our dreaded enemies didn't really occur to me until later.

"They don't ask a lot of questions when you sign up," Cayal told me with a smile. "And we didn't even have to lie, did we, Lukys?"

"Not once," he agreed, "has anybody asked us if we're immortal."

"You're incorrigible. The pair of you," I said, smiling at the audacity of them. Cayal wasn't nearly so maudlin in those days, and Lukys was always a disarming charmer when the mood took him. I doubt the Holy Warriors stood a chance, once those two decided to join up. "But take Kentravyon *out*? I hate to be the harbinger of doom here, lads, but Kentravyon's as immortal as any of us. Taking him out isn't really an option."

"We can't kill him," Cayal agreed. "But we think we can immobilise him."

"Which will last right up until the next High Tide and then not only will you have one very pissed off Tide Lord to deal with, but one looking to even the score with you."

"Not if we freeze him."

I stared at Cayal, not even attempting to hide my scepticism. "*Freeze* him? How?"

It was Lukys who answered me. "We figure there's just enough power left in the Tide to do it. But it'll take a few of us. Kentravyon can draw on the same power as us, so no single Tide Lord could do it alone, because he'd be able to counter anything we threw at him just as easily."

"And you think if a few of us wield the Tide together, we can do this?"

Lukys nodded unsmilingly. I don't think I realised how serious they were until then.

"How many is a *few*?" Cooperation between us is rare. Even if such a bizarre idea might work, I couldn't imagine how they were going to get enough of us together to make it happen.

"Lukys thinks it'll take at least four of us. I say we'd be safer with five."

"I count only three of us."

"Brynden's agreed to help," Lukys told me.

"That's four. Who were you planning to recruit as number five? Tryan or Elyssa?"

"Pellys," Cayal replied.

I laughed aloud at the suggestion.

"My sentiments exactly," Lukys said with a frown. "However, Sparky here didn't like my suggestion about how to secure Elyssa's cooperation."

"I'm not sleeping with her, Lukys," Cayal said in a tone that made me think they'd had this discussion before, a number of times.

"So, there you have it, old girl," Lukys said to me. "Sparky's too shy to get us some reliable help, so we're stuck with the Lord of the Lunatics."

I shook my head at the absurdity of the idea of involving Pellys in anything that required coherent thought. "He doesn't even know which way is up! Tides, you can't rely on him. Anyway, I thought Pellys wasn't speaking to anybody at the moment."

"I should be able to talk him into it," Lukys assured me. "If we decide we need him."

I was silent for a time, trying to think through the implications of this unprecedented plan. "Once you freeze Kentravyon, then what?"

"We'll have to take him to Jelidia. Store him somewhere he's not likely to thaw out."

"What happens next High Tide? Won't he be able to thaw *himself* out?"

Cayal shook his head. "Lukys thinks if we freeze his brain, and it stays frozen, even at High Tide he won't be aware enough to do anything about it."

"And the Holy Warriors? They'll all pack up and go home, I suppose, when they learn Kentravyon is no longer a threat?"

"He claims he's the One God," Cayal said with a shrug. "And the Warriors happily buy into that. Kentravyon had to explain the rest of us away, so he told them we draw our power from him. If he goes, the rest of us—according to his doctrine—cease to exist."

That seemed a reasonable assumption, although I still wasn't convinced. "And when were you planning to do this thing?"

"The sooner the better," Lukys said. "The Tide slips away a little more each day. If we leave it much longer, there won't be enough power left to try it."

I looked at the two of them, with their smooth, reassuring smiles, certain there was some ulterior motive behind this rare act of civic-mindedness. I wasn't sure if either Lukys or Cayal really cared that much about the fate of the other immortals and the Tides know they'd done nothing to stop the slaughter of the millions of mortals Kentravyon was responsible for in years gone by.

And it wasn't as if *they* were being persecuted. They were Holy Warriors, for pity's sake. For all intents and purposes, these two scoundrels were helping to *organise* the persecution of the immortals. Surely, there was some other reason they wanted to end it.

On the other hand, someone had just tried to burn me alive. I wasn't feeling all that fond of the mortals of Amyrantha right then, either.

"If I help you do this," I asked, "what's to stop you doing it to me, or one of the others?"

"The very nature of this enterprise requires us to cooperate, Maralyce," Lukys pointed out. "How often do you think that's going to happen?"

He had a point.

"Count me in then," I told them with a sigh. "Let's put an end to this nonsense."

We shook hands on the deal and then Cayal passed a flask around to seal our agreement.

Barely two months later, we were standing at the foot of Kentravyon's mountain in Corcora—Lukys, Cayal, Brynden, Pellys and I, with the Holy Warrior army at our backs under Kinta's command—bracing ourselves to bring down a Tide Lord.

Chapter 22

"Tides, you can't stop there," Declan complained, when Maralyce abruptly stopped talking, rose from the table, and headed for the door.

"I'm a Tide Lord, Declan Hawkes," she reminded him, jerking the door open to a blast of icy air. "I can do anything I like."

With that, she stalked out into the darkness, slamming the door behind her, leaving Declan alone with his grandfather.

"You shouldn't aggravate her, lad."

He turned to stare at the old man. "You've heard this story before, I suppose?"

Shalimar nodded. "And quite a few others."

"You and the Tide Lord seem to be pretty thick."

"There's a lot you don't understand, Declan," the old man replied.

"I'm getting *that*."

"You shouldn't judge things when you don't know the whole story," Shalimar advised, draining the last of his tea, which must have been stone cold by now.

Declan was rapidly losing patience with his grandfather's evasive answers. "So *tell* me the whole story, then."

"It's not mine to tell."

"You're a member of the Cabal, Pop. Worse . . . you're a senior member of the Pentangle. You're sworn to *protect* the Lore. To add to it, with every scrap of knowledge you can find. How long have you been keeping your friendship with Maralyce from the Keeper?"

"I've not kept anything from Tilly that would make much of a difference to the Cabal."

Declan gasped at his grandfather's words. "If what Maralyce is saying is true, they found a way to destroy a Tide Lord. What part of *that* do you think the Cabal isn't interested in hearing about?"

Shalimar shook his head. "Weren't you listening, boy? It took five Tide Lords to take Kentravyon down. And he's not dead. He's just frozen."

"So Maralyce claims."

Shalimar snorted at Declan's implication. "She's not lying."

"How can you be certain?"

"I just am."

Declan rolled his eyes, starting to wonder if Maralyce really had ensorcelled his grandfather. He was about to say as much, when the door opened again and the Tide Lord stalked back in clutching an armful of split logs, accompanied by another blast of chilly mountain air, slamming the door behind her with her foot.

"You still here?" she demanded of Declan, as she walked to the fire, dumped the wood on the floor and began to stoke some life into it again.

He looked up at her, his gaze flat and unfriendly. "I'm waiting to hear the rest of the story."

Unaccountably, Maralyce smiled as she turned from the fire. "You think I'm going to tell you how to kill a Tide Lord, do you?"

"Assuming it's possible . . ."

"It's not," Maralyce informed him flatly. "You should listen to your grandfather."

"Then tell me what happened to Kentravyon."

"All in good time. Why don't you tell me something?"

"Like what?"

"What's your favourite colour?"

He stared at her as if she was mad. "*What*?"

"Your favourite colour. I wouldn't have thought it a hard question."

"Why would you *care*?"

The immortal shrugged. "I might yet decide to kill you, boy. I'll need to know what colour to paint your headstone."

He shook his head, quite convinced that like Kentravyon, immortality had driven her crazy. "You're insane, aren't you?"

"Quite possibly."

Declan looked at his grandfather, hoping for help, but the old man was staying determinedly neutral.

"Your favourite colour," Maralyce insisted. "What is it?"

"Blue," Declan snapped.

"We distracted him."

"*What*?"

Maralyce took the seat she'd vacated a few minutes before and continued as if she'd never left. "That's how we defeated Kentravyon. Brynden, Pellys and I distracted him. Blew the top off his wretched mountain, actually, so he got his ground-shaking after all, just not the one he was hoping for. That gave Lukys and Cayal the opportunity to sneak up on him. It took the two of them together to do the deed. And they didn't have long. I know Lukys was fairly certain they wouldn't be able to do it while Kentravyon was swimming the Tide."

"You said the Holy Warriors went with you to confront him. Didn't they know who you were?"

The immortal smiled in remembrance. "Now you see that was the *true* brilliance of Lukys's plan." Clearly, she had a great deal of admiration for the Tide Lord. "After I agreed to help them, they trussed me up again and we returned to the Holy Warriors' camp where Lukys announced they'd been able to torture the secret of killing an immortal from me. I played along, of course, and let them keep me chained as a prisoner, spitting and cursing with great gusto every time someone came near me."

"And they *believed* him?" Declan asked.

She nodded. "You have to remember, Lukys hadn't just joined up a few days before. He'd been working this scam for years. The Warriors trusted him implicitly, and Cayal, too. When your most loyal and decorated officers ride into camp with a Tide Lord in tow, claiming they've discovered the secret you've been hunting for the past few hundred years, why would you doubt them?"

"That explains three of you," Declan said, finding himself being drawn into this fascinating tale, despite his doubts about the truth of it. "How did the others become a part of the invasion of Corcora without being discovered?"

"Interesting creatures, you mortals." Maralyce shrugged. "Keep falling for the same old tricks, over and over. Ever noticed that?"

"What do you mean . . ."

"Brynden and Kinta did the same as Lukys. They posed as high-ranking Holy Warriors visiting from Torlenia—no stretch for someone with their military background—and brought Pellys with them. I've no idea what Lukys said to him to get him to cooperate, but he seemed quite calm about posing as their prisoner. When Brynden arrived claiming they'd also managed to extract the secret of killing an immortal from their prisoner, all it did was confirm Lukys's story. They had their stories worked out in advance, of course, with enough similarities to verify their account and enough differences to make them appear unrehearsed. It was a masterful performance. You really should be thankful we don't get together more often, my lad. We can be pretty dangerous, when we're getting along."

"Didn't the Holy Warriors figure it out?"

She nodded. "Of course, they did. Eventually. It was too late for them to do anything about it, by then."

Declan still wasn't convinced. "The Holy Warriors had an army . . . and the Tide was on the way out. Had been for a century, to hear you tell it. How could the Tide Lords have had the power to do anything?"

Maralyce frowned. "Combine the power of the Tide Lords and you wind up with something that's much greater than the sum of its parts, my lad, rather like an orchestra. That's something you need to remember," she added in an ominous tone. "As the Tide retreats we lose the ability to do much damage individually, but we can still combine our power for a long while after the Tide's peaked."

Declan glanced at his unusually silent grandfather. "Is that little snippet one of those things you think the Cabal doesn't need to know?"

"They know," Shalimar replied, frowning. "And watch that tongue of yours, lad. You act as if I'm a traitor."

"I'm not entirely convinced you're not, Pop."

Shalimar glared at Declan for a moment and then rose stiffly to his feet. "More tea?" he asked Maralyce.

"Please."

The Tide Lord turned her attention back to Declan as Shalimar bent over the fire to stoke it up. "You're an unforgiving little sod, aren't you?"

"You have *no* idea."

"Well, I know where you get that trait from. Where were we?"

"You were blowing the top off Kentravyon's mountain."

"Which we did in quite a spectacular fashion," she told him with a wistful smile. "I'm not one for throwing the landscape around as a rule, but I must admit, that day was rather . . . entertaining. I think we took the whole mountain range out in the end."

"At which point I imagine the Holy Warriors realised they'd been duped, too."

Maralyce nodded. "I suppose. Wasn't paying much attention, truth be told. It takes a lot of concentration to swim the Tide in concert with someone else. Brynden's control was fine, but we had Pellys helping us and he was all over the place."

"What about Lukys and Cayal?"

"They were concentrating on finding Kentravyon. Nobody had seen him for decades, by the time we arrived. He'd been holed up in his temple, licking his wounds, trying to find a way to regain lost ground ever since his last miracle fizzled. Lyna had left him by then, too, so there wasn't much keeping him in touch with the real world. Lukys reasoned he'd be clinging to the Tide like a limpet, too afraid to let it go, for fear of losing even more control. That's why we had to shock him. We had to do something to make him let go, even if only for an instant. Being something of a loner, it probably hadn't occurred to him he'd be able to cheat the retreating Tide for a while longer by teaming up with another Tide Lord. And even if he did realise it, we only needed an instant for Lukys and Cayal to strike."

"What did the Holy Warriors do when they realised their One God was defeated?"

"They fled, for the most part. The land around Kentravyon's stronghold in Corcora was in chaos after the mountain blew, and as Lukys predicted, many of the survivors believed the rest of us immortals must have perished along with Kentravyon. Brynden wasn't quite so confident, and I'm fairly certain he and Kinta spent the next century or so wiping out every last outpost of Holy Warriors they could find."

"Your plan worked well, then."

"Like a charm," Maralyce agreed, "which is something your Cabal needs to remember, my lad. Cayal and Lukys, with the Tide on the way out and only a split second to act, were able to immobilise Kentravyon sufficiently to freeze his brain, and then the rest of him, and do it well enough that he's not awoken since. There are no more dangerous Tide Lords in the universe than those two, when they act in concert."

Declan digested the warning silently, not sure at what point he'd started to believe Maralyce. The warning didn't offer any comfort, however. It angered him. "You're only warning us about them *now*?"

It was Shalimar who answered him, and his answer shocked Declan almost as much as the discovery of his grandfather sitting in a Tide Lord's kitchen sharing tea.

"You've got it wrong, Declan," the old man corrected. "Maralyce has done more than warn us of the danger." With his hand protected by a scrap of towel, he lifted the cast-iron kettle onto the table with a grunt, and added, "She was the one who retrieved what was left of the information the Holy Warriors had gathered on the Tide Lords during their hundred-year history and passed it on to Lyrianna of Lebeken."

Declan stared at Maralyce in amazement. "*You* gave all that information about how to defeat a Tide Lord to the founder of the Cabal of the Tarot?"

"Fool," Maralyce said as she took the kettle from Shalimar and refilled the teapot. "There *was* no Cabal of the Tarot. Lyrianna of Lebeken didn't gather the information to create your wretched Tarot. I did."

Chapter 23

It became obvious to Warlock after a few weeks in the royal household that King Enteny and Queen Inala were more than a little suspicious of Kylia's behaviour, both toward her new husband and around her constant companion, Jaxyn Aranville. She'd come to them—in theory—an innocent young girl, but the effort required to maintain the persona of Kylia was boring the immortal witless and occasionally she forgot herself.

Diala was starting to let the mask slip and Warlock wasn't the only one who noticed. Although they never said anything outright, the king's disapproving looks when the young princess chose Jaxyn's company over her husband's, the queen's less than subtle remarks about inappropriate friendships for a married woman, and their disapproval at some of the comments she made when she was feeling particularly impatient were becoming more and more frequent.

As the days went by, Kylia seemed less and less inclined to appease her in-laws, which worried Warlock a great deal, and not only because of what it might mean to Glaeba. The Tide was on the way back, which meant the confidence of the immortals was growing apace. The danger Warlock feared, however, was that as he became more and more a fixture in the royal household, Declan Hawkes would be less and less likely to want him to leave. It was only a matter of a couple of months now before Boots was due to whelp.

Hidden Valley seemed further away now than it had when he didn't really believe it existed.

Warlock knew the Tide was on the turn, just as he knew in this unholy alliance it was Jaxyn, not Diala, who wielded the true power. By all accounts—according to Crasii Lore—Diala's power was limited to healing (or destroying things) on a small scale. The Immortal Prince had confirmed as much when he'd related his tale to the Duchess of Lebec while still a prisoner in the cell opposite Warlock in Lebec Prison.

Diala and Jaxyn could both manipulate the elements, it was true, but of the two, only Jaxyn was a true Tide Lord. Only Jaxyn could bring about the sort of cataclysmic event that might result in the death of millions. Diala, so the Lore and the Immortal Prince claimed, could barely raise a storm in a teacup.

Her increasing willingness to flaut convention, however, risking the wrath of the court gossips and her husband, did not augur well for Glaeba's future. Particularly as she seemed to care less and less that she was antagonising the king and queen.

Perhaps the Tide was turning faster than Shalimar anticipated. Perhaps the immortals were getting ready to make their move, not in the year or two that the old Tidewatcher had predicted, but much, much sooner.

And that meant it wasn't likely that Warlock was going home anytime soon.

Jaxyn had developed something of a routine in the palace. It mostly involved keeping the young prince out until the small hours of the morning, which meant Mathu slept a good part of the day away, leaving Jaxyn and Diala to their own devices. Jaxyn was always up and about, bright and cheerful, first thing in the morning, ready to be of service to the ladies of the court. He was supposed to be representing the interests of the Duke of Lebec, but if he actually did any work, it wasn't when Warlock was around to witness it.

Today, as usual, Jaxyn was waiting for the king and queen and the princess as they crossed the manicured lawns below the palace and approached the royal barge tied up at the palace dock. It had been decided last night at dinner that everyone would go boating on the lake this morning. The weather had been particularly fine these past few days, so Queen Inala had decided they should make the most of it and take the royal barge out.

The excursion was for more than recreational purposes. Such an outing would give the royal family an excuse to sail past some of the nearer villages, where their presence would undoubtedly be remarked. They would stop for lunch at one of them—unannounced—bestowing their royal largesse on the village and ensuring the continuing loyalty of their subjects, who considered it an unimaginable honour to meet the king and queen in person.

The royal barge was quite elaborate, designed for little more than pleasure cruising up and down the lake shore. Painted green, its brass-work glinting in the sunlight, it had a crew of nearly thirty, many of whom were simply on board to serve the royal family and their guests. There were another score of amphibious Crasii responsible for towing the craft, who were already slipping into their harnesses, while the barge's captain yelled orders at the rest of his crew, the pitch of his calls increasing in urgency when he spied his royal passengers approaching.

Warlock walked behind the royal party, along with another dozen slaves, including the queen's personal chef and the king's huntmaster. Warlock wasn't sure what the huntmaster was supposed to do aboard a barge in the middle of the lake, but he seemed a regular guest on these excursions. Perhaps the king planned to stop later in the day and do some hunting in the forests that bordered much of the lake's eastern shore.

The royal party stopped when they reached the dock. The queen glanced around her, frowning, as if only just realising her son was missing.

"Where is Mathu?" she asked, directing her question to Kylia.

The princess smiled brightly at her mother-in-law. "Still asleep, Mother. He got in very late last night."

The queen frowned. "Didn't you remind him that we planned to go sailing today?"

"I did," Kylia assured her. "But he just grunted at me, rolled over and went straight back to sleep."

"It's my fault, I fear, your majesty," Jaxyn confessed, interrupting with an apologetic bow. "I didn't mean for us to stay out so late."

"*You* appear to have had no trouble getting out of bed this morning," the king remarked, turning his attention from the barge to the young lord. He looked even more unhappy about his son's absence than the queen.

"I probably didn't drink as much," Jaxyn admitted with a smile. "Would you like me to fetch him for you?"

"I would," the king announced. "In fact, you can inform my son that we're expecting him to join us on the royal barge within the hour."

"Oh!" Kylia exclaimed in disappointment. "Do we have to wait for him, Papa? It's such a lovely day. We'll miss the better part of it if we have to hang around here while Mathu gets dressed."

"Don't you *want* your husband to join us?" the queen asked with a suspicious frown.

"Of *course* I do," she replied with a laugh. "But I don't think we should lose the day just because Mathu's a silly sleepyhead. Can't we go on without him? Jaxyn could fetch him out of bed and make him row out to us once he's ready, couldn't he? It'd do him the world of good anyway— a just reward for being so thoughtless about your plans."

The queen thought on it for a moment and then glanced at her husband, who shrugged and nodded in agreement. "The exercise will do him good, I suppose. Damn that boy for being so irresponsible."

"I'll have him clean, dressed and on board within the hour," Jaxyn promised. "May I borrow Cecil to give me a hand? I'll need someone who knows his way around his highness's wardrobe if we're to get our recalcitrant prince ready in time."

With a frown, the king absently waved his hand in Warlock's general direction and turned his attention back to the barge. Like the good slave he was pretending to be, Warlock bowed to the king and turned to follow Jaxyn. As he did, he caught the look that passed between Diala and the Tide Lord.

It made the hair stand up on the back of his neck.

Something is going on, Warlock concluded, a shiver of fear running down his spine to the very tip of his tail, wondering what the two of them had planned.

Is Mathu's absence this morning deliberate? Are they planning to do something to him?

The death of the crown prince would serve little purpose unless Kylia was pregnant, Warlock decided, fighting back a sudden panic attack. *Was* she pregnant? Warlock had seen no sign of it, but that didn't make it impossible. Given she was sleeping with a mortal, there was no reason why she couldn't be with child, he supposed.

Perhaps that's their plan. Perhaps they intend to kill Mathu and then announce Kylia is pregnant with the next heir to the throne?

It seemed a very roundabout way of doing things, though, even for a Tide Lord.

He would find out soon enough, however. And the tragedy was, there was little Warlock could do to stop Jaxyn doing whatever he desired. Declan Hawkes had warned him that he might face a test to prove he wasn't a Scard. Was the test going to be today? Was it going to be standing back and letting a Tide Lord kill the Crown Prince of Glaeba?

Am I going to have to witness a murder, just to prove I'm a loyal servant of the immortals?

Is that what Declan Hawkes *wanted* him to do? To stand by and do nothing?

He's the King's Spymaster. Surely his mandate includes protecting the crown prince from harm?

Then again, Warlock might be imagining things. Jaxyn might mean to do exactly as he stated. He might go upstairs, wake the prince, demand he dress, warn him his father was annoyed and then help him row out to the barge for a pleasant day on the lake with the king and queen . . .

But Warlock hadn't imagined the look that passed between Jaxyn and Diala.

With a conviction that bordered on a premonition, he knew somebody was going to die today.

The uncertainty what to do about it, however, ate at Warlock like a canker as they crossed the lawn on their way back to the palace.

Is this what I agreed to? he wondered, staring at the back of Jaxyn's head as if the answer lay somewhere ahead of him. *Stand by and do nothing to prevent the death of an innocent young man for the greater good of mankind?*

And what about Crasii-kind? How would complicity in such a crime aid his own people—the slaves of Amyrantha?

It won't aid them at all, he realised with a sigh.

But even if he wanted to, even if Jaxyn *was* heading back to the palace to murder Prince Mathu, not fetch him for an outing on the lake, there was not a thing Warlock could do to stop him and if he *tried* to stop him, he would end up just as dead as poor Prince Mathu might soon be.

For the first time since being recruited into the Cabal of the Tarot,

Warlock began to understand what Declan Hawkes had been getting at when he asked if he thought himself up for the job.

This is the test. Not a test to see if I can follow the orders of a Tide Lord so they believe I'm a Scard. This is a test to see if I have the fortitude to go on.

That, he knew, was the bigger picture. From the moment Jaxyn and Diala had set their power-hungry sights on Glaeba, the royal family was probably doomed. But after they'd taken power, *that's* when it would be important for the Cabal to know what the two immortals were planning.

And what choice do I have, in any case? If I object to anything Jaxyn does, Warlock reminded himself, *if I so much as flinch, I will die.*

By the time they entered the palace, Warlock was trembling with anticipation and fear. He forced it under control. It would take nothing more innocuous than a simple glance over his shoulder for Jaxyn to realise the Crasii was fretting about something. If he noticed that, Warlock was on the fast road to annihilation.

You can do this, Warlock told himself with a confidence he didn't feel. *You can carry this off.*

Forcing his tail up a little, so it appeared he had nothing to worry about, Warlock hurried after Jaxyn toward the lower atrium and the stairs that led to the family suites on the upper floors of the palace, deeply afraid of what the Tide Lord had in mind.

Chapter 24

Arkady's next meeting with Chintara was due several days after Tiji arrived from Glaeba with her disturbing news that Declan Hawkes suspected the Imperator's Consort might be the immortal Kinta.

She wasn't nearly as nervous about the meeting as she thought she might be. Perhaps it was her previous friendship with the consort. Perhaps it was the knowledge that Kinta was merely immortal, rather than a Tide Lord capable of tearing the world apart in her wrath. Maybe she was becoming jaded with the whole notion of Tide Lords. Arkady smiled at the thought, glancing through the perforations at the front of her carriage. She turned to look at the little chameleon.

"What do you need me to do?" she asked, lifting the shroud so she could see the Crasii without obstruction.

"Stay in the doorway long enough for me to slip in behind you before they close it," Tiji replied. "And if you could keep their attention from the door, that'd be good too. It's hard to stay camouflaged when I'm on the move."

"And after we're inside?"

"Forget about me, your grace."

Arkady frowned, acutely aware that she was leading this strange young Crasii into terrible danger and feeling a responsibility for seeing she made it out again in one piece. "Is there nothing else I can do to help?"

Tiji shook her head, as she lifted her thin linen shift over her shoulders unselfconsciously, and laid it on the seat beside her. Arkady tried not to stare. It wasn't easy. The naked chameleon was humanoid in form, but her silver-scaled skin and complete lack of hair marked her as something quite alien.

Tiji seemed to know what Arkady was thinking. "This is what I do, your grace. And I mean it when I say you have to forget I'm there. You'll give the game away if you're constantly looking around the room trying to find me."

"Won't Kinta be able to sense you?"

"We're not even sure it *is* Kinta, your grace."

Arkady smiled. "Won't Lady *Chintara* be able to sense you?"

"No more than she can sense any other Crasii."

"And if she really is who Declan fears she is?"

"Then we'll get a message back to Glaeba, your grace, and wait until we see what the Cabal has to say about it, before doing anything else."

That made sense. Arkady was relieved. She wasn't sure how she'd deal with orders to confront another immortal, no matter how friendly she seemed. "How will you get back to the embassy?"

"I'll find a way."

"I could send a carriage . . ."

Tiji seemed amused by the suggestion. "I think a carriage parked outside the royal palace emblazoned with the Glaeban coat of arms would kind of give the game away, don't you?"

"I could send a *hired* cab," Arkady said.

The Crasii smiled in appreciation, but she clearly didn't seem to think she needed help. "I'm grateful for the offer, really I am, your grace, but I've done this sort of thing before. Truly, I can find my own way home."

Arkady studied the Crasii for a moment, wondering where she found her confidence. She seemed so small, so fragile, her long slender limbs so naturally graceful, yet so delicate. "Does Declan have you doing this sort of thing often?"

"It's what I *am*, your grace. And when you think about it, there's not a lot of other useful occupations for a chameleon Crasii."

"Isn't it dangerous?"

"Not unless I do something stupid. And I do have an unfair advantage over humans when it comes to sneaking in and out of places I don't belong, you know."

Arkady shook her head in bewilderment at the Crasii's blasé attitude. "I'm not going to rest until I know you're safe."

"Which is very nice of you, your grace, but unnecessary."

"I can see why Declan is so fond of you," Arkady told her with a smile.

"Funny, I could say the same about you," Tiji replied with a grin, but before Arkady could ask what she meant, the carriage rocked to a halt inside the entrance to the royal seraglium.

Arkady dropped the shroud back into place and turned her attention to the door, which opened before she could stop the doorman outside from doing his duty, but when she turned to warn Tiji to hide, the little Crasii had vanished, leaving only the slightest warping in the upholstery. At least Arkady imagined she could see where the Crasii had been sitting only a few moments before, but it was impossible to be certain, so she took a deep breath, offered her shrouded hand to the doorman and stepped out of the carriage.

"Ah! Arkady! You're here at last. What do you think of these?"

After shedding her shroud and handing it to Nitta, Arkady crossed the main hall to where Chintara was standing by the central couches, studying several bolts of cloth spread out over the sofas for her examination. There must have been a score of them, all thin, expensive, almost transparent silks, exquisitely dyed, some in geometrical patterns and some worked with gold thread in delicate floral sprays.

"They're lovely," Arkady said, as she stopped to examine them. "What are they for?"

"I'm having a dress made for a very special occasion. I like the gold, but the blue might suit my colouring better, don't you think? Or the burgundy?"

Arkady hesitated before she replied, recalling Cayal once describing Kinta as someone who favoured leather over cloth. The delicate fabrics laid out before them seemed a far cry from the tastes of that woman. Maybe Declan was wrong about Chintara. Maybe she wasn't an immortal at all. Maybe she was just someone who happened to be blonde and statuesque with an interest in the history of the immortals.

It could be argued that, except for her hair colour, Arkady fitted the same description.

"What's the occasion?" Arkady asked, resisting the temptation to glance around to see if Tiji had followed them inside.

"I'm meeting an old . . . *acquaintance*. I want to make a good impression."

"I'm sure you will, my lady," she assured the consort.

Chintara didn't seem nearly so certain. "We haven't seen each other for a very long time and we didn't part friends. I want to make sure everything is perfect when we renew our acquaintance."

"What were you wearing the last time you saw him?"

Chintara was silent for a moment, and then she looked at Arkady, shaking her head. "I'm not sure I was wearing anything at all."

Arkady smiled. "Your last meeting wasn't here in Torlenia, then?"

The consort frowned. "Why do you say that?"

"Torlenian dress codes would make such a circumstance virtually impossible, wouldn't they?"

"You really are a sharp little thing, aren't you?"

"It's a logical enough conclusion, my lady."

"And one most women would have been too busy judging me to come to. But you're right. It wasn't here. It was . . . somewhere else."

"With less rigid dress codes?"

Chintara allowed herself a small smile. "Yes, with much less rigid dress codes."

"I'm guessing this friend is someone you knew before your marriage to the Imperator, then," Arkady prompted, wondering if she could coax an admission out of Chintara about her true identity.

Are you really an immortal, my lady?

Why yes, Arkady, I am *an immortal hiding here in the royal palace, waiting until my lord and master returns . . .*

"Oh, Tides . . ."

"I *beg* your pardon?" Chintara gasped, a little shocked by Arkady's uncharacteristic curse.

"I'm so sorry, my lady," she hurriedly replied, trying to think up a reason for her outburst. "I just thought of something I should have done before I left home this morning."

"*Really?*"

Arkady shrugged, which gave her the short time she needed to concoct her excuse. It wasn't difficult. She was a practised liar. "I had a new Crasii arrive from home the other day and I'd arranged to meet her this morning so I could organise for her to start her duties. I forgot all about her. She'll still be waiting for me in my sitting room, I suppose."

"Then you have nothing to be concerned about. It is the nature of Crasii to wait on their masters. Literally *and* figuratively."

"You don't have many Crasii servants here, I notice."

"They have their place, I suppose." Chintara shrugged, refusing to be drawn on the subject. "Which one?"

"My *lady*?"

"Which fabric? Before you decided your Crasii was the most important thing in the world, we were discussing which fabric I should choose."

Arkady dutifully turned her attention to the bolts of cloth. "To be honest, my lady, I'm not sure what difference it would make."

"Why do you say that?"

"Well, if you're not meeting with your husband, then you'll be wearing your shroud, won't you? You could be dressed in a hair shirt and hobnailed boots and your friend will never know."

Chintara was silent for a moment and then she shrugged. "This will be a special occasion. I won't be wearing a shroud."

"In that case," Arkady replied with a great deal of caution, "shouldn't you ask yourself what he remembers about you most? And if you want to remind him of that? Or did you want to turn his mind from something that is—quite possibly—a *painful* memory, perhaps?"

For a moment, Chintara let a wistful smile flicker over her face. "You're a very insightful woman, Arkady. And you make a valid observation. I shall have to think on this some more, before I decide."

"Well, if it comes down to it, my favourite is the green," she said, pointing to a bolt of emerald green cloth worked with delicate gold flowers, instead of asking: *Is the dress being made for you to greet your immortal lord and master when he returns?* which is what she really wanted to know.

Surreptitiously, Arkady glanced around the room, but of course, she could see no sign of Tiji. And she needed to find the Crasii; needed to speak with her. She had to know for certain if Chintara really *was* Kinta.

Because it occurred to Arkady at that moment that if this woman truly was the legendary immortal warrior Kinta, then the pieces were rapidly falling into place. Chintara's lord and master wasn't the callow boy Stellan had described. She was preparing for her Tide Lord lover to return.

All that remained for Arkady to discover was *which* Tide Lord lover.

Brynden, the Lord of Reckoning?

Or Cayal, the Immortal Prince?

Chapter 25

Once Warlock and Jaxyn reached Prince Mathu's suite of rooms in the Glaeban Royal Palace, Lord Aranville showed little interest in getting the prince out of bed. He went through the motions, shaking Mathu awake with a less-than-enthusiastic suggestion that he'd better get up because the king was angry with him. Then he ordered Warlock to find the prince something to wear. But the Tide Lord didn't bother to stay in the prince's bedroom. Instead, he strode back to the sitting room and threw open the double doors that led onto the balcony overlooking the lake.

Warlock tried to keep an eye on Jaxyn as he hurriedly assembled the prince's clothes for his outing on the lake. The day was bright, the wind blowing scudding clouds across the face of the sun, making the light brighten and dim erratically.

The immortal stood on the balcony for a long time, still as a mill pond. In the other room, Prince Mathu, rubbing his eyes and cursing, finally dragged himself from his bed and staggered to the wash bowl, where he splashed cold water on his face.

That revived the young prince enough, apparently, for him to notice what was going on around him. Wearing nothing but the braes he'd slept in, he stumbled into the sitting room, squinting in the bright sunlight at Jaxyn's still figure on the balcony.

"What's going on?" he asked, as Warlock followed the prince into the sitting room, carrying the shirt, trousers and boots he'd selected from the prince's wardrobe.

"There's a storm coming," Jaxyn replied, his gaze fixed on the sky.

The clouds seemed to be moving faster. Warlock wondered if he was imagining things, because it looked as if they were deliberately colliding with each other.

"Tides, weren't we supposed to go out on the lake, or something, this morning?" Mathu mumbled, snatching the shirt Warlock was holding for him. Clumsily, he managed to get the shirt on. "I'll bet Mother is furious."

"She wasn't happy," Jaxyn agreed. "But I'd not worry too much, if I were you. I have a feeling they'll be heading back sooner than they planned."

"How can you tell?" Mathu asked, buttoning up his shirt.

"Can't you feel it?"

The prince pulled a face. "My head feels like there's a military band practising on the inside of my skull, Jaxyn," he complained, accepting the trousers Warlock offered him with barely a glance in the Crasii's direction. "I can't feel much of anything beyond that."

Jaxyn glanced over his shoulder, smiling briefly. "There's a storm on the way. A big one."

Mathu didn't notice his companion's smile. He was too busy fighting his way into his trousers. "How can you tell?" he asked, hopping on one foot.

Warlock was wondering the same thing, but then he glanced at the sky again, in time to see the sun blotted out by the rapidly gathering clouds that were now amassing at an unnatural rate. The sense of foreboding he felt on the way here deepened to a palpable fear. The light was dimming rapidly, enough even for Mathu to notice.

Buttoning up his trousers he padded barefoot to the balcony. "Tides! Look at that sky."

"It's going to be a bad one," Jaxyn remarked in a bland voice.

He's doing this, Warlock realised with a stab of apprehension. *Jaxyn is calling on the Tide*. He's *the one summoning the storm*.

It took Warlock a little time to puzzle out why the Tide Lord would bother to summon a storm *now*, when his intended target was standing here, safe as a mill mouse, while his immortal partner in crime was out on the lake . . .

Tides! Prince Mathu was never Jaxyn's target. It's the king and queen.

With every drop of self-control he owned, Warlock stood there, unmoving, holding Prince Mathu's stockings and boots.

You want me to behave like a Crasii? he recalled asking Declan Hawkes the day he and Tiji had arrived in Herino. *To obey the orders of the immortals, even if it means killing an innocent Crasii?*

Even if it means killing ten of them, Declan had replied, and then he'd sent him to the palace.

With his heart hammering, Warlock realised the test Declan Hawkes had warned him of wasn't what they'd imagined at all. The spymaster spoke about killing Crasii; unimportant slaves whose death meant little in the grander scheme of things. Even his earlier suspicion that Jaxyn was on his way here to murder the prince seemed easier to deal with. At least then, had he wanted to stop it, Warlock might have been able to intervene. He was physically stronger than Jaxyn and might have been able to slow him down or somehow make enough noise that the guards might hear them.

It had all been useless and idle speculation. He was standing here now because the Cabal of the Tarot needed someone close to the immortals and somehow, Warlock had been elected. *We must find out what they're planning. That's only going to happen if we have someone in the palace who can get close enough to Jaxyn and Diala to find out what's going on.* He was here to observe. Here specifically *not* to intervene.

But Declan Hawkes had assumed any trial by the Tide Lords to prove the loyalty of their Crasii would involve their own kind. He'd not instructed Warlock to stand by and watch a Tide Lord assassinate the King and Queen of Glaeba.

Warlock was torn with indecision, the rest of the spymaster's warning burned into his brain. *The slightest hesitation and you're blown, my friend. The Tide Lords will know you're a Scard, and they'll kill you. Then they'll wonder why Lady Ponting sent them a Scard as a wedding present and they'll kill her. Then they'll trace your movements back to Aleki and the rest of your brethren in Hidden Valley and kill all of them, too, including your mate and your unborn pups.*

Warlock jumped as lightning split the rapidly gathering darkness, followed by a sharp crack of thunder. While he'd been agonising over what he should—or shouldn't—do, Jaxyn had been busy. To his credit, Prince Mathu seemed to have gathered his wits somewhat, as the storm built up above them. He stood next to Jaxyn on the balcony, staring up at the sky which was so dark now the clouds had turned a sickly dark green.

"Tides! Look at that build-up. We have to get a message out to my father's barge and tell them to head back to shore."

Although Jaxyn was doing nothing obvious to encourage the storm, the sky darkened as the clouds swelled and multiplied with unnatural speed. "I would think they're doing it already," he remarked, glancing at the prince. "A storm like this would be hard to miss."

At the first crack of thunder, it began to rain. By now, the storm had completely obliterated the sun. The morning, which had been so bright only a few minutes before, was full of threat, the charged air sharp with burning ozone. The rain bucketed down, not the gentle, misty Glaeban rain they were so accustomed to—this was a torrential downpour, likely to flood the whole city within an hour, if it lasted that long. The strength of the storm terrified Warlock—not because he was particularly frightened of thunder and lightning, but because of what it meant.

By all accounts, the Tide wasn't even close to peaking yet.

What will they be capable of when it does *return fully?*

"Cecil!" Mathu ordered, the rain washing away the last of his hangover. "Get down to the dock. Tell the boatman I said they'd better be ready for the royal barge when it docks, or there'll be hell to pay."

Warlock guessed as much as heard the order. The prince was shouting to be heard over the wind and rain, the lightning and its accompanying thunder making him hard to understand. Jaxyn remained on the balcony beside him, drenched to the skin, his eyes filled with elation. He was channelling the Tide, manipulating the very forces of nature, the power coursing through him like a powerful aphrodisiac. Mathu didn't notice it, wouldn't have understood what he was seeing if he *had* noticed it.

Warlock didn't hesitate, dropping the prince's boots on the floor and rushing off to do as he was bid. He was glad of the escape. There was nothing he could do here, but at least, if he was down on the wharf, he might be able to do *something* to help.

As he pounded down the palace stairs, through the hall and out into the storm, another thought occurred to him, which spurred him on. *The king's barge is crewed by humans, but it's towed by a score of amphibious Crasii and there's an immortal on board the barge, in a position to issue orders they're compelled to obey.*

Kylia wouldn't—couldn't—drown, but the king and queen were human and mortal and *they* certainly could.

The subtlety of Jaxyn's plan was breathtaking, Warlock realised, as he worked it all out in his head, the partially flooded gravel path from the palace gardens to the dock squelching underfoot as he ran. *Send Kylia out on the barge; she who could order the Crasii around and not be harmed by any danger. Stage a dreadful accident in a freak storm. Keep Mathu—the next in line for the throne and Kylia's husband—away from the disaster, so he would survive to become the puppet King of Glaeba.*

The reason for Jaxyn's frequent outings with the prince became clear now. The young prince's tardiness and subsequent absence from the barge during a family outing wouldn't raise a single eyebrow in the aftermath.

And they've done it in such a way that nobody will ever suspect the sudden and unexpected death of the King and Queen of Glaeba was anything but a tragic accident.

By the time Warlock reached the dock, he discovered any orders the crown prince might have issued regarding the king's barge were redundant. The men on the dock had seen the danger long before the hungover young prince had thought to do anything about it.

As Jaxyn had predicted, the barge was heading back to shore, being tossed about the choppy surface of the lake like a child's toy in a bathtub. The amphibians towing it toward the dock were struggling against the waves, many of which were breaking over the side of the barge, making it surge uncontrollably forward. The first surge had apparently crushed several of the Crasii nearest the hull between the hull and the wharf, and they now hung limp and useless in their harnesses, hampering the efforts of their companions to control the forward momentum of the boat.

Warlock skidded to a halt as the barge and its terrified passengers were making a second attempt to dock. He couldn't see the king or queen on deck, but it was possible they'd been ordered below for their safety. He *could* hear the screams though, even over the drenching downpour, the thunder and the panicked shouts of the stevedores on the dock trying to bring the barge home.

"They'd be better off heading back out into deeper water!" someone shouted beside him. "And waiting until this squall has passed before they try again! Who's on board?"

Warlock turned to find a large, grey-haired man had stopped beside him, drenched to the skin as Warlock was. He knew who he was, although they'd not been formally introduced. This was Daly Bridgeman, Declan Hawkes's predecessor. The old man had returned to Herino to temporarily resume his duties for Declan who'd had to leave the city because of some family business that even Prince Mathu had not known the details of, commenting that Hawkes was always disappearing like that, and giving the spymaster barely another thought.

But here was a man who might be able to do *something*, Warlock reasoned, although he couldn't imagine what.

"The king and queen are on board, sir!" Warlock informed him, shouting to be heard. And then he added as an afterthought, "And the crown princess!"

Before Bridgeman could answer, the barge surged forward again, this time hitting the dock, which shattered under the impact. Warlock winced as several stevedores were thrown into the water, the waves swallowing them as if they were titbits thrown into the lake for the hungry churning waters to devour. For a moment, even the thunder was almost drowned out by the crack of splintering wood. Everyone ignored the amphibious Crasii screaming as they perished, caught between the dock and the massive weight of the barge. Warlock tried to go to their aid—nobody seemed to care what was happening to the Crasii because everyone's attention was focused on saving the king and queen—but Bridgeman's vice-like grip fastened on his arm.

"There's nothing you can do!" he yelled.

Sick with frustration and knowing the old spymaster was right, Warlock turned to look up at the palace behind them, at the balcony where he could just make out the lone figure of Jaxyn standing there in the torrential rain, calmly watching the disaster with the king's barge unfold. There was no sign of Prince Mathu. Perhaps he was already on his way down. After all, his wife and both his parents were on that barge.

Another loud splintering sound caught Warlock's attention over the sound of dying amphibians. The waves had thrown the barge into the shore again, killing more Crasii, and this time, breaching the hull.

"We have to do *something*!" Warlock screamed at Daly Bridgeman, trying to shake free of the old man's grasp. "He's killing them!"

"Which is why we need you here!" the old man replied. And then he pointed to the balcony—to Jaxyn—with that one gesture letting

Warlock know that, like Declan Hawkes, he was much more than just the King's Spymaster. "If the king doesn't survive this, then we're in big trouble, Cecil, and the Cabal is going to need you! Now more than ever!"

The old man's cold pragmatism was too much for Warlock. He tore himself free of Daly Bridgeman's grip and ran toward the shattered dock to help pull the wounded from the water. The rain kept on relentlessly. By now the desperate rescuers on shore had been joined by Prince Mathu and a score of palace guards who'd followed the prince down to see if they could lend their aid.

There was little the rescuers could do, however, except drag the occasional body from the lake and try to avoid the massive barge hurtling itself, time and again, against the shattered dock.

By the time the storm blew itself out several hours later, thirty-seven bodies lay on the grassy shore of the Lower Oran, among them King Enteny and Queen Inala. Seven other crewmembers—two human and five amphibious Crasii—and the Crown Princess Kylia were missing.

Chapter 26

"To kill an immortal you have to attack the problem at the source," Lukys informed Cayal.

The younger man looked across the dune at the Tide Lord with a puzzled expression. They'd come out here into the desert where they weren't likely to be disturbed. The sun was nearing its zenith and the sand stretched out before them like an endless golden sea. Sitting on the crest of the dune, Cayal tried to remember what this place had been like before he'd robbed it of its sea, but it proved too difficult. Or perhaps too uncomfortable.

He gave up, turning his attention to Lukys who sat beside him on the sand. "What are you talking about?"

"I mean, the reason we can't be killed is because, down to the tiniest pore in our magically altered bodies, we're designed to heal. That's all immortality is, you know. Our bodies will repair themselves endlessly, and if they can't, they'll just wait until the environment around our body is more conducive to healing and repair itself, then."

"Hence the reason Kentravyon has stayed frozen all this time," Cayal concluded, as he grasped what Lukys was telling him. He wasn't sure he cared, but long experience had taught him that when Lukys was in a lecturing mood, it was foolish not to pay attention.

"Exactly," the older man agreed, obviously pleased his student was being suitably conscientious. "Kentravyon's not dead, but because his body is frozen, it can't heal itself, either."

"And if we thawed him out?"

Lukys shrugged. "Hour or two later, he'd be fine, I suppose." Lukys smiled. "Rather pissed off, I suspect, but physically as well as anybody else."

Cayal nodded in agreement. He'd always suspected as much. "Let's not thaw him out then, eh?"

"Wasn't planning to," Lukys assured him. "Homicidal maniacs are far too much trouble."

"Do you remember where we stashed him?"

"In Jelidia, I think."

"I mean, *specifically* where we stashed him," Cayal amended with a thin smile.

Lukys shrugged, his gaze fixed on the shimmering horizon. "Not really."

Cayal couldn't tell if he was lying. "Shouldn't we have marked the location of the cave, or something?"

"With what?" Lukys asked. "A big red X?"

That made Cayal smile. "I suppose that would rather defeat the purpose of hiding him, wouldn't it?"

"Rather," Lukys agreed, and then he turned his gaze from the distant horizon and looked at Cayal. "Have you given any more thought to my suggestion?"

"Which one?" Cayal scooped up a handful of burning sand and let it run through his fingers. "You've suggested everything from suicide to creating some sort of interplanetary rift so you can move between worlds since I've been here, Lukys. Could you be a little more specific?"

"I was referring to which of our brethren you plan to approach to aid you in your noble quest for annihilation."

Cayal let the sand dribble away completely before he answered. "I thought I'd take your suggestion and ask Maralyce."

Lukys stared at him for a moment and then smiled knowingly. "Not willing to ask the fair Immortal Maiden for her aid? I thought you *wanted* to die?"

"Not that badly," Cayal replied with a grimace.

His answer seemed to amuse Lukys. "Then maybe you're not as suicidal as you think you are, Sparky."

Cayal was silent for a moment, trying to decide which was worse, getting involved with Syrolee and her wretched clan again, or facing the prospect of eternity.

It was a surprisingly difficult decision.

"Well?" Lukys asked after a time.

Cayal shook his head. "I think I'd rather go on living than do what I suspect I'd have to do to secure Elyssa's cooperation."

"Well . . . Maralyce I suppose is worth a try, but she'll probably say no."

"Why? She likes me."

"No," Lukys corrected. "Maralyce doesn't like you, Cayal, she dislikes you marginally less than the rest of us. That's a long way from being willing to help you die."

"You don't think it's worth asking her then?"

"Let's just say I'm not confident of your chances."

"Who should I ask then? Brynden?" Cayal smiled sourly. "If I tell Brynden I want his help to die, he might oblige. Tides, it's not as if he hasn't tried to kill me before."

Lukys shook his head. "I think you're wasting your time, Cayal, but if you must . . ."

Cayal thought about it for a moment longer and then nodded, thinking it was time to put the unfinished business between him and the Lord of Reckoning behind him.

"Yes," he said. "I think I must."

Lukys smiled. "Well, I suppose the idea has some merit. And I can't think of anybody who'd be happier to see an end to you. Maybe, if you ask him nicely, he'll agree. And as you say, it's not as if he hasn't tried to do you in before."

"I keep getting blamed for that," Cayal complained. "The last Cataclysm wasn't my fault, you know."

"Brynden threw a meteorite at you, for pity's sake," Lukys said. "For stealing his woman, wasn't it?"

"Exactly! It was Brynden who tossed that bloody great ball of rock into the ocean, not me."

"I think the stealing-his-woman part is the reason you traditionally get the blame for it."

"I didn't steal her . . . Tides, it wasn't even my idea. Kinta was the one looking for a way to get his attention."

"Ah, yes," Lukys sympathised. "That terrible, wicked woman who led the innocent young prince astray. Poor you . . . just dragged along for the ride, weren't you?"

"I didn't say that. I just said I wasn't entirely to blame. And I never forced Kinta to leave Tenacia with me. In fact, I wasn't even the one who suggested we leave. She did. Until she got it into her head that we should run away together, Brynden didn't even know what was going on, and I was quite happy to keep it that way, thank you very much."

"You really do have an interesting, if somewhat arcane, code of honour, don't you?" Lukys remarked. "You resent being blamed for the consequences of stealing Kinta from Brynden, yet you happily admit to sleeping with her behind his back. Don't you think your sin was in the act of commission, not the act of getting caught?"

"Sin?" Cayal asked with a raised brow. He worried when people started throwing around the word "sin." It led to all sorts of nasty things that frequently got out of hand. "Tides, you're not thinking of starting a religion too, are you?"

"Haven't the time at the moment," Lukys said with a shrug. "Although I have been giving the matter some thought."

"And you decided it was too much work, I hope?"

"On the contrary. I long ago decided the only way to do it efficiently was to make a big splash so you get everyone's attention and then vanish—preferably with some vague promise you'll return—leaving everybody believing you've gone on ahead of them to paradise, and then just sit back and watch the fun begin."

"What fun?"

"The fun of self-delusion," Lukys said. "That's what faith is all about, Cayal—believing in something so profoundly you'd devote your entire life to it without any proof that it actually exists. Worse than that, it's believing without the *need* for proof. It's believing, even when confronted with definitive proof that you're wrong. A truly effective religion doesn't need gods parading around every year on feast days to assure the peasants they're still on the job. That's what brought Kentravyon down, you know, and the reason Syrolee and her tribe never last much beyond the most recent Cataclysm. Their religions require the physical presence of their gods to maintain them. A truly effective religion needs nothing more than a promise of salvation. It'll outlast the others by a thousand years."

"You know what I think?" Cayal said, scooping up another handful of sand. It was almost too hot to touch, this close to the surface, but he barely noticed. "I think you've spent far too much time thinking about this."

The older man smiled. "Well, I don't have your wide range of hobbies to keep me entertained, Sparky. I have to do something to banish the boredom."

Cayal looked up, a little confused. "My wide range of hobbies?"

"Yes . . . you know . . . trying to kill yourself . . . stealing other men's wives."

"They're not my hobbies!"

"Aren't they?" Lukys stared at him with those pale, all-knowing eyes. "Tell me, honestly, old friend. How long has it been since you slept with another man's wife? Not counting mine."

"I haven't slept with your wife," he protested.

"Of course you haven't. Yet. But that's more lack of opportunity than lack of intent. Anyway, I told her the reason you're suicidal is because you're impotent. She feels very sorry for you. Now answer the question. How long has it been? A century? A decade? A year? Less than that, perhaps . . ."

Cayal looked away, refusing to answer. Lukys laughed. "Tides, it's only been a matter of months? I was wrong, Sparky. It's not a hobby for you, at all. It's a way of life!"

"You see, that's why I want to die, Lukys," Cayal grumbled. "I've had all I can take of you. Speaking of which, other than telling me we need some of the others to help, you're being very cagey about the details of this miraculous cure for immortality you claim to have discovered."

Lukys leaned back on his elbows, stretching his sandalled feet out in front of him, relaxing as if he hadn't a care in the world. "I'm not giving you the details because I don't intend to be killed myself."

"Why should you be killed?" Cayal laughed sourly. "Is it *dangerous*?"

Lukys scowled at him. "You know, jokes like that are much of the reason why I'm willing to help you find a way to kill yourself, old boy."

"There aren't words for the depth of my gratitude."

"Don't take that tone with me, Sunshine. You're the one who wants to die."

"So tell me how."

"There's no need, just yet."

"And when will there be a need, do you suppose?"

"When I say so."

Cayal didn't answer, angry at Lukys's intransigence on the matter, and deeply suspicious of his motives.

The older man could tell he wasn't happy. He reached across and patted Cayal's shoulder. "Take heart. The end is nigh. But we'll do it my way or we don't do it at all. I don't care how you manage it, but you get me another couple of Tide Lords. Ones with the same sort of power you and I can wield and I'll give you the death you're so eager to embrace, Sparky. But until you have the others committed to our cause, I'm not telling you a damned thing about the how. Only that I can."

Chapter 27

It took Tiji hardly any time at all to confirm that the Imperator's Consort was one of the missing immortals.

There was no special trick to it. Any Crasii who came within a few feet of a suzerain knew it instantly. Her species was created for it, specifically designed to recognise and serve their masters—every canine, every feline, even those wretched, unsociable amphibians. Of course, Tiji was a Scard, which meant she lacked the normal Crasii instinct to serve them, but she hadn't lost the ability to identify one from across a crowded room.

She couldn't fail to recognise the sickeningly familiar prickle that washed over her skin as soon as she'd followed Arkady Desean into the consort's presence.

Tiji had slipped unnoticed into the reception hall behind Arkady when they arrived and had taken up a position in the shadows of one of the twelve tall columns supporting the room's impressively decorated domed ceiling. As the two women hedged around the real reason they were both here, speaking of fabrics and old friendships, Tiji let her skin blend with the murals around her, until she became all but invisible. A surface such as this was easy to mimic, although it required her to stay absolutely still to maintain the illusion. Plain backgrounds were harder to duplicate, but once you had them, it was possible to move without being detected.

No such luck here. Tiji sighed as she settled in to wait, realising that if Kinta used this hall as her main living room, she may well have to wait until after dark before she could risk leaving the seraglium. That was really going to be a nuisance, she decided, because now she'd identified Kinta for what she was, her job was done. Tiji had other plans and other places to be.

For one thing, she wanted to do some sightseeing in the Crystal City before anybody thought to revoke her diplomatic status and send her home.

As was often the case when one was trying not to think about standing still, Tiji started to itch in the most inconvenient places. To take her mind off it, she turned her thoughts to escape. Now she'd confirmed Chintara was a suzerain, her task was to escape the palace undetected so she could return to the Glaeban embassy and report her intelligence to the Duchess of Lebec.

Looking around using only her eyes without moving any other part of her body—a skill it had taken years to master—she decided the prospects weren't good. Like Arkady, Tiji had entered the royal seraglium through the front door, which was located inside a guarded and sheltered courtyard. It might be possible, she mused, as the duchess and the immortal chatted like old friends, to slip out of the hall, jump the fountain-fed pool on the other side of the room, slip into the gardens she could see through the open doors and go over the wall, but Tiji really wasn't sure what might be on the other side. If she'd known which wall faced onto the street, she could be over it in a matter of seconds. But there was no way to be certain. Although she'd questioned her at length regarding the royal palace and its surrounds, Lady Desean hadn't really known what lay beyond the outer walls of the seraglium. She couldn't even say which walls connected the seraglium to the rest of the royal complex.

You see, Declan, this is what happens when you send amateurs to do a job, Tiji grumbled silently, as Kinta . . . Chintara . . . or whatever she was calling herself these days, ordered tea for herself and her guest. Several more slaves—human slaves, interestingly—came running at her command and gathered up the bolts of cloth, so the ladies could sit down.

Tiji couldn't really make out what the two women were saying from her position by the column, but she could read their body language. Chintara seemed tense, almost excited . . . her mood—oddly enough—reflected like a mirror in the stiff way Arkady was seated on the edge of the couch. Both women were apprehensive, Tiji could see that, no doubt for entirely different reasons.

The explanation for Arkady Desean's nervousness was easy to figure

out. Here she was, sharing tea and small talk with an immortal—
something the duchess was quite accustomed to, by all accounts—but
clearly something she wasn't at ease with. Had she been so polite, so
ladylike, Tiji wondered, when she was sharing tea and small talk with
the Immortal Prince?

And was that all they shared?

Truth be told, the only reason Tiji had ever suggested there might
have been something else going on between the duchess and the Immortal Prince was to get a rise out of Declan, but as she thought about
it, she began to wonder.

Arkady Desean—by human standards, at any rate—was an extraordinarily beautiful woman. If you believed the rumours, it was her remarkable beauty that saw her elevated from a penniless physician's daughter to
a duchess. The Duke of Lebec, even with his unconventional tastes, had
been struck by her charms. Tiji was fairly certain Declan Hawkes was
utterly spellbound by them.

Why wouldn't an immortal be just as enchanted by her?

Across the room, Chintara laughed at something Arkady said. Turning her attention from Arkady, Tiji studied the immortal for a while, intrigued by the sense of anticipation that seemed to radiate from the
woman. Even Tiji could feel it, despite being so far from the immortal
and her guest she could barely make out their voices. Chintara's excitement puzzled Tiji enough to keep her standing there in the shadows
without blinking or complaining about the oppressive heat.

*The woman's almost ten thousand years old, for pity's sake. Something pretty
special must be about to happen to get her all worked up about it.*

Logically, the consort's excitement had something to do with the returning Tide. Although she didn't command the power of a Tide Lord,
Kinta would be able to feel it, perhaps even wield it a little.

Is it that which has her so animated?

Or was Tiji's original guess about Kinta trying to make up with
Brynden the right one? *Maybe her love affair with Cayal hadn't lasted,*
Tiji had suggested to Declan back in Herino when he'd first received
Arkady's letter. *Maybe this is her way of patching things up with Brynden.*

Was *that* why Chintara was having a new gown made? Was she hoping to impress Brynden?

As she watched them talking, Tiji wondered how long it would take
Arkady to reach the same conclusion. The duchess wasn't stupid, that

much was clear. And with what they already knew, it was hardly a great feat of deductive logic to come up with the reason for Kinta's preparations.

Tides, Tiji thought, wishing she could scratch her nose. *Another wretched Tide Lord back from legend. That's all we need.*

While she had no desire to see the return of the Tide Lords, a part of Tiji hoped she was right, just so she could say "I told you so" to Declan.

She didn't get to do that often.

And if she didn't get out of here soon, she feared, she might not get to tell him at all.

Tiji remained in place while Arkady spent a frustrating hour chatting to the Imperator's Consort, before they were interrupted by one of the palace slaves, informing the Lady Chintara she had another visitor. Kinta smiled apologetically at Arkady and then turned to ask the slave a question. Although Tiji couldn't hear what she said, she assumed it had to do with the identity of her visitor.

The slave leaned forward and whispered something in her mistress's ear. No sooner had she finished speaking, the consort smiled, rose to her feet, and graciously proceeded to kick the Duchess of Lebec out, begging her guest's forgiveness, which Arkady—naturally—was at great pains to give.

The absurdity of their conversation made Tiji want to scream. The two women were polite, apologetic and generously forgiving, as they walked toward the door, closer to where Tiji stood, all but tripping over themselves to assure each other no offence was meant and none was taken.

It was nothing more than lies masquerading as manners. Arkady had a good idea who she was dealing with, and it was very likely Kinta had some idea of Arkady's involvement with Cayal, the Immortal Prince, if the gossip grapevine worked as efficiently among immortals as it did among humans.

But nobody could say what they really meant. Nobody could risk revealing they knew anything at all.

It took a few minutes for Kinta to be rid of Arkady, and Tiji knew she should follow them. In the hustle and bustle of the duchess's departure, she should be able to slip through the seraglium, unseen.

But Kinta's obvious agitation had changed subtly on the news that she had a new visitor. It was no longer pent-up excitement or anticipation

Tiji thought she could see. It seemed different. More aggressive. Even angry.

Curiosity kept Tiji standing still as a rock, a part of the murals, as the duchess and the immortal passed the column where she was hiding. Chintara saw Arkady out and then hurried back to the couches, where she sat down and then immediately stood up again, as if she couldn't decide what pose she should strike for her next caller.

Could it be Brynden is here? Already? Tiji's heart began to race. *Is that what has Kinta so animated?*

Was the Lord of Reckoning about to stride through that door and reclaim all that was his, from his woman to the whole nation of Torlenia, which tradition held he had always owned?

Tiji could barely breathe. She waited, watching Kinta pace, stop, check her reflection in the surface of the shallow pool that ran along the inner wall of the reception room, pace some more, and then hurry toward the door at the sound of it opening.

Ever so carefully, Tiji turned her eyes to the door, a little disappointed to see a shrouded figure step into the hall. A shroud meant a woman, which meant this wasn't the Lord of Reckoning.

It might not be another immortal at all . . .

The thought withered and died as the figure passed Tiji, unaware she was observed. The familiar prickle ran down Tiji's spine at the stranger's approach, almost making the little Crasii whimper with fear. This was—without a doubt—another suzerain.

That accounted for Kinta's agitated demeanour. The only question remaining was: *which one?*

Tiji didn't have long to wait for her answer. When the newcomer reached the place where Kinta waited—much closer than she'd been when talking with Arkady—the figure dispensed with the shroud, revealing another surprise.

It seemed the woman wasn't a woman, after all.

Her visitor was a man; tall, dark-haired, quite handsome by human standards if Tiji was any judge, and if she hadn't known better, the Crasii would have sworn he'd not yet reached thirty.

Kinta looked angry rather than surprised by the identity of her visitor. She stared at him for a long moment and then, with all the strength she could muster, raised her arm and slapped his face, the crack of her blow ringing across the hall.

The man's head was thrown to the side by the force of her rage, but he didn't retaliate, or even seem surprised by this savage reception. Instead, he dabbed at the small bead of blood on his lip and smiled as he looked back at her. "Nice to see you too, *darling.*"

"Tides, you've got a nerve, showing up here."

Her scorn didn't seem to faze him, any more than her slap had. "Yes, thank you, I'm well. How are you?"

"You should leave. *Now.* Brynden will be here any day . . . If he sees you . . ." Kinta was furious, all but growling at him.

The immortal smiled, unconcerned. "He'll what? Throw another *rock* at me? That trick's getting a bit old, don't you think? But never fear, my fickle and faithless lover. I'm not here to cause you trouble."

Kinta snorted with disbelief. "You don't know how to do anything else, Cayal . . ."

Tiji's knees almost buckled. She had to force herself to remain still. She was so startled, she didn't even hear the man's answer . . .

Oh, Tides! she gasped silently. *It's the Immortal Prince.*

Chapter 28

The rhythmic *thunk, thunk* of the axe as Declan chopped firewood for Maralyce was a soothing sound. He'd been at it for most of the afternoon, the mindless task giving him a chance to marshal his thoughts, time to put together everything he'd been told, these past few days, and more importantly, everything he *hadn't* been told. There was an impressive stack of wood piled up under the eaves of Maralyce's small cabin, and Declan was sweating with the exertion despite the cool afternoon.

With a powerful blow, Declan split yet another log, bending down to pick up one of the halves so he could split it into quarters. He placed it on the block, but when he straightened, it was to find Maralyce standing before him. In her hand she held a cup of water, which she offered to him without a word.

Declan hesitated and then accepted the water, guessing this was Maralyce's idea of a peace offering.

"You've done quite a lot," she said, glancing at the woodpile.

He shrugged, and drank the water down. It was cool and tasted faintly stale, but he welcomed the drink. Swinging an axe was thirsty work. "You said you wanted wood chopped."

"Didn't think you'd be quite so willing to do it, though." Maralyce took the empty cup from him but made no move to leave. Declan waited, leaning on the axe, wondering if she had something else to say.

"Your grandfather seems very fond of you," she said, just as the silence was starting to become uncomfortable.

"And I'm fond of him. You seem surprised by that."

"Nothing surprises me any longer."

He smiled. "Then you're one up on me, my lady, because I'm *still* getting over the shock of finding out you and Shalimar are old pals. Not entirely certain I ever will get over it, for that matter."

That seemed to amuse the immortal. "You remind me of him when he was younger."

"Is that a good thing?"

"Depends on the mood I'm in," she said, with a thin-lipped smile. "Will you be leaving soon?"

"You're kicking me out?" he asked, not really surprised. What surprised him was that she had allowed him to stay this long.

"There are other places you need to be, lad," she said. "Other immortals you should be worrying about."

Declan leaned the axe against the block. "You've got me plenty worried all on your own."

"That may be so, but what worries you about me is what I've done in the past, not what I'm planning to do in the future."

Much as he didn't want to admit it, the immortal was right. "Don't suppose you know which immortals I *ought* to be worrying about?"

"Right now? If I were you, I'd be heading for Caelum to find out what Syrolee and her lot are up to."

"Jaxyn and Diala have taken up residence in the Glaeban Royal Palace," he said. "I work for the king. I'm supposed to be looking out for Glaeba's interests."

"You work for the Cabal, boy," she pointed out. "Your responsibilities to Glaeba come a poor second to that."

"I'm not sure King Enteny would agree."

"I wasn't suggesting you ask his opinion."

"Are you the fifth member of the Pentangle?"

His question seemed to amuse her. "Why do you think that?"

"Because whoever it is, they've gone to a great deal of trouble to conceal their identity. I could never understand why. If the fifth member was an immortal—someone like you, for instance—that would explain a lot."

"I gave your wretched little secret society a hand once," Maralyce said, shaking her head. "I've no interest in running it. Still," she added thoughtfully, "you could have the right of it."

"You mean the fifth member of the Pentangle really *is* an immortal?"

She shrugged. "I have no idea. But I wouldn't put it past a few of my brethren to get involved. It'd tickle the fancy of more than one Tide Lord to think they were aiding the humans of Amyrantha in their futile quest to see an end to them. It was that sort of thinking that had Lukys joining the Holy Warriors, you know. There's even one or two who probably think what you're trying to do is a good idea."

Not sure of the reaction he'd get, Declan hesitated before asking, "Like the Immortal Prince, for instance?"

Maralyce smiled. "I suppose you heard he was here recently?"

"How do you think Shalimar found you?"

She sighed. "Poor Cayal. He'd do just about anything if it meant dying."

"He really is suicidal then?"

"Has been for more than a thousand years," Maralyce confirmed with a nod. "It comes and goes, mind you. Cayal gets distracted easily, especially if the distraction is pretty and female, but it's only temporary. Sooner or later, the weight of eternity starts to bear down on him again and all he wants to do is find a way to end the pain."

"Was he distracted while he was here this time," Declan asked as casually as he could manage, "by something pretty and female?"

"With your duchess?" Maralyce asked. She shrugged. "I'm not really sure. I suppose he was."

"But you're not certain?"

"Well, they didn't act like your average pair of lovers, if that's what you're asking, but then your little duchess is hardly average, is she?"

"No, Arkady is anything but average," Declan agreed, wishing Maralyce's vague answer could have been a little more reassuring. "It's too much to hope he's still buried in the bottom of your mine somewhere, I suppose?"

Maralyce laughed. "Cayal? Of course he's not here. He cleared that cave-in months ago. Probably by the time Jaxyn and your precious little duchess were back in Lebec."

Declan had feared as much. "Do you know where he is now?"

She shook her head. "Haven't a clue."

"Will he go looking for Arkady, do you think?"

"He might. I really can't tell you. He didn't exactly fill me in on his plans for the next millennium, you know." She studied him for a moment with an all-too-knowing look. "Ah! I see. Another fool who's a little bit fonder of the lovely duchess than he should be, eh?"

Declan bristled at her implication. "I was just asking . . ."

"Of course you were," she agreed. Then she laughed again. "That girl really knows how to attract trouble, doesn't she? Good thing her husband's such an understanding soul."

"Did she tell you that?"

"She told me more than she probably intended," Maralyce said. "But that really wasn't much. She's very good at keeping secrets, your duchess. Lies like a trouper, too."

"What was she lying about?" He was curious as to what Arkady might have said that would prompt such an observation.

"Everything, far as I could tell. Not that a practised liar would bother Cayal all that much. He'd probably find it attractive, come to think of it."

Tiji's assertion that Cayal and Arkady had developed something much deeper than friendship was starting to feel horribly real. "So there *was* something going on between them?"

"What would you like me to say?"

Declan stared at her, puzzled by the question. "What?"

"Well, this is obviously bothering you, lad. You keep harping on about it. What would you like me to say? Do you want me to tell you nothing happened between your lovely duchess and the good-looking and very-charismatic-when-he-wants-to-be Immortal Prince, so you can feel better? Or do you want me to tell you they were at it like a pair of rutting rabbits the whole time they were here so you can work yourself up into a right old jealous rage?"

Declan gazed at her for a moment and then shook his head. "You know, I think you'd really *like* to see me in a right old jealous rage, wouldn't you?"

She grinned. "The wood you'd have to chop to work it off did cross my mind."

Declan picked up the axe. "I appreciate the thought, my lady, but I don't mind chopping your wood for you, so even if you *could* provoke me into a jealous rage, I don't need one to keep me going."

Maralyce's smile faded. "What's it going to take to *get* you going, then?" she asked. "You're getting a mite too comfortable around here, if you ask me."

He shrugged, hefting the axe over his shoulder. "Soon as Shalimar is ready to go, we'll leave."

"You're assuming Shalimar intends to leave with you?"

"Of course I am. He's *free* to go, isn't he?" To emphasise his point, Declan swung the axe, splitting the halved log into quarters.

Maralyce, although she was standing only inches from the block, didn't flinch.

"Maybe he doesn't want to leave."

Declan picked up the other half of the log and placed it on the block. "He told you that, did he?"

"Did you bother to ask him? Or are you just assuming that what *you* want is the most important thing in the world, so your grandfather will have to go along with it?"

"I'm not the only one with responsibilities to the Cabal," he said, splitting the half-log with a powerful blow. "A moment ago you were telling me off for ignoring them."

Maralyce nodded as he bent down to pick up the pieces, stacking them on the pile before retrieving another log to split.

"Aye . . . and with good cause," she said. "The rise of the Tide, and the immortals it brings with it, is never an easy time, for us *or* for humanity in general. But you're young, Declan, you're strong, you're healthy and—most importantly—you've shown no symptoms, so far, of being affected by the Tide."

He studied her closely for a moment, before asking, "Why would I? I'm three generations removed from Shalimar's immortal ancestor."

"Your immortal ancestor too, you know, lad, much as I'm sure it pains you to acknowledge the fact."

"Do you know who it is—this mysterious immortal ancestor of ours?"

"Fact is, the Tide's on the way back and your grandfather can feel it," she said, ignoring his question. "Worse, it's causing him real pain, and it's only going to get worse as the Tide returns. You shouldn't be thinking about taking him away from here, lad. You should be thinking about making the time he has left as comfortable as possible."

Declan stared at her in shock. "Are you telling me he's *dying*?"

"I'm telling you the Tide is killing him," she corrected with grim certainty. "It's why he came here. To see if I could help."

"Can you?"

She shook her head. "Talk to Cayal, sometime, about the futility of an immortal trying to help a gifted Tidewatcher, if you want to know how helpless I am to do anything for your grandfather."

Declan frowned, remembering the tale Arkady had related to him when she returned from the mountains. The story Cayal had told her. "You're referring to the story he told Arkady? About the little girl, Fliss, and how the Great Lakes were formed?"

"It's not a story, Declan. Even ignoring the rather noble slant Cayal puts on his own involvement, it really happened. The tragedy is, Shalimar's near as powerful as Fliss was and the only thing that's saved him from being ravaged by the Tide until now is that it's been out."

"That's absurd! You're saying Shalimar can *wield* the Tide?"

"What I'm saying, Declan, is that he's not going to live long enough to find out. Fliss was a healthy child. Even with the Tide at its peak, it took the better part of seven years to kill her and she may have lasted quite a few more, before it destroyed her completely, if she hadn't tried to immolate herself. Shalimar, on the other hand, is an old man. I doubt he has the strength to fight the effects for anywhere near that long."

"Does he know?"

She nodded. "He's known for a long time."

Declan glared at her, wishing he could be certain she was lying. Deep down, he felt she wasn't. All his life, Shalimar had been able to sense the Tide—even when it was still far out of a Tide Lord's sensory range. Declan still remembered the headaches that incapacitated his grandfather for days at a time. It was one of the reasons he'd spent so much of his childhood roaming the Lebec slums on his own, looking for mischief. That was how he'd met Arkady. She'd caught him breaking into her father's surgery looking for something to ease his grandfather's pain.

But of late, the old man had said nothing about being in pain. He'd never mentioned any headaches. With a stab of guilt, Declan realised he'd seen Shalimar so rarely since leaving Lebec, he wouldn't have known about them, anyway. His public falling out with his grandfather—staged mostly for the benefit of the residents of the Lebec slums to protect Shalimar from those who feared what Declan's appointment as the King's Spymaster might mean to them—had effectively cut him off from anything but the most casual contact with his only living relative. He cursed himself roundly for not guessing the truth.

Tides, even Arkady nagged me about it, without even knowing why the old man was unwell.

"Why didn't he say something to me?" he asked, as if somehow the immortal had the answer.

Of course, she didn't. Declan knew that, even before she replied, "You'll have to ask him, although I'd rather you didn't, given he extracted a solemn vow from me not to tell you any of this."

Declan sighed. "Can you do *anything* for him?"

Maralyce looked uncertain. "Ease the pain a little, I suppose. But I can't fight the inevitable, any more than he can."

"How long does he have?"

"Until the Tide peaks, is my guess. That could be a few months; it might be a few years."

Declan's sense of helplessness was almost overwhelming. "Is there *anything* I can do?"

"Let him die with hope," Maralyce said.

"What do you mean?"

"I mean you need to do *something*, Declan. I don't know what, and I've no idea how, but you need to find what the Cabal has been seeking for the past few thousand years. Your grandfather will die by the time the Tide peaks, my lad, make no mistake about it. If you want him to die happy," she shocked him by saying, "find a way to put an end to the Tide Lords."

Chapter 29

Arkady Desean was pacing the floor of the seraglium like a caged cat when Tiji returned to the Glaeban embassy. At the sound of the door opening, she looked up, sagging with relief when she spied the little Crasii.

"Tides! You're safe!"

Tiji was genuinely touched. She'd not expected the duchess to care about her fate one way or the other.

"I told you, your grace, I'm pretty good at what I do."

"Please, sit down," Arkady urged. "You must be exhausted. I know I am."

Tiji smiled, not at the offer of a seat so much as the idea she was tired. Arkady Desean might well be drained by the stress of their intrigue, but that was simply a mark of how unprepared she was for this kind of life. Tiji wasn't feeling exhausted. Just the opposite. She was quite exhilarated.

"Can I get you anything?" the duchess asked, as Tiji took the offered seat.

She shook her head. "Truly, your grace, I'm fine."

"Did you learn what we needed to know . . . I tried to look for you, but . . ."

"I know you did, your grace, I was there."

"Is Chintara . . . is she who we think she is?"

Tiji nodded. "She most certainly is, your grace."

Arkady didn't look surprised. "But you can only tell she's immortal, can't you? How do we confirm *which* immortal?"

Tiji hesitated. This could get a little awkward if she handled it the wrong way. "I was able to establish that too, before I left," she admitted.

The duchess seemed impressed. "You *were*? How did you manage that?"

"I waited around to see who her other visitor was."

"Yes, I saw a woman waiting for admittance to the reception hall when I was getting into the carriage," she confirmed. "She was shrouded so I couldn't see her face. Who was she?"

"Had you donned your own shroud by then, my lady?"

Arkady shook her head. "I waited until I got into the carriage. Every moment I don't have to spend wearing that wretched thing is a blessing."

Tiji wasn't so sure blessing was the right description. "That could prove a bit of a problem, your grace. If you were seen."

"Seen by whom?"

"Chintara's visitor was shrouded like a woman," she informed the duchess carefully. "But that was just to get himself through the gates of the seraglium."

"The visitor was a man, then," Arkady concluded with an admirable lack of histrionics. "Was it Brynden?"

Tiji shook her head. *Here goes nothing* . . . "It was the Immortal Prince, your grace."

Arkady hesitated for only a fraction of a second and if Tiji hadn't been looking for it, she may have missed it altogether. "What did he want?"

"I'm really not sure. He spent a lot of time asking about Brynden. You know, where he was, the mood he was in . . ."

"You learned where *Brynden* is hiding?"

"No," Tiji said, shaking her head. "Kinta wouldn't answer anything but the most banal of his questions. I got the feeling they didn't part friends the last time. In fact, she slapped his face before she even said hello."

That made Arkady smile, although whether it was the idea of someone slapping Cayal, or because it confirmed the rift between the Immortal Prince and his former lover, Tiji had no way of telling. "Did you learn where Cayal is hiding? Where he's staying in Ramahn?"

"Why, your grace?" the little Crasii asked, before she could stop herself. "Are you planning to visit him?"

Arkady's smile vanished, along with her friendly demeanour. "I beg your pardon?"

You've done it now, Slinky. "I just meant, your grace, that given our lack of resources, knowing the exact location of the Immortal Prince probably wouldn't be of any use to us, right now. It's enough to be able to warn the Cabal he's here in Torlenia, don't you think?"

Arkady took a long time to answer. Perhaps she was debating the wisdom of Tiji's advice. She could have been trying to decide what Tiji knew or suspected about her relationship with the Immortal Prince. Assuming there *was* a relationship, which was really nothing more than speculation on Tiji's part.

But then the duchess stunned Tiji with both her lack of embarrassment and her honesty. "If Cayal saw me in the seraglium, there's a real danger he'll come looking for me," she said.

"How big a danger?" Tiji asked warily.

"Almost a certainty," Arkady replied.

Tiji nodded, trying to gather her thoughts. The Crasii was stumbling about in the dark here and Arkady wasn't reacting the way Tiji expected her to. The first thing Tiji needed to do was establish *exactly* what she was dealing with.

"So you and Cayal had . . . something going on?" she ventured.

"I slept with him, Tiji, is that what you wanted to know?"

"Well, yes, but I didn't think . . ."

"What? That I'd be quite so willing to admit to it?" Arkady shrugged. "I'm not a fool, you know. If Cayal is here in Ramahn and he saw me at the palace, there's a good chance he'll try to contact me. You are the only ally I have in Torlenia who believes the Tide Lords exist or know what they're capable of. It would be idiotic beyond reckoning for me to try to hide something like that from you."

Tiji was silent for a moment, as she was forced to rethink almost every assumption she had ever made about Arkady Desean.

"Does Declan know about you and Cayal?"

"I told Declan everything I could," the duchess answered.

The chameleon frowned. "I'll take that as a *no*."

Arkady looked uncomfortable, but not guilty. "He didn't ask, Tiji, and I didn't volunteer the information. My husband knows."

"Well, that's not a lot of help, given he doesn't even believe the Tide Lords exist."

A fleeting smile crossed the duchess's face. "Declan's not a fool either, Tiji. If he didn't ask, I'm sure it's because he either guessed the truth or he didn't *want* to know. Either way, what Declan does or doesn't think, right at this moment, is irrelevant. The point is, Cayal and I developed a friendship of sorts. And I'm not just talking about sleeping with him—believe it or not, that was an entirely different matter. I was talking to Cayal in prison for months before he escaped. He's depressed, suicidal and doesn't care much who he offends. If he's coming here and I can use that friendship to gain information for the Cabal, then we'd be foolish not to take advantage of the situation, don't you think?"

Tiji didn't answer, wishing someone *had* thought to revoke her diplomatic status and send her home. She wasn't ready to make a decision like this. She was a slave. She was trained to gather information, not decide what to do with it. She certainly didn't have the authority to order a duchess to become a spy.

But Arkady was looking at her like she expected an answer.

"Perhaps we should get word to Declan . . ."

"Cayal could be on his way here now," Arkady pointed out. "I really don't think we have the time."

"What do *you* think we should do?" she asked, to stall having to come up with an answer of her own.

"I think we should take advantage of whatever is at hand."

"Like the Immortal Prince, for instance?"

"And Chintara . . . or Kinta, if you'd prefer to call her that. You claim she *slapped* him?"

Tiji nodded. "Like she really meant it, too."

"Then perhaps that's where we start," the duchess announced with a determined set to her shoulders that Tiji really didn't like the look of. "Isn't the purpose here, after all, to gain intelligence about the Tide Lords in the hope of finding a weakness? If Kinta and Cayal are at odds, she may be willing to share what she knows about him."

Tiji shook her head. "I don't think so, your grace. That would mean confronting Kinta and telling her you know who she is."

"Exactly."

"But you don't know what she'll do."

"I doubt she'll strike me down," the duchess replied, quite unconcerned. "I'm still the wife of the Glaeban ambassador and she's still the Imperator's Consort. That's a fiction she needs to maintain until Brynden returns. And it's not as if I'm going to burst in there and threaten to blackmail her. On the contrary, we have a great deal more in common than we first assumed."

"Like what?" Tiji asked, not liking this plan at all. "You've both been dumped by the Immortal Prince?"

Surprisingly, Arkady wasn't offended by the suggestion. "In a manner of speaking. There were extenuating circumstances, but in the strictest sense, you're right. Cayal was happy to see us go our separate ways once I was of no further use to him. It wouldn't surprise me in the slightest to learn he'd done the same to Kinta."

That was something Tiji hadn't known, only guessed. *Tides, could this get any messier?* Still, it suggested an interesting twist to Arkady's relationship with the immortal. "You must hate him a lot for doing that to you."

Somewhat to Tiji's surprise, the duchess shook her head with a sorrowful little smile. "My life would be a lot less complicated if that were actually the case, Tiji."

The Crasii was shocked by such an admission. "But you just said he used you and then he abandoned you. How could you still love . . . or ever trust again . . . someone who did that to you?"

Arkady studied her for a moment, and then nodded, as if she'd come to a conclusion about her companion. "You've never been in love, have you, Tiji?"

"What's that got to do with anything?"

"If you had, you'd understand relationships are never so black and white."

"They certainly don't seem to be when *you're* involved," Tiji agreed, a little shocked at herself for daring to voice such an opinion aloud.

Fortunately, the Duchess of Lebec was more tolerant than the average high-born Glaeban. She smiled. "I fear you're coming to know me far too well, Tiji. A scary thought, given the brevity of our acquaintance."

Tiji shook her head. "I still don't think you should just barge into the royal seraglium and accuse the Imperator's Consort of being an immortal, your grace."

"Is there any doubt in your mind that she isn't?"

Reluctantly, Tiji shook her head. "None at all."

"Then the die is cast. Before long, she'll be announcing it to the whole world, Tiji. What do we have to lose?"

Chapter 30

It was a few days after his conversation with Maralyce before Declan made the decision to move on, but not, as he'd originally intended, to return to Herino. He was heading for Caelum, certain that was where he was needed most.

Declan had stopped pressing Shalimar to leave with him. Now that Maralyce had alerted him to his grandfather's condition, it was clear the old man was in constant pain. The shuffling walk Declan had always attributed to advancing decrepitude, he knew now was caused by the oncoming Tide. The constant grimaces every time the old man sat down or tried to climb to his feet had a far more ominous source than simple stiffness of the joints. Knowing he was helpless to do anything to ease his grandfather's hurts just made it that much harder to watch.

"Shouldn't you be heading *home*?" Shalimar asked, as he watched Declan stuffing the supplies Maralyce had begrudgingly allowed him into his pack. The old man was sitting at Maralyce's table, nursing a chipped cup of warm tea. He hadn't moved since Declan started packing.

"I know what's happening at home," Declan said. "But I've no idea what's going on in Caelum. For all I know, Jaxyn's presence in Glaeba with Diala is part of a much grander scheme the Empress of the Five Realms has in store for us. I think I'd like to find out before I recommend any course of action to the Cabal."

Shalimar glared at Maralyce. "Did you put him up to this?"

The immortal shrugged. "I might have mentioned that with the Cabal being run from Glaeba these days, it was far easier for others to keep an eye on what was happening there, than in other places."

"I left Daly Bridgeman in charge," Declan reminded his grandfather. "He was going crazy in retirement. He won't mind if I take a bit longer to get home." He tied the pack off and dumped it on the floor. "There's an argument my position as the King's Spymaster is redundant, anyway," he added. "Given the immortals are on the loose."

"You just can't walk away from your responsibilities like this, Declan. I thought I taught you better than that."

"My responsibility is to the Cabal of the Tarot, isn't it? The whole spymaster thing has always just been a convenient front for what was really going on. Why are you worried I'll get in trouble for neglecting my pretend job?"

"Let him go, old man," Maralyce said, before Shalimar could answer him. "Jaxyn and Diala might be planning to move on your king, but the fate of a child hangs in the balance in Caelum. In the general scheme of things, Declan probably can't stop what's going to happen once the Tide has returned, but perhaps, if the Caelish are warned, they'll not throw away the life of a child on something so futile."

"You don't think the Caelish deserve everything likely to happen to them?" Shalimar said, directing his question to Maralyce. "This ridiculous custom of theirs—marrying off children to secure the throne— that's what's going to land them in this mess you're predicting."

"I doubt they intended it to go this far," Maralyce replied. "In fact, as far as I can recall, it started out as a way of protecting the heir to the throne. They have no concept of, or wish for, a regency in Caelum, so if the heir is too young to rule, the only option is to find a spouse for them who can run the show until they come of age."

"But Caelum already has a queen," Declan said, wondering how far in the past she was referring to. With her lifespan, she might be referring to a custom that had its start half a millennium ago. "What need to hand the reins of power to a child and an unknown or untested pretender now?"

Maralyce shook her head. "Queen Jilna was the wife of the late king, not a direct descendant herself. The throne belongs to her child and she's only clung to it as long as she has because she's been actively and openly searching for a husband for her daughter."

Declan studied Maralyce with a curious frown. "You're remarkably well informed about the goings-on in Caelum for someone who claims they have no interest in the affairs of our world."

"An hour and a few ales at Clyden's Inn every decade or so is enough to catch anybody up on current affairs," Maralyce said. "You should keep someone permanently stationed in the corner of Clyden's taproom, you know. You'd get more useful intelligence from that place in a week than half a dozen informers hanging around the streets of Lebec could stumble across in a month."

"I'll bear that in mind," Declan said. He turned to Shalimar. "What do you think I should do?"

"Go home," his grandfather replied. "But as you're obviously not going to listen to me, my suggestion would be to make contact with the Caelish spymaster and warn him their soon-to-be king is an impostor."

Declan wasn't sure there was much point in that. "Do you really think that will stop them?"

"Might slow 'em down a tad," Maralyce suggested.

"Or tip Syrolee's hand that the Cabal is on to them?"

"It's a risk," Shalimar agreed. "But a fairly safe one, I think. Even if the immortals remember the Cabal of the Tarot from before the last Cataclysm, I doubt they'll think we represent any sort of real danger to them."

Shalimar was probably right in that. There was a reason, after all, that the Cabal went to such pains to maintain secrecy. "Then that's what I'll do. I'll talk to Ricard Li when I get to Caelum and warn him of the danger. Which really just leaves getting there." He turned to Maralyce. "Do you know the way to Caelum?"

"West," the immortal replied unhelpfully.

"I was hoping you'd be a little more specific."

"You want me to reveal every secret track through my mountains, do you? Just because you're too lazy to go the long way round?"

"Time is of the essence, my lady."

"To you, maybe, boy. It means absolutely nothing to me."

Declan looked at his grandfather.

The old man shrugged, and took a sip of his tea. "Don't ask me, lad. I've no idea how to get to Caelum from here."

He turned back to Maralyce. "I can cut through the mine, can't I?"

Declan waited a long time before Maralyce reluctantly nodded. "I suppose."

"How many weeks would it cut off the trip?"

"Most of 'em."

"What do you mean?"

"You could be on the other side of the lake in four days," she admitted with some reluctance. "If I was in the mood to show you the way. Which I ain't."

Declan turned to his grandfather for help, certain there was nothing he could say that would influence the immortal.

"You could give him a map," Shalimar suggested.

"He'd be hopelessly lost within a day."

"At least you'd be rid of me," Declan pointed out.

At that suggestion, her eyes lit up. "*Promise*?"

"Promise what?" Declan asked with a smile. "To be gone or to be hopelessly lost within a day?"

The immortal shrugged. "Don't much care, one way or the other, just so long as you're out from underfoot."

"Give me the map, my lady, and you'll not hear from me again. For a good long while," he added as an afterthought.

Maralyce shook her head. "Tides, you're as bad as he is."

"Who?"

"I think she means me," Shalimar said. He smiled fondly at the cranky immortal. "Thank you, Maralyce."

"Don't thank me, you foolish old man," she complained, turning to take down several sheets of paper and an ink pot from the shelf by the door. "He'll get himself killed, sure as I'm immortal, and I ain't going looking for him to give him a decent burial just to make you happy, neither."

Several hours later, his pack on his back, a lantern in one hand and Maralyce's precious map in the other, Declan turned to his hostess, studying her curiously in the cool, late afternoon sun. He'd already said goodbye to his grandfather in the cabin. Shalimar didn't come to see him off, having decided the wind was too cold for his tired old bones. It had been a brusque and entirely uncomfortable farewell.

Although neither of them was willing to admit it, they'd both known it was likely he'd never see his grandfather again.

"How far has the Tide come in, anyway?" he asked, forcing the notion of Shalimar's impending death from his mind. He couldn't afford to dwell on that now. And hard as it was for Declan to accept the fact, in the care of Maralyce the old man was probably in the best place he could be to face the onslaught of the rising Tide.

"What do you mean?"

"I mean how much power do you . . . or to be more specific, do the *other* Tide Lords have by now?"

Maralyce hesitated and then she turned and waved her arm. Across the yard, a pile of loose shingles stacked beside the lean-to began to scatter and tumble across the muddy yard as if being tossed by the breeze.

Declan watched the demonstration with interest. "Ah, the old falling shingles trick. I'll be on the lookout for that one."

"Don't get smart with me, boy," Maralyce said.

"I'm sorry, but I'm not sure I get the point of your demonstration."

"Tide magic is elemental, Declan," she explained. "That's what we do. It's *all* we can do. The extent to which we control the elements varies, according to individual talent and our willingness to master what we do. That makes Lukys the most dangerous of us all, because that's pretty much all he does—look for ways to hone his skill. The only other immortal who was ever his student for long enough to be anywhere near as dangerous is Cayal. The rest of them think they know it all, so they tend to be a great deal more ham-fisted when it comes to settling their disputes."

"It's not lack of power that causes the Cataclysms," Declan said. "Is that what you're saying? It's a lack of finesse?"

She nodded. "That's one way of looking at it."

"So what do I have to fear?"

To Declan's surprise, Maralyce answered him without hesitation. "Syrolee, more than most, is the one to watch out for. She's not even as powerful as Engarhod, and she certainly wields nowhere near the power Elyssa or Tryan can summon when they're in the mood. But she rules the roost, make no mistake about it. Whether through fear, emotional manipulation or just outright sneakiness, Syrolee is the empress of that family, sure as she used to be Empress of the Five Realms."

"But what can she actually *do*?"

"Not much, when it comes to the Tide. Tryan and Elyssa, though . . . by now they'll be able to affect the weather, manipulate water, air, earth and even fire to some degree. We could rustle up a fairly short, localised storm at a pinch, but it's a bit early for any of us to be able to cause the sort of calamitous weather Cayal is famous for." When she noticed his expression, she frowned. "Don't glare at me like I'm trying to dodge the question. It's really not an easy thing to answer. We all have different areas that interest us; all have different reasons to have mastered what we know. I can tunnel through a mountain with a wave of my hand, but I could never have caused the storm that flooded Glaeba and gave rise to your Great Lakes."

"So the short answer," Declan concluded, adjusting his pack to a more comfortable position, "is that you really don't know what the others are capable of."

The immortal thought on that for a moment and then nodded. "Pretty much."

"You've been a great help, my lady."

She glared at him. "Don't get snippy at me, boy. I've done more for you and your kind than any of the others of my kind, and all out of the goodness of my heart, and for no other reason. A bit of gratitude wouldn't go astray, you know."

Declan smiled. "Forgive me, my lady. I am grateful to you, everything you've done for us and everything you're going to do to ease Shalimar's pain."

"That'd be a real nice apology if I thought for a moment you meant it."

"Family shouldn't need to apologise to each other," Declan said, watching her closely.

Maralyce didn't reply. In fact, she didn't react at all to his suggestion. She just turned her back on him, heading back to the cabin.

"Does Shalimar know you're his mother?" he called after her.

After a few steps she stopped and turned to look at him. The immortal seemed to debate something within herself and then she shrugged. "Reckon he must. He ain't stupid. We just never talk about it."

"You'll take good care of him, won't you?"

"I'll see him through it," she agreed, which Declan figured was as close as she was likely to come to admitting she cared for the old man, or that she had any familial ties to him.

He grinned then, wondering how far he could push her. "May I call you Great-grandmamma?"

Maralyce's eyes narrowed. Her voice was flat. "Only if you want me to strike you down where you stand, boy."

Declan didn't doubt for a moment that she meant it. "Will I see you again, my lady?"

"Maybe. I ain't goin' nowhere."

With that, Maralyce turned back toward the cabin and disappeared inside, leaving Declan alone in the chilly yard, standing at the maw of the mine, armed with a lamp, a hand-drawn map and not much more than the word of a grumpy immortal to see him through the labyrinthine tunnels to Caelum on the other side.

Chapter 31

Arkady barely slept after her discussion with Tiji. The knowledge Kinta was immortal, the news Cayal was here in the city . . . It was too much to take in all at once. She tossed and turned all through the steamy night, her skin clammy, her pulse racing, and woke the next morning feeling as if she'd spent all night engaged in hard physical labour.

She'd decided nothing, resolved nothing and achieved nothing. By the time she sat down to breakfast with Stellan, Arkady had no idea what she was going to say to Kinta when she confronted her, or what she would do if Cayal showed up.

A part of her was terrified by the prospect of meeting Cayal again, another part excited, yet another part coldly indifferent to the notion. Her feelings for the Immortal Prince were complicated. Part love, part contempt, part fear, part fascination, part lust and part gratitude, if it was possible to feel all those emotions for one person, at the same time.

"You look distracted this morning."

Arkady realised Stellan was speaking to her. She picked up the teapot and poured herself a second cup, mostly to give her something solid and practical to do. "Am I? I'm sorry. I don't mean to be rude. More tea?"

"You weren't being rude," Stellan assured her, pushing his cup across the small breakfast table toward her. "You just seem to be miles away."

"It was so hot last night. I didn't sleep well." She figured she was better telling a half-truth than a complete lie.

"What are your plans for the day?" he asked, accepting the fresh cup of tea. "Are you staying in, or planning to beggar me in the Ramahn silver markets?"

She smiled, appreciating his attempt to lighten the mood. "Much as beggaring you sounds like fun, Stellan, I'm actually due back at the palace. The Imperator's Consort has summoned me, yet again."

He sipped his tea, nodding. "You two seem to be firm friends these days."

"We have a great deal in common," Arkady said, certain Stellan would be horrified to realise their most common ground was whatever patch of Amyrantha the Immortal Prince was standing on.

"It's causing a great deal of comment."

"Is that a bad thing?"

"I haven't decided yet. It's certainly got the ambassador from Senestra in a flap. His wife's attempts to befriend the Imperator's Consort resulted in her being imprisoned for a week. And all over something she was wearing, as he tells it."

"According to Kinta, it had nothing to do with what she was wearing. The woman called her a slut."

Stellan's eyes widened. "Surely not?"

Arkady nodded. "That's what the consort told me. The ambassador is a member of some strict Senestran religious cult that still worships the Tide Lords. They were having a discussion about heirs one day, and the ambassador's wife asked Chintara when she was planning to produce one for Torlenia. Chintara made some flippant comment about it happening in the fullness of time, but in the meantime, the practising was a lot of fun. At that, the silly woman went crazy, according to Chintara. She started ranting about a union between a man and woman being sacred and how sex was only for the purpose of procreation and how it was an offence against the Lord of Temperance to indulge in anything smacking of recreational copulation. Kinta got so sick of her lecturing she had the woman tossed in a cell until she calmed down."

"Are you serious?" Stellan chuckled. "Tides. I don't blame her. I would have done the same."

Arkady laughed too, more over the knowledge Stellan had no notion who the Lord of Temperance was, than the humorous anecdote she'd just related. "Not sure how the story the consort had her thrown in a dungeon for wearing the wrong colour got started, but Kinta assures me that's what really happened."

Stellan's smile faded. "That's the third time."

"The third time?"

"The third time you've called the Imperator's Consort Kinta, rather than Chintara."

"It's a nickname," she said. "A diminutive of her proper name. As you say, we've become firm friends."

"You certainly have," Stellan agreed. Arkady couldn't tell if he believed the lie. "You will try to avoid offending her and getting yourself thrown in gaol, won't you?"

She smiled. "I'll do my best, Stellan."

Before her husband could answer, Dashin Deray interrupted them. A slender, short-sighted young man, he was the younger son of the ruling family of Whitewater and Stellan's deputy here in Ramahn. He bowed to Arkady and then turned to the ambassador to inform him an important message had arrived from Herino by bird. Stellan drank down the last of his tea and with an apology and absent-minded kiss to his wife's cheek, hurried off with Dashin to attend to business.

As soon as they were gone, Arkady jumped to her feet, tossed her napkin on her uneaten breakfast, and hurried back to the seraglium where her phaeton was waiting to take her to the royal palace.

Her heart pounding, she settled in to the seat and pulled her shroud down over her face as the carriage jerked forward. Somehow, between the embassy and the palace, she needed to prepare herself for what might happen when she confronted the immortal posing as the Imperator's Consort, and told her the game was up.

"Are you unwell, Arkady?" Chintara enquired as the Duchess of Lebec took a seat opposite her in the main reception hall of the royal seraglium. "You look quite flushed."

"I'm quite well, my lady," she replied, smoothing down her skirts so her companion wouldn't notice how hard her hands were shaking. "Can I . . . may I ask you a question?"

Chintara seemed intrigued. "That *was* a question, Arkady."

"Another one, then."

"Ask away."

"Would you consider us friends?"

Chintara was silent for a moment, studying her guest, and then she shrugged. "I suppose I would."

"And would you agree friends should be honest with each other?"

Chintara laughed. "Tides, Arkady! You sound as if you're about to tell me I have bad breath or an offensive body odour."

"Actually, Chintara, I was going to ask you if you were immortal," she said, "and if your real name is Kinta."

Her words silenced Chintara's laugh as if a bucket of cold water had been thrown over her. The consort rose to her feet. "Let's take a turn around the gardens."

Arkady did as Chintara bid, following her out through the arched doorway into the extravagantly lush gardens, relieved the woman hadn't struck her down where she stood. Chintara's reaction surprised her, though. She'd been half expecting her to laugh off the accusation; to deny it and accuse Arkady of being crazy.

The consort remained silent, however, leading Arkady through the dense foliage of the seraglium gardens until they reached the rotunda in the centre. Several cushions and a low table took up most of the small pavilion that seemed to have been carved from some sort of blond wood that certainly wasn't native to this land. In fact, it was like nothing Arkady had seen since arriving in Torlenia. Chintara indicated Arkady should take a seat, but she remained standing, walking to the edge of the small platform to look out over the gardens.

"There's a saying here: the seraglium walls have better hearing than the canines."

"You've not answered my question," Arkady reminded her.

"What would be the point?"

"I expected you to deny it."

"Then you're one up on me, my dear, because I never—not even for a moment—thought you even believed in the immortals, let alone knew how to spot one."

"You're not the first one I've met," Arkady told her.

That got Kinta's attention. She turned from examining the gardens and sat herself down on the cushions opposite Arkady, staring at her with a piercing and quite unsettling gaze.

"You've met *another* immortal?"

A little surprised at how ridiculously ordinary the conversation seemed, she nodded and held up her hand, counting them off on her fingers. "I've met Jaxyn, who's currently in Herino. And I've met Diala—only I didn't know it was her at the time. And Maralyce—"

Kinta looked shocked. "You've met *Maralyce*, too? Tides, woman, how did you manage that?"

"It's a long story," Arkady said, before adding, carefully, "and I've met Cayal."

A tense silence descended over the rotunda. The temperature seemed to drop. Arkady knew she was imagining it. Kinta wasn't powerful enough to control the weather like that, but it felt real, just the same.

"Recently?" the immortal enquired in a flat, dangerous voice.

"Several months ago," she explained. "He was incarcerated in Lebec Prison for a time."

"What was he doing in prison?"

"I believe he was trying to get himself beheaded."

A humourless smile creased the immortal's lips. "As we're here discussing him, I think I'm safe in assuming he was unsuccessful in his quest?"

"He was. But he escaped and took me hostage. That's how I met Maralyce. He fled into the Shevron Mountains and took me with him."

Kinta nodded. "Maralyce would aid him if he asked. She owes him a debt."

"For what?" Arkady asked, before she could stop herself.

"He and Lukys saved her from a marauding mob, once. She remembers that sort of thing."

"What about you?"

"What about me?"

"Would *you* aid him if he came to you for help?"

"Do you think he might?"

Arkady didn't answer, letting Kinta draw what inference she would from her silence.

It didn't take the immortal long to come to the right conclusion. "You know he's here in Ramahn." Not a question. A flat statement of fact.

"I've heard rumours. I've not seen him myself, though."

Although she said nothing, this answer seemed to please Kinta.

"I am curious," Arkady added, aware she might be pushing her luck too far. "I thought your love affair with Cayal ended with the last Cataclysm."

Kinta didn't answer immediately. Arkady let the silence drag on, mostly because she had no idea what to say, either.

"Who told you that?"

"It's common belief among us mere mortals."

To Arkady's intense relief, a small smile flickered across Kinta's unlined face. "You mere mortals, eh? Trust me, Arkady, there is nothing *mere* about *you*."

"I appreciate the compliment, my lady, but . . ."

"But you want to know what happened?"

Arkady nodded.

"Are you asking as a historian or as a woman?"

"Pardon?"

"I mean, my dear, is your interest in the events that brought about the last Cataclysm historical or personal?"

For no good reason she could think of, Arkady responded with the truth. "A little of both, actually."

Her answer didn't seem to surprise Kinta in the slightest. *Maybe, when you're as old as she is, nothing surprises you anymore.*

"There's not much to tell, Arkady. Immortal we may be, but we brought all our human failings with us. It was just one of those things that happen . . ."

"Just one of those *things*? It ended in a global catastrophe, my lady."

She shrugged, as if such minor inconveniences were of no concern. "We had no way of knowing how it would end. If one rules their life by the vague notion of what *might* happen, they'll never do anything. Fear paralyses all living creatures, Arkady. You should remember that."

"But you and Brynden were together for so long . . ."

"And we will be again, the Tide willing," Kinta said, confirming what Tiji had suspected all along. Kinta was here in the palace to secure the throne of Torlenia for the Lord of Reckoning.

"Will you tell me what happened?"

"Are you sure you *want* to know?"

Cayal had asked her the same question once. Settling back against the cushions, Arkady nodded. There was no going back now.

"Yes, my lady," she said. "I *really* want to know."

Chapter 32

We were always friendly, Cayal, Brynden and I, although I'd hesitate to call us friends. My Brynden is not easy to befriend, truth be told. He's an abrupt and pedantic sort of fellow. He's a warrior.

Fyrennese warriors have a very strict code of honour. Other immortals have laughed at this, over the years, but Cayal understood, I think. He might have teased Brynden about many of his peculiarities, but the Immortal Prince was wise enough never to mock a warrior's honour.

This was back before the last Cataclysm. The last Tide was a small one, not long out, not long in returning, but we'd barely recovered from the devastation. Amyrantha wasn't nearly as sophisticated as it is now. The mortals were on the uphill climb back to civilisation, but they weren't there yet.

Syrolee and her lot had settled in Tenacia once more, but what happened with Kentravyon scared them. We'd never acted in concert before. I'm not even sure if they realised we could. Whatever the reason, news that a group of us had banded together and immobilised Kentravyon—more or less permanently—put the fear of the Tide into Syrolee and Engarhod.

For the first time in five thousand years, they asked for a meeting. They wanted to make peace, they claimed; to delineate the boundaries of each Tide Lord's territory during the coming High Tide.

It wasn't a bad idea, actually, even if it was motivated by nothing but abject terror, so we agreed to the meeting. With the Tide on the rise, for the first time in thousands of years, all the immortals began to gather in the one place.

The meeting was to take place in Tenacia and Syrolee took her role as host very seriously. She provided us with a villa just outside the partially rebuilt city of Libeth. It was a sumptuous mansion, a relic of the previous age, restored almost to what it had been in its heyday. It was just a house, really; somewhere we could live while the negotiations were going on, Crasii slaves to wait on us hand and foot, the best foods, copious amounts of wine, and endless entertainments . . .

Syrolee had good reason to try to make us comfortable for an extended length of time. Finding an immortal with no wish to be found is no easy task, even for another immortal. We were among the first to get there. Cayal and Lukys had already arrived—they'd been on their way back from Jelidia after checking on Kentravyon when they got Syrolee's invitation, I believe. Word arrived not long after Brynden and I did, that Maralyce was due within the month. Of the lesser immortals, not all had been contacted yet.

Pellys had been located, however—in Senestra. He was quite taken with the amphibious Crasii, many of whom had made their home in the Senestran swamps after the last Cataclysm, so he wasn't that hard to locate. Brynden and Lukys offered to travel to Senestra to fetch him.

I stayed in Libeth. In the villa. With Cayal.

You'll get no prize for guessing what happened. We were stuck in that villa with nobody but ourselves for company for months. The other immortals hadn't arrived. Cayal and Tryan had both given their word—albeit reluctantly—they would stay away from each other until the negotiations started, and in Tenacia, that meant not venturing far from the villa . . . this was Tryan's turf, after all.

Neither of us meant for it to turn out the way it did. It just happened. Not right away, of course, but you know how it is, when you're stuck somewhere with someone and there's nothing else to do and nowhere to go. You start to talk, first about ordinary, mundane things, and then as the nights grow longer, and the weather grows colder, you move a little closer for warmth and you find yourself pouring your heart out to somebody who nods and smiles sympathetically in all the right places. Before long, you start to think this is the soul who *really* understands you. The one destiny *wanted* you to meet . . .

You even start to wonder if *this* is the man you're meant to be with, not the man you've spent the last seven thousand years loving.

Tides, I don't know what I was thinking. I told Cayal things during those long cold nights I've never shared with Brynden. As I mentioned before, my man is an abrupt, unsympathetic sort of fellow, not the kind to sit up half the night letting you ramble, while you try to explain something to him that you can't even explain to yourself. And it wasn't all me. Cayal did the same—this was a mutual sharing of dark secrets and hidden longings. He told me some amazing things about his life; some of the things he'd done and more than one thing he wished he hadn't. I'm quite sure he'd never told another living soul the thoughts and feelings he shared with me that winter. And while I'm loath to admit it now, at the time it was cathartic for both of us.

There are some things you can only tell another immortal. Things only another immortal would understand.

And it was the first time, I think, Cayal openly admitted he was trying to find a way to die.

In hindsight, I think that's what weakened my resolve.

God, women can be fools. In fairness to Cayal, I really don't think he told me of his wish to end it all just to invoke my sympathy. He was beyond that, by then. He really, truly wants to die, and I think he told me about it because he thought I might understand why.

I don't, in case you're wondering. I cannot conceive of not wanting to live. For me immortality is a gift, a precious gift, to be rejoiced in every day. For Cayal it has become a burden, every day another to be borne rather than relished, to be endured rather than enjoyed.

I remember the moment it changed from friendship to danger like it was yesterday. It had been unseasonably warm, so we'd gone out onto the terrace to watch the sunset. There was a fountain in the centre of the courtyard. It no longer worked but there was still a pool at its base. We'd kicked our shoes off and were paddling in the cool water. It was stocked with brightly coloured decorative fish—by Syrolee, I presume—that swam past us, kissing our toes gently as we sat on the edge of the pool. I remember laughing and snatching my feet out of the water as one brushed against the sole of my foot.

"Tides, I wish I could still laugh like that," Cayal sighed.

I looked at him. "Is something wrong with your throat?"

"Something's wrong with me."

That struck me as being very funny. "Would you like my help compiling a list?"

"Haven't you ever wanted to die, Kinta?" He wasn't smiling, but I didn't realise yet that he was serious.

"Tides, no! Why would I want that?"

"Because this is never going to end."

"And this bothers you, does it?"

"Doesn't it bother you?"

"Not in the slightest."

He was silent for a time before asking, "How many languages can you speak?"

I shrugged. "Fourteen, perhaps, maybe more. I've never really counted."

"And what happens when you know them all?"

"What?"

"When you've done it all? Seen it all? Been everywhere? Thought everything? What then? Will you just do it all again?"

"That's an absurd question," I said. "When would we ever reach that point?"

"We're immortal, Kinta. Sooner or later, there will be nothing left for us to do, nothing to see, nothing to experience. I'm already sick of it. I can't bear the thought of spending eternity like this."

"Get yourself beheaded," I joked. "Then you can start all over again."

Cayal didn't share my amusement. "That's a stupid idea."

"It worked for Pellys."

"Have you *seen* Pellys?" he asked.

"I don't think he was all there before you lopped his head off, Cayal. You can't blame the decapitation for that."

"Don't you remember what happened when I did? He destroyed Magreth while his head was growing back."

"And you're concerned about doing something similar, are you? How remarkably conscientious of you, Cayal."

"I want to die, Kinta. I'm not really interested in taking half the planet with me."

"Noble sentiments, my friend, but hardly reason to stop you if you were serious about it."

"What do *you* suggest, then?"

"Have yourself decapitated at Low Tide." I wasn't serious. I certainly never thought he'd try it.

There's a lot I was wrong about when it came to dealing with Cayal.

But I was warming to this idea, even if I thought it ludicrous. "Think about it. There'd be no Tide magic to run out of control while your head's growing back and you're still figuring out which way is up. When you've recovered, your mind will be a blank slate and you can start all over again. You never know, maybe the next Cayal won't mind being immortal."

I looked at him, expecting to see him smiling, but he was staring at me, silent, watchful, thoughtful . . .

There is a moment that comes between a man and a woman, a moment in which fate gives you an opportunity to go on, or turn away. This was that moment for Cayal and I, and I blame myself as much as him for not turning away. It's a moment that demands mental, rather than verbal communication. You're both wondering "should I or shouldn't I," hoping somehow with a look, a blink, a twitch, perhaps, the other will tell you what you want to know and you won't have to be the one who makes the first move and risks the rejection you're half expecting. It's a moment that lasts for a fraction of a second, and yet—when you're experiencing it—that fleeting moment feels like an hour.

I can't tell you who moved first, only that we kissed and the result was too explosive to comprehend.

Cayal was desperately seeking a reason to live, and I think I was looking for a taste of the passion I'd once shared with Brynden. When we were young and first in love, we were so *alive*, more alive than we'd ever been, before or since, even with immortality thrown in for good measure. Tides, I let Brynden immolate me to prove his love, that's how passionate we were for each other, and for a time, I thought I'd recaptured that feeling with Cayal.

This may sound odd, but when I was with Cayal, I didn't feel immortal.

The urgency of mortality was upon me, and I think that's what seduced me, rather than Cayal.

They say love is blind, but lust has no sense or feeling at all. And I was lost to it.

Much more than Cayal, I learned later.

But that was a problem for another time. For the present, we were alone, the Tide was rising rapidly and our emotions with it. We were quietly desperate for something we didn't even know we wanted. Neither of us stopped to think of the consequences of our affair.

And then Lukys arrived back in Libeth, announcing that Brynden and Pellys were only days behind him.

Cayal, quite matter-of-factly, suggested we put an end to our affair as soon as he heard Brynden was on the way home. I was stunned, hurt and not nearly so ready to admit this had been nothing more than a fling. Tides. I'd risked everything for this. I wasn't prepared to just shrug it off and pretend it had never happened. It wasn't in my nature. It's not in the nature of any Fyrennese warrior to walk away from something they had committed their heart to.

We have the courage of our convictions, we Fyrennese.

We're prepared to stand by what we've done.

We would, I informed Cayal, confront Brynden. We'd tell him the truth. We'd explain it wasn't a deliberate betrayal. And when this meeting of Syrolee's was done, we would leave and go somewhere we could be together.

Cayal was less than enthusiastic about my decision, but I was too taken with my plans for this brave new future to notice. And I'd forgotten what drove him. This was a man looking for a way to die. His lust for me wasn't love; it was his desperate need to find some reason to live. I couldn't see that defying Brynden might just be the out Cayal was looking for.

After days of disagreeing with me, he changed his mind, seemingly on a whim. But he didn't want to confront Brynden, he just wanted to leave. He told me he just wanted to be with me. Forever.

And I believed him.

Before Brynden arrived back in Libeth, we'd fled, looking for somewhere—so I thought—where we could be free to love each other for the rest of eternity, as I was convinced destiny had deemed we must.

Tides, what a fool I was. I think I knew Brynden would follow us. I'm certain now Cayal knew he would. We certainly made no real attempt to hide our trail. When I questioned him about it, Cayal promised me there was nothing Brynden could throw at us he couldn't counter. I had no reason not to believe him. He's a Tide Lord, after all, as is Brynden. They are as powerful as each other. Cayal may even have had the edge, in an open battle of wills.

In fact, in hindsight, I'm quite certain he could have stopped Brynden. If he'd wanted to.

And that was my mistake. He didn't want to.

I'd forgotten Cayal wanted to die.

The Immortal Prince didn't run away with me because he feared Brynden's wrath. He ran away with me to provoke it.

You know the rest, I suppose. It's the stuff of legend, after all. Your silly Tarot has the right of it, for once. Brynden found us eventually— I'm fairly certain that was Cayal's doing, too—and he brought the wrath of the heavens down upon us.

We were in a ship at the time, sailing toward the Glaeban mainland. The flaming rock he threw at us was the size of a house and it hit us square amidships. I suspect Brynden had help. The hit was too precise to be a random or chance encounter, and Brynden would never have thought about pulling a rock from the heavens down upon us on his own. Lukys was with him in Tenacia, remember, and this reeks of something he'd have a hand in. He may have combined his power with Brynden's to do it.

I wouldn't have thought the Tide high enough or any of us powerful enough to do such a thing on their own, but with Lukys, you can never be sure.

That was your last Cataclysm, by the way. Even with the Tide up, there was little any of the immortals, even the Tide Lords among us, could do to fix the damage caused by a meteor so large smashing into the ocean, although I hear Tryan and Elyssa did try to ease the backlash as best they could. Syrolee had plans to rule the world, after all, and a global catastrophe was likely to interfere with that. Their efforts did little, in the end: barely a century later the Tide receded and—as we always do—the immortals stumbled back into hiding to wait until it returned.

Chapter 33

If Kinta had any more to add to her tale, Arkady wasn't going to hear it today. Nitta arrived with lunch, interrupting them. She was more than a little grateful for the distraction. Some elements of Kinta's tale were horribly reminiscent of her own encounter with Cayal, forcing her to look at her relationship with the Immortal Prince through rather more cynical eyes.

The way it came about, the isolation, the long talks in the middle of the night, the heart-to-heart exchanges that preceded any physical contact . . . Even the desperate need to find something to live for that seemed to pervade everything Cayal did and said, and the callous and unthinking way he'd brushed Kinta aside when he realised Brynden was heading home—all of it was hauntingly familiar.

Arkady hoped none of her anguish reflected on her face. She feigned boredom as Nitta stood at the entrance to the rotunda supervising the other slaves laying out the meal of sliced meats, flat bread and various exotic fruits beaded with condensation. After a time, even Kinta grew impatient with their fussing and ordered the slaves gone.

Once they were alone again, the immortal fixed her gaze on her companion. To Arkady's intense relief, Kinta didn't seem to think her tale was anything more to her audience than a fascinating anecdote about the strange and sometimes irresponsible behaviour of the immortals. "So, now you know the sordid truth."

"Have you spoken to Brynden since the Cataclysm?"

"Not in person."

"But you're hoping to see him soon."

Kinta smiled. "You seem very certain about my intentions."

"You're consumed by preparations for an upcoming meeting with someone you hope to impress, my lady. I can't imagine any other soul on Amyrantha who'd fit that description."

"I'm not used to having a mortal read me so easily."

"I meant no offence."

"I'm not offended, Arkady. Disturbed a little, but not offended."

"Have you been able to heal the breach between you and Brynden?"

"I'm in the process of doing so."

"By handing him the throne of Torlenia?"

Kinta leaned back against the cushions. "You think that's what I'm doing?"

"You married the Imperator of Torlenia for some *other* reason?"

"I might have."

"My husband describes him as a callow boy. That's not the sort of man a Fyrennese warrior would choose as a husband unless there was something else in it for her."

"You dare a lot to accuse me of such a thing, Arkady. Aren't you worried I'll have you thrown into a dungeon?"

"Actually, I think you're relieved to have someone you can talk to," Arkady said, aware of the risk she was taking, but reasoning she was long past the point where it mattered. If Kinta was planning to do anything to her, it would have happened when she first accused her of being immortal. "How did you manage it, by the way? In a society as constrained as this one, you wouldn't have had the opportunity to seduce him."

"It was an arranged marriage," Kinta replied. "All high-born marriages are brokered in such a fashion in Torlenia. He'd never laid eyes on Chintara before the wedding. Tides, I don't think her own father had seen her since she was twelve."

"What happened to the real Chintara?"

"She's dead."

Arkady wasn't sure how to respond to such a brazen admission, and in the end, she didn't have to. Kinta must have guessed what she was thinking.

The immortal laughed. "Tides! You think I murdered her and left her lying on the side of the road somewhere, don't you?"

"You'd not be the first immortal to do such a thing. And her name *is* the Torlenian derivative of your Fyrennese name."

"Don't be absurd, Arkady. You're thinking of a chinta, which is nothing but a smelly little rodent. Chintara had her name chosen for her long before I came along to replace her."

So much for that clever theory, Arkady thought, wondering at the bizarre coincidence that had led Declan to conclude the Imperator's Consort was an immortal because of her name, when in fact, it was nothing but serendipity.

"Rest your mind, Arkady," Chintara continued. "The real Chintara died of natural causes. It was dysentery, if you must know. She came down with it on the journey to Ramahn from her home in the lowlands. I happened to be staying in the village where she took ill, posing as a travelling herb-woman, for want of a better profession. Healers tend to be welcome more often and questioned a little less, when they move among strangers. I was called in to treat her, but she was beyond my ability to help by then without magical intervention and remember, this was more than five years ago. There was no sign of the Tide returning. When her chaperones tried to impress upon me how vital Chintara's survival was, because she was the intended bride of the Imperator of Torlenia, I saw an opportunity."

"So you killed her?"

"Of course not, although I'll admit to not breaking my neck with my efforts to save the poor girl. She died later that night, and would have done even if I hadn't been there. I put on her shroud and told her chaperones—who were all too well-bred and well-mannered to ever look upon the face of their princess—that I was feeling much better, and was ready to continue my journey. We arrived in Torlenia a week later. I married the Imperator, did my duty as his wife and then set out to find Brynden."

"The Imperator must have been very young when you married him."

"Barely fifteen," she agreed.

"That must have been difficult for you."

She smiled. "And rather more than my new husband bargained on. What I've done is probably repugnant to you, Arkady, I realise that. I'm sure, in your perfectly proper world, you'd never dream of marrying anyone for such a cold and calculated reason. But I like to think my young and inexperienced husband has gotten something out of this subterfuge."

"It would account for your influence over him," Arkady said, wondering what Kinta would do if she had any notion of how cold and calculated her own marriage to Stellan had been. "Having the resources and wealth of the Imperator's name to search for Brynden can't have hurt, either."

Kinta shrugged, clearly seeing no reason to apologise for what she'd done. "One would be a fool not to take advantage of such a rare stroke of good fortune, don't you think?"

"You found Brynden?"

"It's not a hard thing to do, if you know where to look."

"Fortunate for you the Tide is now turning."

"I've been alive for eight thousand years, Arkady, and I'm still not prepared to say for certain there's no such thing as fate or destiny."

"Has Brynden forgiven your indiscretion with Cayal?"

"It would appear so. As I said, we've not had a face-to-face conversation since he left Libeth to look for Pellys. It's difficult to read nuances of expression when the message is delivered second-hand."

"Brother Ostin," Arkady said, recalling the saffron-robed monk she'd met in the seraglium several weeks ago. "He's your contact to Brynden, isn't he? What was he saying when I arrived . . . something along the lines of his lord anxiously awaiting the return of his queen to his side, his companion to his table and his lover to his bed?"

"So you were eavesdropping."

"The comment struck me as being rather romantic, my lady."

"And very unlike Brynden," Kinta said. "Hence the reason I worry about the real meaning of his words."

"And what of your husband, my lady?"

"What of him?"

"When Brynden returns, what will happen to the Imperator of Torlenia?"

Kinta was silent for a moment and then she shrugged. "I will leave that decision to Brynden. How do you know the Tide is on the way in?"

"Cayal told me."

That didn't seem to surprise her. "Pity he left his run so late."

"What do you mean?"

"Well, if he was in Glaeba trying to get himself beheaded at Low Tide, he left it too late, didn't he? The Tide is on the way back. If he still holds to his intention to end his suffering without taking the rest of us with him, he's out of luck for the next few hundred years at least."

"Is that how long a High Tide lasts?

"Near enough," the immortal agreed. "This one may last longer. The Tide's been out a very long time which may mean it will come back harder, faster and longer than it has in the past."

Arkady filed that away for future reference and then, while Kinta was still in a garrulous mood, she asked, "What do you think Cayal will do now?"

"I'm not sure. He wants to meet with Brynden."

Arkady hadn't expected such an honest answer, nor had she expected Kinta to so readily confirm Cayal's presence here in Ramahn. It was further proof of what Arkady had begun to suspect months ago, ever since she'd arrived in this city and been so inexplicably befriended by this strangely powerful, yet vulnerable woman—Kinta, the Immortal Charioteer, was glad of someone she could talk to.

But even so, given what she'd just learned about the history between Cayal and the Lord of Reckoning, it seemed a risky ambition at best.

"Did he say why he wanted to meet Brynden?"

"No, but I can guarantee he's up to something."

"But you've no idea what?"

Kinta shook her head. "I'm certain of only one thing, Arkady. If Cayal has a plan, it has something to do with his wish to end his own life, which means if he succeeds, that could signal the end for all of us."

Chapter 34

By the time Arkady returned from the palace, Stellan's preparations to leave Ramahn and return to Glaeba were well advanced. He'd spent the day in a daze, going through the motions of making arrangements for his absence, settling affairs that couldn't wait, sending apologies for invitations he had no choice but to decline, all the while numb with shock over the news that had arrived this morning at breakfast. By the time he'd sent for Arkady to tell her, she'd already left for the palace.

But she was back, the servants informed him, and if ever he needed his wife's understanding and support, it was now.

He looked up from his desk as the door opened. Arkady had already dispensed with her shroud and was wearing a simple gold gown that emphasised her height and slender grace. She looked curious rather than concerned by his summons. "There was a message waiting for me in the seraglium saying you wanted to . . . Tides, Stellan! What's wrong? You look awful!"

"The king is dead."

She looked at him blankly. Perhaps she hadn't heard what he said.

"The King and Queen of Glaeba are dead," he repeated, rising to his feet, his voice lacking any emotion.

"But . . . but . . . *how* . . . ?"

He sympathised with her shock. He'd felt just as stunned when he'd gotten the news. "A tragic boating accident on the lake during a freak storm, according to the message I got this morning. I don't know anything else, at this point, only that I must return to Herino immediately."

"Is Mathu all right?"

"Yes, of course," he replied, wondering why his wife's first thoughts were of the crown prince and not his niece. "So is Kylia, in case you're interested."

"Yes . . . of course I'm worried about Kylia. She wasn't hurt, was she?"

"No, thank the Tide, although it was a close call. She was missing for a time, but washed up on the lake shore a couple of hours after the storm hit. The letter I have speaks of her survival as nothing short of miraculous."

"Oh, Stellan, I'm so sorry." She crossed the room and came around the desk to embrace him, and for a moment he relished the contact, then he pushed her away, with the disturbing feeling she was apologising for Kylia's survival rather than sympathising with his grief for his dead king and cousin.

"I'm leaving tonight."

"Did you want me to start packing?"

"I haven't the time, Arkady. I need to finish up here and get back to Herino as quickly as possible so I'll be taking the fastest, not the most comfortable route."

Needing no further explanation, she nodded in understanding, which is what made her such a good wife for a man in his position. "You're next in line for the throne until Mathu produces an heir."

He wished she sounded a little more enthusiastic about the idea. "It's not just that, Arkady. Enteny was more than my king or my cousin. He was my friend."

"The friend who exiled you for saving his son from embarrassment." She moved away from him, putting the desk between them.

"This is no time for recrimination," he said, surprised at the bitterness in her voice. There was more than just a rift between them these days, he realised, more than a little sad to have lost his easy friendship with her.

"Would you listen to me if I asked you not to go?"

Stellan stared at his wife. "Not go? How can I *not* go, Arkady? Why would I not return home to see my cousin laid to rest and his son crowned king?"

"Assuming Mathu is ever *crowned* king."

"If you know something that suggests he might not be," Stellan said, appalled by her suggestion, "please tell me what it is. But if this is just some sort of misguided attempt to seek revenge for our exile, then I'll thank you to show some respect for the dead, and let me grieve for my family in peace."

Arkady didn't reply. Stellan had no way of telling if it was because she was feeling chastised or rebellious. Since she'd helped the murderer Kyle Lakesh escape from prison, since her return from the mountains after he abducted her, she had become a stranger to him. He no longer knew what drove her, no longer understood anything about her.

"It matters little what I know or what I believe, Stellan. You don't believe *me*, that's what counts."

"I've got Dashin investigating likely places for you to stay while I'm away," he said, deciding to change the subject. There was no answer to such an accusation, and even if he wanted to go down that path, he didn't have the time to fight with Arkady now.

"What's wrong with me staying here?"

"You can't stay here, Arkady. A woman alone in a house in Ramahn is considered scandalous."

"This is an embassy, not a house, and I'll be sharing it with several other wives, scores of servants and a dozen high-ranking embassy officials. Not exactly how I'd define *alone*."

"Be that as it may, a married woman staying here in the embassy compound while her husband is out of the country is out of the question. I suggest you select one or two slaves you wish to take with you and get them to start packing. The best option so far seems to be the Caelish embassy seraglium."

"You're not serious, are you?"

"Of course I'm serious. Dashin was heading there after he presented my petition to the Imperator."

"What are you petitioning the Imperator for?"

"We live in Torlenia at his pleasure. I need his permission to leave." When Stellan noticed the alarm on her face he added, "It's a formality, Arkady, nothing more. Dashin will inform the Imperator's aides of the king and queen's death, request his leave to attend their funeral, and then he'll advise the Caelish ambassador of this development and request asylum for you in his seraglium until I return."

"But there are other wives here . . . Dashin's staying in Ramahn, isn't he? And his wife? Surely they are sufficient chaperones? I'm a grown woman, for pity's sake!"

"I don't make the rules here, Arkady. I'm just compelled to abide by them. You are an ambassador's wife and as such, only another ambassador or higher is considered suitable as a guardian."

"This is ridiculous."

"I'm sorry our king and queen have perished at such an inconvenient time for you, my dear."

"That's not what I mean, Stellan, and you know it."

Before he could respond, there was a knock on the door, followed by Dashin Deray stepping into the office without waiting for permission to enter. He held a small packet of documents tied with a red ribbon, which he handed to Stellan, before he turned and bowed politely to Arkady.

"My condolences on your loss, your grace," he said.

"Thank you, Dashin," she replied in a neutral tone. "You were able to secure Stellan's travel papers, I see."

"Yes, your grace," he agreed. "The officials at the royal palace were most sympathetic. They've even offered to order all flags in Ramahn flown at half-mast as a measure of respect for the loss of our king and queen."

"Fancy the Torlenians willing to make such a sacrifice for us. What's next, I wonder? A national day of mourning, perhaps?"

"Arkady . . ." Stellan warned, glancing up from the packet of papers Dashin had brought him, all of which seemed to be perfectly in order. "Please . . ."

Arkady glared at him defiantly, and proceeded to drop that subject for one even more contentious. "And what of *my* imprisonment, Lord Deray? Have the Caelish offered this beggar a bed, or is your next call to the Senestrans, to see if they can put me up?"

Dashin glanced at Stellan for a moment before answering. "On the contrary, your grace. I haven't even been to the Caelish embassy. There was no need."

"Had they already heard?" Stellan asked.

"No, your grace. I already had an invitation."

"From whom?" Stellan and Arkady asked in unison.

"From the Imperator's Consort," he answered, looking at Stellan. "As soon as she got word of the accident in Glaeba and realised you were leaving Ramahn, she sent word offering Lady Desean sanctuary in the royal seraglium until your return."

Stellan looked at Arkady, expecting some sort of reaction to this news, but she hardly seemed surprised at all.

"What did you tell her?" Arkady asked.

"That you'd be honoured to accept, of course. What else could I say?" He turned to Stellan. "I trust I did the right thing, your grace. I know I should have consulted you first, but the consort's offer shocked me so much I couldn't think of any logical reason why Lady Desean might refuse."

Stellan studied Arkady for a moment. "Are you all right with this?"

Arkady nodded. "It's a solution, I suppose. If I have to stay in Ramahn, I'd rather stay here, but that's not likely."

"You know it isn't. Still this is a remarkable offer. It augurs well for Mathu's future relationship with Torlenia."

"And that's all that matters, isn't it?" Arkady seemed unimpressed. "Torlenia's smooth relationship with Glaeba. Always the politician, aren't you, Stellan?"

Her accusation wounded him. He certainly didn't think he deserved such a disdainful tone. "It's my job to watch over things like the relationship between Torlenia and Glaeba, for my new king as diligently as I did for the old."

"Your new king may not be quite the king you had in mind," she said.

"What are you talking about?"

She sighed. "Tides, Stellan, if only I could explain . . ."

"I wish you would."

Arkady hesitated, choosing her words carefully. "Mathu's . . . going to be influenced. By people who don't necessarily have his best interests—or yours—at heart."

"Tides, you're not going to start . . ." He stopped when he realised Dashin was still in the room. "I won't have you maligning people you don't . . . agree with, just because you don't like them, Arkady."

His wife, also aware that they were not alone, glanced at Dashin and then shook her head. "I'm not trying to malign anyone. I'm saying that things might not be what they seem and you need to be careful of who you consider friends."

"I know who my friends are."

For a moment, Arkady looked as if she was going to explain her quarrelsome attitude, but apparently she thought better of it and shrugged.

"Do what you have to, Stellan. Just don't be surprised if things don't turn out quite the way you expected." She turned to Dashin. "Did Lady Chintara say how many attendants I would be allowed to bring with me?"

"The invitation specifies no more than one or two, your grace. Apparently everything else you need will be provided in the royal seraglium."

"Then I will retire to our seraglium to pack. Clearly, I'm not needed here." She turned for the door, stopping when she reached it. "Stellan?"

"Yes?"

"Will you promise one thing?"

"If I can."

"When you get home to Glaeba, be very careful. Mathu may not be the man you think and his wife—the girl you believe is your niece—is certainly *not* the innocent you assume. Nor is Jaxyn Aranville the friend you believe. If you have any brains at all, you'll trust nobody, except . . ." Her voice trailed off, as if any warning she delivered was useless.

"Except who?"

She shrugged. "I was going to say Declan Hawkes, but I've a feeling such a warning would be a waste of time."

Her suggestion made him smile. "You think the only person I can trust in Glaeba is *your* good friend, the King's Spymaster?"

Arkady didn't share his amusement at the idea. "What I *think*, Stellan, is Enteny and Inala's death was no accident. If I'm right, as second in line to the throne, you are a danger to those who have other plans for Glaeba, and they're likely to do whatever it takes to be rid of you. Return home if you must, bury your king and queen and crown their son heir, but mark my words, the future is not what you imagine. Worse, it's something you *cannot* imagine. There may even come a time when you learn your friends are really your enemies, and a man you think of as your enemy now may well prove to be your only friend."

With that ominous warning delivered, Arkady let herself out of the office leaving Stellan and Dashin staring after her, the resounding slam of the door the only sound lingering in the uncomfortable silence that followed her departure.

Chapter 35

Lon Brandor and Tenry Crow, the bodyguards Aleki Ponting had assigned to watch over Shalimar Hawkes—and who Shalimar had sent on a wild goose chase to Caelum to be rid of them—were waiting on the appointed day in the taproom of The Lone Traveller's Inn on the outskirts of Cycrane, just as Shalimar had said they would be. They were surprised to discover Declan had come to meet them, although not surprised to learn their mission to Caelum was a ruse. Both longstanding members of the Cabal of the Tarot, they'd worked that much out for themselves weeks ago.

They hadn't been idle, however, and were able to bring Declan up to date regarding the gossip around Cycrane about the upcoming marriage of Princess Nyah and the handsome young duke, Tyrone, son of the formidable Grand Duchess of Torfail. The marriage, according to the rumours Tenry and Lon had heard, was eagerly awaited by everyone in Caelum with the possible exception of the bride, who had taken an unreasonable dislike to her future husband.

Queen Jilna, tolerated by the people of Caelum because she was the mother of their rightful heir, rather than a "proper" monarch, was becoming increasingly unpopular, as word spread that she might be forcing this marriage on her daughter. As Declan listened to Tenry's summary of the goings-on in Cycrane for the past few weeks, he shook his head, wondering at the mindset of these people. They could apparently see nothing wrong with marrying off a ten-year-old child, yet they were concerned the poor child might not like the groom.

"Nobody has any idea who the Grand Duchess of Torfail and her son really are, I suppose," Declan asked, taking a swig of foaming ale. He would have preferred to have a chance to clean up first, after his week or more wending his way through the labyrinthine tunnels of Maralyce's mine, but Lon and Tenry had been waiting for him when he arrived.

"Nobody suspects they're immortal, if that's what you're asking," Tenry said, after glancing around to check there was no danger of their being overheard. The older of the two, he did most of the talking. "But since it got about Princess Nyah ain't exactly in love with Lord Tyrone, there's plenty of people questioning who they are and where they come from."

"And where the little princess is," Lon added.

Declan looked at him. "What are you talking about?"

Tenry shrugged. "There's a new rumour doing the rounds that Princess Nyah is missing."

"Are you sure it's only a rumour?"

"Nobody's sure. That's the problem," Tenry said. "Way we heard it, there was a big to-do the other day at the palace. Some traditional function they always hold before a royal wedding. I'm not sure exactly what it was about, but I do know the little princess didn't show up. The official story was that she wasn't feeling well. The unofficial story is that she hates her future husband so much she's run away."

Declan smiled at the irony. "If it's true, then Caelum's ten-year-old heir might be the smartest person in the whole damned country. Have you made contact with Ricard Li yet?"

"Wasn't aware you wanted us to. Is he even a member of the Cabal?"

Declan shook his head. "That doesn't mean we can't warn him the Grand Duchess of Torfail is an impostor."

"That's more your area of expertise than ours," Tenry said. "In fact, Lon and me, we have a rule about trying not to run afoul of the local law."

"Can't blame you for that. What will you do now?"

"Depends on you, sir. If there's nothing you want us to do here, and you don't need us to go after the old man, we'll head back to Hidden Valley. Always something to do there, particularly now, with the old king gone."

"What old king?"

"Enteny," Tenry said. "Who else would I be talking about?"

"King Enteny is *dead*?"

"Been dead better part of a fortnight." The older man studied Declan with a frown. "Him and Queen Inala both. Ain't you heard?"

"I've been out of touch." *Tides, there's an understatement.*

"You surely have, sir, if you ain't heard 'bout it. Freak storm on the
lake, it was. Only a fluke the crown prince weren't on board with 'em,
neither."

Declan was stunned. And overwhelmed with guilt. He was the King's
Spymaster . . . he should have been in Herino . . .

And what could a spymaster do to fight a freak storm? he could hear his
grandfather asking.

"You're right. You two need to get back to Glaeba," Declan agreed,
needing time alone to digest this news. "I'm sorry you got sent on a
wild goose chase."

"Weren't so bad," Tenry said with a shrug. "Got to see Cycrane.
Hadn't done that before."

"Do you need money?"

Tenry shook his head. "Lord Aleki saw to it we was well provi-
sioned."

Declan rose to his feet, offering his hand to the men. "Then I wish
you luck on your journey home, gentlemen. Tell Lord Aleki I'll be
home as soon as I'm able."

"You'll need the luck more than us, I s'pect," Tenry replied, shaking
Declan's hand. He slapped his companion lightly on the shoulder.
"C'mon, Lon. If we get a move on, we can catch the first ferry across the
lake in the morning."

Lon rose to his feet, pushing his stool back. Tenry turned to leave and
then changed his mind and added, "Watch yourself on the streets
here, least 'til you get yourself cleaned up. The city watch is pretty intol-
erant, 'specially in regard to disreputable-lookin' characters, and to be
honest, sir, you're a fairly disreputable-lookin' character at the moment."

Rubbing his grubby, unshaven chin, Declan nodded in agreement.
"Thanks for the warning, Tenry."

"Then we'll be off, sir, and good luck to you."

Declan watched them leave and then swallowed the last of his ale, still
too shocked to comprehend the news that Enteny and Inala were dead.
A freak storm, Tenry said. Was it true? Or had the Tide returned faster
than they'd calculated it might?

Fast enough for Jaxyn and Diala to move on the Glaeban throne already?

Declan felt nauseous at the very idea.

The Cabal had thought they had months, even years, before any of the Tide Lords made a move against the mortal population.

So much for that idea . . .

He glanced around, wondering what he should do first: turn around and head straight home, get cleaned up, or try to make contact with the Caelish spymaster, Ricard Li.

Given Tenry's warning about his disreputable appearance, he decided on getting cleaned up first. Even if he left Caelum this minute, he was days away from Herino. There was nothing he could do now, and he was here in Cycrane, so he might as well try to do something useful before he headed back to Glaeba. Besides, finding a bed for the night and a much-needed bath meant he wouldn't have to deal with his other problem for a little longer, which was how exactly he was going to make contact with Ricard Li, anyway.

In the normal course of events, had he still been at home in Herino, before setting foot on Caelish soil, he would have sent a letter through long-established channels, setting up such a delicate meeting well in advance. A Glaeban spymaster certainly wouldn't arrive unannounced in the Caelish capital expecting to be treated like an honoured guest. In fact, explaining his presence here, or how he crossed Caelum's borders without detection, was going to be hard enough to explain away, let alone the massive breach of protocol preceding it.

But it was a problem for later. First he had to find the man.

Declan left The Lone Traveller's Inn and headed toward the city, cursing his own foolishness for staying in the mountains for so long, cursing Tilly for sending him after Shalimar, cursing Shalimar for leaving Lebec . . . It was late, the lights of the city bright against the dark backdrop of the Caelish highlands. He shivered a little, shouldering his pack a little higher as he walked, the wind carrying a bite that owed as much to the altitude as it did to the fickle mountain weather.

As was the case in most cities Declan had visited, the outskirts of Cycrane were home to the poorest and most marginalised citizens, particularly the free-born Crasii, who—like their cousins in Glaeba—were not considered human, and therefore not deserving of humane treatment. The streets were rank and badly maintained, as if the noses of the nobility didn't reach this far, so it didn't matter how bad they smelled.

Declan breathed through his mouth as he walked, hoping the inn he sought wasn't much further.

Although he'd been to Cycrane before, he wasn't familiar with the city's layout. The inn he was looking for—the closest thing to a safe house Glaeba owned in the Caelish capital besides its embassy—was run by a widow named Toshina Hanburn. The Widow Hanburn had lived in Cycrane most of her adult life, but she was a loyal Glaeban and more than happy to offer sanctuary to the odd countryman in need of a discreet place to do business.

Another few blocks, during which at least three human whores and one beggar had propositioned Declan, and the inn was in sight.

"Hey, mister!"

Declan turned to find a ferrety little man in a grey coat following him down the street. "What?"

"Looking for a bit of fun?"

"No."

"Got a female feline on heat . . . give you a night you ain't ever gonna forget . . ."

He stopped and turned to face the man. Mistaking his actions for interest, the pimp hurried forward. Declan grabbed him by the shirt front and slammed him up against the closed shutters of the shop behind him. "Do I look like the sort of pervert who screws animals?"

You probably do, a little voice in his head replied, recalling Tenry's comment about his disreputable state. Perhaps that's why the man had singled him out.

"Er . . . now you come to mention it . . . not a bit."

Declan let the man go. "Piss off."

With no further encouragement, the pimp did just that. Declan breathed a sigh of relief and continued on toward the inn. The windows were lit with a soft yellow glow that illuminated the wooden footpath outside in a patchwork of darkness and light. If he needed any further confirmation the Glaeban king and queen were dead, he found it as he drew closer. Either side of the door were poor copies of the official portraits of the king and queen of Glaeba, both banded with black mourning cloth.

Tides, how could it happen so quickly? Was it really an accident? Declan thought it unlikely. Maralyce had warned him before he left the mine that the others might already be capable of affecting the weather.

Picking up his pace, Declan hurried forward, turning into the alley beside the inn with the intention of entering by the back door. The Widow Hanburn might not mind his arrival in principle, but she wouldn't want it remarked upon, either. As Tenry Crow had pointed out, and his encounter with that slimy little panderer had just proved, Declan was a fairly disreputable-looking character at the moment.

The alley was dark and smelled of rotting garbage. Slipping his pack from his shoulder, Declan was two steps into it when something struck him on the back of the head. With a grunt, he fell face first into the muddy lane.

He barely had time to register he'd been attacked before he was hit again and tumbled into a dark well of unconsciousness.

Chapter 36

"Tides, you didn't kill him, did you?"

Declan groaned, rolling onto his back, a little surprised to discover hard floor beneath him rather than mud, which was the last thing he remembered. The voice was gruff and impatient and vaguely familiar.

"He's waking up," another unseen voice remarked.

Declan tried to speak, but discovered all he was capable of was another incomprehensible groan. His mouth was dry and he was certain his head had been cleaved in two. He felt rather than saw a figure squat down beside him. A moment later cool water dribbled across his lips.

"Thank you," he managed to croak.

"You're welcome."

Tides, I know that voice.

"Of course, I should just hang you as a spy and be done with it, you miserable Glaeban pig, but I need a favour, so I'm willing to give you a moment to explain yourself, before I decide whether or not to string you up."

"Ricard Li." Declan forced his eyes open and looked up. Sure enough, the Caelish spymaster was kneeling over him holding a waterskin. He took the offered skin, drank a few more mouthfuls of water and then rolled onto his back. "How did you find me?"

Ricard smiled humourlessly. "Followed those two thugs of yours around for a month. I was about to call off the surveillance as a complete waste of time, actually, when lo and behold, who should turn up tonight at The Lone Traveller's Inn, but the legendary Declan Hawkes himself."

"I was on my way to find you, Ricard." Declan pushed himself up on his elbows and looked around. They were in some sort of cellar, the only light coming from a lantern sitting on a barrel off to Ricard's left. There were several other men in the room, but he couldn't make out their faces in the gloom.

"I'm sure you were."

"I wouldn't risk coming to Cycrane without telling you."

"Funny, you seem to have forgotten about letting me know you crossed the border. Slipped your mind, did it?" Despite his words, Ricard offered Declan his hand and helped pull the Glaeban to his feet. "Which also begs the question how you got here. By the look of you, I'd say you did it by tunnelling through the mountains on your belly using nothing but your bare hands."

Declan glanced down at his filthy clothes with a shrug. "You'd be surprised how close to the truth that is, Ricard."

"Well, fascinated as I am by the how, I really am rather more interested in the why, my shady young friend. My people tell me you've been gone from Herino for a month or more, which I find astounding, given what's going on there at the moment. So, if you like the way that pretty head of yours sits on your shoulders, you'd better pray I don't find out you've been here in Caelum all that time."

Declan feigned wide-eyed surprise. "You have *spies* in Herino? Who'd have thought?"

"Don't give me any lip, Hawkes. Believe me, I'm not in the mood for it. Your king and queen are dead. You should be in Herino. What are you doing here?"

His head still pounding, Declan glanced around, spying a small barrel near the taller one where the lantern rested. "Mind if I sit down?"

Ricard didn't reply, but he made no move to prevent Declan from taking a seat.

"Tides," he groaned, feeling the back of his head gingerly and coming away sticky with blood. "What did they hit me with?"

Ricard smiled, not in the least apologetic. "I warned my lads you might take a bit of putting down. You disappointed them, actually. Didn't even put up a fight."

"That tends to happen," Declan agreed, "when someone jumps you from behind and hits you with a *tree* trunk."

"You'll get over it. A less tolerant sort of fellow might even point out that you wouldn't have been hit at all if you'd stayed on your side of the lake where you belong." Ricard's smile faded. "Which brings us back to *why* you're here in Caelum, at a time like this. A question you seem to be avoiding."

Declan shook his head, regretting the motion the moment he did. "I came to warn you."

"You couldn't just send a message?"

Declan shrugged, which was almost as painful as shaking his head. "I was in the neighbourhood."

Ricard was not amused. "And what warning is important enough to bring the King's Spymaster of Glaeba to Caelum to deliver it in person, instead of him staying at home where he's needed in a time of crisis?"

"This is about *your* future king, not mine."

Ricard didn't visibly react to the news. "Do tell."

"The Grand Duchess of Torfail is not who you think she is."

"And you came *all* this way to tell me? Why, Declan? Because you think we're stupid here in Caelum?"

"Of course not! I just wasn't sure if . . ." His voice trailed off and he nodded in understanding, which sent even more shooting pains up his skull. *I really* need to stop doing that. "You know about them."

"You don't think the first thing we did when the Grand Duchess and her son arrived out of nowhere with an offer for our crown princess's hand, was check up on them?" Ricard glared at Declan, obviously insulted. "Is that how you do things in Glaeba? Tides, no wonder you're sitting here as my prisoner."

"I'm your *prisoner*?"

"Until I decide otherwise."

"I'm curious, then, Ricard. If you know the Grand Duchess is a fraud, why have you let things go this far? I hear the wedding's scheduled to take place in less than a week."

Ricard frowned. "And every recommendation *you* ever made to Enteny was accepted without question, too, I suppose. How did you get into Caelum without coming through one of the ports?"

"I came through the mountains," Declan replied, honestly enough. *No need to go into details . . .*

"Can you go back the same way?"

"I wasn't planning to."

"What if I needed you to?"

Declan's eyes narrowed. "Ah. I see! Now we're getting to the favour part, aren't we?"

"I have a package," the Caelishman said, taking a seat on the barrel opposite Declan. "A very important, extremely valuable package. It needs to be . . . hidden for a time. Out of sight."

"And you want me to hide it for you?"

"The last place anybody would look for this package is in Glaeba."

"Then why not take it to Glaeba yourself?"

"My movements tend to be . . . noticed. As do those of my men. You're not known here, Hawkes. Tides, nobody even *knows* you're here. You could slip back into Glaeba the way you came in and take our package with you. All you need do after that is keep it safe until I send someone to collect it."

"Suppose I decide to steal this valuable package of yours for myself?"

Ricard stared at him evenly. "Then I will devote every breath I take until the day I die to bring about your extermination, Declan Hawkes. You can count on it."

Declan sighed. It was easier and less painful than shaking his head. "How big is this package of yours?"

"About yea high," the Caelishman replied, holding his hand up at shoulder height.

"It's a *person*?" Declan asked, wondering if he should just take the offer of a hanging and be done with it.

"Not just any person." He glanced over his shoulder, jerking his head at one of the unseen figures lurking in the shadows. A moment later, Declan heard a door opening and closing somewhere off to his left, and then footsteps coming closer.

Shortly after that, one of Ricard Li's henchmen stepped into the light. He was holding the hand of a little girl no more than ten years old. She was dressed in a rumpled but expensive pink gown, her dark hair tangled and fallen out of what had obviously once been a very elaborate arrangement. The child's eyes were swollen, her face tear-stained and pale.

"Declan Hawkes, spymaster to the King of Glaeba," Ricard said, rising to his feet and indicating with his hand that Declan should do the same. "You have the honour of standing in the presence of her most August Highness, Crown Princess Nyah of the Royal House of Korell."

Declan was still trying to take that in when Ricard turned to him and added calmly, "And we need *you* to get her out of Caelum."

He gazed at the little girl for a moment and then turned to Ricard Li. "Are you *insane*?"

The spymaster shrugged. "Desperate would describe our situation more accurately, I think. Why else would we involve a Glaeban?"

Declan was staggered. "But . . . Tides . . . you've kidnapped your *own* princess?"

"I ran away," Nyah said, before Ricard could answer. "Nobody kidnapped me. Master Li is helping me hide, that's all. I didn't know where else to go."

Declan sank back down on the barrel, torn between what his common sense was telling him to do—which was to get out of this any way he could—and the spectre of this child in the bed of a Tide Lord known as Tryan the Devil. He studied the little princess for a moment and then looked at the spymaster. "Who else knows you've got her?"

"Only the men in this room. And you."

"Do you trust them?"

"It's *you* I don't trust, Hawkes."

He threw his hands up. "Then why ask *me* to do this? Am I the only man in Caelum who knows the way across the Lower Oran?"

"I trust you have the resources to keep her hidden, but more importantly, I trust your word, Hawkes. You Glaebans are always making such a fuss about your damned honour, I figure it's time I put it to the test."

Declan couldn't believe what he was hearing. "So you'll give your crown princess into my care and hope I'll smuggle her out of the country and keep her safe, based on nothing more than my word? Tides, you were right the first time, Ricard. I *do* think you're stupid."

The spymaster seemed unconcerned. "Maybe I am. But I'm a pretty good judge of character, Hawkes, and I figure I've got you pegged. Besides, unlike you, I'm not foolish enough to think *you're* stupid. I'm sure you'll very quickly come to realise the political favour your country will gain from helping us is worth far more than the trouble you'll bring down on Glaeba if you refuse."

Ricard had the right of it. Declan had realised that much, half a heartbeat after Ricard told him what he wanted. "Does anybody realise she's missing, or is the story she's ill still holding up?"

"You could speak to me like I'm in the *room*, Master Hawkes," the little girl said, glaring at him.

Oh, and she's a brat, too, Declan thought. *This just gets better and better.*

"So far, nobody suspects the truth, but I doubt that'll last much longer."

"Not even Queen Jilna?"

"Queen Jilna is rather too . . . taken . . . with her guests from Torfail to be thinking clearly. We felt it safer for everybody if she not learn the whereabouts of her daughter."

"Tides, Ricard, this is treason."

"Not if we're acting under the orders of Caelum's true heir, who we need to get out of the city tonight, by the way. Over the border by tomorrow night would be even better."

If he returned to Glaeba through Maralyce's mine, Declan could do what Ricard Li wanted, but travelling through the mine was no easy thing, as his current disreputable state could attest to. He doubted a spoiled child raised in the Caelish palace, whose most common form of exercise consisted of walking up and down an enclosed gallery with the other ladies of the court, would have the stamina or the fortitude to negotiate her way through the darkness of the mine.

"She'll never make it," Declan said.

"We can stall any pursuit for another day, perhaps . . ."

"That's not what I mean. The way I came into Caelum . . . it's not for the faint-hearted. I doubt your little princess here would survive the first hour before she's screaming at me to bring her home."

"I can do whatever I have to, Master Hawkes," Nyah declared, squaring her shoulders. "All *you* need do is keep me safe."

Declan recognised that look. Even if Ricard wasn't standing there threatening him with this absurd plan, the child was set on it. But as Shalimar was fond of saying, *sometimes the best way to be rid of a stupid idea is to follow it through to its most absurd conclusion.* He turned to Nyah. "You'd have to agree to follow my instructions, your highness. Without questioning them. Without arguing about them."

"I can do that," she said with a nod.

"And you'll have to cut your hair."

"*What?*" both the princess and the spymaster said at the same time.

"The best disguise is to dress you as a boy. Even if I could get you across the border, I'd still need to get you through the city first." He turned to Ricard. "Cut her hair, smear a bit of mud on her face and dress her like a boy. We'll be able to walk down the main street in broad daylight and I guarantee, nobody will suspect who she is."

Ricard thought about that for a moment and then nodded. "He has the right of it, your highness. Dressed as a boy, you'd be much safer."

Nyah glared at Declan rebelliously for a moment and then she nodded. "If I must."

"I think it's a good idea. You'll find it easier crossing the mountains in trousers, too."

Well, that plan to deter them from this idiocy worked well, didn't it, Declan? He sighed. *Tides . . . now I'm talking to myself. Maybe that blow on the head did more damage than I thought.*

He turned to Ricard, shaking his head, not caring about the pain. "This will never work. She has no concept of what she's getting into, Ricard."

"No, but she's pretty clear on what she's running away from," the spymaster replied. "So are you, I'm fairly certain. Don't you think it's worth the life of a child to put yourself out a little?"

"My king is dead. I need to get back to Glaeba. By the fastest route possible. What you want will mean adding days, perhaps weeks to the trip. And what, in the name of the Tide, am I supposed to do with her once I get there, anyway?"

"Keep her safe until we send for her."

"And when will that be?"

"When we've killed the Grand Duchess of Torfail and her son," Ricard announced.

Declan stared at him for a moment and then closed his eyes. *Tides . . . this is a nightmare . . . they have no idea who they're dealing with.*

"Well?" Ricard prompted. "We don't have all night for you to debate this with yourself, you know, Hawkes."

Opening his eyes, Declan glanced at the child again, with her spoiled pout and her pretty, crumpled dress. But even if she was the most obnoxious brat that ever lived, no child deserved what awaited this girl. Underneath it all, he suspected, she was quietly terrified. And smarter than she looked if she had the sense to run from a Tide Lord.

"By the time this is done, Ricard Li, you'll be sending me *copies* of your own intelligence reports, to save me the trouble of spying on you myself, you'll owe me so many favours."

The older man smiled. "You'll do it then?"

Declan nodded, regretting the action for much more than just the pain it caused in his head. "I'll do it."

"There!" Ricard said to the princess. "I told you I'd find a way out of this for you, your highness. It's all settled. You're going to Glaeba."

Chapter 37

Declan Hawkes had been right about one thing, Warlock mused, as he let himself into the royal suite, carrying Queen Kylia's breakfast tray. Now he'd proved his credentials as a doting slave to the suzerain, he was never doubted again. Since the death of King Enteny and Queen Inala—where he'd stood by and done nothing to raise the alarm or try to prevent it—he'd been by Kylia's side. Not once had she ever so much as glanced in his direction with an uncertain look, even when discussing the most treasonous of plans with her partner in crime, Jaxyn Aranville.

The immortals were smart enough to insist only Crasii serve them in the royal palace. There were no mortal human ears around Jaxyn or Diala to overhear their plotting, no human eyes to witness their scheming, and no human hearts to be overcome by guilt or conscience. The Crasii were bred to be obedient to their masters and Warlock had proved he was that.

The Tide Lords didn't fear betrayal by their slaves because the Crasii were incapable of it.

This morning was proving to be a perfect example of how things were in the palace these days. Mathu was long gone, up at the crack of dawn to deal with the numerous demands on him now he was the un-crowned King of Glaeba, so Kylia was taking her breakfast in bed, where she'd been joined by Jaxyn Aranville.

As far as Warlock could tell, the two immortals weren't sleeping to-gether. He suspected this was because Diala didn't entirely trust Jaxyn—a wise precaution—or perhaps the reverse was true. Given what the

Immortal Prince had told Warlock and the Duchess of Lebec about this woman—known among even her own kind as the Minion Maker—not trusting her probably wasn't a bad idea.

Whatever the case, the soon-to-be Queen of Glaeba was sitting in bed, propped up by a mountain of pillows, while Jaxyn sat on the window seat chatting to her. Warlock placed the tray on her lap with a polite bow.

"Will there be anything else, your majesty?"

He'd stopped calling her "highness" the moment they'd found her downstream from the ruined dock, collapsed on the shores of the Lower Oran, about an hour after the royal barge was smashed against the wharf. Although she was sobbing and clearly distressed, Warlock knew it was an act. He thought she must have jumped clear when the boat first slammed into the pylons. Diala was immortal, so there was no danger of her drowning. She might, however, have had some trouble explaining away broken bones that healed within an hour or cuts that stopped bleeding and sealed themselves while you watched.

"Just wait over there until I'm finished," she said, waving a hand in the general direction of the other side of the room. "You can take the tray back to the kitchens when I'm done."

It was a habit of Diala's to make her slaves wait around while she ate. Even more humiliating was her suggestion they might like to eat the scraps when she was done, something Warlock had been forced to swallow his pride to do, on several occasions.

"As you wish, your majesty."

Diala ignored him after that, as Warlock retreated across the room to stand in the corner. Diala's attention was fixed on Jaxyn and the conversation Warlock had interrupted with his arrival. "Mathu got a message last night. Stellan Desean is on his way home from Torlenia for the funeral."

"That's hardly news. He's the king's cousin."

"Aren't you worried?"

Jaxyn shrugged, unconcerned. "It was a freak accident caused by an unseasonable storm. He won't suspect anything."

"I'm not suggesting he'll think Enteny and Inala's death is anything else," Kylia said, biting into her toast. "But with Enteny dead, doesn't that make him heir to the throne, now?"

"I hadn't thought of that." Jaxyn frowned, rubbing his chin. "Don't suppose *you* feel like getting pregnant in the next week, do you? Give young Mathu the heir he craves—not to mention so desperately needs?"

"Don't be ridiculous."

He smiled. "Just a thought. We could kill Stellan, I suppose."

Diala shook her head. "Too many deaths too soon and people will start to talk. The Tide's not up far enough for us to take this country on our own. Besides, killing him won't solve the problem. Arkady is already pregnant, remember? She carries the Desean heir, so if Stellan dies, his son will be next in line for the throne after Mathu and we're no better off than we are now."

"So? We kill them both."

"You can't. Arkady's staying in Torlenia. Stellan's on his way back alone. I imagine he doesn't want to risk her travelling in her condition."

Jaxyn was silent for a moment, pursing his lips. "The problem, then, is not killing the Desean line, but discrediting it."

"How are you going to do that?"

He looked at her, shaking his head. "Tides, Diala, you lived in Lebec Palace with us. You saw what was going on. You're not that naive, surely?"

Warlock wondered what they were talking about. They both seemed to know what it would take to bring down the Duke of Lebec, but—rather inconveniently—didn't feel the need to explain it for the benefit of the spy standing in the corner of the room. Warlock hadn't known about the duchess being pregnant, either. He was glad to hear it, certain she must be delighted by the news.

Diala swallowed another mouthful of toast and washed it down with a sip of tea before she answered Jaxyn. "If you tell Mathu about Stellan's sexual proclivities, you'll have to admit your own involvement with him. What's the point of bringing Stellan Desean down, if you go crashing down with him?"

"But I was his innocent victim," he said, smiling in a manner that made Warlock's blood run cold. "He's so much older than me, after all. And he's a duke. How could I refuse him? He forced himself on me. Over and over and over. It was . . . terrible."

Diala laughed. "Tides, Jaxyn, you'd better look a little more put out than that, if you're planning to convince anybody you were being taken by force. It does pose an interesting question, though."

"What question?"

"Well, with dear old Uncle Stellan playing for the other team, I wonder how Arkady got pregnant?"

Reeling a little from this startling news about the Duke of Lebec, Warlock expected Jaxyn to reply with something flippant, but his reaction was quite the opposite. The Tide Lord closed his eyes for a moment and then began to swear in a language Warlock had never heard before. He cursed for a full minute, Diala looking on curiously, before he finally stood up and began pacing, his anger a palpable force Warlock could feel from the other side of the room.

"Tides, I should've guessed," Jaxyn eventually said in Glaeban.

"Guessed what?" Diala asked, anxious to discover—as Warlock was—what had prompted his unexpected outburst.

"Who fathered a child on her."

"It wasn't *you*, was it?"

He glared at her. "Think about it, Diala. She was interrogating Cayal every day at the prison and then she conveniently disappeared into the mountains with him for a week."

Warlock's heart sank at Jaxyn's words, certain he had the right of it. He'd seen the way Arkady and Cayal reacted to each other. Their eventual mating wasn't only likely, it was probably inevitable.

Without the advantage of Warlock's first-hand knowledge of their relationship, however, Diala scoffed at the very idea. "You think *Cayal* is the father of her child? How do you figure that? When you got back from your heroic little rescue mission, you told me you saw no sign of any affection between them. You said Cayal couldn't have cared less that you'd come for Arkady."

"I'd forgotten who I was dealing with," Jaxyn said. "The man who'll walk away from any soul on Amyrantha—once they're of no further use to him—and the Queen of the Liars herself. Tides, Arkady has faked being the love of Stellan's life for the better part of seven years. She wouldn't even break into a sweat pretending there was nothing going on between her and Cayal."

Diala seemed more amused than worried by the idea. "It makes no difference, Jaxyn. If you expose Stellan for what he is, the scandal will ruin his whole house and Mathu will have no choice but to disinherit him, along with any child Arkady might be carrying, regardless of who fathered the brat."

"I'll bet he was laughing at me the whole time."

Diala rolled her eyes. "Oh, *please*, can we not get all tied up in knots over Cayal and what he may or may not have been thinking three months ago? I thought you'd be long past caring what he did, anyway."

"I would be," Jaxyn said. "If only he'd stop doing it around me."

"Doing *what*?" Diala asked. "He's crazy, Jaxyn. Has been for a thousand years or more. He wants to die, for pity's sake, and he seems to have chosen making you dedicate your life to being rid of him as his method of achieving it."

"He's up to something."

"He's always up to something. We're all up to something." She leaned back against the pillows with a sigh. "It's what we do, Jaxyn."

Diala's reassurances did little to soothe the agitated immortal. "This is Glaeba. Cayal's traditional stomping ground. If he was planning to make a comeback with the Tide returning . . ."

Diala smiled, picked up the teacup. "Ah, yes, I can see now, how he must have been sitting there in Lebec Prison planning to take over the whole country from his cell . . . still, he is *crazy*, I suppose."

Jaxyn was not amused. "Don't mock me, Diala. You underestimate Cayal. You always have."

"And you're jealous of him," she said. "Although I've never really understood why."

To Warlock's surprise, Jaxyn didn't even try to deny Diala's accusation. "It's because he always gets what he wants."

"I don't know," Diala said with a shrug. "He doesn't seem to be having too much luck with this 'goodbye cruel world' campaign of his, so far, does he?"

Jaxyn turned on her. "Tides, how can you be so dense? Suppose Cayal *does* eventually find a way to die?"

"Then we'll be well rid of him."

"Then we'll no longer be immortal," he pointed out, impatient with her lack of comprehension. "If one of us can die, Diala, we *all* can. Think about that."

Clearly, Diala hadn't thought what Cayal's successful suicide might mean to the rest of them, but even now, she seemed far less concerned than her companion. "It's all hypothetical, Jaxyn. He's been trying to kill himself for more than a thousand years and he hasn't succeeded yet. I'll worry about no longer being immortal when he does."

Jaxyn stared at her for a moment and then threw up his hands, muttered a curse under his breath and headed for the door.

"Where are you going?"

"To see Mathu. If I'm going to expose Stellan Desean as deviant, I'll need to do it before he gets here."

Diala smiled. "Well, try not to look *too* thrilled while you're describing all the gory and graphic details, Jaxyn. You don't want Mathu thinking you *enjoyed* it."

Jaxyn stopped and turned to face her, his eyes full of anger. "Are you *threatening* me?"

Warlock thought that a rather silly question. There was an implied threat in her words that even *he* got.

"I'm just saying . . . you need to be careful, that's all."

The Tide Lord shook his head, smiling dangerously. "Diala, my precious, if you so much as *hint* to Mathu that I was a willing participant in Stellan Desean's perversions, I will order every male Crasii in the palace to swear you've been having your way with them on a daily basis, starting with your tame hound, Cecil, over there in the corner. If you think our young king won't like what *I've* been up to, imagine what his reaction will be to that."

Diala's smug expression faded. She glanced at Warlock. "Cecil, I am your mistress. You were given to me. You are not to follow the orders of Lord Jaxyn, is that clear?"

"To serve you is the reason I breathe, my lady," he replied, wishing they would leave him out of it.

"Cecil, come to heel!" Jaxyn countered, which left Warlock in an untenable position. He was a Scard, and not naturally inclined to do anything these monsters ordered him to do. Worse, he had no idea how a real Crasii would react to two such conflicting orders from those he was compelled to obey. He hesitated, knowing his indecision could be fatal, and then decided to do as Jaxyn commanded.

He crossed the room to where Jaxyn waited, and then bowed. "My lord?"

Jaxyn gave Diala a triumphant look. "See? They'll do whatever I ask."

"He had to think about it, though," she said, apparently putting her Crasii's indecision down to the conflicting orders he'd been given, rather than the fear that he might not want to obey them at all. "Cecil, come away from him."

This time he didn't hesitate. He dutifully walked to the bed, and once again, treated Glaeba's future queen to a courtly bow. "As you wish, your majesty."

Diala gave Jaxyn an *I-told-you-so* sort of look, but Jaxyn didn't try to countermand the order again. Instead, he muttered another curse in the language he'd used earlier and strode from the room, slamming the door behind him.

Diala smiled, turning her attention to Warlock. "You're mine, Cecil. Pay no attention to him."

"To serve you is the reason I breathe, your majesty."

"And if anybody ever asks you about it, you're to say you've seen Jaxyn looking at other men, the way decent men look at pretty women."

You treacherous little bitch.

"As you wish, your majesty."

She smiled even wider, pleased with his obedience. "There's a good boy, Cecil. Would you like to eat my crusts?"

Chapter 38

The runaway heir to the Caelish throne proved only a slightly less troublesome travelling companion than Declan feared. Despite being barely eleven years old—she'd had a birthday while Declan was in the mountains with his grandfather—she was spoiled, snippy and impatient, and expected him to wait on her hand and foot. In fact, she considered her new guardian to be so far below her socially, he suspected she wouldn't have spoken to him at all, had not her very survival depended on it.

Things changed, however, once they reached Maralyce's mine. Even Declan found the crushing darkness unnerving. It terrified Nyah. They weren't in the tunnels more than ten minutes before a small hand snaked into his in the darkness, gripping it with all her eleven-year-old strength, which was considerable. She held on so tight, in fact, that Declan had to warn her to ease up a little, because his fingers were starting to go numb.

Ricard Li's men had offered to see them clear of the city, but Declan declined his help. As the Caelish spymaster himself had pointed out, his movements were noticed. If nobody knew Declan Hawkes was in the city, then nobody would know to follow him out of it. Once Nyah's hair had been trimmed to a boyish crop—a traumatic event during which Nyah sat quietly sobbing as her long dark hair fell in ragged clumps onto the cellar floor—and with her dressed in the nondescript clothing of a street urchin, she looked nothing like the girl who'd demanded Declan acknowledge she was in the room.

"How long before we stop for a rest?"

Declan looked down at the little princess, raising the torch higher to see her face more clearly. The darkness was complete, not a thing visible beyond the circle of light thrown by the torch's steady, golden flames. "A while yet. We've only been walking for about an hour."

"How can you tell?"

"I just can."

"Are you sure you know where you're going?"

"Haven't a clue."

Even in the inadequate torchlight, Declan caught the fleeting look of panic on Nyah's face before she realised he was teasing her. "Are you always this disrespectful of your betters?"

"I'm famous for it," he replied, pulling her forward as he resumed walking. The tunnels were smooth here, and quite wide. They'd yet to reach the narrower parts of the mine which meant crawling on their hands and knees through passageways he could barely squeeze through.

He hadn't told Nyah about those tunnels yet.

"If you betray me, I'll have Ricard Li kill you where you stand," she announced without preamble, about ten minutes later.

"Ricard did mention something about that." He wasn't sure if she was threatening him, or just trying to fill the overwhelming silence with conversation and had nothing much else to talk about.

"Or if you try to take advantage of me . . ."

Declan stopped again, staring down at the child. "Take *advantage* of you?"

She stuck her chin out defiantly. "I know how the world works. You're common-born, after all, and I'm a princess . . ."

Declan rolled his eyes. *Tides, what sort of nonsense do the Caelish feed their children?* "You're a right pain in the backside, is what you are, your highness. And in case it's slipped your notice, you're a child; a very scared and frightened child, granted, even though you're too damned stubborn to admit it. But you may put your mind at ease. In Glaeba we prefer to copulate with people old enough to spell the word."

Oddly, that did little to reassure her. "Don't you think I'm pretty?"

"I think you're a child."

"Lord Tyrone told me I was pretty."

Declan shook his hand free of hers and pointed down the tunnel back the way they'd come. "Why don't you go back home and marry him, then, if it's so important someone thinks you're pretty. It's that-away, in case you're wondering."

Tears welled up in her eyes, spilling onto her cheeks, streaking the dirt on her face. "Mama was right. All Glaebans are pigs!"

"This would be the same loving mama who arranged for her ten-year-old daughter to marry a Tide Lord?"

"I'm eleven!"

"Whatever." He lifted the torch and headed down the tunnel again without waiting to see if she was following.

Stranded in the darkness, Nyah wasted no time scurrying after him. "And what do you mean, Mama arranged for me to marry a Tide Lord? The Tide Lords aren't real. They're just pictures on Tarot cards."

Declan cursed his slip of the tongue, and then decided it mattered little. The Tide was on the way back. The whole world would know the truth soon. And this child deserved to know it more than most, even if she was a brat. He stopped and waited for her to catch up. "Your precious Lord Tyrone is really Tryan the Devil. The Grand Duchess of Torfail—she's Syrolee, Empress of the Five Realms."

Nyah was impressed. "Does that mean Lady Alysa is really Elyssa, the Immortal Maiden, too?"

"Almost certainly."

At some point, Nyah's cold little hand had found its way back into his, and they'd resumed walking. She thought about this new information for a moment and then shook her head. "You're making this up."

"Why? Because Mama told you all Glaebans are liars too?"

"Because it doesn't make sense. If the Tide Lords are real, what are they doing in Caelum? We're not that important. Wouldn't they be trying to take over Glaeba?"

"Ah, so you think Glaeba is more important than Caelum, do you?"

"You're twisting everything I say around."

"I am," he said. "That wasn't very nice of me. And for your information, they *are* trying to take over Glaeba. Only it's Jaxyn and Diala—the Lord of Temperance and the High Priestess—who are making themselves at home in my country, which is why I'd *really* like to get back there."

She was silent for a time as they walked on through the black, oppressive silence, and then out of nowhere, she said, "I'm sorry about your king and queen being dead."

The apology surprised him. He glanced down at her. "So am I."

"Did the Tide Lords kill them?"

"I don't know for certain, but I'm guessing they had a hand in it."

She digested that and then asked in a small voice, "Will they kill Mama?"

Declan wasn't sure how to answer. Or rather, he had no way of knowing how she might react to the truth. In the end, he settled for an answer that lay somewhere between the truth and the reassurance she was looking for. "I suppose it depends on whether or not they perceive the current Queen of Caelum as a threat."

"Would they have killed me, if I hadn't run away?"

"Maybe," he said. "On the other hand, they're immortal, so they may have been willing to sit back and wait for you to die of old age before they made their move."

"They didn't wait for Queen Inala and King Enteny to die of old age."

"No, they didn't."

Once more she fell silent. A short while later, the tunnel widened even further, opening up to a larger cavern, from which three other tunnels branched off. Even though he still had Maralyce's map, Declan had marked the one he'd come through on the way here, so he decided to stop for a time. He raised the torch to look around, found an ancient wrought-iron bracket set into the wall off to his left to hold it, and ordered Nyah to rest.

"Why are we stopping?"

"The next tunnel is narrower," he told her. "Much narrower. You need to rest while you can. We'll be going deeper into the mine from now on, which means it'll get hotter and occasionally wetter, too. Much as I find you a riveting conversationalist, your highness, there'll be no strolling along chatting for a while after this."

Nyah took a drink from the waterskin and passed it back to Declan. She'd stopped wiping his germs off before she drank from it, he noted, biting back a smile.

"I was supposed to marry Prince Mathu, you know," she said, settling herself against the wall with her knees pulled up under her chin. "Mama was really cranky when Duke Stellan came to tell us he didn't want me."

"It had nothing to do with what Mathu wanted, Nyah," Declan tried to explain. "In Glaeba, we toss men in gaol for marrying little girls, we don't give them a crown for it."

"Why do you keep calling me a little girl?"

"Because—by Glaeban standards, at any rate—you *are* a little girl."

"Does that mean I'll be treated like a little girl when we get to Glaeba?"

"We certainly won't be lining up potential husbands for you."

She looked rather worried to learn that. "What *will* happen to me then?"

Declan shrugged. "We'll arrange something."

"Will I have to keep pretending I'm a boy?"

"Possibly. It's a safe disguise when people are looking for a little girl."

"Will you take me to Herino? Or somewhere else?"

"I really haven't thought that far ahead yet, your highness."

"Well, you should," she commanded. "I'm the rightful ruler of Caelum, you know. I *deserve* to be treated as such."

What did I *ever do to deserve* you? But he was smart enough to realise this child was much more cooperative when she thought she was being treated in the manner to which she was clearly accustomed. "I'll make sure everyone is aware of your exalted rank, your highness," he promised, climbing to his feet. *Because that's what you do when you're trying to hide something—tell everyone about it.* "You ready to go?"

"Is it far?"

"This next narrow bit only lasts for an hour or two. After that the going gets easier again for a while."

She climbed to her feet, brushing the dirt from her filthy trousers as if it made the slightest difference. "How do you know your way through here, anyway?"

"I have a map."

"But these tunnels must be ancient. Where did you get a map?"

"My great-grandmother gave it to me."

"Is it some sort of family heirloom?"

Declan smiled, lifting the torch from the bracket. "You could say that."

She looked around, frowning. "Your ancestors were probably smugglers, if they used this place. Or worse."

"Much worse, I fear," Declan agreed. "It's that tunnel off to the left. Come on." He turned toward the marked entrance, and then stopped when he realised Nyah wasn't behind him. "Is something wrong?"

"You don't seem too bothered by the idea your ancestors were smugglers."

Declan crossed the cavern in two steps and took her by the hand. "Nyah, my mother was a whore, my grandfather is a charlatan and my great-grandmother once blew the top off a mountain because someone pissed her off. *Smugglers* for ancestors? Tides, I should be so lucky."

"What about your father?" she asked, resisting him as much as she dared.

"What about him?"

"You didn't say what he did."

"Don't know what he did," Declan said as he pulled her along behind him. "Did you miss the bit about my mother being a whore?"

Nyah shook her hand free of his and stopped, glaring at him in the gloom.

"That means you're a bastard."

"Both literally and figuratively," Declan agreed. "Which also means I'm not averse to leaving you in the dark, your *highness*, to find a way out of here on your own if you don't shut up and start walking."

She stood defiantly for a moment, weighing up the advisability of calling his bluff, perhaps, and then apparently thinking better of it, she tossed her head and stalked past him toward the tunnel.

"Ricard Li will be hearing about this," she declared with haughty disdain.

Won't make any difference, Declan decided as he headed off after the little princess, *'cause the next time I see that flanking Caelishman, I'm going to kill him.*

Chapter 39

Exhausted and still numb with grief, Stellan arrived in Whitewater City a little over ten days after he'd left Ramahn. From there he'd intended to hire another barge to take him north to Herino, but was relieved to find an escort waiting for him, sent by Mathu, to bring his cousin home.

Stellan was impressed, even touched, Mathu would think of treating him with such honour at a time like this, and willingly gave himself over to the care of his escort. The guard of honour was a mounted troop of feline Crasii, commanded by a human captain named Martan Derill, along with two other human lieutenants he never bothered to introduce. The younger son of one of Herino's many noble families, Captain Derill was polite yet distant toward his charge, and offered little in the way of conversation on the ride north.

He did tell Stellan what he knew of the circumstances of the king and queen's death as they rode, although it proved to be little more than the duke already knew. There had been a freak storm. The king and queen were among the score of victims. Princess Kylia was miraculously thrown clear and rescued sometime afterward. Prince Mathu had slept in, that morning, and by a mere stroke of good fortune had not been among the casualties.

As he had no wish to be King of Glaeba, Stellan was more thankful for Mathu's survival than he could put into words. He was bereaved by the loss of Enteny, certainly, and a little concerned that Mathu might not be ready to become king in such dramatic circumstances. But he felt the boy had promise and was looking forward to the opportunity to act as mentor and advisor to the young king, once his father and mother were laid to rest and the coronation was done with.

It surprised Stellan a little to discover how much he was looking forward to the future under Mathu's reign. The young prince's time in Lebec had shown him to be a good-natured, if a little too easily distracted, young man, with a great deal of potential. With the right guidance, he had the makings of a great king; more tolerant than his father, with luck, and certainly more popular.

These thoughts occupied most of Stellan's time on the journey home. It took another six rainy days of hard riding and frequent changes of horses before the island of Herino appeared on the horizon. Stellan breathed a sigh of relief when he spied it. It wasn't quite as comforting as the sight of Lebec might have been, but it was near enough to make Stellan grateful to be home.

He would see Lebec again soon. But there was a king to bury and another to crown. Mathu needed his counsel. One of the young king's first official decrees, Stellan hoped, would be to recall him and Arkady from the ambassadorial post in Torlenia he currently occupied, and have Stellan appointed to the court, perhaps Chancellor of the Exchequer, or even First Minister. Karyl Deryon's position of Private Secretary to the King might also be available, soon. Lord Deryon was an old man, after all, and with the death of Enteny was likely to take this opportunity to retire.

Whatever post he was appointed to, Arkady would be delighted, Stellan knew, wondering how she was managing as a guest of the Imperator's Consort in the royal seraglium. He was glad she'd been offered the chance to stay at the palace. It augured well for the negotiations about the Chelae Islands.

With luck, by the time Mathu officially recalled them, Arkady might have achieved what centuries of Glaeban and Torlenian diplomats had failed to do—sorted out who owned the islands and reached an equitable agreement about where the line between Glaeban waters ended and Torlenian waters began.

But that was for the future. For now, Stellan was home and anxious to meet with Mathu. When they arrived at the palace, another troop of palace guards was waiting for him. With a great deal more ceremony than Stellan thought the occasion warranted, they fell in either side of him and escorted him, not to the private chambers of the king where Stellan expected to meet with his cousin, but to the throne room, a cavernous marble-tiled hall, lacking any sort of warmth or familiarity.

The escort stopped at the entrance, indicating the duke should continue alone. Stellan stepped into the hall, glancing over his shoulder as the doors closed behind him with a faintly ominous boom. Turning back, he spied Mathu seated on the throne at the other end of the hall.

"What's this then?" Stellan asked, his boots echoing through the chilly hall as he approached the throne. He stopped at the foot of the dais and bowed to the new King of Glaeba, who was dressed quite formally, a golden coronet circling his forehead, his expression grim. "You've no need to impress me, Mat."

"Welcome home, Stellan."

He stepped a little closer and held out his hands. "There aren't words to describe the depth of my grief, Mathu, or my sympathy for you and Kylia. How are you holding up?"

Mathu deliberately ignored the gesture. "I'm fine, thank you. How is your wife?"

Stellan lowered his hands, putting Mathu's cool welcome down to the uncertainty of a young man, barely twenty years old, who—in the worst possible circumstances—finds himself a king. "She was well enough when I left Ramahn."

"Her pregnancy progresses well, then?"

Stellan shook his head. He'd decided on the way here he wouldn't lie to Mathu the way he'd lied to Enteny. A new king was a chance for a new start. While there were some things he could never confess, clearing up the mess he'd made by claiming Arkady was pregnant seemed a good place to begin. "She's not pregnant, Mat. She never was. Your father was pressuring me about an heir, and we were facing exile . . . it was stupid, I know, but telling him she was expecting a baby seemed like a good idea at the time."

"And what's one more lie to a man like you, eh?"

A feeling of dread began to radiate out from Stellan's gut. This meeting here in the throne room, Mathu's cold, monosyllabic answers . . . "Is there something wrong, Mat?"

"You will address me as *your majesty*."

"Tides, I hope you're joking," he replied, frowning.

"You think it's a joke that I expect you to treat me with the respect due your king?"

"Considering how many times I've bailed you out of trouble, your *majesty*, I think it's an insult, actually."

"Oh, and you care about insults, do you?"

"A great deal more than you do, it would seem. What's going on here, Mathu?"

For a moment, the young king seemed to relax, and the Mathu Stellan knew so well was seated there on the throne, not the icy monarch who'd greeted him a moment ago. It didn't last. The king frowned, fixing his gaze on some point over Stellan's head to avoid looking him in the eye. "There have been . . . accusations . . . made about you."

"What sort of accusations?"

"I'd rather not repeat them."

"If you're going to treat me like a leper because of them, I'd rather you did."

Mathu squirmed uncomfortably on his gilded throne. "There are claims . . . that you have been . . . seeing men."

"I see," Stellan replied, forcing himself to remain calm, despite the sickening dread threatening to bring him to his knees. "And *seeing* is a crime under your rule, is it, your majesty?"

"Don't be obtuse, Stellan. You know what I mean."

"Actually, I'm not sure I do."

Mathu swallowed hard and seemed to sit a little straighter in his throne before he replied. "You've been accused of being a sodomite."

Although his heart was hammering, and his palms began to sweat, long practised at denying such things, Stellan laughed at the very suggestion. "Tides, you're not taking such a ridiculous accusation seriously, are you?"

"I probably wouldn't have," Mathu agreed. "Except this accusation comes from an impeccable source."

"What impeccable source?" he asked, racking his brains to think of who would level such a charge at him, or what they hoped to gain by it. Was this Reon Debalkor's revenge for Mathu running away from Venetia and coming to Lebec? Payback for inadvertently foiling Reon's plans for his daughter to marry Mathu? Or was it someone else? Someone clearing the decks for their own personal rise to power? He'd known there would be competition for the positions closest to the new king, but who wanted one badly enough to discredit him in such a manner?

More importantly, who even *suspected* the truth, let alone had enough evidence to convince Mathu of it?

"The charge comes from an eyewitness. The man you raped and sodomised for the better part of a year while he was in your service."

Even now, Stellan couldn't imagine who Mathu was referring to. "That's ridiculous! I'm a married man. And I've never raped anybody, male *or* female. If you don't believe me, ask Jaxyn. Or Kylia . . ."

Mathu's eyes narrowed in disgust. "Tides, Jaxyn was right. You're so depraved you don't even see it, do you? He said you'd claim he was your willing partner, when in fact he was too traumatised and threatened by you to resist. As for Kylia, you'll not want to call her as a character witness. Jaxyn confessed to Kylia, fearful of how your sick desires would affect her, when she first returned to Lebec from that school you abandoned her to, leaving you free to pursue your . . . sick and perverted hobby—"

"Hang on! You're saying *Jaxyn* is accusing me of this?" Stellan felt as if he'd been gutted.

"And lucky for you the accusation came from him and not one of your other fancy boys," Mathu said. "At least Jaxyn Aranville cares enough about the royal family to bring this directly to me, and not make it public."

"Jaxyn would never . . ." Stellan began, trying to imagine what had prompted the young man to betray him. Was *he* the one who hungered for a position close to the king? Had Stellan laid the foundations for his own downfall by sending Jaxyn to court, where he'd gotten a taste of the power he could wield if he had the ear of the king? "I'd like to speak with him."

"Who? Jaxyn?" Mathu shook his head. "Not a chance. I'll not have you intimidating or manipulating him into changing his story."

Stellan felt physically ill. "Am I to be given a chance to defend myself against these charges?"

Mathu shook his head. "I'm not prepared to bring the entire family down because of your sick appetites, Stellan, which is exactly what would happen if I announced your depravity to the whole world in an open court. The stink of such a scandal would taint our family for generations to come."

He relaxed a little, seeing a glimmer of hope. "Then what *are* you planning to do?"

The king shrugged. "Charge you with something else, I suppose. The result will be the same, we just won't have to admit to your degeneracy publicly."

Stellan stared at him in shock—this news even more appalling than the realisation Jaxyn had betrayed him. "You'd trump up charges against me?"

Mathu glared at him, angry, hurt and still not sure of himself, Stellan suspected, despite his posturing. "Don't look at me like that, Stellan. You don't own the high moral ground here. You've lied to me. You lied to my father. You've indulged in the most base and degrading perversions for nothing more than your own pleasure . . . Tides . . . there's no end to the list of your crimes. Don't you dare suggest *I'm* the one in the wrong because I choose to punish you in a manner designed to protect my throne. Your niece is my wife. I cannot—*will* not—damage her reputation by having it sullied with any mud that might stick to yours. Tell me, does Arkady know the truth about you? Is she part of this sick charade?"

For Arkady's sake, Stellan couldn't afford to answer that question. As his accomplice, she stood equally culpable. It would be safer for her if people thought her duped along with the rest of the world.

"You're a better man than this, Mathu. And I'd hoped you'd be a better king."

"Suit yourself, Stellan," Mathu said with a shrug. "You've made your own bed. Now you can lie in it. Alone."

Mathu rose to his feet and called out for the guards, who'd obviously been waiting for his command.

Before he had time to protest, Stellan was under arrest, being led in disgrace from the throne room, not to take up an honoured position at the side of his king, but to face an uncertain future and false charges laid against him.

He walked with his head held high, his soul shredded inside, trying not to dwell on the fact that he'd been betrayed, not only by his king and his niece but by the one person in the whole world he would have sworn had loved him.

Chapter 40

Declan and Nyah were almost through the mine, within hours of reaching the surface, when the cave-in hit them.

There was little warning of the impending disaster. One moment they were making their way along a wide and seemingly sound tunnel, the torch flickering steadily as they walked. Nyah was chatting away about her pony, or some such triviality that Declan really wasn't listening to . . . and then a crack sounded through the mine like a tree trunk snapping and a nightmare exploded around them.

They had only a few seconds and it wasn't nearly enough to get clear, even if it had been possible to tell which direction the trouble was coming from. The torch died in a heartbeat, smothered by the choking dust as Declan tossed it aside and grabbed Nyah—who was screaming hysterically—pushing her down so he covered her body with his. Nyah's screams stopped as she hit the floor, or they were drowned out, because after that, all Declan could hear was the crashing cacophony of falling rocks filling the blinding dust-filled darkness that made it seem as if they were breathing in the very rock holding up the walls. Falling boulders pounded against his arms and his pack, as he bent over his precious charge, his knees buckling under the onslaught. Beneath him Nyah lay quiet and unresisting, surprising Declan with her equanimity during such a terrifying time.

Although it seemed like an eternity, it must have been only a few minutes before the rocks stopped falling, a few minutes after that before the rolling echoes faded into the distance.

Coughing up dust, Declan felt about the floor of the cavern until he recovered the torch. Nyah was still silent, thankfully, as he shook the dust from the torch, then found his flint in his pocket to light it again. After a few false starts, the torch sputtered into life. Declan held it up and looked around, relieved beyond measure to discover the way forward was still open. The cave-in had been right behind them, and the way back was now almost completely blocked. Ahead of them, it seemed clear.

Coughing up another lungful of dust, he turned to Nyah. "Tides, that was close!"

She didn't respond. In fact, she wasn't moving, just lying there, her eyes closed, limp against the rock fall.

"Nyah?"

When she didn't respond, Declan wedged the end of the torch between the fallen rocks and shook her gently. "Nyah? It's over now. You can open your eyes."

She still didn't react. Didn't so much as flinch at his touch.

"Oh, no, you don't, you wretched child," he said, quashing down the panic that began to bubble in his gut. He felt for a pulse beneath her ear and found it after a moment, thready and weak, but it was there.

When his hand came away, however, it was slick with blood.

"*No, no, no . . . no . . .* don't you *dare* do this to me," Declan muttered, lifting her limp body forward to discover she was bleeding from a nasty gash on the back of her head. He cursed savagely—at his own inability to protect her as much as her stupidity for getting in the way of a falling rock—while he gingerly felt around the wound, trying to determine how serious it was.

It was impossible to tell. Between her dark hair, the inadequate light and the choking dust, he could barely make *her* out, let alone judge the extent of her injuries.

And she was still unconscious, which worried him a great deal more than the blood.

He laid her down gently and sat back on his heels. They were, as far as Declan could tell, only a few hours from the surface and the shelter of Maralyce's cabin. But a few hours—if Nyah was bleeding internally—might be a death sentence.

It would be faster, he knew, to leave her here. He could make it back to the cabin in half that time, unencumbered by an unconscious child. And Maralyce was a Tide Lord, after all. If this child was badly wounded and had any hope of recovery, it was at the hands of someone able to wield Tide magic, the ultimate source of healing in the universe.

But he had no guarantee Maralyce would agree to follow him back down into the tunnels to rescue and treat a dying child.

Suppose she wasn't badly hurt? Suppose he left her here in the darkness, only to have her regain consciousness minutes after he left? Even if she wasn't hysterical within a matter of seconds at the thought of being abandoned in these oppressive black tunnels, she was just as likely to try finding her own way out of the mine.

A wrong turn would see her lost down here forever.

With a sigh, Declan climbed to his feet, groaning as every ripening bruise he'd acquired during the cave-in made its presence felt. He adjusted his pack and then scooped Nyah's limp body up, before awkwardly trying to pick the torch up without setting her hair alight. When that proved too difficult, he rearranged the child until she was draped over his left shoulder. He bent down, collected the torch and raised it up, hoping he was right and that it wasn't far to the mine's entrance and the safety of Maralyce's cabin.

Because if he was wrong, and something happened to the heir to the Caelish throne while she was in his care, Declan was in no doubt that Ricard Li would make good on his promise to devote his every breath until the day he died to bringing about Declan Hawkes's extermination.

It was dark when Declan finally emerged from the tunnels into the littered yard outside Maralyce's cabin, relieved and exhausted, the weight of his still-unconscious burden seeming to grow heavier by the minute. His leg muscles were trembling and he was staggering by the time he reached the door of the cabin. Relieved beyond measure that aid was within his grasp, he tossed aside the remains of the torch and turned the latch without knocking, kicking the door open with his boot to find Maralyce and Shalimar playing cards at the table, a cheery fire in the hearth.

His grandfather looked up and smiled, as if he'd only just stepped outside for some fresh air. "Declan! You're back!"

"Help me," he said, pushing past them and through to Maralyce's bedroom at the back of the cabin. He lowered Nyah onto the fur-covered pallet, checked her pulse again—which was much stronger—and then turned to Maralyce, who'd followed him into the room. "She's hurt."

"I can see that."

"Can you help her?"

"Dunno."

"*Will* you help her?"

"Who is she?"

"The Crown Princess of Caelum."

Maralyce peered at the little girl for a moment. "Funny, don't re-member leaving one of them layin' about down in the mine."

If he thought it would do any good, Declan would have cheerfully throttled the woman, right at that moment. "There was a cave-in. She hit her head."

"So you broke my mine while you were at it, too, did you?"

"Will you just do *something* for her?"

"What makes you think I can?"

"You're a Tide Lord, aren't you? And the Tide's on the way back? Surely there's something you can do?"

Maralyce frowned at him. "Funny how it ain't so bad me bein' a Tide Lord, soon as you need something from me."

"Stop tormenting the lad, Maralyce," Shalimar called from the other room. "Have a look at the child, for pity's sake."

Without actually saying she would help, Maralyce pushed past De-clan and bent over the little girl to examine her. After a moment, she straightened and turned to him. "Go boil some water."

"Why? What's wrong?"

"Nothing. I just want you out of the way."

Declan glared at her and then stormed out of the room to find his grandfather staring at him, still seated at the table with a rug over his legs, despite the warmth of the cabin. "Please tell me you were joking when you told Maralyce just now you've *kidnapped* the Crown Princess of Caelum?"

"If I was joking, Pop, I'd have thought up something funny." Declan shrugged off his battered pack and collapsed onto the chair so recently vacated by Maralyce. There wasn't a muscle he owned, right now, that wasn't complaining. "Besides, I didn't kidnap her. Ricard Li gave her to me."

Shalimar's eyes widened in surprise. "Gave her to you? For *what*?"

"To stop her marrying Tryan, if you must know," Declan said, stifling a yawn. Even though he'd only just sat down, he was so exhausted the warmth of the cabin was already making him sleepy. "It seems the Cael-ish weren't ignorant of the suspicious origins of the Grand Duchess and her family, after all."

"They *know* about the Tide Lords?"

Declan shook his head. "They knew Syrolee and Tryan were frauds, that's all. They've yet to learn the truth about who they're dealing with."

Shalimar shook his head despairingly. "So you agreed to bring their little princess back *here*? Tides, Declan, have you lost your mind?"

Declan was disappointed Shalimar, of all people, couldn't see the jus-tice in what he'd done. "What was I supposed to do, Pop? Stand back and let them have her?"

His grandfather shrugged. "Of course not . . . it's just . . . it compli-cates things. How are you going to keep her from them, anyway? If Syrolee has her eye on the Caelish throne for Tryan, she won't let something like this pass unremarked."

"I'll have to hide her somewhere."

"Somewhere the Tide Lords won't find her? Good luck."

Before Declan could respond, Maralyce emerged from the bedroom, wiping her hands on her trousers. "That's a nasty bump she's got on her head."

"Will she be all right?"

"Maybe."

"She's been unconscious for hours."

"Probably got sick of listening to you. I know I'd want to retreat into a coma if I had to listen to your complaining for days on end."

Declan was too tired to react to her needling. "Is she going to be all right?"

"She'll be fine."

"How long before she can travel?"

"With that sort of head wound? A week or two, maybe."

Declan was so weary he wanted to weep with it, but he didn't have a week to spare. He certainly didn't have two. "I have to get back to Herino."

"Thought you'd decided Daly Bridgeman was more than capable of covering for you?" Shalimar reminded him.

"That's before I learned Enteny and Inala are dead. The Tide Lords have made their first move on Glaeba, Pop. I need to get back."

Shalimar glanced up at Maralyce for a moment and then looked back at Declan. "Leave her here."

"You plannin' to ask *my* opinion on that, old man?"

"I don't have to, Maralyce," Shalimar replied. "You don't want Tryan getting his hands on that little girl any more than Declan does. Besides, where would she be safer? Nobody knows she's here, and even if they did, nobody knows how to find this place. And if the worst should happen and they *do* come for her, you're the only one on Amyrantha with the ability to stop another Tide Lord from taking her away."

"Tides, I should have drowned you at birth," Maralyce muttered, stalking from the cabin, slamming the door behind her so hard the whole cabin shook with it.

"She'll be all right in a little while," Shalimar told Declan with a smile. "You look like hell, by the way. Is that your blood?"

Declan shook his head. "I think it's Nyah's."

"Is that her name?"

"She's a brat."

"I'm used to brats. I raised you, didn't I?"

Declan allowed himself a weary smile. "Do you think Maralyce will begrudge me her hearth for the night? I'm so tired, I'm going to *fall* down, if I don't get some sleep soon."

"Make yourself at home. Did you want something to eat?"

He shook his head. "I'm too tired to eat. Too tired to think."

"Get some sleep then, lad. We'll talk again in the morning."

As Shalimar predicted, by the following morning Maralyce seemed resigned to having another houseguest. Nyah was awake and asking for food, which Declan took to be a good sign, and Shalimar seemed to find it entertaining to have someone other than Maralyce for company.

After explaining to the little princess that his grandfather would keep her hidden until he could send someone for her, she agreed to stay put, probably so grateful she had finally stopped running that she didn't care where Declan left her, as long as it meant she wasn't required to walk another step. Once he'd slept, eaten and washed some of the grime from his sorely bruised body, he almost felt fit enough to continue his journey.

By midmorning, he'd said goodbye to Shalimar and Nyah and was heading down the trail toward the three graves lower down the mountain. Maralyce walked with him for a time, not saying a word, until finally they reached the place where, almost two months ago, Declan had stood by these graves and wondered if Shalimar was already dead.

"You know you can't win this fight of yours, don't you?" Maralyce asked, as Declan stopped to adjust his freshly stocked pack.

"We have to try, though."

"You're trying to hold back the Tide, lad. Even the Tide Lords can't do that."

"I know," he said, turning to look at her. "But that's what it is to be mortal. We're compelled to hope."

She treated him to a rare smile. "Then I hope you die young and quickly, lad. Disillusionment's a bitter way to spend your old age."

He smiled back. "You know, that's probably the nicest thing you've ever said to me."

"Don't let it go to your head. And watch out for Jaxyn when you get to Herino. He's a treacherous little bastard, and Diala's not much better."

"I'll be careful."

"Sure you will . . . and I'm going to die tomorrow." And with no further ado, she turned and headed back up the trail, without even saying goodbye.

PART III

Now morn has come,
And with the morn the
Punctual tide again.

—"Flood-Tide,"
Susan Coolidge (1835–1905)

Chapter 41

Even with the horse he commandeered at Clyden's Inn, it still took Declan two hard-travelling weeks after he left Maralyce's mine before he arrived in Herino.

When he got there, it was just in time for the trial of Stellan Desean, the Duke of Lebec, who—he was stunned to learn while on his way through Lebec Province—was charged with the murder of the King and Queen of Glaeba.

He'd been planning to stop in Lebec on the way to Herino, anyway, to see Tilly Ponting and tell her everything he'd learned these past few weeks, including the disturbing revelation that Maralyce was now sheltering both Shalimar and the Crown Princess of Caelum.

The news about the Duke of Lebec's arrest put paid to that idea.

As Maralyce had suggested, Clyden's Inn was the best place in Glaeba for gossip, and nobody was talking of anything else, particularly at an inn located in the duke's own province, where he was both well-known and well-liked.

As soon as he reached the capital, Declan headed for the palace. It was late, but still quite warm and sure enough, a light still burned in the window of his office. Travel-stained and only marginally less weary than he had been when he'd staggered into Maralyce's cabin a fortnight ago, he let himself in through the back entrance to the palace and made his way upstairs. When he opened the door, he found Daly Bridgeman sitting at his desk, hunched over a document he seemed to be studying intently.

A big, hirsute bear of a man, Daly was almost seventy, although to look at him you'd never know it. Like Declan, he was a member of the

Cabal of the Tarot first, spymaster to the Glaeban king a distant second. He'd also been appointed at the urging of Karyl Deryon, and like Declan, had used the post to watch over the Glaeban throne, and hopefully protect it from the Tide Lords—something he'd done for thirty years prior to his retirement and been far more successful at than Declan.

He scowled at the interruption and he then realised who it was who'd dare disturb him. "You're back."

"You see, that's why you're such a legend, Daly. Nothing gets past you."

The old man pushed himself to his feet, tossing the letter he'd been reading on the table. "Glad you've still got your sense of humour, Declan. Trust me, you're going to need it."

He stepped into the office and closed the door behind him. "You're talking about Desean's arrest?"

Daly nodded, still scowling. "It's all yours, son. I've had a gutful."

"Is it true?"

"That he's being tried for the murder of Enteny and Inala? My word it is."

"Is he guilty?"

"Guilty as I can make him."

Declan stared at the old man, a little bemused. "What do you mean?"

"The charges are a sham. Enteny's death was an accident and everybody knows it."

"Then why are they charging Stellan Desean with murder?"

"Because Diala wants him out of the way."

With a muttered curse, Declan sank down into the chair opposite the desk. Daly also resumed his seat.

"What happened?"

"There was boating accident. A freak storm, so I'll let you guess who engineered it. In fact I know Jaxyn did, because that Scard of yours saw it happen."

"Warlock?"

Daly nodded. "Smart dog, that one. Knows how to play the game like a pro. He's got Kylia wanting him to follow her around like a lap dog, so there's not a lot she and Jaxyn get up to we don't hear about eventually. That's also how I know that once the king and queen were dead, it occurred to our two scheming immortals that even with the king out of the

way and Mathu on the throne with Diala pulling the strings, Stellan Desean was still next in line and his wife was pregnant—"

"*Was* pregnant?"

"Seems that was a lie, too. I feel for the man, truly I do, but Desean's
been very careless. He's handed his own head to them on a platter, you
know."

Declan didn't visibly react to the report that Arkady wasn't pregnant,
but it was welcome news, nonetheless. If she had been pregnant, he was
fairly certain there could only have been one candidate for father and it
wasn't her husband. He'd spent a lot of time, lying awake at night, trying to convince himself Arkady would never have been stupid enough to
get involved with an immortal, with little success.

But that was something he could worry about later. Right now, there
were other, more pressing issues to be dealt with and none of this was
making sense.

"Does that mean Jaxyn and Diala are going after *all* the heirs to the
throne?"

"Not sure they need to worry about all of them. Next in line after
Desean is Reon Debalkor of Venetia, and he only has daughters. He's as
unpopular as Desean is popular, and a sick old man, to boot. Nobody is
going to rally behind him to take the Glaeban throne from a pretender
once Mathu is disposed of. I doubt they even consider him a threat."

"Even so, Mathu and Stellan are good friends. How did Diala . . . or
Kylia . . . whatever her name is . . . ever convince Mathu to turn on
him? I would have thought Stellan Desean first in line to replace Karyl
Deryon."

"And he would have been," Daly agreed, "if a certain matter of his
less-than-conventional sexual preferences didn't come to light."

Declan sagged in his chair, shaking his head. It was only a matter of
time, he supposed, before the truth came out. "Tides . . . how did *that*
happen?"

Daly looked at him in surprise. "You *knew?* Ah . . . of course . . . your
girl married him, didn't she? You would've checked him out very thor-
oughly. Still, it explains a lot. Always thought you took the whole thing
about a duke marrying a commoner a bit too hard."

"Arkady is just a friend," Declan corrected. "And I took it hard because she married him to secure her father's release. If I'd thought she
really loved him, I would have been much more . . . sympathetic."

Daly smiled. "Well, you tell yourself whatever you have to, son. In the meantime, our problem is that Mathu knows the truth about Desean, because Jaxyn spun him a fairly horrific tale about how the evil duke had kept him as his sex slave for the whole time he was Kennel Master in Lebec. Kylia backed him up—and that lovesick boy would believe night was day if Kylia told him it was—and that was pretty much the Duke of Glaeba's death knell. He's been disinherited, stripped of his title, his assets seized by the crown . . ."

"That won't hurt the royal coffers. Desean's a very wealthy man."

"*Was* a wealthy man," Daly said. "And soon he'll be a dead one."

"I still don't get why he's being charged with the king's murder. Surely, if Jaxyn's prepared to testify against him, the sodomy charge alone would bring him down?"

"I suspect Mathu doesn't want the scandal attached to publicly admitting one of the most popular dukes in Glaeba—and his own cousin—is a sodomite. He's had me fabricating evidence against Desean, so he can be rid of him some other way."

"But . . . what evidence is there to fabricate? It was a freak storm."

Daly shrugged, as if this was the easiest part of his job. "And all I need is a couple of bribed sailors to claim they were paid to sabotage the royal barge's steering lines by one of Desean's agents, and a couple of amphibious Crasii to swear the ship was out of control before the storm struck, and we'll have our case for murder."

Declan remained unconvinced. "I still don't see how it'll pass even the most casual scrutiny. What motive could Stellan Desean possibly have for killing the king and queen?"

"Are you kidding? He was already in exile. Everyone in Glaeba knows that. And then he lied about his wife being pregnant. And the accident—which should have included Mathu's death, except he slept in that morning—would have made Stellan Desean king. Tides, Declan, it's such a good motive, you have to wonder why he *didn't* try to kill them, not doubt that he did."

Sadly, Declan was forced to acknowledge that Daly was right. "Has Arkady been arrested, too?"

Daly shook his head. "She's still in Ramahn. Although what will happen to her there once the news about her husband reaches Torlenia is anybody's guess."

"What are we going to do?"

"*We* aren't going to do anything, my boy," Daly announced, rising to his feet. "I'm walking away from this mess, fast as my weary old legs will carry me. There's a whole lot of fish in the Upper Ryrie demanding my attention, and I don't intend to neglect them a moment longer than I have to. You're back, and it's all yours, my young and tireless friend, with my blessing. *You* can deal with arranging for the trial and execution of an innocent man any way you see fit."

Declan didn't blame Daly for feeling that way. His own inclination was to turn around and ride straight back to Maralyce's mine where the worst he had to deal with was hiding the missing heir to the Caelish throne, his dying grandfather and the irascible immortal who was watching over them.

He wouldn't run away, of course, but it was a very tempting thought.

"Has Mathu been asking where I am?"

"He did when he first came to me with this, so I gave him the story about you seeing to your sick grandfather. Did you find him, by the way?"

Declan nodded.

"Well, something's gone right then. The king will be glad you're back. Got the impression he thought he might have had less trouble convincing *you* that framing the Duke of Lebec for murder was a good idea, than he did me."

"You objected?"

"Of course, I objected. But Diala's leading our naive young king around by his cock at the moment, so not much else is getting through to him."

Declan sighed, wondering how things could have gotten so bad, so quickly. Was it always like this for the Cabal? *Do we always spend hundreds of years planning and scheming and kidding ourselves we have everything under control, and then the Tide comes back and we discover how badly we've been deluded?*

"Where's Desean now?"

"In the tower cell of Herino Prison."

"Have you spoken to him?"

Daly shook his head. "I'm due at the prison first thing tomorrow morning to take his confession."

Declan looked at Daly in shock. "He's *confessing* to this?"

The old man nodded. "Seems our selfless sodomite is planning to be a real little trouper about his arrest, to spare his good friend, King Mathu, any further embarrassment. And another reason I'm glad you're back. You can deal with that nasty little piece of theatre, too. I want no part of it."

"I'll talk to him," Declan promised. "See if I can't talk some sense into him."

"You'd best not mention anything about the Tide Lords," he suggested. "Not if you expect him to listen to you. Desean may have the right of it, though. If he confesses to the murders, he saves himself a whole lot of pain and humiliation, not to mention ensuring a speedy execution. He's a realist. He knows there is no way out of this jam, so he's taking the path of least resistance. Not sure I'd have the courage to do the same, but then, I always did think Stellan Desean was a cut above your average high-born flunky." Daly walked around the desk as Declan rose to his feet. "How come you never said anything about him, anyway, if you've known all along? You could have brought him down years ago."

"To what purpose?"

He smiled, and treated Declan to a playful—and very painful—punch on the arm, which landed right on top of a few other choice bruises that he'd collected on his way through Maralyce's mine. "You might have stood a chance with that girl of yours, if she wasn't married to Desean. You may yet, if you play your cards right."

"Arkady is just a friend," Declan insisted. "And I never exposed him for just that reason. Besides, he was always discreet in his affairs, and as far as I could tell, he wasn't hurting anyone else."

"Well, that's all very tolerant and understanding of you, Declan. I just hope your fondness for the good duke's pretty young wife doesn't mean we've played right into the hands of the Tide Lords trying to take over Glaeba." The old man walked to the door and then stopped and turned to look at him. "I'll come by in the morning after you've spoken to Desean to collect my things and bring you up to date on everything. In the meantime, you should get some rest. You look like hell."

"Goodnight, Daly."

The old spymaster let himself out of the office and closed the door behind him.

Weary beyond words and still reeling from all he'd learned in the last hour, Declan walked around the desk and sank into the seat so recently vacated by Daly Bridgeman. Leaning back in the big leather chair, he put his feet on the desk and closed his eyes for a moment, hoping to push the world away for a time just to let him catch his breath.

He wasn't very successful. On top of his need to bring the news about Nyah to the Cabal, word would soon arrive from Caelum that she was missing, which was liable to spark an international incident if there was even a hint of his involvement. Even if there wasn't any talk of Declan Hawkes being implicated in her disappearance, logically if the child wasn't in Caelum then she almost had to be in Glaeba, and the Empress of the Five Realms wasn't going to be foiled so easily.

And now there was this mess of Stellan Desean's to deal with. The King and Queen of Glaeba were dead. Arkady's husband was about to confess to two murders he had nothing to do with to protect someone else's reputation.

The new King of Glaeba was married to an immortal scheming to take his throne and a Tide Lord stood at her right hand, poised to aid her in her quest.

Even worse, Arkady was trapped in Ramahn with no idea she had lost everything and was about to be stranded by her husband's noble and entirely idiotic idea of being loyal to the throne.

Nor did Declan have any idea where Tiji was or if she was in a position to help Arkady, and no way to get word to her.

And Shalimar was dying.

Tides, no wonder Daly wants to go fishing . . .

Chapter 42

There was a certain amount of freedom in being exposed, Stellan discovered. A weight lifted off his shoulders after a lifetime of lies. He was disgraced, disinherited and doomed, and yet slightly euphoric about the whole thing. It was strange, but of all the consequences he had expected of being discovered, that was the one he hadn't considered. Stellan was no longer required to pretend to be something he was not, and that made the rest of it bearable.

His cell was large, by normal standards, and quite well lit, given it was in the corner tower of Herino Prison, rather than a dungeon underground. Reserved for prisoners of the highest rank, it boasted a small fireplace and an alcove with a narrow drain where he could relieve himself out of the view of his guards. The tower cell overlooked the lake, its surprisingly large window affording quite a spectacular view of the Upper Oran and the faint purple smudge of the Caterpillar Mountains on the horizon, on the other side of the lake. There were no bars on the window. Perhaps they thought the four-storey drop to the lake below sufficient deterrent. Or maybe nobody had ever tried to escape from here.

There was a real bed in the corner of the cell, with a mattress that had seen better days, and two thin blankets to ward off the night-time chill. The ultimate luxury, however, was a small desk and stool, where he was able to put his affairs in order, before his trial and the inevitable execution that would follow.

He'd written a number of letters, so far. One to Kylia, apologising for not being a better guardian, and trying to explain that her impression of him was the result of things he couldn't explain. There was another to Arkady, thanking her for being a much better wife than he'd been a husband, and begging her forgiveness for the trouble now likely to befall her because of his sins. The letter he was working on this morning was to Jaxyn, but he was having no luck composing it. Despite everything he wanted to say to his former lover, what he really wanted to know was *why*?

"I'm not disturbing you, am I?"

Although he'd heard the door to the outer guard room opening, he'd assumed it was just one of the guards moving about. He hadn't realised the visitor was for him. Stellan looked up, surprised to find Declan Hawkes standing on the other side of the bars.

He laid down his pen and rose to his feet. "Any interruption is welcome to a man in my position."

It was raining outside, the gentle patter of the raindrops on his windowsill barely audible in the background, the window misted and opaque. Between the irregular light and the bars separating them, Hawkes's expression was impossible to judge as he stood there, studying the prisoner. He seemed neither angry nor reproachful, which surprised Stellan a little. This man, he was sure, would have walked through fire to protect Arkady, and he must know what Stellan's downfall would mean to her.

The spymaster glanced over his shoulder at the guards standing either side of the outer door. "Leave us."

The felines obeyed without question, leaving them alone.

Stellan watched the guards leave, wondering if Hawkes had sent them away so there wouldn't be any witnesses. "That was unnecessary. There's no need to beat me into submission, Master Hawkes. I will confess."

"To what? Rank stupidity?"

The disgust in Hawkes's voice didn't surprise him. Declan Hawkes was the King's Spymaster. He would have been told the true reason for Stellan's incarceration.

"You have to know, Declan, in spite of my crimes, I've never hurt Arkady. I never meant her to be hurt." He shrugged, unable to think of any other way to explain himself. "I can't help what I am."

"I couldn't care less what you are," the spymaster said. "Any more than I care who you do it to. What I care about, your *grace*, is that you're going to give up without a fight."

Stellan was stunned. "You think I should *fight* this? What do you want of me, Hawkes? To expose my king to ridicule and scandal? And what of the effect on Arkady? Have you thought of what would happen to her if it became known she was nothing more than a willing front for my malfeasance? She'd be shunned, ostracised—"

"As opposed to being crowned queen of the Herino social set, I suppose," the spymaster cut in, "which is sure to happen once her husband confesses to murdering the king, the queen and a couple of dozen innocent bystanders."

Stellan threw his hands up, certain there was nothing he could say that would satisfy this man. "Think of me what you will, Master Hawkes. I have chosen the manner of my death, and I intend to go to it honourably."

"Tides, but you're a selfish bastard."

Stellan had expected Declan to accuse him of all manner of sins, but selfishness wasn't one of them. He was offended by the very suggestion. "I would have thought my actions quite the opposite. By confessing to Enteny and Inala's murder, I spare my king, and my family, the shame of everyone knowing what I am."

"What you *are*, Stellan Desean, is the only man in the country with a chance of opposing your king's enemies, who intend to dispose of him and take Glaeba's throne the moment all the other likely contenders to the crown are disposed of."

Stellan stared at the spymaster. "Do you know of such a plot?"

Declan glared at him. "I'm standing here looking at it in action."

He shook his head, unwilling to believe such a far-fetched tale. "You're imagining things. Who would do such a thing?"

"Hmmm . . . I wonder . . ." Declan said. "Let's start with your lover who betrayed you to the king, shall we? Oh, and then there's your niece . . . did you know she's *not* your niece? The real Kylia is probably dead, I'm sorry to report. This one's real name is Diala, she's a great deal older and a lot less innocent than she looks, by the way, and she's known your little friend Aranville for far longer than you can imagine."

Stellan shook his head. "No . . ."

"The two of them dug this trap for you months ago, your grace, and you walked into it with your eyes wide open. Jaxyn Aranville has his eye on the throne. He has done since the moment he first leant over and started whispering sweet nothings in your ear, and you thought you'd fi-

nally found true love. The only thing standing between him and
Glaeba's crown are her rightful heirs. Well, he's disposed of Enteny and
Inala. Diala has Mathu wrapped around her little finger, so he'll be allowed to stay around for a bit—long enough to dispose of the truly dangerous contenders, like you—and then they'll get rid of him, too. His
grieving widow will become queen and then, in a groundswell of approval and affection for the tragic young bride, she'll marry the late
king's closest friend and advisor—and his new Private Secretary, in case
you haven't heard—Lord Aranville. Even allowing for a decent period
of mourning, I give them a year before we're all bowing down to King
Jaxyn and Queen Diala."

Stellan was appalled by the inconceivable horror of Declan's scenario. "You're seeing guilt where none exists."

"There's an epitaph you might want to consider for your *own* headstone, your grace."

"You're speculating, Declan. You have no proof."

"You *are* the proof," the spymaster said. "Can't you see that? Or is it
that you just can't bring yourself to acknowledge that you might have
been so comprehensively duped? Not that I blame you. After all, you
were the one who brought Jaxyn Aranville into your home. And the
one who mistook an impostor for his own niece and then introduced
her to the crown prince. Don't think I'd be looking too kindly on my
involvement in this sorry business either, if I were you."

Stellan shook his head, unable to comprehend the depths of resent-
ment that must drive this man. "If this is your way of getting even
with me for taking Arkady from you . . ."

"You're a flanking fool, Desean."

"Perhaps. But I'm not as blind as you claim. And you have plenty of
reason to want to destroy me."

Declan rolled his eyes. "If I wanted to destroy you, my lord, I could
have brought you down any number of times before now. Tides, I've
covered for you, more than once."

That news was almost as unbelievable as the notion Jaxyn and Kylia
had conspired to destroy him and were planning to murder Mathu so
they could take the throne. "What are you talking about?"

"You don't recall that trip you took to Venetia about three years ago?
You met a man there in Reon's court? He was bookkeeper, I think."

"Bruse Decalle," Stellan said, remembering the handsome young man who had been so passionate and keen for an affair and then vanished without explanation before they were due to leave the city.

"He was a plant. A deliberate attempt to seduce you into doing something foolish."

"But that was more than two years before I met Jaxyn . . ."

"He wasn't put in your path by Jaxyn. This was Reon Debalkor looking for a way to curb your influence with the king. He's suspected the truth about you for years. According to my information, he was ready to move on you quite some time ago, but then you blew his case away by marrying Arkady. He's been waiting like a spider ever since, just looking for a chance to get the proof he needs, to take his accusations to the king."

There was a ring of certainty about Declan Hawkes's tale Stellan couldn't argue with. "How is it you know this?"

"Because I'm the one who made sure the proof never got back to the Duke of Venetia."

His eyes widened in horror. "You *killed* Bruse Decalle?"

"I saved your neck, your grace. And your duchy, while I was at it."

"*Why?*"

Declan shrugged. "The consequences to Arkady should you be exposed aside, my job is to protect the Glaeban throne. I happened to think at the time—along with a large majority of Glaeba's population—we were safer with you third in line to it, than Reon Debalkor."

Stellan sank down onto the stool, staggered by the news. "How many others?"

"Three or four. Not all of them required such drastic measures. A few of them we scared off. One we bought off."

"Does Arkady know?"

"Of course not."

"I don't know what to say."

"How about: thank you, Declan, for repeatedly saving my neck, and in return I won't confess to a score of murders I didn't commit, but rather, I'll fight these pernicious charges until I can make the king see reason and he banishes those two vipers he's nesting with, who are planning to steal his throne?"

Stellan looked up at the spymaster, smiling. "You do have a way of boiling things down to their essence, don't you?"

"Is that a yes?"

Stellan shook his head. "You don't know what you're asking."

"I see. You'd rather have Mathu lose his crown, than you lose your reputation, is that it?"

"You haven't convinced me his crown is actually at risk."

Declan was silent for a moment, and then he shook his head. "Tides, you're a bigger fool than I feared."

"Perhaps," Stellan agreed. He rose to his feet, squaring his shoulders with determination. It was time to get this done. "Now, do you want my confession or not?"

The spymaster stared at him for a moment, clearly disgusted with his resolve to see this through, and then he shook his head. "To hell with your confession. You want to be a martyr? You want to see this charade through? Fine. You can stand up in an open court and tell the whole world how you plotted to murder your king. I'm not going to help you kill yourself."

"Daly Bridgeman said if I confessed then we could avoid a trial."

"Well, you're out of luck," Declan said. "Daly's gone fishing."

With that, the spymaster turned on his heel and stalked out of the guard room, leaving Stellan staring after him, Arkady's parting words in Torlenia ringing in his ears.

There may even come a time, she'd said, *when you learn your friends are really your enemies, and a man you think of as your enemy now may well prove to be your only friend.*

If only there was a way to tell if she was referring to Declan Hawkes.

Chapter 43

Arkady Desean surprised Tiji by refusing to take her into the royal seraglium as her servant. She made the announcement as she was sorting out the garments she wanted loaded into her trunks before she left for the palace that afternoon.

"But you need someone with you who you can trust, your grace," Tiji pointed out, not wanting to be the one to explain to Declan how she had let the duchess march unaccompanied into the heart of the enemy's stronghold without at least putting up a token fight about it.

Arkady was adamant. "Kinta despises the Crasii. Bringing one into the seraglium would cause nothing but trouble. I'm sorry, Tiji, but it's just not possible."

"I could sneak in . . ."

"What would be the point? You're far more use to me—and the Cabal—out here. In fact, you should probably think of returning to Glaeba. I'm sure Declan has much more useful things for someone of your unique talents to be doing than following me about Ramahn."

The little Crasii scowled. "Declan will run me through if I let you out of my sight."

The duchess looked up from her packing. "*Declan* will run you through?"

"He's very fond of you, your grace. If I go back home and tell him I left you at the door of the royal seraglium in Torlenia with an immortal waiting for you on the other side, he'll chop me into little pieces and feed me to the canines."

Arkady smiled. "I think you're exaggerating, Tiji."

"And I think you underestimate Declan Hawkes's feelings for you, your grace."

Arkady's smile faded. Tiji winced. She hadn't meant to voice *that* thought aloud.

"And what, *exactly*, do you mean by that?" the duchess asked in a tone that made it quite clear who was the master and who was the slave. For a common-born physician's daughter, she had it down pat, too, Tiji decided, wilting a little under Arkady's withering glare. It was the first time the duchess had pulled rank on the Crasii since Tiji had known her.

"I just meant . . ." she began, wishing there was some tactful way out of this. "Declan's known you a long time. He thinks of you like a . . . sister . . ."

"Is that right?"

"Absolutely!" the little Crasii said, grabbing on to the idea with both hands. "He says it all the time. Lady Desean is like a sister to me, he says . . ."

"He calls me Lady Desean?"

"Well . . . yes . . ."

"You know for a spy, you're a terrible liar, Tiji."

"So's he," Tiji said, figuring she'd already put her foot in it, so she might as well have her say and be done with it.

"I beg your pardon?"

"Declan Hawkes," she said. "He's a terrible liar, too. He tries to pretend he doesn't care what you're up to, or that you're married to someone else, or what might have happened between you and the Immortal Prince, but he does. It eats him up inside."

Arkady was silent, too shocked perhaps to respond.

Good one, Slinky. Now's when you find out she's best friends with an immortal because she really is *an evil bitch who enjoys tormenting poor Crasii who've dared offend her . . .*

The duchess stared at her for a moment longer and then turned back to her packing. "Pass me that shawl on the dresser, please."

Worried by the abrupt change of subject, Tiji did as she was asked, waiting for the explosion she was sure must be coming any moment now.

"Would you ask Corianne and Valorey to make sure they're ready by the time the royal carriage gets here?" She was taking two human servants, Glaebans both, to serve her in the palace. The duchess was all business now, as if the conversation of a few moments ago had never taken place.

"Your grace . . ."

"That will be all, Tiji."

"I didn't mean to . . ."

This time Arkady did look up. Her gaze was frosty, any glimmer of friendship Tiji might have once thought possible between them smothered by her presumptuousness.

"Didn't mean to *what*, Tiji? Offend me? Embarrass Declan? Insult my husband?"

She shrugged. "I just thought . . . maybe you didn't know . . ."

Arkady seemed to debate something within herself for a moment. "It's not me who's ignorant of the facts here, Tiji, it's you. I'm sure you're very loyal to your master, and I know he thinks highly of you, but don't you dare presume to know anything about my relationship with Declan Hawkes, what he thinks of me or what I think of him."

"I'm sorry, your grace, truly, I never meant to offend you."

"I'm sure you didn't, Tiji. Just as I'm sure you're never going to bring this up again, are you?"

"Of course not, your grace."

"Then do as I ask, please. Find Corianne and Valorey and tell them I expect them to be ready to leave within the hour. Once that is done, you may make whatever arrangements you need to make to ensure your safe return to Glaeba. If you need money, speak to Dashin Deray. He'll see you have sufficient funds for the return journey."

"You're sending me home?"

"Your work here is done," Arkady said, folding the shawl and placing it on the pile she intended to pack. "I'm sure Declan has more important things for you to do."

Tiji debated arguing the point, but—even with diplomatic status—she was still a slave and not in a position to defy a direct order from an ambassador's wife. "What did you want me to tell Declan when I get back?"

"What he sent you to Torlenia to find out. That his suspicions were correct. Chintara *is* the immortal Kinta, and she appears to be paving the way for the Lord of Reckoning to take control of the country, as soon as the Tide is sufficiently high for her to risk it. I have befriended her, and will find out what I can."

"He knows that already. We sent him a letter telling him all of this.

Your husband took it with him and promised to deliver it personally, remember?"

"Then I'm sure Declan has need of you in other areas."

"But . . . if I leave, how will you get a message to him?"

"The same way I did before you arrived. I'll write to him."

"Suppose your mail is intercepted by Kinta?"

"I'm a resourceful person, Tiji. I'm sure I'll find a way."

Tiji shook her head, wishing her diplomatic status gave her more than the ability to flag down passing ships. "Your grace, I really must object . . ."

"Object all you want," Arkady said, her attention fixed on her packing. "My mind is made up."

Tides, why doesn't she get her servants to do that like any other noblewoman would, and pay attention? This is important.

"But if anything should happen to you . . ."

"Then it won't be your fault. And you can tell Declan I said that." Arkady straightened up and turned to face Tiji. "You may go."

"But . . ."

"I *said*, you may leave. Now."

Defeated, and with no notion of how she was going to explain her dismissal to Declan when she got home, Tiji bowed to her mistress.

"To serve you is the reason I breathe, your grace."

She turned on her heel and strode from the room, not waiting to see the human woman's reaction. She didn't need to. Arkady Desean was a smart woman. The Duchess of Lebec wouldn't mistake her meaning for anything other than the criticism is was meant to be.

To serve you is the reason I breathe is what all grovelling, spineless Crasii told their immortal masters, even when they were asked to do stupid, dangerous things that wouldn't help anybody.

Shrugging on the long-sleeved, hooded robe the slaves of Torlenia favoured, Tiji slipped out of the palace and went for a walk to cool her temper. She couldn't believe she was being sent home. She couldn't believe she'd been so foolish.

She couldn't imagine how she was going to explain this mess to Declan.

The area around the embassy was quiet; tree-lined streets and broad avenues where the cutthroat business of government and diplomacy took place beneath a veneer of tranquil civility. Tiji headed south, toward the markets, where the slaves of the city, human and Crasii alike, gathered to gossip and shop while on their masters' business. Tiji liked the Ramahn markets. They were full of strange sights and exotic smells and weird, haunting music from the countless Crasii buskers, who despite their apparent poverty played strange stringed instruments carved out of buffalo horn, or polished ebony inlaid with mother of pearl.

Tiji had always been intrigued by the Torlenian capital, surprised at the diverse population. Every human race on Amyrantha seemed to be represented in this vast city, along with every Crasii she had ever seen or heard of, too.

Except there were no chameleon Crasii.

There were never any chameleon Crasii.

It was midmorning by the time she reached the markets. Already, some of the stall owners were closing up for the midday break. Almost everything but the taverns in Ramahn closed midmorning, reopening again midafternoon once the heat of the day had passed.

Tiji had no destination in mind. Not really. She'd spent much of the walk here replaying the conversation with Arkady Desean in her mind, trying to think of a way she could have handled it better. Or what she could do to fix things.

Not a lot, she concluded. Tiji had crossed the fine line between servant and friend. She'd assumed Arkady would react to her comments about the supposed relationship between her and the spymaster the same way Declan did, which is to say he barely reacted at all. He would just automatically deny it and move on, without so much as missing a beat.

The Duchess of Lebec, however, wasn't as comfortable with the notion that someone knew or suspected there might be—or might once have been—something between her and Declan Hawkes. Pushing through the crush toward a stall selling the spicy strips of horsemeat jerky she'd developed a taste for since coming to Torlenia, Tiji wondered if that was because Arkady was genuinely offended by the idea, or if she'd inadvertently rubbed the scab off an old wound.

Maybe there really was something between them . . .

Tiji froze, mid-stride, as she felt the taint of a suzerain. It was a fleeting contact, and one she'd been too preoccupied to pinpoint, but it was there, on the edge of her awareness.

Somewhere nearby, there was an immortal lurking.

All thoughts of what may or may not be going on between Declan Hawkes and Arkady Desean evaporated. Tiji closed her eyes, letting the crowd jostle around her, ignoring their curses, and let her senses roam out, searching for the source of the taint. It was hard to focus with the noise and the heat. When her search achieved nothing, she opened her eyes and looked around, standing on her toes to see over the heads of the other slaves, which proved pointless, because even on her toes, she only reached the shoulder of the average canine. Muttering a curse she pushed back against the flow of people. There was a tavern ahead. Cayal's Rest, the hanging sign announced in several languages. Tiji frowned.

Surely Brynden's not hiding down here in a tavern called Cayal's Rest?

Tiji pushed her way across the dusty market to the tavern, stopping when she reached the entrance. The taint was stronger here and there were no signs saying Crasii were forbidden. Taking a deep breath, she stepped inside, the taint of the suzerain almost overwhelming in the gloomy, confined space of the taproom.

She spied him immediately. Not Brynden, as she'd feared, but Cayal—the Immortal Prince himself—standing at the bar in the tavern named after him, nursing an amber-coloured glass tumbler of something potently alcoholic. Tiji could tell that by the smell of it, too, even from across the room.

She froze again, her natural instinct to take cover in camouflage taking over. It was a waste of time, of course—not only was she wearing a robe, which meant that was the camouflage her skin tried to emulate, she was blocking the light from outside and not hiding her presence from anyone.

"Come in or go out," the barman called to her. "Don't just stand there blockin' the wretched door."

"I'm looking for my master," she said, glancing around the taproom as if she had a purpose here. "He's a tall fellow. Missing his left ear."

"Ain't seen anyone like that in here. You buyin' or leavin'?"

"Sorry to bother you, sir," she said, bobbing a quick curtsey. Cayal hadn't even looked in her direction.

But then, why would he? Even when the Tide was at its peak, he couldn't tell a Scard from a Crasii.

Tiji fled the tavern and didn't stop for a whole block before she leaned up against the wall of a bakery, breathing hard.

Tides, Cayal is here. She'd known he was in Ramahn, of course, but she'd never expected to run into him like this.

What should I do?

What would Declan *want me to do?*

The answer was easy. There was no question of what Declan would want her to do. What's more, now she'd been dismissed by Arkady Desean, she was free to do it.

Tiji would follow the Immortal Prince. Wherever he might lead.

Chapter 44

Tilly Ponting arrived in Herino for the funeral of Enteny and Inala and to bear witness to the coronation of the new King and Queen of Glaeba. More importantly, she arrived in time to host an emergency meeting of the Pentangle, the ruling body of the Cabal of the Tarot.

That she was helpless to stop the coronation of an immortal as Queen of Glaeba had visibly aged her, Declan thought when he arrived at her townhouse. She opened the door to him herself, not saying a word until they reached the parlour where Lord Deryon, Aleki Ponting, and Markun Far Jisa—the only Senestran member of the Pentangle—and another man Declan had never met before were waiting, gathered around the table. The stranger was Torlenian, Declan guessed, with pale eyes that didn't seem to fit in his dark skin; he looked to be in his thirties, and was a wealthy man, if his embroidered silk coat was anything to go by.

"I believe you know everyone, Declan," Tilly said, indicating he should take a seat. "Except Ryda Tarek."

The Torlenian rose to his feet and offered Declan his hand across the table. "Ah, the King's Spymaster. I've heard quite a bit about you, Master Hawkes."

Declan shook his hand, a little puzzled. The man's handshake was firm and confident. Tilly noticed Declan's expression and smiled. "It's all right, Declan. Ryda is one of us."

"You're a member of the Cabal?"

"And then some," Markun Far Jisa chuckled.

Declan's eyes widened. This then, must be the fifth member of the

Pentangle. The man whose identity had always been such a closely guarded secret. The one Maralyce speculated might be immortal. He didn't look like a Tide Lord, but things must be dire indeed, to bring him out of hiding.

"You honour us with your presence, sir."

Ryda Tarek smiled sourly. "I'd prefer it wasn't necessary, but things are moving quickly and so must we."

Declan nodded in agreement and took a seat next to Markun. He hadn't seen the Senestran since he'd rescued Tiji from the freak show in Senestra, and they had no time to catch up now. He was here to report what he'd been up to.

It remained to be seen how the Cabal would react to his news.

"How is your grandfather, by the way?" Ryda asked, as Declan pulled his chair in a little closer and accepted a glass of wine from Tilly.

"He's getting by," Declan said, taking a sip, impressed that Tilly had laid out the good stuff for this meeting. "The Tide's return is causing him pain."

"Is that common among Tidewatchers?" Tilly asked, directing her question to Ryda.

He nodded. "It will only get worse as the Tide nears its peak. Have you considered the possibility of killing him sooner?"

Declan coughed, choking on his wine. "*What*?"

Ryda shrugged apologetically. "The return of the Tide is going to decimate your grandfather, Declan—do you mind if I call you Declan? The torment Shalimar faces will become intolerable eventually. It would be an act of mercy to end his suffering before it reaches that point."

"And you know this *how*, exactly?"

"Ryda Tarek is the most eminent Tide Lord scholar on Amyrantha," Markun explained. "There is nobody who has studied them longer or knows more about them."

Declan thought he looked a little young for such a glowing endorsement, but he said nothing, just glowered at the man, relieved, for the first time since Shalimar had left Lebec, that he was safe in the company of Maralyce, out of the reach of men like Ryda Tarek and their dubious notions of mercy.

"We'll miss Shalimar's counsel," Markun said, clapping Declan's shoulder in a comforting manner. "But he's probably better off where he is."

"Which brings us to the question of *where* exactly he is," Tilly said, fixing her gaze on Declan. "Would you like to enlighten us?"

No, Declan thought. *I wouldn't.* But he knew it was a rhetorical question, posed out of nothing more than good manners. There was no choice here.

"He's with Maralyce at her mine in the Shevron Mountains."

"*She's* holding him prisoner?" Lord Deryon asked in the awkward silence that followed.

Declan shook his head. "He's staying with her by choice."

"That makes no sense," Markun said, shaking his head. "He's spent his whole life fighting against the evil of the Tide Lords. Why would he seek one out now?"

Lord Deryon nodded in agreement and turned to Declan. "I find it amazing that she's allowing him to stay. Is he there to learn what he can from her?"

Ryda Tarek answered before Declan could say a word. "He's with Maralyce because he's old, he's sick and he's only going to get worse. He's done what most old people do when they find themselves in that predicament, my lord. They go home to their families."

Even Tilly blanched at that suggestion. "Maralyce is somehow related to Shalimar?"

"I'm sorry. I thought you all knew." Ryda's perceptive gaze fixed on Declan. "Maralyce is Shalimar's mother."

Declan was grateful he knew this already. Ryda Tarek had been watching him closely as he broke the news, trying to judge his reaction. Forewarned, Declan was able to weather the dramatic announcement without so much as blinking.

"You don't look surprised, Declan."

"Shalimar's a Tidewatcher. I've always known he had to have an immortal parent. Like you, Lord Deryon, I couldn't imagine what my grandfather was doing with Maralyce or why she was allowing him to stay. Once I figured that out, the rest of it made sense."

"Well, I'm glad it makes sense to you, my lad," Tilly said. "Because it doesn't make any sense to me. How can she be his mother? She was what . . . in her fifties when she was made immortal?"

"That makes her unlikely to bear a child, Tilly," Ryda pointed out. "It doesn't make it impossible. Immortality preserves her and keeps her healthy. And I don't think she was that old. Late forties perhaps."

"Do we know this for a fact?" Aleki asked. "Or are we just speculating?"

"It's a fact," Ryda assured him. "Maralyce spends most of her time alone, but she does come down from her mountain, from time to time. About eighty years ago she was in the mood for some company and needed supplies, so she decided to visit civilisation for a few days. She met a man at Clyden's Inn, I believe. They got drinking together, one thing led to another, and a few months later, Maralyce realised she was pregnant. She didn't want a child, and after nearly ten thousand years, she was too set in her ways to even consider keeping it, but it's extremely difficult to induce an abortion in an immortal for any number of reasons. So she carried him to term and after Shalimar was born, she trudged down the mountain to Lebec and left him on the doorstep of the first house she came to that had human, rather than Crasii, females coming and going from it. It was a brothel, but she didn't know it at the time, and I'm not sure that would have affected her decision to abandon him there, in any case. The whores found the baby, took it in and raised it between them. When Shalimar was about seven, Maralyce got curious about him and returned to Lebec to find out what had happened to her son. That's when she discovered he was a Tidewatcher and told him what he was."

Declan stared at Ryda. "How do you know all this?"

"Shalimar told me. Didn't he tell you?"

Declan shook his head, glancing around the table. They all looked as stunned as he was at the news. He didn't doubt the veracity of the tale for a moment. It fitted with everything he knew about his grandfather, his own origins, and everything he'd seen and heard, growing up in the Lebec slums.

As always, it was Tilly who recovered first. "Does this mean Maralyce is on our side, this time?"

"Begrudgingly," Declan replied. "She's not interested in becoming involved in our battles, but I kind of forced her into helping a bit . . ."

"Tides, Declan, what have you done?" Lord Deryon asked.

Taking a deep breath, Declan told them about his trip into Caelum, and the fate of Nyah. The Pentangle listened in silence as he related his tale, giving him no indication of what they thought of his interference with the plans of the Empress of the Five Realms, for her son to take the throne of Caelum, by kidnapping their crown princess.

"So," he said, after he'd explained it all. "Right now the Crown Princess of Caelum is safely tucked away at Maralyce's mine . . ."

"Which would explain why the Caelish are threatening to declare war on us," Lord Deryon added with a frown.

"They *are*?" Tilly asked.

"We had an envoy arrive at the palace earlier today. They've no evidence, thank the Tides, but they're fairly certain someone smuggled her over the border. The letter the envoy carried from Queen Jilna demanded Nyah's immediate return or they'll come looking for her themselves."

"Does Syrolee have any idea, I wonder," Aleki mused, "that Jaxyn and Diala are about to gain control of Glaeba?"

"What difference would that make?" Lord Deryon asked.

"Well, if they knew Jaxyn was here, wouldn't they assume Nyah's kidnapping was something he cooked up?"

"I don't see that it makes that much difference," Tilly said.

"Actually, Aleki's got a point," Ryda said. "If Syrolee gets wind of Jaxyn and Diala in Glaeba, that's exactly what she'll think. It would never occur to her that mortals, on their own, might try to thwart her plans by kidnapping that little girl."

"What are you suggesting?" Declan asked. "That we deliberately set Syrolee and Jaxyn at each other's throats to take the suspicion off the Cabal?"

Ryda nodded. "That's exactly what I'm suggesting."

"They're Tide Lords," Declan reminded him. "We have a word for what happens when Tide Lords turn on each other, Master Tarek. It's called a *Cataclysm*."

"Tide's not up far enough yet to cause a Cataclysm," Ryda said, shrugging. "We'll be fine for a few years."

"Oh, well . . . if we've got a few years before they destroy us all . . ."

"Settle down, Declan," Tilly said. "Ryda has a point. If the Tide Lords realise their neighbouring country—be it Caelum or Glaeba—is also under immortal control, they'll focus their efforts on protecting themselves from each other. We should be able to operate under their noses for quite a while longer."

"Or we'll all be destroyed that much sooner because they're out to ruin each other."

"I think you worry unnecessarily, Declan," Ryda said. "The point is, sooner or later, one of the Caelish immortals is going to run into one of the Glaeban immortals, anyway. We might as well manage things in a way that suits us. And as Tilly says, while they're focused on each other, they'll be leaving us alone."

"Funny, I always thought the aim of the Cabal of the Tarot was to prevent the Tide Lords from gaining power and abusing it. I didn't realise we'd changed our charter to aiding and abetting them."

"We've done no such thing," Tilly assured him. "But I think Ryda has the right of it. If we can distract the immortals for a time, we'll have that much longer to formulate our own plans."

"Which involves what, exactly?" he asked. "Smoothing the way for the Tide Lords to gain total world domination?"

"Not at all," Ryda said. "We're going to find a way to kill them."

Declan glared at him. "Not very clear on the meaning of *immortal*, are you, Master Tarek?"

Ryda smiled, unperturbed by Declan's sarcasm. "You're not seeing the bigger picture here, Declan. The Immortal Prince already wants to die and my sources tell me he may have found a way. If he succeeds in ending his life, then we have what we need to put an end to all the immortals."

"You want to *help* them?"

"I want to do whatever it takes to rid this world of them," Ryda replied. "Even if that means—in the short term, at least—giving them exactly what they want."

"And if we fail?"

The older man shrugged. "Then we're no worse off than we are now, are we?"

Chapter 45

Patience was a skill Cayal thought he'd mastered eons ago. It surprised him a little to realise he hadn't mastered it at all. He was impatient to find Brynden. He was impatient to secure the aid of the other Tide Lords Lukys said he needed to bring about the concentration of power the older man was insisting they must channel to end it all.

In short, he was impatient to die.

He swallowed the last of his mead and slammed the glass down, tossed a couple of coins onto the counter beside it, and turned for the door of the Cayal's Rest, wondering what he should do next. Ramahn irritated him. Torlenia in general irritated him. The mortals of this country cursed his very name—albeit not without cause. He'd only come back here in the first place because of Arkady Desean, and he'd not so much as laid eyes on her.

He knew where she was, of course. She was an ambassador's wife, after all, tucked safely away behind the walls of the Glaeban embassy where Cayal had no hope of getting in to see her by normal means. His only chance of meeting her was if he scaled the walls of the embassy seraglium, risked being caught and—more than likely—run through for his trouble.

It wouldn't kill him, but being run through was *painful*. Now Lukys had given him a purpose in life, he wasn't at such a loose end any longer that he was willing to risk it again, just for a few moments alone with a woman just as likely to snub him as fall into his embrace.

He needed to forget about Arkady. Put her out of his mind.

A man really only had room for one obsession at a time.

I don't need you, Arkady Desean, he told her, afraid this tendency he'd developed lately for having silent conversations in his head with people who weren't there was a sign of impending madness. Which begged the question: was the madness *impending* or had it already arrived? Was this death wish just another symptom of his tumble into the abyss of insanity?

Would an insane man even notice he was insane?

Cayal growled at himself for being a fool. He needed to forget Arkady Desean. He was too old, too weary and too anxious to die, to have the energy left to indulge in love. When he thought about her, it was with longing, but it was a longing he couldn't afford to indulge. If Lukys was right, then when the Tide peaked this time, he could die.

He refused to allow love for a woman, or even the need for her, to distract him from his purpose.

Cayal needed to focus on the matter at hand. He wanted to die. Lukys had found a way, but it required the power of several Tide Lords to do it. Somehow, he had to convince three of the others he needed their help, while assuring them no harm would come to them.

Such a thing was unlikely. As Lukys had pointed out, if one immortal could die, they all could. Better to stick with the story Lukys had devised: Lukys wanted to leave Amyrantha. If they could combine their power, channel it in a concentrated stream, it might be possible to open a gateway to another world.

A world where there were no other Tide Lords.

A world where an immortal would be God.

Unlike Syrolee or Jaxyn or even Kentravyon's desire for divinity, Lukys wasn't interested in gaining a measure of control over a few million peasants. Not for him the danger of a faltering miracle or a cohort of immortals banding together to defeat him. Lukys's plans were much bigger than that. If Cayal read Lukys right, he wanted to be a true God and had spent most of the past thousand years looking for ways to refine his control of the Tide to accomplish it.

But he wasn't content. Not for Lukys the crude notion of diverting rivers or setting off volcanoes. He wanted to control matter, the very stuff from which the universe was made. His definition of divinity went much further than Kentravyon's limited vision. He wanted as much control over the tiniest particle as he had over weather or the orbit of Amyrantha.

That wasn't the story Cayal intended to tell Brynden. All the immortals knew about Lukys's obsession with controlling the Tide, and because he didn't pick fights with the others, it had always struck them as a fairly harmless pastime. No, Brynden wanted vengeance and Cayal intended to give it to him.

If and when Cayal found him.

Kinta had been unhelpful, to say the least. He hadn't told her why he wanted to find Brynden, of course. She was understandably suspicious of his motives, and there was nothing he could think of to say that might have set her mind at ease. She'd been remarkably easy to locate, but that was, once again, because of Lukys. He'd been living here in Torlenia for quite a while now. He may have sensed her presence in the city, or just put two and two together. Either way, it wouldn't have taken him long to figure out who Lady Chintara really was.

However he'd managed it, he was right. Kinta was posing as Lady Chintara, the Imperator's Consort, and she was getting everything ready for Brynden's return.

His return from where?

He was likely to be in Torlenia somewhere. Since first coming to this wretched continent before Cayal had dried up the Great Inland Sea with his rage, Kinta and Brynden had been almost permanent fixtures here.

Cayal wasn't sure why. Maybe they liked the people. Maybe they found them tractable. Gullible, even. They were certainly loyal. Cayal had always thought it odd that so much of Torlenia's history had been destroyed when Brynden sent that meteorite hurtling into the ocean after him and Kinta, and yet they remembered his laws.

Even the shrouds worn by the women of Torlenia were the result of an angry proclamation Brynden made a thousand years ago, after Kinta and Cayal had fled Tenacia. The enraged Tide Lord had returned to Torlenia just long enough to curse all women in general, Torlenian women in particular, issue his wretched decree that they all wear sheets, and then turn his attention to tracking down his missing lover and her paramour so he could throw a flaming rock the size of a small house at them.

That was something else Cayal had always wondered about: which came first—Brynden's proclamation that adultery was punishable by stoning? Or the meteorite he threw at the fleeing lovers, which became a symbol of what he thought a just reward for all unfaithful women?

Cayal hesitated on the threshold of the tavern, glancing around the marketplace. It was midafternoon. A few of the more enthusiastic merchants were rolling up their shutters, or rekindling their small cook-fires, hoping to get a head start on the competition. In this city of too many people and not enough firewood, few poor homes had kitchens. People bought their meals in the marketplaces, the cost of it directly related to the fuel the stallholder cooked with.

That was another reason Cayal disliked Torlenia so much. Flatbread—or any sort of bread for that matter—cooked over a camel-dung fire tasted like shit. Cayal hadn't had a decent meal since leaving Lukys's luxurious villa near Elvere. He understood now why Lukys had taken a wife. Oritha was more than just useful in the bedroom. The girl could cook, too.

Stepping down into the street, Cayal glanced up at the sun. He could feel the power of the Tide Star rising, even here. Across the way, more stallholders were opening their shutters.

And in the distance, from the tower at the Temple of the Way of the Tide, the huge bronze bells began to toll, announcing to the residents of Ramahn that the midday break was over. The sound rolled over Cayal like a warm benediction. He smiled.

The bells of the Temple of the Way of the Tide. Brynden's way.

More importantly—Brynden's temple.

"May I help you, brother?"

Cayal looked around curiously. He'd never had reason to enter a Temple of the Way of the Tide before. Not surprisingly the building was large, but austere and undecorated, just the way Brynden liked it.

The monk who'd greeted him at the entrance had a shaved head and wore a saffron-coloured robe. He was thin to the point of emaciation, but his eyes were bright and he sounded as if he genuinely wished to aid this lost soul who had wandered onto hallowed ground.

"I'm looking for Brynden."

The monk smiled. "As are we all, brother."

"I meant *literally*."

"The Lord of Reckoning is only found through study, purity of thought and deed, and the rejection of all worldly values, brother."

"So, I couldn't just make an appointment then?"

Somewhat to Cayal's surprise, the monk had a sense of humour. He smiled. "No, brother, that's not how we find the Lord of Reckoning."

"How *do* I find him then? I mean other than study, purity of thought and . . . what else was it you said . . . the rejection of all worldly values?"

"Are you serious in your desire to seek him out?"

"It's a matter of life and death."

"Then you might consider joining us."

Cayal smiled. "*Join* you?"

"The Lord of Reckoning judges men only by what is in their souls, brother. If you wish to seek enlightenment, which is the only path to his side, then you need to consider how badly you want it. There are no half-measures with the Way of the Tide."

Cayal stared at the monk. "*That's* how you get to meet with Brynden? You become one of his minions?"

The monk shrugged. "I didn't say it would be easy, brother."

"Tides! You're serious."

Cayal's cursing did nothing to dent the monk's infuriating calm. "The rejection of all worldly values is just that, brother. The rejection of *all* of them. One cannot reject the values one has no time for and keep those he likes. The Way of the Tide requires total dedication. If you wish to find the Lord of Reckoning you must look into your own heart first."

"And then what?" Cayal asked, thinking this idea was a complete waste of time.

"If you feel you are ready, then you may come back here."

"To pray?"

"To join us," the monk said. "If you wish to become one with the Tide, it is the only way open to you. Every month we take on a new cohort of novitiates. You are fortunate, brother. The next cohort leaves in three days' time."

"Leaves for where?"

"For the abbey, of course."

"You don't teach your novitiates here?"

The monk shook his head. "One could not possibly seek the Way of the Tide amid the distractions of the city. All those seeking to join us are escorted into the desert—away from venal temptation—where they can meditate, contemplate, study in peace and eventually find the Way of the Tide."

"This abbey of yours? Is it the old one near Elvere?"

The little man smiled. "If you want to know that, brother, be here at dawn three days from now, willing to change your life, with your heart open to the teachings of the Lord of Reckoning. You'll not find it—or him—any other way."

The monk bowed, still smiling, and turned his back on Cayal, heading back into the cavernous temple.

Cayal stared after him, shaking his head.

Tides, Brynden, he said, starting up yet another conversation in his head with someone who wasn't there. *I actually have to join your miserable religion to find you?*

Even Kentravyon wasn't that strict.

Chapter 46

Once Arkady moved into the royal seraglium, she began to wonder if it had been such a good idea. Although she was treated with nothing but the greatest respect, she couldn't help feeling this was a cage, and she was the tame canary trained to sing for her mistress's entertainment.

Kinta was a gracious hostess, but now she had access to Arkady all day and all night, she seemed to want to spend every moment of it either interrogating Arkady about her own life, or trying to get Arkady to reassure her that she was going about getting Brynden back the right way. Her insecurity struck Arkady as being very strange until she realised that here was a woman who had spent the past eight or nine thousand years with the same man, until her fling with Cayal. Kinta couldn't remember the last time she'd tried to entice a man—not one that mattered to her—and that included her affair with Cayal, who as far as Arkady could tell (and based on her own experience), had done most of the seducing.

Kinta's insecurities reassured Arkady. It was comforting to think that even with immortality and the ability to wield the Tide, they suffered from the same uncertainties mortals were doomed to suffer. Kinta had betrayed Brynden. Now she was sorry and desperate to get him back, just as desperate to prove her love by handing him the throne of Torlenia.

This didn't augur well for the current Imperator, however.

It was unlikely, Arkady mused, as she took her seat opposite Kinta in the pavilion in the centre of the gardens, that there would be an Imperator Number Sixty-five.

"Is something the matter?"

Arkady shook her head as she smoothed down her skirts. They often retired to the pavilion these days, where they were unlikely to be over-heard. As usual there was a platter of sliced fruit between them and a jug of wine. Kinta seemed to have a limitless capacity for alcohol. "Why do you ask?"

"You're frowning like someone just ran over your favourite Crasii."

"I was thinking about Stellan."

"And this makes you frown?"

"He faces a difficult time in Herino."

"Does he know what awaits him there?"

"If you mean does he know there are two immortals in the palace, then no. He doesn't believe you exist."

Kinta smiled. "He'll find out the hard way that he's wrong, then?"

"That's what worries me."

"Perhaps it's fortunate you stayed in Ramahn. Neither Jaxyn nor Diala will brook any interference in their plans."

"Are you speaking from experience, my lady, or because that's what you'd do in their place?"

"Both," Kinta replied. "Are your quarters comfortable?"

"More than comfortable, thank you."

"I'm glad you agreed to come here."

"Dashin Deray was under the impression the suggestion I stay here at the palace was more in the nature of a command than an invitation, my lady."

Kinta seemed amused. "It wasn't, but I'm glad he mistook it for such. Oh, what is it now?"

Arkady glanced over her shoulder in the direction Kinta was look-ing. Hurrying along the path was Nitta.

"My lady, your grace," the slave puffed as she climbed the step to the rotunda.

"I gave instructions that I was not to be disturbed, Nitta."

"I know, my lady, but the Imperator is here. He wants to see you. And Lady Desean."

"Did he say why?"

Nitta shook her head. "Just that he must see you immediately."

"*Tides,*" Kinta muttered under her breath. "Ask my husband to join us here, Nitta." The slave curtseyed and hurried back to the hall to pass on the invitation. Kinta sighed. "He'd better have a good reason for this. I've warned him about disturbing me when I'm entertaining."

"Should I find a shroud?"

Kinta shook her head. "Not in here. Besides, it'll do him good to gaze upon another human female. The Tides know he doesn't get to look at many of them." The immortal rose to her feet smiling broadly.

Arkady did the same and turned to find a heavy-set young man walking up the path behind her.

"Husband! What a pleasure to welcome you into my domain. It is such an honour. Are you here to demand your conjugal rights?"

The Imperator stopped on the bottom step and looked up at Kinta, blushing a deep shade of crimson. *Stellan is right*, Arkady decided as she looked at him. *He's just a boy.*

"Er . . . no . . . my lady . . ."

"Then to what do I owe the pleasure of your esteemed company, my lord?"

"It's about Lady Desean." The young man turned to Arkady, but looked away when she caught his eye. "I have a message about her from the Glaebans."

"A message?" Arkady asked, before Kinta could terrify the boy into being too frightened to say anything.

"Actually, my lady, it's not so much a message, as a . . . a warrant."

"A *warrant*? A warrant for what?"

The Imperator looked away. He was so nervous he could barely speak. "For your arrest . . . and return . . . to Glaeba, your grace. You've been charged with . . . high treason, along with your husband."

Arkady stared at the Imperator, too stunned to speak.

Kinta seemed as shocked as Arkady. "What could Lady Desean have possibly done to deserve such a charge?"

"The warrant says she aided her husband in the murder of the king and queen."

"That's ludicrous!" Arkady finally managed to sputter. "There must be a mistake."

"The document bears the seal of the King's Private Secretary, your grace. Lord Aranville, himself, has signed the warrant and sent an escort to take you home."

"*Jaxyn* signed the warrant?"

She said that as much for Kinta's benefit as she did for the Imperator.

The immortal didn't miss it, either. "Thank you for bringing this news personally, my lord. Is the escort waiting for Lady Desean now?"

"They're at the Glaeban embassy. I mean, they couldn't come here armed and demanding one of my guests. But they're expecting an answer. They've asked that I send word when Lady Desean is ready to leave."

"Then that is what we shall do, husband. Send word to the Glaeban embassy that the Duchess of Lebec will be ready to leave with them in the morning."

"She's not a duchess, any longer."

"I *beg* your pardon?" Arkady said.

"Your husband has been stripped of all his titles . . . and assets, your grace," the Imperator explained, all but cringing at the idea of delivering such dire tidings. "The warrant explicitly states that. And that you are to be treated accordingly."

"They've taken Lebec from him?" Arkady felt faint.

"That is my understanding of the matter, your grace. I'm sorry. I quite liked him . . . considering he was Glaeban."

Kinta glanced at Arkady and then turned to her husband. "I shall see everything is in order, husband. You may go."

The Imperator was too overwhelmed by his wife to do anything but turn on his heel and hurry back down the path of the seraglium. Arkady didn't even notice he'd left. She collapsed onto the cushions, her head spinning.

"Are you all right, Arkady?" Kinta asked.

"I can't go back."

"It won't be easy, I'll grant you . . ."

"No, you don't understand, my lady. That warrant is signed by Jaxyn Aranville."

"You think he has designs on you?"

"I know he does," Arkady said, fighting down a wave of overwhelming terror. "But if it was just about sex, it wouldn't matter so much. I've been used like that before. I can survive it. This is about tormenting Stellan."

"Your husband?"

Arkady nodded, wondering how much she could risk confiding. And wondering if—given Stellan had been disinherited and charged with regicide—it made the slightest difference any longer. "The relationship between Jaxyn and my husband is . . . Tides, it's just too complicated to explain. What I'm certain about, though, is that Jaxyn wants me back because he wants to prove to me he's won, and to Stellan that he was a fool. I don't care what happens to me, but I can't do that to Stellan."

Kinta nodded and sank down on the cushions beside Arkady. "You have the right of it, I fear. Jaxyn always was a vengeful little prick."

"Can I ask for asylum, my lady? Here in Torlenia?"

"You could," Kinta agreed. "But if you do, I will advise my husband to deny you."

"But you know what will happen to me if I return to Glaeba." Arkady stared at her in shock. "*Why?*"

"For exactly the reason I just gave you. Jaxyn is a vengeful little prick. I'm planning to hand Brynden a throne, Arkady, not a country on the brink of war over you with another Tide Lord."

Arkady shook her head, wondering why she'd been foolish enough to imagine, even for a moment, that any immortal would think of something other than themselves.

"Then I am doomed, my lady. Shall I give Jaxyn your regards when I'm in chains and on my knees before him?"

Kinta frowned. "I suppose there's no chance you will agree to keep my presence here in Torlenia a secret from Jaxyn and Diala? Or my plans for Brynden?"

"Not much chance at all, my lady," Arkady said, meeting the immortal's gaze with unflinching determination. Two could play this game.

The immortal was silent for a moment as she debated something and then nodded. "Very well."

"You'll speak to the Imperator about granting me asylum?"

The consort shook her head. "That would precipitate the very war I'm trying to avoid. No, it would be easier if you just weren't here."

"I have no money, my lady, no title, no status and I barely speak the language here."

Kinta smiled sourly. "I wasn't planning on tossing you over the walls and leaving you to fend for yourself, Arkady. The purpose of helping you escape would not be to facilitate your immediate recapture."

"Then what are you planning, my lady?"

"I will send you somewhere Jaxyn will never find you, my dear."

"Where is that?"

"I will send you to Brynden."

Chapter 47

Tilly Ponting had laid out all the major cards of the Tarot on the table for the others to see. Declan studied them with a frown. Now he could put faces to some of the names, the cards seemed much less benign, almost sinister, as they tracked the history of the Tide Lords in colourful—and seemingly harmless—artwork.

A thousand years from now, will there be others sitting around a table like this, looking at this record of living history, wondering if there's anything they *can do to stop the immortals?*

The deck Tilly used was a special one. This was not the deck she rolled out to tell fortunes at parties. This was the Lore Tarot. The one that told the truth.

"Historically, as far as I can tell, Jaxyn and Diala have never been allies before," Tilly remarked, as she laid out the last card.

"Diala made Jaxyn immortal," Ryda Tarek agreed. "But neither of them is trustworthy nor particularly trusting. I'd suggest their alliance this time is one of convenience rather than a meeting of minds."

Declan nodded. "That would fit with what Warlock has observed."

"Warlock?"

"Declan's been able to get a Scard onto Diala's staff," Karyl Deryon explained. "He's been very useful."

Ryda looked across the table at Declan. "Diala has a *Scard* on her staff and doesn't know it? That's brilliant. How did you manage that?"

Declan shrugged. "All her staff are Crasii. Immortals are no better at spotting Scards than we are, until they do something they're not supposed to. We just had to be certain she didn't suspect his willingness to follow her orders is driven by choice rather than compulsion. The credit for staying close to her this long belongs to Warlock, not to me."

"I'd like to meet this Scard of yours."

"I'll send a note to the palace asking him to attend us, shall I?"

"Declan, stop it!" Tilly said. "Ryda has risked a great deal to come here. We all have."

"Does the Tarot give us any idea how this is likely to play out?" Aleki asked, saving Declan from having to apologise to either Ryda or Tilly.

Tilly shook her head, pursing her lips as she studied the Tarot cards. "Except for Brynden's almost inevitable rise in Torlenia, these power alignments are all new. We've not seen Jaxyn and Diala together before, and once Tryan finds Princess Nyah and marries her, he will be King of Caelum, leaving Syrolee in a subordinate role, which is extraordinary."

Ryda smiled. "And Cayal worries that he's seen it all."

"You know that for a fact?" Declan asked.

"Why else would he want to die?"

Once again, Aleki interrupted before their sniping could escalate into a full-blown argument. "Speaking of Cayal, do we know where he is? Or what he's planning?"

"He's in Torlenia."

They all turned to stare at Declan. This was news that had arrived in the dispatches Stellan Desean had brought with him from Ramahn. The letter was from Arkady—in theory—a boring and seemingly trivial description of life in the seraglium. Underlying Arkady's message, however, was a much more comprehensive coded report from Tiji, in which she revealed, among other things, that she had seen Cayal.

"What's he doing there?"

"I'm not sure. The word I have is that he met with Kinta, but she wasn't happy to see him."

Lord Deryon looked very worried. "Is he planning to challenge Brynden for control of Torlenia?"

"Unlikely," Markun said. "If he's looking for a way to die, he'll not be looking to set himself up as a potentate, particularly not in a country ruled by a man who tried to crush him with a meteorite the last time they ran into one another."

"Maybe he still feels something for Kinta?" Tilly suggested.

"Even if he did, I doubt he'd act on it," Ryda said. "But there is another possibility."

Declan glared at him. "Are you planning to share it with us, or are you just pausing for dramatic effect?"

"Cayal wants to die. As you so rightly pointed out, that's no mean feat for an immortal. Maybe he needs help."

"Magical help?" Tilly asked.

Ryda nodded. "If there was a way for Cayal to end his life by ordinary means, he would have found it long ago. I'm suggesting he needs help. Who better to approach than the man who wants you dead?"

Although Ryda's words made perfectly good sense, something else occurred to Declan that made his blood run cold as he remembered Maralyce's tale about what the Tide Lords had been capable of when they banded together to bring down Kentravyon. At that time the Tide had been on the wane. How much more damage could they do if they got together when it was on the rise? "If Cayal needs the help of another Tide Lord to die, then they'll be channelling the Tide, won't they. And a lot of it."

Ryda nodded. "More than likely."

Declan pointed to the Tarot on the table. "Cayal decapitated Pellys and half a continent disappeared into the ocean. What's a couple of Tide Lords channelling enough power to *destroy* one of them going to do to the rest of us?"

"If it *is* only a couple of them."

Declan looked at Markun. "What do you mean?"

"You're assuming he only needs the aid of one Tide Lord. What if he needs more than one?"

Declan didn't answer right away. He didn't really need to. The look of every face in the room said it all. Except for Ryda Tarek, who was smiling.

"What's so funny?"

"Not funny, my passionate and pessimistic young friend. Ironic."

"*Ironic?*"

Ryda leaned back in his seat and cast his gaze over them. "We sit here plotting the demise of the Tide Lords. For centuries, people like us have sat around tables like this, studying the Tarot, looking for patterns and praying to gods we're fairly certain don't exist, to deliver us from their clutches. And here we stand, on the cusp of succeeding, only to discover that in the process of destroying them, we may have to destroy ourselves.

"That, my friends, it the very essence of *ironic*, don't you think?"

———

It was after dark when the meeting broke for a chance for everyone to stretch their cramped legs, ease their aching bladders and silence their growling stomachs. Tilly took the opportunity to pull Declan aside in the hall outside her parlour, to find out what was happening with Stellan. When he told her of the former Duke of Lebec's noble plan to confess to crimes he had nothing to do with in order to spare Mathu any further embarrassment, Tilly cursed like a deckhand for a full minute before she was calm enough to speak coherently.

"The man has lost his mind."

"No, he's lost everything else, but he's still sane. From where he sits, this is the most logical thing to do."

"We can't afford to have Stellan Desean executed."

"With the Tide on the rise, I don't see that it makes that much difference in the long run, Tilly. He's not of the Cabal."

"No, he's the heir to the Glaeban throne. Until the Tide is up, Jaxyn can't make a move on it unless there are no other contenders."

"You'll get no argument from me about that. I'm quite certain he wants to be rid of Desean so he can take the throne now, without waiting until the Tide has returned enough for him to take it by force."

She nodded. "Being subject to Diala's whim must irk him." She frowned in thought for a moment and then looked up at Declan, who was easily a head taller than her. "You know, even if that wasn't his plan, I'd be tempted to try to thwart it, just on principle."

Declan stared at her. "How? By busting him out of gaol?"

Tilly pursed her lips for a moment and then nodded. "It would complicate things nicely."

"You don't think with the Crown Princess of Caelum missing things are not complicated enough?"

"He's a friend, Declan."

"He's *your* friend, Tilly. Not mine."

Her eyes narrowed as she glared at him. "You're not objecting to this because of Arkady, are you?"

"Are you suggesting I'd be happy to let him die because I'm jealous?"

"Are you?"

"That's insulting, Tilly."

She smiled. "It was, and I'm sorry. You'd not let anything so trite interfere with something this important. I do know that. Tell me why you don't think we should help him."

"We'd be drawing attention to the Cabal. You just said it in there a moment ago. If the Tide Lords can be distracted, we can stay out of sight and work unhindered for that much longer. Break Desean out of gaol and we might as well open a shop in the main square of Herino and hang out a sign saying we're back in business."

"Could you do such a thing without implicating the Cabal?"

Declan hesitated and then nodded with a great deal of reluctance. "Maybe."

"*Will* you do it?"

"Are you ordering me as Guardian of the Lore, or asking a favour?"

"A favour, Declan, nothing more. Stellan Desean is a good man. He doesn't deserve this."

He looked down at her, shaking his head. "I can't promise anything, Tilly. And I won't risk my people for him, either. But I'll see what I can do."

"That's all I ask, dear." She stood on her toes and kissed his cheek. "And let's just keep this between us, eh?"

"Afraid the great Ryda Tarek won't approve?"

"You shouldn't mock him, Declan. Ryda's a loyal member of the Cabal. And he knows so much about the Tide Lords, I'm embarrassed to call myself Guardian of the Lore when he's near. You could learn a great deal from him."

"He wants us to help them gain control, Tilly."

"Only in so far as it helps us."

"Are you sure about that?"

"What motive could he have to aid them, other than to further our cause? No mortal with his understanding of the Tide Lords could possibly do anything else."

Tilly's logic was sound, but that didn't alter Declan's gut feeling there was something not quite right about Ryda Tarek.

"If you say so."

"I do. Now go and fetch something to eat and then let's get back in there and work out what, in the name of the Tide, we're going to do next."

Chapter 48

Having overheard Cayal's discussion with the monk at the Temple of the Way of the Tide, Tiji thought she was safe to return to the embassy and collect her things. Cayal's intentions were clear. He was looking for Brynden—although Tiji had no inkling as to why—and the only way to find him was to find his abbey. Even the Cabal had heard the rumours that Brynden was holed up somewhere in the desert, posing as a brother of his own sect. The chances were better than even that Cayal knew it too, and was planning to join the monthly caravan from the Temple of the Way of the Tide to find him.

When she returned to the Glaeban embassy, she discovered the place in an uproar. There were guards everywhere and a troop of felines who hadn't been here a few days ago, when Tiji had first discovered Cayal. Pushing through the chaos in the halls, she finally cornered Dashin Deray. He was in Duke Stellan's office, going through the contents of his desk. A feline stood by, watching him closely, as the young man loaded a stack of the Duke's personal correspondence into a leather satchel.

"My lord?"

Dashin glanced up, frowning when he spied the chameleon. "I thought you'd left for Glaeba already."

"There were some things I had to do first. What's going on?"

Dashin Deray glanced at the feline watching them with a dark, unblinking stare, before fixing his attention on Tiji. "The Duke of Lebec has been charged with ordering the death of King Enteny and Queen Inala. He's been disinherited and will stand trial within the month."

"You're kidding."

Dashin glared at her. "It would be a poor attempt at humour if I was."

"Tides! That's unbelievable! Is it true?"

"Ask your master," Dashin suggested in a tone that left little doubt about what he thought of the King's Spymaster. "He'll be the one manufacturing the charges against the duke."

"Declan Hawkes would never do such a thing," she said, knowing full well he probably would, if he thought there was a good enough reason to do it—particularly if it suited the aims of the Cabal. "Where does that leave the duchess?"

"Under the same cloud of suspicion as the duke. We have a warrant for her arrest, signed by the new King's Private Secretary, Lord Aranville. I've sent word to the palace seraglium, but we don't have a response yet."

Tiji felt her blood run cold. "Jaxyn Aranville is now the King's Private Secretary?"

Dashin nodded. "You seem surprised."

I shouldn't be, Tiji thought. *This is the way they play the game.* "I'm just surprised old Lord Deryon finally retired. I liked him. Do you have any orders for me from Master Hawkes?"

Dashin shook his head. "Were you expecting any?"

"Not really. Just thought I'd make sure. Lady Desean said you'd give me money if I needed it."

He sighed. "How much?"

"Enough to get me by for a month or so. There's something I have to check on. I might be gone for a while."

Dashin Deray thought about it for a moment, weighing up his reluctance to give this slave with diplomatic papers a single fenet, against the inadvisability of interfering with the business of the King's Spymaster.

"Very well." He took a sheet of fresh paper, picked up a pen, dipped it in the crystal inkwell and scribbled out a note which he signed with an impatient flourish and then handed to her. "Take this to the Quartermaster. He'll see you have whatever you need."

"Thank you, my lord."

Tiji was almost out the door when he called after her. "Whatever it is you're up to, Tiji, don't expect us to come to your rescue if you get yourself into trouble. Our job here at the embassy is to preserve the good relations between Glaeba and Torlenia, something I'm not certain your master appreciates."

"I'll be a good girl," she promised with a demure curtsey, biting back the desire to add, *as if I'd ask a pompous, stuck-up windbag like you for help, anyway.*

Once she had her money and had retrieved the few possessions she carried—not to mention the precious diplomatic papers—Tiji made her way to the Temple of the Way of the Tide.

She had debated long and hard about the best way to follow Cayal across the desert. She couldn't just tag along behind him. Tiji's ability to blend with her surroundings depended on her flesh being in contact with whatever she wanted to emulate. Travelling the desert naked would kill her within a day or two. That left joining the same caravan as Cayal as a slave—which meant no freedom of movement at all, even if she could find a way of achieving a placement on such short notice—or travelling as a diplomat.

For obvious reasons, she settled on the latter. Tiji considered this an excellent use of her precious diplomatic status, which up until now had proved more decorative than useful. It was true that Declan had warned her not to commandeer any ships. He hadn't said a word about desert caravans, though.

The saffron-robed monk who met her at the entrance to the temple was the same one who had spoken to Cayal. He eyed her up and down with a frown before asking what she wanted.

"I wish to join the caravan leaving tomorrow for your abbey."

He shook his head and turned away. "We have no need of your kind, here or at the abbey."

"I'm not offering my kind, brother. I am an envoy of the Glaeban king." She waved her royal warrant in front of him. He turned, snatching it from her hand and then examined it with a suspicious glare.

"This looks genuine." The monk seemed shocked.

"That would be because it is."

He handed her back the document, which she carefully folded and returned to its leather wallet.

"What business does an envoy of the Glaeban king have with the Temple of the Way of the Tide?"

"I have a message for the head of your order on behalf of King Mathu. He has long been an admirer of the Way of the Tide."

That got the monk's attention. "Go on."

"I am to present a letter, asking that a teacher be dispatched immediately to Glaeba, so my king may begin his instruction."

The monk held out his hand. "That is great news indeed. I'll see the letter gets to him."

"Did you miss the part where I said *I* am to present the letter to him, my good man?" she asked, in a tone that would have done the Duchess of Lebec proud.

The monk frowned. "We do not allow your kind in our abbey."

"Then I shall return to my king and inform him you are not interested in showing Glaeba the path to enlightenment. Good day to you, brother."

Tiji turned on her heel and headed down the steps, not in the least surprised when the monk called her back before she'd taken two or three of them.

"Wait!"

She turned to look at him. "Was there something else?"

"You'll have to be segregated, both on the journey and when you reach the abbey."

The little Crasii made a great show of debating the matter. "I suppose I can live with that. You will see to it, of course, that I am attended in the manner to which I am accustomed?"

The monk frowned. "You want me to provide you with servants?"

"If I am to remain apart from the rest of your caravan, brother, then I will need someone who can fetch my meals and provide a way of communicating between me and your guides, will I not?"

With some reluctance, the monk nodded. "I'll see what I can arrange."

"Then I will be here at dawn tomorrow," Tiji promised. "And you can sleep easy tonight, brother, knowing you have been instrumental in bringing the Way of the Tide to all Glaebans."

At dawn the following day, shrouded like a human female, Tiji arrived at the temple to meet up with the caravan. The forecourt was crowded when she arrived, with a score of snorting, spitting camels, rough cameleers who seemed to be cursing the beasts and each other with equal ferocity, and a small clutch of mostly young, nervous-looking men, obviously the acolytes intending to follow the Way of the Tide.

There was no sign of Cayal as yet, nor could Tiji sense him. She wasn't worried. Cayal wanted to find Brynden and this was his only way. He really had no choice but to join them. Even as she'd stood blended to one of the tall sandstone columns at the front of the temple the other day when Cayal had enquired about Brynden, she could tell he was desperate. She could also tell how much the idea of even pretending to follow Brynden's Way of the Tide irked him.

One way or another, though, he'll have to join the caravan, she reasoned. *But probably not until the last minute.*

Tiji pushed through the crowd and climbed the steps to the temple where the brother she had spoken to the day before was standing, overseeing the chaos.

"Ah! You're here."

"Was there some reason you thought I might not be?" Tiji enquired, hoping she sounded imperious. She felt more than a little silly wearing the shroud.

"You bring me a double-edged sword, Crasii," the monk told her. "A message of great hope delivered by an abomination. I have mixed feelings." He smiled thinly and pointed to another shrouded figure standing in the shadows of the columns behind him, a small sack and a full waterskin at her feet, which was all the luggage a slave would be permitted to bring on a journey such as this. "I do, however, have the servant you requested. If you ladies would like to wait here, I will have the cameleers fetch you when it's time to leave."

Tides, he believed me! was Tiji's first reaction to discovering she now had her very own servant. She bowed to the monk, glanced around hoping to catch a glimpse of Cayal—to no avail—and then stepped into the shadows to greet her new companion.

The slave was taller than her by more than a head. Tiji looked up and met her eyes. The shrouded woman examined her for a moment and then her eyes widened in shock

"*Tiji?*" she hissed. "Tides! What are you doing here? I thought you'd gone back to Declan."

"Your *grace?*" Tiji glanced over her shoulder. Nobody was paying any attention to them. But Arkady's presence here was a complication she didn't want or need. "Your grace, you can't come with us."

"I'm not here by choice, Tiji."

The little Crasii frowned, wishing she could read the duchess's expression under that irritating shroud. "If this is about Cayal . . ."

"Cayal? What's Cayal got to do with anything? Haven't you heard? There's a warrant out for my arrest."

Tiji stared at her, remembering what Dashin Deray had told her about the charges against the Duke of Lebec. "That still doesn't explain what you're doing *here*, my lady, lining up to cross the desert to find the Way of the Tide."

"I'm here because Kinta offered me a way to escape Jaxyn."

"By sending you to Brynden? There's a mixed blessing, if ever I saw one."

"In this case, Tiji, I think the devil I *don't* know is the safer option to the one I do. What are you doing here, anyway? Kinta said I would be posing as the servant of a Glaeban diplomat."

"That's me. I joined the caravan to follow Cayal."

Arkady fell silent for a moment. "Cayal is here?"

The Crasii shook her head. "Not yet. But I'm expecting him."

Arkady's eyes closed, and then she opened them and looked straight at Tiji. "For the first time since coming to this place, I think I'm going to be glad of this wretched shroud."

"You and me both, my . . . Tides, I can't keep calling you that. And Arkady's probably not a good idea, either, given you're on the run, the Glaebans will be hunting you and the Immortal Prince is likely to roll up any time now."

"Call me Kady." She smiled. Tiji could tell by her eyes, even though the shroud covered the rest of her face. "That's what Declan used to call me when we were children."

"That's awfully close to your real name."

"But a name I'm likely to answer to without thinking," she said, reminding Tiji this woman was nobody's fool. "Our ruse will become instantly apparent if I don't answer to what is supposed to be my own name."

With some reluctance, Tiji had to concede she had a point. She never got to say so, however, because at that moment the monk returned with the head cameleer so he could instruct the two women on the finer points of riding a camel across the harsh Torlenian desert.

Chapter 49

Although she'd been warned by Kinta that the immortal was planning to send her to Brynden, Arkady had not expected to be dragged from her bed while it was still dark, hurriedly dressed in an outfit borrowed from Kinta's slave, Nitta, and hustled out of the royal seraglium to meet up with a caravan travelling into the desert. She was still rubbing her eyes as Kinta explained there was a female Glaeban travelling to the abbey in need of a servant, which was the perfect cover for a fleeing, not to mention disinherited, duchess.

"You will have to behave as a servant does," Kinta instructed, as Arkady pulled the shroud over her head.

"I wasn't born a noblewoman, my lady," Arkady assured her. "I'm sure I'll manage."

Somewhat awkwardly, Kinta hugged her. "I have enjoyed having you as a friend, Arkady. I hope the future is kinder to you than the past few days have been."

"I hope so too."

"Would you do me a favour?"

"Considering the favour you're doing me, my lady, it would be churlish of me to deny you."

Kinta held out a letter sealed with the royal seal of Torlenia. "Would you give this to Brynden for me?"

Arkady accepted the letter and nodded, as she slipped it inside her vest. "Do you have a message for him, too?"

"Just tell him I miss him."

"I will," Arkady promised, turning for the carriage that was to deliver her to the temple.

"It might be prudent not to mention you've met . . . certain other people."

Arkady glanced around at the servants and carriage driver waiting for her to leave and nodded in understanding. "I'll be careful."

"Good luck, Arkady."

"Goodbye, my lady."

Although she was nervous about what the future might hold, things were happening too fast for the full impact of her changed circumstances to make themselves felt. In fact, she'd not really begun to worry until the Glaeban diplomat turned out to be none other than Declan's pet chameleon, Tiji.

Arkady quite liked the little Crasii. At least she had, right up until she started to get a little bit too familiar with her comments on the relationship she imagined between the Duchess of Lebec and the King's Spymaster. But there was no time now to question Tiji on how she came to be part of this caravan. To further complicate matters, the news Cayal might be in the vicinity had Arkady's pulse racing so fast that when the cameleer addressed the two shrouded women in a torrent of quick, unfamiliar words, Arkady only understood about a third of what he said. When he finally drew breath, expecting the women to nod in understanding, Arkady touched Tiji's shoulder.

"My lady," she said, just on the off-chance the cameleer spoke Glaeban, "if our lives depend on what he just said, then we're in trouble, because I barely understood a word of it."

"He said camels always try to intimidate their riders. We must be strong and forceful and refuse to let them bully us."

"He used all those words to say that?"

"No, he also said that even the most obnoxious creature can be brought under control by a good sharp twist on their nostrils. Oh, and he said that when you're fixing the head rope, make sure you don't stand in front of them."

"Why?"

"You stand in front. You get puke," the cameleer informed her in broken Glaeban, making Arkady glad she'd not assumed he didn't speak her language.

"I think he means they'll spit on us," Tiji said.

But the cameleer shook his head. "Camel no spit. Camel puke. You stand in front. You get puke. No water. Puke smell bad."

Despite the language barrier, Arkady thought she understood what he meant. They were crossing the desert. There would be no spare water for washing, even if one wound up wearing the contents of a camel's stomach. She nodded and replied in the little Torlenian she knew. "I get it. No water. No washing."

"You drink. No thirsty, still drink." The cameleer pointed to Arkady's waterskin. "Drink all that. Each day. Otherwise, go poof!" He emphasised his words with a dramatic wave of his arms, disturbingly reminiscent of an explosion.

Arkady frowned. His warning made no sense to her at all. "I'll go *poof*?"

Clearly irritated by her lack of comprehension, the man rattled something off to Tiji, who then turned to Arkady. "He's saying the water will evaporate out of the skin if you don't drink it. He also says that if you wait until you're thirsty, it's too late, you're already dehydrated. Our water ration is one skin per day. They'll fill them up each night when we make camp."

The cameleer then launched into another lecture, the only word of which Arkady thought she knew was "stones." Once he was done, the man strode down the steps of the temple, urging them to follow with an impatient arm wave. Arkady picked up her sack, which contained the few personal items a slave was allowed to posses, such as a comb and another dress borrowed from Nitta, and her waterskin. She turned to Tiji. "What was that last bit about?"

"Stones," the little Crasii replied. "You'd better take mine, too."

"What?"

"My luggage roll and waterskin," she said, pointing at the items in question which lay at her feet. "You're my servant, remember?"

Arkady cursed for not thinking of it herself. It was a long time since she'd waited on somebody else. It seemed she'd grown more accustomed to being a duchess than she imagined.

"Of course, my lady," she said, picking up the other sack and water-skin. They began walking down the steps toward the camels. "What was he saying about stones?"

"Once we're out in the desert we'll have to use them for . . ." The Crasii hesitated, as if she was searching for the right words. ". . . for matters of personal hygiene."

Arkady was fascinated. "Really? I always thought one would use sand for that sort of thing. I suppose rocks make more sense, when you think about it. Sand would tend to get into some rather awkward places, and I'll bet it rubs like a hasp file—"

"Stop it!" the little Crasii hissed. "Servants don't talk so much. In fact, they shouldn't talk at all." Tiji looked around to see if they were being observed, before lowering her voice and adding, "Tides, my lady, you've got the Glaebans after you for conspiring to murder their king, you've got one untrustworthy immortal sending you off to visit another, and any minute now the Immortal Prince—who just happens to be a lover of yours—is liable to show up. Any normal person would be incoherent with fright by now."

"Cayal is a *former* lover," Arkady corrected in a voice just as low, determined to clear that awkward misconception up at the outset. "And I always keep a cool head in a crisis, Tiji. I'm famous for it. They used to call me the Ice Duchess in Lebec, you know . . ." She stopped and stared at the camel. "Tides, they don't seriously expect us to ride that thing, do they?"

"Little one in front, big one at the back," the man holding the lead rope on the only camel left without passengers said to them, urging the two shrouded women forward. Even Arkady knew enough Torlenian to understand the command. She glanced around to find most of the other camels pushing to their feet, each one of them carrying two riders, except for a string of pack animals at the rear who were laden with water-skins and presumably their bedding and tents and tent poles.

Without so much as stopping to think about it, Tiji scrambled into the large wicker saddle, as another man relieved Arkady of their luggage and proceeded to tie it onto the back of their saddle. The camel turned its ungainly head and stared directly at Arkady with dark, malevolent eyes.

She hesitated, certain the creature could smell her fear.

Refuse to be intimidated, she ordered herself. *It's just like a big lumpy horse, really.*

The man holding the beast waved to her. "You there! Hurry-hurry! Sun coming."

"You heard the man, Kady," Tiji said. "Hurry-hurry." Arkady couldn't see her face, but the silver skin around the Crasii's eyes was crinkled in what she suspected was amusement.

Arkady braced herself, stepped forward and lifted her leg, which immediately got tangled in her shroud. She stumbled, falling against the camel, who bellowed loudly in protest. On her second attempt she managed to wedge herself into the uncomfortable saddle. She had time only to breathe a sigh of relief before she squealed in fright as the creature lurched to its feet. She was thrown backward as it pushed up on its forelegs and then tossed forward with even more force as it found its hind legs, banging her head painfully on the crossbar that separated her seat in the double saddle from Tiji's.

All around her the men laughed, and one of them shot a rapid burst of Torlenian at Tiji, who responded with a reply just as incomprehensible.

"What did he say?" she asked, looking down at the ground, which seemed much too far away for safety.

"Something along the lines of 'the big clumsy one is going to give us many amusements on this journey.'"

Arkady didn't think her inexperience was particularly funny, but she cared little for what the Torlenian cameleers might think of her. She had more immediate concerns. "Have you felt any sign of Cayal, yet?"

The little Crasii accepted the reins and a long riding crop that looked like a leather-bound fly-whisk from the man holding the lead rope before she answered, settling back against the saddle with the ease of someone in command of the situation. She seemed to know what she was about, which was of some small comfort to Arkady, but not much.

"I can't feel him at all."

"Perhaps he's not coming."

"Or he'd rather follow the caravan than join it," Tiji suggested.

The caravan began to move off, the snaking line of camels ahead of them heading out into the street as the sun began to lighten the sky. Already the heat of the coming day was making its presence felt. Arkady couldn't imagine what it was going to be like once they reached the open desert.

With a flick of her wrist, Tiji tapped the camel's neck with the crop and they lurched forward. Arkady clung to the saddle with grim determination, wondering if being arrested and taken back to Glaeba was really such an awful fate.

At least in Glaeba, they had horses.

"Are you all right, my lady?" Tiji asked, without taking her eyes off the camels in front of them.

Arkady leaned forward to speak into her ear. "You're supposed to call me Kady, remember?" They turned into the street, the camels apparently content, for the moment, to behave in an orderly fashion.

"I am frightened, Tiji," she admitted after a time, glad nobody else could hear them. "I'm not cold or unfeeling, just really good at pretending I am."

"You'd make a good spy."

Arkady let out a short bitter laugh. "Me? I don't think so. I've been spectacularly unsuccessful in that regard, thus far."

"Declan has faith in you."

"Could we not think about Declan Hawkes, please?"

The Crasii turned in her saddle to look Arkady in the eye. "Actually, my lady, I think you should think about him. A lot. Particularly if Cayal turns up."

Tiji, it seemed, hadn't learned her lesson from the last time they'd had this conversation. Nor was she ever likely to, given their roles had been reversed and Arkady no longer had the power to threaten the Crasii with anything.

Denied any sort of effective response, Arkady leaned back in the saddle and chose to remain silent as the sun burned the night away and the camel lurched beneath her like a small boat on a choppy swell, wishing she could decide what was worse—the idea of seeing Cayal again or the thought of *not* seeing him again.

Chapter 50

Warlock had thought his life couldn't get any more fraught than it already was, right up until a few days ago when Jaxyn had called him into the office of the King's Private Secretary—so recently vacated by the involuntarily retired Lord Deryon—to inform him a delegation was arriving from Caelum. Jaxyn wanted Warlock to act as Lord Torfail's manservant while the Caelish emissary and his sister were guests in Herino.

Warlock all but choked on the news, covering his shock with a coughing fit. Lord Torfail was the immortal Tryan, among the worst of Jaxyn's immortal brethren and something the Tide Lord clearly didn't have a clue about. Warlock knew about Tryan and Elyssa being in Caelum, because Tiji had told him about their presence in the Caelish palace on their way from Hidden Valley to bring the news to Declan Hawkes and the Cabal. It never occurred to him, until that moment, the news might not have reached the ears of Jaxyn or Diala.

Tides. Dealing with two suzerain is bad enough. Now I'm going to have to deal with four of them.

And then another, even more depressing thought occurred to him.

I'm never going to see my pups.

Warlock was still brooding over that realisation as he glanced across the rain-sodden lawn at the King's Spymaster, standing a dutiful pace behind Lord Jaxyn Aranville, the new King's Private Secretary, as they waited for the Caelish barge to dock. There was a persistent rain falling, but it seemed, somehow, to be falling *around* Jaxyn rather than on him. He wasn't yet strong—or foolish—enough to announce who he was by blatantly walking through the rain untouched by it, but he clearly didn't intend to suffer any undue discomfort, either. Declan Hawkes, barely three feet from the King's Private Secretary, was drenched.

Hawkes was here at the behest of the King's Private Secretary, because of the missing Caelish princess. As usual, the spymaster didn't even acknowledge Warlock's presence when he arrived, treating him with the same ignorant disdain as any suzerain. Warlock was grateful for his disregard, while desperate to speak with him. His safety lay in his ability to fade into the background with almost, but not quite, the same skill as a chameleon. Tiji disguised her presence by blending with the background. Warlock survived by being part of it.

The trouble was, time was growing short. In about six weeks, Boots was due to whelp. Anxious as he was to do what was asked of him for the Cabal who had offered him and Boots shelter and a safe place to raise their pups, he wanted to go to be there for them, too. The added complication of the arrival of even more Tide Lords in Herino didn't augur well for Warlock's plans in that direction.

The amphibians brought the barge into the newly repaired dock with an impressive degree of control. A few moments later the gangway was pushed out from the barge and landed with a thump on the wharf, followed by several armed felines who hurried to take up position as an honour guard. Each one wore a red sash to indicate their rank in the royal household, and the weapons they carried—although shiny and impressive even in the rain—were purely decorative. Warlock knew how much the felines hated to be encumbered and their claws were weapon enough on their own to deter any aggressors. But they looked imposing on parade and this was all about making a point. The Caelish were convinced their princess had been kidnapped and spirited over the border to Glaeba and they were here to get her back.

But before they even got around to discussing poor little Princess Nyah, the two immortals descending from the barge were about to get a very rude shock when they realised who the new King's Private Secretary and the new Queen of Glaeba were.

Warlock glanced at Declan again, but the spymaster looked relaxed, albeit rather wet, his thumbs caught in his belt, watching the docking as if nothing was out of the ordinary. If he was worried or even remotely interested in this historic meeting, he gave no outward indication of it.

Two cloaked figures appeared at the head of the gangway, but Warlock couldn't make them out clearly through the rain. Then Jaxyn's posture altered slightly, as if something had alerted him to the impending danger at almost the same time as Warlock sensed the suzerain on the boat. It was obvious the pair on the boat felt the presence of another immortal, too. The female leaned into her companion and said something to him. He shook his head and then offered her his arm and the two of them walked down the gangway to confront their welcoming party.

Jaxyn held his ground on the lawn, forcing the others to come to him. Standing just behind and to the left of Jaxyn, Warlock studied them as they approached. The pair were exactly as Cayal had described them. Tryan was almost too handsome to be male, while his sister, although her body was as perfectly formed as immortality could make it, was a bland, pale creature with wide-set eyes and a jawline that disappeared into her neck before it ever managed to form a chin.

They stopped a pace from Jaxyn and stared at one another for a long, tense moment, before Jaxyn stepped forward and offered Tryan his hand. There were too many mortals here watching for any of them to say what they really wanted to.

"Lord and Lady Torfail, I presume? Welcome to Glaeba."

"*You're* Lord Aranville?"

"Fancy that."

"Well, that explains a lot," Elyssa said, glowering at Jaxyn. "What have you done with her?"

"Done with whom?"

Tryan glared at him. "Really, Lord Aranville, are you that dense?"

"Ah, you mean your missing princess? Terrible tragedy. I hear the wedding can't proceed until she's found. How that must break your heart, Lord Torfail. And your mother's, too."

"We want her back!" Elyssa hissed, but Tryan jerked her arm sharply to shut her up before she could add anything further.

"I'm sure you do, Lady Alysa," Jaxyn agreed. "And to that end, allow me to introduce Declan Hawkes, the King's Spymaster."

Right on cue, Declan stepped forward and bowed to the visitors from Caelum. "My lord, my lady."

Jaxyn clapped Declan on the shoulder. "I have put Master Hawkes in charge of the investigation to discover if the suspicion that your betrothed has been brought across the lake into Glaeba has any basis in fact. Trust me, if Princess Nyah is here, our spymaster will know where to find her."

"That's a bit like asking the fox to guard the chicken coop, isn't it?" Tryan asked. "He's probably the one who's got her stashed somewhere. On your orders, I wouldn't be surprised to discover."

"My lord, you may rest assured," Declan said, his manner so earnest even Warlock believed him, "Lord Aranville has *never* given me any such order. If your princess is in Glaeba, he knows nothing of it."

Tryan seemed unimpressed by the assurance. "You seem to have the hired help nicely trained, Lord Aranville. Do they jump through hoops and play dead when you command it, too?"

"Oh, yes," Jaxyn replied, clearly considering himself the victor in this first encounter with his immortal brethren. "Shall we get out of this rain and go somewhere we can discuss this in . . . a less public forum?"

Tryan nodded his agreement, as if only just realising that in addition to the many Crasii forming the honour guard to welcome them to Herino, there were a lot of humans within earshot who were not ready to learn the truth.

"This is Cecil," Jaxyn said, motioning the Crasii forward. "He will show you to your rooms and see to it you have everything you need."

With a glare at Jaxyn, they turned to Warlock. The stench of the suzerain was on them both. It made his stomach churn, but he was getting used to the sensation now. Besides, Warlock had another distraction. As he turned toward the palace, he caught sight of Jaxyn leaning toward Declan Hawkes.

Only his sharp canine hearing allowed him to hear the Tide Lord telling the spymaster, "Whatever you have to do, Hawkes, if that child is in Glaeba, I want you to find her."

"Are you so anxious to appease Caelum, my lord?"

"Appease be damned," the Tide Lord replied in a low voice. "I want you to find her and then I want you to kill her. Under no circumstances is that man to be allowed to take the throne of Caelum."

"If you would follow me please, my lord, my lady?" Warlock said, one eye and both ears fixed, not on the Caelish suzerain, but on the conversation going on between Declan Hawkes and the Tide Lord.

"Wouldn't it be quicker and easier to just kill Lord Torfail then?" Hawkes asked. "I mean, we've no idea where the child is, but I can locate Torfail for you in a snap."

Tides, that man likes to live dangerously.

Unfortunately, before Jaxyn could answer the spymaster's loaded question, the feline honour guard fell into place around them, forcing Warlock and the visitors from Caelum to turn for the palace, and he heard no more of their conversation.

Once they were dry and changed, Warlock led Lord Torfail and his sister through the palace to the office of the King's Private Secretary. Tryan strode into the room, slamming the door behind him with such force he almost amputated Warlock's tail before he could snatch it clear. He then turned on Jaxyn, wasting no time on pleasantries.

"We want her back!"

"I don't have her," Jaxyn said, looking not at Tryan, but at Elyssa. He smiled at her as if she was something rare and lovely to behold. "It's been so long since we've seen each other, Elyssa. You look charming in that colour. I wonder why I never noticed it before."

The young woman beamed at him, which infuriated her brother. "Tides, Lyssa, you're not going to fall for that, are you? Jaxyn's lines are older than he is."

"He was just being polite."

"No, he was trying to distract you. Pay attention. Where is she, Jaxyn?"

"Hard as this may be for you to grasp, Tryan, my old friend," Jaxyn said, taking the seat behind the desk. "I really have no idea where your child bride is. And to be honest, until you sailed into my kingdom an hour ago demanding her back, I really couldn't have cared less about her fate. Would you like some wine?"

Jaxyn snapped his fingers at Warlock, who was waiting by the door. He hurried to the sideboard, filled three glasses which he placed on a silver tray before turning to offer the wine to the suzerain, taking care to serve Jaxyn first. It wouldn't hurt to let Jaxyn believe Warlock was loyal to him above all others of his kind.

"*Your* kingdom?"

"It will be soon enough."

"Why should I believe you, Jaxyn?"

"What reason do I have to lie?"

"You could have taken the little girl to stop Tryan becoming King of Caelum," Elyssa suggested, taking the wine Warlock offered her without so much as glancing at him.

"Still the family's master strategist, I see." Tryan frowned, but Jaxyn's sarcasm went right over Elyssa's head. "Look . . . I had no idea you were even in Caelum, just as I'm quite sure you had no idea Diala and I were here in Glaeba."

"Diala's here, too?" Tryan asked, taking a seat opposite Jaxyn. He smiled coldly. "So you're the Minion Maker's minion, these days?"

"Only in her wildest dreams. I hear Mummy's going to let you be king this time."

"Only in Tryan's wildest dreams," Elyssa said, taking the other seat. "Mother is going to change the laws once Tryan is married to Nyah so she can be empress again."

"And you're going to let her, I suppose? How forceful and manly of you, Tryan."

"Don't think you can insult me and I'll run away crying, Jaxyn. Are you sure you don't have the girl?"

"Quite sure."

"Someone in Glaeba does."

"Then we'll just have to find her for you," Jaxyn promised.

"This spymaster of yours, is he any good?"

"Who? Hawkes?" Jaxyn shrugged. "He seems capable enough. I've not been here long enough to be certain. His mother was a whore, so the rumour goes. You and he have quite a lot in common, now I think about it."

"Well, I hope you're right," Tryan said, ignoring the jibe about his mother. "Can't say I'm blessed with the same good fortune in Caelum. In fact, I'm still not entirely certain our spymaster, Ricard Li, isn't the one responsible for Nyah's disappearance."

"Then why aren't you back home, tearing his fingernails out with a pair of horseshoe pliers, and leaving me in peace?"

"Because even if he *was* involved, the only place she could have been taken on such short notice is Glaeba."

"He doesn't have the authority to order the Queen's Spymaster to do anything until after the wedding," Elyssa added, apparently finding the idea quite entertaining. "That's the real reason he came here himself."

Tryan glared at his sister. "Shut up, Lyssa."

"Why? Jaxyn's not stupid. He'll have worked that much out for himself already. Where's Diala?" She addressed the question to Jaxyn, ignoring her brother.

"Oh, you wouldn't have heard, would you? Diala's moved up in the world. She's our crown princess—and very soon to be crowned Queen of Glaeba—Kylia."

"That Stevanian slut is married to Prince Mathu?" Tryan asked. "I thought he married some cousin of his."

"He's King Mathu now. And yes, he married the former Duke of Lebec's niece, who is cousin to the king." The Tide Lord spread his hands and smiled. "You know how it works, Try. The niece goes away to school for a while, and when she comes home everyone remarks on how much she's grown and how much she's changed. . . . She meets a prince, they fall in love . . ."

"Tides, we should have tried Glaeba first," Elyssa said, downing her wine in a gulp and then holding it out for a refill.

Warlock hurried to comply with her unspoken order, afraid to do anything that might anger his masters and see him excluded from this most fascinating meeting. He wasn't sure at what point his stomach overcame the nausea and he stopped being afraid. Perhaps it was listening to these powerful beings squabble like petulant children. Despite listening to Cayal's tales, he'd never witnessed these people when they were alone with each other, just being themselves. It was possible nobody who could look at them objectively ever had. Certainly no human alive and probably precious few Crasii had seen anything like it and it was proving an enlightening experience. Until that moment, it had never really sunk in that Tide Lords were just ordinary humans endowed with a gift they were not equipped to deal with, rather than magical beings deserving of awe.

Tryan shook his head as Warlock stepped back from filling Elyssa's wine. "There would have been no point coming here, Lyssa. Glaeba's heir is a nineteen-year-old boy. Taking Glaeba's throne required the skills of a shameless trollop, not a prince."

"You do your sister a vast injustice, Tryan," Jaxyn scolded. "I'm sure Elyssa could trollop shamelessly with the best of them if the occasion called for it. And since when have you been a prince?"

"My mother is Empress of the Five Realms."

Jaxyn was unimpressed. "You could check with Cayal—being a real prince, he'd know for certain—but I suspect self-appointed titles don't actually make you royal."

Before Tryan could answer that, Elyssa was leaning forward in her chair. "You've seen Cayal?"

Jaxyn studied her for a moment and then, with a heavy sigh, he shook his head and addressed her brother. "Tides, she's not *still* nursing a crush on that suicidal loser, is she?"

"I don't have a crush on him," Elyssa objected, even as Tryan nodded in agreement to Jaxyn. "I just like to know where everyone is, that's all."

"Well, if you're looking for him, precious, go ask Maralyce. Last I saw of the Immortal bloody Prince, he was trying to dig himself out from under the mountain I'd just dropped on him."

"So Cayal's out of the picture?" Tryan asked, sitting a little straighter.

"For a while," Jaxyn agreed. "You owe me one, Tryan."

"We'll see. In the meantime, I want my fiancée back."

"Never fear, Hawkes is on the job. I've already told him to drop everything else until she's either found, or we have proof she's not here."

"That's very thoughtful of you, Jaxyn."

"You don't rock my boat, Tryan, and I won't capsize yours." Jaxyn rose to his feet and smiled at his guests as if he was nothing more than a gracious host welcoming two honoured visitors to Glaeba. "And now, if you will excuse me, I'm going to visit our future queen and suggest she control herself at dinner this evening. Wouldn't do at all for our new queen to start throwing things at the Caelish delegation when she realises who you are, would it?"

"You just tell that pretentious little whore to keep her mouth shut," Tryan suggested, rising to his feet, "and we'll all get along just fine."

"I'll be sure to give her your regards," Jaxyn said. "And I'm sure she'll see reason. After all, once we find your little princess for you, we're going to be neighbours, aren't we?"

Chapter 51

Cayal watched the temple caravan snaking toward the Tarascan Oasis from the rocky outcrop surrounding the tented settlement on three sides. Between the bubbling springs here and the protective wall of rocks, the oasis was a natural resting place for travellers crossing the vast arid inland of Torlenia, and the closest thing to a real town anywhere in the Great Inland Desert.

The caravan approaching the oasis was relatively small, no more than twenty or thirty camels, and only half that carrying passengers. The rest were pack animals carrying water, food, shelter and tent poles. Knowing Brynden's love of austerity, the caravan guides would have provided their passengers with only the bare essentials, Cayal suspected. These were acolytes on their way to follow the Way of the Tide, after all. Nobody made that journey unless they were ready to eschew all worldly comforts.

Which was much of the reason Cayal decided to go on ahead of the caravan, rather than join it. He was nowhere near ready to eschew all worldly comforts. Nor did he need a caravan to guide him. Cayal knew where Brynden's abbey was. He'd been there any number of times in the past.

But on those occasions, he'd been invited. Even welcome. Approaching Brynden's lair this time was rather more problematic.

A problem he considered himself close to solving as the caravan drew nearer and he spied two shrouded females riding toward the end of the line. Although he could tell nothing of their identities, given how anxious Kinta was to patch things up with Brynden—something his own arrival might well jeopardise—it seemed logical she would come to Brynden herself to warn him.

After all, who else could she trust to deliver the news that the Immortal Prince was in the vicinity?

Even if it isn't Kinta, Cayal reasoned, as he watched the caravan wending its way between the dunes toward the Tarascan Oasis, *those two females are headed for Brynden.* Cayal had a much better history getting what he wanted out of women than he did out of men.

He watched the caravan for a while longer, letting the late afternoon sun burn down on him as he soaked up the rising Tide. It was about a third of the way back, he estimated, closing his eyes for a moment to relish the sensation. At this rate, he had a year, maybe a little longer, before it peaked.

In that time he had to convince several other Tide Lords to help him.

And then it would be over.

It was after dark before Cayal approached the camp set up by the temple cameleers. This journey was a regular monthly occurrence for them. They had established their encampment with practised efficiency, and then left their passengers to their meals as they went off to attend their camels, refill the caravan's depleted waterskins, and catch up with their friends from the other outfits camped at the oasis, of which there were, in Cayal's estimation, at least another four caravans.

There was a tavern tent close to the centre of the settlement, where the cameleers would drink themselves into oblivion the first night they spent in Tarascan. It was a tradition almost as old as the oasis. The excessive drinking was limited to the first night, however, because one needed the next day to recover and the day after that to be certain there was no more alcohol left in one's body to dehydrate it once they hit the open desert.

So he had a day or two, he estimated, while the cameleers rested their camels, their passengers, and their sore heads, before they headed out again.

Cayal doubted that was enough time to convince Kinta to help him. It certainly wasn't enough time to convince a complete stranger to act as his emissary. But right now, he didn't have much choice if he wanted to approach Brynden without starting a minor war. So Cayal waited until he spied the small shrouded female from the caravan slip away furtively (probably off to find herself a cameleer for the night) before he glanced around to be certain he was alone, and then headed for the women's tent.

He lifted the flap and looked around. As he'd suspected, the tent was plain and unadorned with anything but the most rudimentary pallets for sleeping, laid out either side of the wooden centre pole, which held two flickering candles in small brackets attached at head height, where a thin band of polished metal served to protect the pole from the flames as well as reflect the light. The tent proved to be empty, but for another dark-haired servant kneeling over the luggage in the corner. She was unshrouded—not unexpected in the privacy of a sleeping tent—and had her back to him.

"Where is your mistress?" he asked in Torlenian, certain he'd only seen two women in the caravan. This dark-haired one—so obviously dressed as a slave—seemed to be the taller one. The one he'd hoped was Kinta.

The slave refused to answer him, remaining on her knees with her face turned away. She'd heard him speak. He saw her back stiffen in alarm at the sound of his voice, but she seemed reluctant to face him.

He was in no mood for some slave-girl's prudish Torlenian sensibilities. *Damn Brynden and his wretched shroud laws. Silly cow probably hasn't let a man look at her since she was twelve.* In three strides, he was across the tent. He caught the girl by the arm and pulled her to her feet. She didn't protest. But she did keep her face averted until it was obvious nothing would save her from his unwelcome gaze.

Then she squared her shoulders and looked him in the eye.

As if she was too hot to touch, he let her go, too dumbstruck to speak.

"Hello, Cayal."

"*Arkady?*"

"You remember me, then?"

Her cool reception was almost as surprising as her unexpected presence here in the oasis. "What . . . what are *you* doing here?"

"I could ask you the same thing."

She was calm and much less surprised to see him than he was to see her. Cayal drank in the sight of her, a part of him rejoicing in the idea he'd found her again, another part of him wanting to flee, aware this woman was a real danger to his plans. Cayal desperately wanted to die. He didn't want or need the distraction of a woman who—with very little effort—might provide him with a reason to live.

"But I thought . . . where's Lady Chintara?"

"Back in Ramahn." Arkady sounded puzzled and then she seemed to realise what he was getting at and nodded in understanding. "I see . . . you thought the other woman travelling with us was Kinta, didn't you. You're mistaken, I fear. She sent me on this journey, but I'm travelling with a Glaeban diplomat, not your immortal companion."

"And you're dressed as her servant," Cayal noted with a frown. "What happened?"

She shrugged philosophically. "The House of Lebec has suffered something of a downturn in its fortunes since we last met."

Cayal took half a step closer, torn with conflicting emotions. He wanted to take her in his arms. He wanted to breathe in the essence of her. Run his fingers through her hair. Run his hands over every part of her body. He wanted to devour her.

Almost as much as he wanted to flee this place and never lay eyes on her again . . .

He contained his tormented desires with an effort. "I hope your change of fortunes wasn't my fault," he said, searching her face for some sign that she was even half as rattled by this unexpected encounter as he was.

Arkady shook her head, sparing him a sad little smile, which made him realise that for her, the meeting wasn't quite as unexpected as it had been for him. "If it's any indication of how far the great House of Desean has fallen, my part in your escape and our subsequent . . . adventures . . . are the least of my problems."

"Jaxyn's responsible for this, isn't he?" he said. While the downfall of her family was something to be concerned about, he was relieved, in a way, that being stranded in the Great Inland Desert posing as a servant to a Glaeban diplomat was the worst that had befallen her. He'd seen the look on Jaxyn's face in Maralyce's mine when they spoke of Arkady. The man was capable of much worse than this.

"Jaxyn *and* Diala, I suspect."

He wasn't expecting that. "Diala? What's that nasty little slut got to do with you being here in the deserts of Torlenia?"

"She's Jaxyn's new playmate."

Cayal took another step nearer and studied her closely for a moment. "Did Jaxyn hurt you?"

She shook her head. "Not physically. I've been here in Torlenia for the past few months, so I'm out of his reach for the time being. But he's not been idle. Since we left Glaeba he's destroyed my husband's reputation, forced the king to disinherit him—and me along with it—trumped up charges against us both, had himself appointed to the role of the new King's Private Secretary and I suspect he had a hand in the untimely demise of the former King and Queen of Glaeba. Kinta thought I'd be safer at the abbey, where Jaxyn wouldn't think to look for me."

Tides, would things never change?

Of course they won't change, he reminded himself silently. *That's one of the reasons there's no point going on.*

"So it's business as usual now the Tide's on the turn, then." He reached out to touch her face, but she leaned away from him.

"Don't, Cayal."

"Why not?"

"I haven't washed in days. I must smell awful."

"We're in the desert, Arkady." Giving in to temptation, he took her hand and drew her closer, breathing in the musky, tantalising scent of her. She resisted for a moment and then relented, letting him pull her to him. When he spoke again, his lips brushed against her cheek, making every word a kiss, every breath a caress. "Nobody's washed for days. We all smell the same."

Arkady closed her eyes as he spoke, her head tilting back ever so slightly. He knew the effect he was having on her, just as he was quite sure she was aware of the effect she was having on him, just by standing there, so vulnerable and yet so dangerous to him. His lips sought hers tentatively, expecting her to resist. When she didn't fight him, he pulled her closer and kissed her with a longing that shocked them both.

And for a fleeting moment she was kissing him back, her mouth open, hungry and wanting, as they teetered on the edge of true lunacy . . .

And then sanity prevailed and he pushed her away.

"Tides . . ." he said, shaking his head in denial, as if that would somehow shake off the effect she had on him. "I hate what you do to me . . ."

She stared at him in shock. "*Excuse* me?"

"A thousand years I've been looking for this chance . . . and then you come along . . ." She was staring at him with a hurt, uncomprehending expression. "Oh, what's the point of trying to explain? You wouldn't understand."

"*I* wouldn't understand?" She sounded wounded and more than a little angered by his inexplicably erratic behaviour. "You barge in here uninvited; you kiss me one moment, tell me you hate me the next . . . Tides, Cayal, I'm not the one who can't make up his mind about what he wants."

"Then make up your mind."

"About what?"

"About us."

"There is no *us*, Cayal."

"Just say the word and there will be." He took her by the arms and pulled her to him again until her lips were so close to his he could almost feel their soft yielding pressure beneath his. "Tell me that's what you want, Arkady, and I'll give you the world. Come with me now. Forget hiding out in Brynden's wretched abbey. I can protect you from Jaxyn and Diala. I can protect you from anyone. Tides, I'll conquer Glaeba for you, if that's what you want. I'll make you her queen . . ."

She seemed unimpressed. "Listen to yourself, Cayal. You don't want me. You don't even *know* me. If you did, you'd not define what you think I desire in terms of how much of the world you can conquer on my behalf."

"Then what do you want, Arkady?"

"Whatever I want, Cayal, I'm fairly certain it's not being the pretty distraction you need to give your life meaning while you wait for the end of time."

He let her go roughly, shaking his head. "Tides, you *have* been getting cosy with Kinta, haven't you?"

Arkady rubbed her arms where he'd gripped her, glaring at him. "We have a lot in common, Kinta and I. Particularly when it comes to *you*."

Cayal couldn't believe he was hearing this. Not from Arkady. "Oh . . . what . . . so now you're angry with me because you don't like the way I treated some woman you barely know, a thousand years before you were even born. Is that it?"

Arkady met his gaze without blinking, not so easily intimidated as that. "You used her, Cayal. You seduced her and then you ran off with her. Not because you loved her. Not even because you felt something for her. It was the ultimate act of selfishness. You did it to make Brynden try to kill you."

"I can't be killed, Arkady, I'm immortal."

"But you never stop trying to find a way around that inconvenient state of affairs, do you?"

She was right of course, which was the torment and the temptation of her. Arkady Desean seemed to know him better than he knew himself, at times. She saw through him. Saw *into* him. And yet, but for a night of reluctant confessions of secrets he was sure she'd shared with nobody else, he knew so little about her.

Or what she was doing here in the Tarascan Oasis. "Why are you really going to Brynden? Are you Kinta's gift to him?"

"Don't be ridiculous. I told you what I'm doing here. Kinta's sending me to Brynden's abbey to hide. She's doing it to protect me from Jaxyn."

"I could protect you from Jaxyn."

That didn't seem to impress her much at all. "And who would protect me from you, Cayal?"

There was no answer to that. And there was so much more he wanted to say to her. So much he *couldn't* say, so much he couldn't even put into words. He wanted her to understand his pain, but if she understood him, he'd never want to let her go. He couldn't risk pursuing even the vague hope of a future that included this woman.

The Tide was on the rise. Cayal couldn't wait another thousand years to end this; certainly not for the promise of a few days, months or even years of short-lived and ultimately painful happiness.

He would never admit such a need, however. He couldn't afford to if he intended to die.

Cayal's expression hardened and he stepped back from her.

"Go to him, then. Find your illusion of sanctuary with Brynden. I don't need you anyway." He turned on his heel and headed for the entrance, adding, "I don't need anybody."

"Which is probably why you want to die, Cayal."

He paused for a moment on the threshold of the tent and then stalked out into the cold darkness of the desert night.

Chapter 52

Arkady was still trembling from her encounter with Cayal when Tiji returned. Tiji, curse her reptilian senses, guessed the truth the moment she stepped into the tent.

"He's been here, hasn't he?"

"Who?" Arkady asked, knowing full well who Tiji meant.

The little Crasii lifted the shroud over her head and tossed it to the corner. "I can smell him, my lady."

Arkady sighed and sank down on the pallet. "I was going to tell you."

"Sure you were," Tiji agreed, taking the pallet opposite. "What did he say?"

"I'm not really sure he said anything of substance."

"Why don't you let me be the judge of that?"

Arkady frowned. "Do you think *me* incapable of judging such a thing objectively?"

"Frankly, my lady, I do."

She paused and then shrugged. "We spoke of . . . insignificant things, Tiji," she said, quite certain she didn't want to share the details of her encounter with Cayal with this strange creature.

Tiji wasn't fooled. "So you came up for air long enough to speak, then?"

"I *beg* your pardon?"

"I can't smell the suzerain in the tent, my lady. I can smell him on *you*."

Arkady felt her face redden. "Very well, if you must know, he kissed me."

"Funny, I didn't hear you screaming in protest. And I'm pretty sure I wasn't so far away I wouldn't have heard you, my lady."

"I'm not that big a hypocrite," she said, amazed at how much reproach this little silver-skinned Crasii could cram into a couple of sentences. "And if it's any consolation, right after he kissed me he told me he hated me."

Tiji didn't seem impressed with that information, either. "He's got an odd way of showing it. What else did he say? After he got through kissing you and then hating you, that is."

"I don't have to listen to this," Arkady said, attempting to stand.

Tiji shoved her back down with a surprising amount of force. "No, you don't. Pardon me for thinking the fate of every mortal on Amyrantha is slightly more important than your feelings."

Arkady took a deep breath, and then shook her head, wondering at what point her life had begun to spiral so completely out of her control. "Tiji, I'm not trying to be difficult. It's just . . ."

"What?"

"Cayal seems very confused. One moment he's offering to conquer the world for me, the next he's telling me I'm spoiling all his fun, just by being alive. I don't know what to tell you because I really don't know what he's planning."

The Crasii thought on it for a moment. "What did he say, my lady? *Exactly?*"

Arkady tried to recall her conversation, a little embarrassed to discover that what she remembered most vividly about their meeting wasn't anything Cayal had said. "He said something about looking for this chance for a thousand years . . . and then I'd come along, as if that somehow spoiled things . . . and then he said, 'What's the point of trying to explain? You wouldn't understand.' "

"Looking for what chance?"

Arkady shrugged. "To die, I suppose."

The little Crasii's eyes lit up with the possibilities. "Tides, you don't think he's found a way, do you?"

"To die? Of course not. If he'd found a way to end his life, Cayal would have taken it by now, I'm sure."

The Crasii shook her head. "But it may not be that simple, don't you see? He's immortal and he's already tried pretty much everything he can think of. If he thinks he's finally found a way to end it all, whatever it is, it won't be an easy one." She pursed her lips thoughtfully. "Do you suppose that's why he's looking for Brynden? Maybe he needs another immortal's help?"

Arkady shook her head. "If what Kinta told me was accurate, Tiji, I think it doubtful Brynden would spare Cayal the time of day, let alone aid him in putting an end to his suffering."

"On the other hand, if you're trying to kill yourself, who better to aid you than the man who wants you dead?" The Crasii fell silent for a time, deep in thought, and then she fixed her unblinking gaze on Arkady. "Will you see him again?"

"Who? Cayal? How should I know?"

"You didn't make plans to meet up again after I fell asleep?"

"*No.*"

"Pity."

Arkady stared at the Crasii in confusion. "You think it's a *pity*? A moment ago I was betraying every mortal on Amyrantha simply because I let the Immortal Prince kiss me. Now it's a shame I'm not making plans for a late-night assignation with him? You're as confused about what you want as he is."

"I'm very clear about what I want, my lady. I want the Tide Lords gone. It's a shame you're not so dedicated to the cause."

A thousand arguments leapt to mind, as Arkady listened to this impudent, outspoken slave admonish her for her sins, both real and imagined. She wanted to tell her to mind her own business. She wanted to tell Tiji she knew nothing about what she felt for Cayal, or Declan, or the price of silk in the Ramahn markets, for that matter.

But in the end, she said nothing, because she realised there was nothing she could say that would appease this feisty little Crasii. "What do you want of me, Tiji?"

"Talk to Cayal again. Find out if he really *has* found a way to die. It would be nice if you could find out exactly what it is, too, and when he's planning to do it. And where. And who's going to be helping him."

"Anything *else*?"

"The location of all the other immortals on Amyrantha would be handy." The Crasii smiled then, adding, "While you're about it."

Arkady wasn't amused. "And how does this fit into your rather impertinent suggestion that I should be focusing my thoughts on Declan Hawkes, if the Immortal Prince shows up?"

Tiji had the decency to look a little shamefaced. "I probably shouldn't have said that."

"No, you probably shouldn't have."

Tiji was silent for a moment, and then she asked, "Are you in love with Declan, my lady?"

"No," Arkady stated emphatically. "And just so we're clear about it, I'm not in love with the Immortal Prince, either. Now, did you want me to talk to him again, or not?"

"It's too good an opportunity to waste, my lady. Do you think he'll tell you anything?"

"I have no idea, Tiji. Do you know where I can find him?"

She nodded. "One of the canines in the tavern told me where his tent is." She leaned over and scratched out a rough map of the tent city on the floor and then pointed to the larger circle she'd drawn in the sand. "The tavern tent is here. Cayal is staying over here. It's the third one on the right."

"Then I'll go and speak to him." Arkady rose to her feet and looked down at the Crasii, a little fed up with her well-meaning disapproval. "And I'll do whatever I have to, Tiji. For the sake of all the mortals *and* the Crasii on Amyrantha."

Without waiting for the Crasii to answer, she picked up her shroud off the pallet and headed for the entrance of the tent.

"Did you want me to wait up?" Tiji called after her.

Arkady decided not to dignify that impertinent remark with a response. She pulled the shroud over her head as she stepped into the darkness to the distant laughter of drunken cameleers.

Before she had a chance to stop and consider the enormity of what she was about to attempt, Arkady hurried in the direction Tiji had told her Cayal's tent was located. The night was chilly, the vast darkness sprinkled with stars. Glad of the protection of the shroud, she didn't stop to admire the sky, however. Not only was she taking a considerable risk roaming the camp unescorted, she was dressed as a slave. Arkady's lowly status meant she'd lost any protection her rank might once have afforded her.

As it turned out, Arkady had nothing to fear from the men of the Tarascan Oasis. This was their first night here. There wasn't a cameleer in the oasis who wasn't in the tavern tent getting drunk, and the remainder of the caravan passengers, like the young acolytes heading to Brynden's abbey to seek the Way of the Tide, or those heading back from the abbey, were hiding in their tents, either meditating or resting their aching bodies, pounded so mercilessly by the unforgiving saddles they'd spent the last hundred miles trapped in.

Cayal's tent, when she found it, was right where Tiji said it would be. Bracing herself, she pushed open the flap and stepped inside.

It was one of the tents set up by the proprietors of the tavern tent for visitors who wished something a little more salubrious than the shelters they were travelling with. It boasted two rooms, a carpeted floor, a double pallet in the sleeping chamber and an elaborate wrought-iron brazier in the centre of the main room, to ward off the chilly desert nights.

But the brazier was cold, the candles unlit, the tent deserted. There was no sign of Cayal.

Not sure if she was relieved or disappointed, Arkady searched both rooms of the tent to be certain and then hurried back to her own tent.

Tiji looked up frowning as Arkady dropped the tent flap back into place. "That was quick. What happened? Is it all over between you already? Or is the Immortal Prince not as enchanted with you as we'd hoped?"

"He's gone."

The Crasii scrambled to her feet and closed her eyes for a moment, before she opened them and began cursing like a cameleer.

"You can't sense him any longer, can you?"

Tiji shook her head. "Tides, we've lost him."

"No," Arkady said, lifting the shroud off. "I don't think we have."

"You know where he's going?"

"If he was here in Tarascan, Tiji, surely there's only one place he could be going."

The little Crasii thought about it for a moment and then nodded in agreement. "You're right. He's on his way to visit Brynden. He'll be heading for the Abbey of the Way of the Tide."

"As are we, Tiji," Arkady said. "As are we."

Chapter 53

Stellan Desean was only days away from his trial when Jaxyn Aranville finally decided to pay him a visit. Warned in advance by the guards that his visitor was on the way up, he had time to compose himself before confronting his former lover.

Stellan was under no illusions, any longer, about Jaxyn Aranville. He'd heard enough from the guards to know Hawkes was telling the truth about how he'd been used; how he'd been set up to clear the way for Jaxyn to take first the Duchy of Lebec and then the Glaeban throne. He no longer felt betrayed. Now he just felt stupid and gullible.

And foolish for not listening to Arkady.

Somehow, Arkady had known. Whether she had merely sensed the young man's evil, or had something concrete on him—Stellan thought that unlikely; Arkady would not have hesitated to show him evidence of Jaxyn's treachery if she'd had it—she had warned Stellan, from the very first moment he'd stepped foot in their home, that Jaxyn was not to be trusted.

If only he had taken that warning for what it was—Arkady's genuine concern for him—instead of dismissing her warnings out of hand as the foolish fears of a woman whose position was threatened by her husband's love for another.

When Jaxyn arrived he was dressed much more formally than his position as the Kennel Master of Lebec had ever required of him. And on the fourth finger of his left hand sat the heavy ducal signet of Lebec. With a single word, Jaxyn ordered the Crasii guards from the tower as Stellan rose to his feet. He stared at his former lover through the bars, disappointed to discover that after weeks of imagined conversations with this treacherous young man, now he was here, standing before him, Stellan couldn't think of a thing to say.

"My, my . . . how far the mighty have fallen," Jaxyn remarked as soon as they were alone, glancing around the tower cell with interest. "Although they tell me this is the deluxe accommodation here. Hate to see where the commoners are kept if this is the *good* bit."

"Hello, Jaxyn."

The young man fixed his gaze on Stellan and smiled, as if he was genuinely pleased to see him. "Tides, but you're a civilised fellow, aren't you? If our places were reversed, I doubt I'd be as polite to you."

Stellan refused to be needled. "I'm still trying to work out what I ever did to make you betray me so heinously."

"You were of no further use to me," Jaxyn said with a shrug. "No . . . that's not really true. It's more that you were in my way. Becoming a liability. That's all it is. Don't take it personally."

"I loved you, Jaxyn."

The young man seemed unmoved.

"I thought you loved me."

"How unfortunate for you."

Stellan was staggered by his casual disregard of everything that had passed between them. "You *said* you loved me."

Jaxyn folded his arms, staring at him through the bars. "And you believed me, Stellan, because you wanted to. You should have listened to Arkady, you know. She had me pegged from the moment we first met."

Stellan didn't need to be reminded of that. "What about Kylia?"

"What about her?"

"I hear you've corrupted my niece, too."

Jaxyn laughed. "*Corrupted* her? Tides, who have you been talking to?"

Stellan didn't answer, keeping his expression blank, privately appalled to think he had ever considered this young man capable of love or honour.

"Well, it's of no matter really. I hear you've decided to stand trial, after all. That's very courageous of you."

"It has nothing to do with courage," Stellan said. "If I'm to be falsely accused, then I want my day in court."

"You don't hope justice will prevail, surely? I hear Hawkes has a whole legion of willing witnesses ready to swear you're responsible for the king and queen's death, along with a dozen other sundry offences and probably the last Cataclysm as well." Jaxyn seemed very amused. "Not surprising really. I mean, you stole his girl, didn't you? He must have been waiting years for a chance like this. And I have to say, Stellan, the King's Spymaster didn't so much as blink when I told him what I wanted him to do to you."

"I'm sure he's done a fine job of fabricating evidence against me, whatever his motivation," Stellan said, wondering if there was a grain of truth in Jaxyn's accusation about Hawkes biding his time for revenge. "However, it would be more expeditious, don't you think, to tell the truth?"

Jaxyn turned to look at the duke in surprise. "You'd willingly stand trial for the *truth*? My, what a difference a couple of weeks in a cell can make in a man. Aren't you worried a confession that you're a practising sodomite will embarrass your precious young king?"

"My precious young king is currently arranging to have me tried for a dozen murders he knows I didn't commit," Stellan pointed out. "I rather think Mathu's honour could already be judged as questionable, don't you?"

Jaxyn smiled. "I should tell him you said that. We could add slander to the list of charges against you. And it wouldn't take much to get him excited about the idea, trust me. Mathu's already smarting over the notion that you've been lying all these years. Not to mention his shuddering disgust of the realisation that you've actually seen him naked."

Stellan shook his head, wondering why it had taken a prison cell to make him see this man for what he really was. "This isn't about the list of charges against me, though, is it? Or Mathu's unfounded fears. This is about hiding the truth. The truth that will bring *you* down along with me, Jaxyn. The truth that would seriously interfere with your plans, I suspect."

"And what truth is that?"

"Why don't you tell me?"

Jaxyn laughed. "Why? Do you think I came here to gloat? Do you imagine you can goad me into laying out my intentions for you, so you can pass the information on to your friends outside—assuming you have any left—so they can put an end to my evil plans for taking the throne of Glaeba?" Jaxyn walked back to the bars, grabbed them and thrust his face between them, grinning like a fool. "Or maybe the Cabal of the Tarot is back? Is that it, Stellan? Someone's told them the Tide is on the turn? Maybe you're an agent for the Guardian of the Lore. Is that it?"

Stellan took a step backward, shaking his head. He'd never heard of the Cabal of the Tarot or the Guardian of the Lore. "*What?*"

Jaxyn studied him for a moment longer and then pushed off the bars, laughing at his own outburst. "Never mind. Can I get you anything? More paper, perhaps, so you can write your confession in great and glorious detail, and be done with this nonsense?"

"I've told you. I changed my mind. I will not confess to false charges. I'll plead guilty to the truth, I've enough honour in me to do that. But I'll not be remembered as a man who murdered his king—and his friend—to suit the purposes of an amoral fortune hunter."

"Tides!" Jaxyn said, his smile fading. "Now you sound like Arkady. And speaking of the lovely Arkady, she'll be here soon, did you know that? I signed the warrant for her arrest myself. It was my first official act as the King's Private Secretary. How about that? Me . . . signing the order to bring Arkady home?"

Stellan's stomach constricted at the thought of Arkady being dragged into this fiasco. Until now, knowing she was safe in Torlenia was the only thing that had kept him from being sick with worry about what might become of her. "There's no need to involve my wife . . ."

"Oh, yes, there is," Jaxyn said, with a vehemence that startled Stellan. "That common-born whore spent the better part of a year looking down her nose at me. Time to redress the imbalance, don't you think? My felines will have her back here any day now. She'll find it a lot harder to look down her nose when she's on her knees, I can promise you that."

"Arkady never did anything to hurt you, Jaxyn."

"Tides, but I've never met a man so blind as you!" Jaxyn shouted, grabbing the bars again. "She's more dangerous than a hundred sodomites lining up to expose me. She *knows*, Stellan . . . and she's not afraid. And if that isn't irritating enough, the stupid bitch—after all the chances I gave her—ran off with that . . . that . . . royal *cloaca*, like he was some sort of . . ." He stopped, as if he'd only just realised he was ranting like a madman. He took a deep breath. "Well, suffice to say, I look forward to seeing your lovely wife again. And showing her the error of her ways."

Stellan looked at him in horror, wondering if it was possible that Jaxyn wasn't entirely sane. Other than the clear threat to Arkady for sins against Jaxyn that seemed mostly in Jaxyn's mind, Stellan had no idea what the young man was raving about. Nothing he said was making sense.

"I must sound like a madman," Jaxyn said, calm and in control now, as if he knew what Stellan must be thinking of his unexpectedly manic behaviour.

"Please, Jaxyn, don't harm Arkady."

"Then confess to killing the king," Jaxyn suggested. "Or so help me, I will drag this farce of a trial out until she returns from Torlenia and then I will bring her here in chains and make you watch as I strip her naked and humiliate her in ways you—in your wildest nightmares—can't even imagine."

Stellan felt sick with fear—not for himself, but for Arkady. He could think of nothing short of giving in to this man that would save her, and yet that notion felt almost as intolerable. "May . . . may . . . I have some time to consider my decision?"

"You've got one day," Jaxyn said, after thinking about it for a moment. "After that, the trial starts, and I will lose all patience with you. I'm sure you understand what that means."

"I'll send word when I've decided," Stellan said with a nod, wondering what he'd achieved with buying himself another day. *Probably only a chance to dwell on the awful future awaiting both Arkady and me.*

Jaxyn smiled. "You're a fool, Stellan, but you're not stupid. I'm sure you'll make the right decision."

Without waiting for his answer, Jaxyn turned and left the guard room. The door hadn't even had time to close before the feline guards filed back to take their positions again.

One day, Stellan had gained. One day to sign his own death warrant, or risk Arkady being tortured and degraded in the hands of a madman for the crime of being married to the Duke of Lebec, for the crime of protecting his secret.

Stellan turned away and walked to the large bay window, staring out at the clouds scudding across the sky, driven by a wind he couldn't feel locked in this cell. It had seemed so simple before.

He looked down wistfully at the long drop to the water below, wondering if he could break the window and jump before the guards in the outer guard room got to him. Probably not. And there was no guarantee the fall would kill him. The tower sat on the edge of the lake. Unless the water was particularly shallow, or concealed a bed of hidden rocks, a fall might simply result in multiple fractures and his rapid recapture.

Stellan was a little surprised to find himself examining the option of suicide so dispassionately. Even more surprised to find himself rejecting the idea. Maybe, despite all that had befallen him, he wasn't quite as ready to die as he'd imagined he was.

Allowing himself to be framed for murder, Stellan realised, was tantamount to the same thing.

"Sharisha?"

The feline in charge of his guard moved closer to the bars. She was a tabby, a distinct "M" marking her forehead. Stellan had been here long enough to learn her name, but she wasn't one of the more garrulous guards so he'd not often spoken to her. "Sir?"

"Would you deliver a message for me?"

She watched him with great suspicion. "That would depend on who you wished your message delivered to, my lord."

"Declan Hawkes."

The feline thought about it and then nodded, seeing nothing wrong with passing on a message to the man who was—for all intents and purposes—her boss. "What did you want to tell him?"

"Can you ask him to visit me? Tell him I said we need to talk."

"You're planning to confess, then?"

"Just ask him to come, Sharisha. Please. And tell him it must be today."

The feline nodded again and turned from the bars. She called a tallish black-and-white feline to her, whispered something in her ear, to which the black-and-white saluted and then hurried from the guard room.

"Grella will deliver your message. I've no guarantee she'll be able to find Master Hawkes, however. He may not even be in the city."

"He'll be here," Stellan said, taking a seat on the small stool at his desk.

Jaxyn Aranville has signed a warrant for Arkady's arrest and sent people to Ramahn to her bring back to Herino.

Declan Hawkes wouldn't be anywhere else.

Chapter 54

Arkady surprised herself, once they reached the open desert. When they'd started out from the Temple of the Way of the Tide in Ramahn, she had thought she would never despise anything quite so much as she did the wretched beast that carried her across the sand. By the time they left Tarascan and reached the open desert again, she had changed her mind. On this ugly creature's broad feet and spindly legs rested her very survival. Two days into the desert, Arkady was patting it fondly and calling it by name.

Its name turned out to be Terailia, which was Torlenian for "nasty bitch," she discovered a few days after they set out, not "sand dreamer" as their cameleer had tried to convince them, to the guffaws of his companions. Terailia was aptly named; a cantankerous cow with little patience and the tendency to nip at anything that came within reach of her, but for some reason she took a liking to Arkady that bordered on obsessive. Although Tiji was a competent enough rider, as soon as they dismounted, she would let nobody but Arkady tend her.

The cameleers had warned all their passengers to take great care to secure their camels when they stopped each day. According to their guides, no matter how well you treated them, they were sly, untrustworthy creatures with a tendency to abscond if you failed to hobble them, or tie them to something solid.

Arkady quickly learned how to attach the hobbles around Terailia's front legs while she was kneeling. It proved less difficult than she feared. All the camels in the caravan were accustomed to being secured in such a fashion, and usually offered only a token resistance, although the hobbles did make standing an awkward affair. She thought the practice cruel until she noticed a beast one of the acolytes had failed to secure, hopping away on three legs the moment he thought the coast was clear. The incident had everyone in the caravan—with the possible exception of the hapless acolyte who'd had to retrieve and resecure the beast—holding their sides with laughter, which surprised Arkady, because she was starting to think there wasn't much left in this world to laugh about.

Life took on a rhythm of its own in the desert. She would fall exhausted into her bedroll at night under the vast desert sky and sleep like the dead until the cameleers roused them at moonrise for another few hours of trekking. Then they would stop while it was still dark and allow their passengers and camels to rest for a while—sleep if they were lucky—only to be shaken awake again before dawn to have breakfast, saddle the camels, pack up the camp and be on their way before the sun seared its way over the horizon. Arkady had learned to drink the bitter Torlenian green tea, eat with her fingers and to check the sand for snake tracks, scorpion tracks and especially the symmetrical stitch pattern the poisonous hakar beetles made before she lay down to sleep, after another of the acolytes was bitten and left weeping in pain for the next two days.

The shroud she had cursed so roundly every day since coming to Torlenia became a blessing. Protecting from the sun, it was loose enough to allow the air to circulate next to her body and it also meant she could wear minimal clothing underneath. The smell of her unwashed body faded into the background and she no longer noticed it over the reek of the camels and the need to conserve water. She conscientiously drank the last drop in her waterskin each day, watched the dwindling supplies on the pack-camels, and told herself these men made this journey on a regular basis and they were in no danger of running out of water.

The desert surprised Arkady. She had expected nothing but endless days of boring, rolling sand dunes, and while there were plenty of dunes, for long stretches the ground was hard, rocky and scattered with pale green and silvery vegetation, clinging to the rocks with grim determination. According to the cameleers, it rained here once a year if you were lucky. These tough little plants were thriving on what they'd managed to collect in a shower of rain months past.

Arkady admired their tenacity, wishing she was as resolute.

There were rocky ridges poking up out of the sand every now and again and they rode in their shadows whenever they could, glad of the shelter and the chance to stop squinting in the harsh light. Occasionally they would crest a ridge and the whole daunting vista would lie shimmering before them. On those days, Arkady found it easy to imagine this place had once been the bed of a vast inland sea, the heat mirage making the air appear liquid, enhancing the underwater illusion.

It seemed as if they were constantly stopping and starting. The cameleers drove them hard from before sun-up until midday, when it simply became too hot for man or beast to keep moving. The whole caravan would rest then, munching lethargically on dried camel jerky and dates while they waited for the sun to move on. Midafternoon, at some point Arkady could never really identify, the cameleers would sense the sun had passed its zenith and they would climb to their feet yelling "hurry-hurry" to their passengers, as the camels were freed from their hobbles so they could resume their journey. They would travel until after dark, turning in some time before moonrise to sleep the sleep of the truly exhausted, until they began the whole process again the following day to the persistent cries of "hurry-hurry."

On their fourth day west of Tarascan, one hundred and twenty miles of desert behind them and another two hundred ahead, Arkady witnessed her first sandstorm.

It crept up on them slowly. At first it was nothing more than a vague uneasiness that permeated the caravan. Even Arkady, for whom everything in the desert was new, could sense the subtle change in the atmosphere. The camels grew increasingly fractious; the acolytes looked at one another with questioning, puzzled frowns while the cameleers sat a little straighter in their saddles, tense and alert, like startled rabbits sniffing the air for danger.

And then someone noticed the horizon moving closer. The sky had taken on a decidedly pink cast. At almost the same time as Tiji pointed west, saying, "Tides, look at that . . ." one of the cameleers let out a ululating cry of alarm.

"What's happening?" Arkady asked the frantic cameleers, shouting to each other, arguing in Torlenian so rapidly Arkady had no chance of following their conversation. They were pointing and gesticulating toward a rocky ridge jutting out of the sand a bare mile north of them, while others shook their heads and waved their arms around frantically.

"There's a storm coming," Tiji said, although she seemed to be having trouble making out what the cameleers were shouting at each other. "They're arguing about whether we should dig in here or head for that ridge, I think."

"Wouldn't we be safer over there?"

"That's what Farek is saying. The others are objecting because they think we won't make it, or because it's haunted, I'm not sure which."

Arkady shook her head, clinging to the crossbar as Terailia backed up skittishly, sensing something was amiss. "Haunted, did you say? Tides, that's just our luck, isn't it? We're stuck in the open desert with a sandstorm about to descend upon us and the only shelter for ten miles is *haunted*?"

Before Tiji could answer, the cameleers began to dismount. Seeing her companions kneeling to disgorge their passengers, without prompting, Terailia did the same. Farek, the head guide, began to run down the line shouting "hurry-hurry, get bed-rolls, hurry-hurry" at the acolytes. He stopped when he reached the women. By then Terailia was on her knees and Tiji had already climbed off.

"What's happening?"

"Big storm. You hurry-hurry," he said in Glaeban, probably for Arkady's benefit. "Must get in bedroll. Must stay in bedroll. Hurry-hurry."

"Aren't they going to pitch the tents?"

Farek shook his head impatiently at Arkady's question. "Tent just blow away. Go poof! Bedroll better. Bedroll low. Keep back to the wind. Stay in bedroll 'til sand stop blowing."

"What about the camels?" Tiji asked.

"Hobble camels. Camels fine. Can see in sand."

With that strange assurance, Farek continued along the line of camels, yelling "hurry-hurry" to everyone he encountered. Arkady climbed off Terailia and reached for the hobbles hanging from the back of the saddle.

"Do you think it's a bad one?" she asked, as she pushed the camel's huge head aside to avoid being spat on while she secured the hobbles.

"Is there such a thing as a *good* sandstorm?" Tiji asked, quickly shaking the bedrolls out with one eye on the western horizon.

With a feeling of creeping panic, Arkady tied off the hobbles and turned to the west. The horizon was already closer, the sky no longer pink, but a dark rusty colour. The air was strangely still, charged with anticipation. Had it not been for the advancing darkness, and the pervading sense of fear radiating from the cameleers, Arkady would not have believed there was a storm on the way.

"Hurry-hurry!" Farek yelled as he scurried past them. "Back to the wind. Keep back to the wind."

"How long will it last?" Arkady called after him.

"Hours, days . . . who knows? Keep waterskin close. Back to the wind. Hurry-hurry."

Even before he'd hurried out of earshot, the wind began to pick up. It was faint at first, but decidedly gritty. Arkady hurried to Tiji's side and with a last worried glance over her shoulder at the advancing storm, she lay down beside her. "Are you sure this is the right way?"

"Storm's coming from thataway so we face thisaway," the little Crasii said. "Back to the wind, remember?"

"I hope this works," Arkady said, glancing around. By now the camels were all hobbled and turned loose and everyone was climbing into their bedrolls, pulling the canvas covers over themselves for protection. Although they seemed to know what they were doing, Arkady didn't miss the concern on the men's faces. They were genuinely afraid, she realised, and that frightened her more than the dark sky or the gritty wind. These men must have suffered through many a sandstorm. For this one to scare them meant it was a bad one.

"Hurry-hurry."

She pulled her waterskin under the cover with her, feeling the wind pick up, buffeting even the low profile she offered, lying on the sand. She waited, holding her breath, which she let out impatiently when she realised what she was doing.

And then the light vanished completely and the storm hit.

The noise was unbelievable, the illusion of being in the middle of an inland sea more intense than ever because the wind sounded like nothing so much as waves breaking on a distant shore, the feel of it almost as solid as water. Arkady lay there, terrified; unable to move.

Arkady cowered in her sandy cocoon, her heart pounding, as the sand whipped around her, the weight of it making it hard to breathe. She tried to remember to sip water from the skin, but time had dilated and blurred until her whole world was defined by nothing more than the muted sound of the wind, the heavy weight of the sand that was piling up on top of her, and the terrifying realisation that she was being buried alive.

Maybe this, she wondered, her heart clenched with fear, *is how I die.*

After some unimaginable time, Arkady woke and realised not only had she managed to sleep, but the waterskin was empty. She could feel the sand built up behind her and then on top of her.

But even through that, she could hear the still-raging storm.

It was impossible to judge how long she'd been here, no way to tell if it was still day or if night had fallen. The crashing sound of the wind had faded a little, insulated by the increasingly heavy layer of sand covering her. The air in her tiny bedroll cave was growing stale. Her heart began to race even harder as Arkady began to fear she would suffocate before the storm had a chance to blow itself out.

Once the thought of suffocation occurred to her, the threat began to fill Arkady's thoughts, blocking out everything else. Her breathing grew shallow. The air tasted increasingly vile. Every orifice seemed filled with sand.

On the brink of panic, she tried to push back the cover of the bedroll but the weight of the sand pinned her to the ground. Frightened to find she couldn't break free, she scrabbled to get clear, her fear of being scoured by the storm seeming insignificant now, outweighed by her desperate, panicked need for air.

As soon as she exposed a corner of the bedroll to the storm in her struggles, the wind whipped the canvas out of her hand and she was open to the elements, protected only by her shroud. The wind-driven sand stung like a million tiny needles slicing into her. She was blind, her eyes tightly shut against the abrasive gale. No longer sheltered by either the canvas or the layer of sand that had blown over it, she was vulnerable and very likely about to die. The crashing-wave cacophony hurt her ears, making it impossible to hear, almost impossible to think.

Arkady's mouth and nose filled with sand; every breath she took was laden with grit. She could feel the thin shroud she wore shredding in the wind. Truly frightened and certain this was how it would all end, she would have wept if there had been enough moisture left in her to squeeze out the tears . . .

She dared open her eyes a fraction, looking around for Tiji, but her vision was limited. Even if she'd been able to see more than a few inches in front of her through the stinging gale, with the sand piled up against the prone bodies of the caravan passengers, there was no sign of the little Crasii.

"Tiji!" she cried, her voice carried away by the wind, her mouth filling with sand. She spat the sand out and cried out again, tried to push up onto her hands and knees, knowing it was useless as she choked on the swirling dust, but desperate, none the less, for some proof that she wasn't the only person left alive in this maelstrom. That the others hadn't already suffocated and her death was just taking a little longer . . .

And then, without warning, the gale ceased.

Her ears ringing with the unexpected silence, Arkady waited for a moment before she dared open her eyes. Pushing herself up, she looked around, horrified to discover the storm still raged about her, but somehow she was no longer touched by it, protected by an invisible bubble of calm.

"Arkady?"

Gasping from this unexpected bounty of fresh air, black lights swimming before her eyes, she thought she imagined someone speaking her name. Perhaps her foolishness had killed her, and she was suffering some sort of hallucination as she died . . .

"Tides, woman, what were you thinking?"

The voice was real, she realised, and surely no death would involve having to spit out so much sand before she could respond. Feeling dizzy and disoriented, Arkady turned, the shroud blocking her view. Impatiently, she pulled the remnants of the shredded garment aside.

Inside the inexplicable bubble of tranquillity she now inhabited stood another figure, untouched, and apparently unbothered, by the raging sandstorm. Slowly, Arkady attempted to climb to her feet and turned to face him, shaking, terrified, yet somehow not surprised to find him here.

He was, after all, a Tide Lord. The elements were his to command.

"Cayal," she managed to croak.

And then she fainted.

Chapter 55

The summons to attend the disgraced Duke of Lebec in the tower cell of Herino Prison didn't surprise Declan when it was delivered. It just couldn't have happened at a worse time. With Tryan and Elyssa in the city, the duke's trial beginning tomorrow and the alarming news that unbeknown to the spymaster, Jaxyn Aranville had already dispatched his own troop of Crasii to Torlenia to arrest Arkady, Declan didn't have the time or the inclination to waste another hour listening to Stellan Desean's impractical and inconvenient notions of honour.

On the off-chance he wasn't planning to merely bemoan his unfair lot in life, Declan decided to pay the duke a visit. It was late, the night dark and overcast and threatening more rain. In the distance, over the glassy black waters of the Lower Oran on the Caelish side of the border, silent lightning flickered sporadically, warning of the coming storm.

Declan entered the prison hoping for something more than another fruitless discussion about the honour of the Deseans and the need to protect Glaeba's new king. But even if Stellan wasn't planning to fight the charges against him, he could—at the very least—tell Declan what arrangements he'd made for Arkady before he left Torlenia. Once word reached the southern capital of the fall of the House of Lebec, she would lose all the protection her position as Stellan's wife might once have afforded her.

Only the knowledge that Tiji was in Torlenia with diplomatic papers, independent of anything that might befall Arkady, gave him some measure of hope. He had no way of getting a message to the Crasii. He just had to hope she knew him well enough to understand that once things turned sour for Arkady, he would expect the little Crasii to do whatever it took to keep Arkady safe.

Not trusting any of the Crasii guarding Desean, Declan dismissed them as soon as he arrived, fairly certain his visit would be reported to Jaxyn within the hour. That made his position all the more untenable, particularly in light of his promise to Tilly Ponting to aid the duke if he could. Right now, Declan enjoyed the tenuous, if not complete, trust of the new King's Private Secretary. For someone so highly placed in the Cabal to have that kind of access to a Tide Lord, right at the beginning of his climb to power, was unheard of in the history of the Cabal. Declan wasn't sure he wanted to jeopardise that for the sake of a man for whom he had decidedly ambivalent feelings.

"Thank you for coming," Desean said, as the last of the Crasii filed out of the guardroom. The room was gloomy, Desean's cell lit with only a single candle, which shaded the duke's face and made him look much older. Or perhaps he really had aged these past few weeks. The threat of disgrace and death could do that to a man.

Declan stopped a few feet from the bars. "I don't have long, your grace. What do you want?"

"Jaxyn Aranville has issued a warrant for Arkady's arrest."

"I know."

"Can't you do something?"

The spymaster stared at him in amazement. "Can't *I* do something? Tides, she's in this mess because she married *you*."

"You're the King's Spymaster, Declan."

"And you're the king's scapegoat, in case you haven't noticed. What makes you think I can do *anything* to save Arkady from what you've brought down on her?"

The duke was silent for a moment, as if he was struggling with himself about something. Then he squared his shoulders, as if his decision was made. When he spoke, he sounded much less uncertain. "Did you speak to her, Declan, after she returned from the mountains?"

"You know I did."

"And did she share her ludicrous theories with you? About the Tide Lords?"

Declan kept his expression blank. "Yes."

"Did *you* think she was crazy?"

Where's he going with this? "What does it matter what I thought?"

Again the duke faltered for a moment, before he braced himself to continue. "Jaxyn came to visit me earlier."

"I'm sure you two had a lot to discuss," Declan said, growing impatient with this seemingly aimless conversation. "Was that all you wanted to see me about, your grace? I have your trial tomorrow, you know. It's hard work keeping all these dishonest witnesses in line. I really haven't the time to stand here catching up on old times." He turned away, a little disappointed but hardly surprised this meeting had proved so futile.

"Jaxyn said something to me earlier, Declan," Stellan called after him. "Something that didn't make sense at the time. But then I started to think about some of the things Arkady said when she returned from the mountains and I've begun to wonder . . ."

Declan stopped, turning back to look at the duke. "That's all well and good, your grace, and much as I'd like to stand here and chat about it—"

"She *knows*, Stellan . . ." the duke said, cutting him off. "That's what he said to me. *She knows, Stellan, and she's not afraid.*"

Declan stepped a little closer to the bars. "Did he say *what* she knows?"

Stellan shook his head. "He was rambling. Almost incoherent. He said *she knows*, and then he said something about that not being irritating enough. He said the stupid bitch, after all the chances he'd given her— his exact words, by the way—had run off with 'that royal *cloaca*' . . ." The duke shrugged. "I've no idea what a cloaca is, but the royal reference was clear enough." Declan knew what the Crasii insult meant, and was quite sure a man as cultured and polite as Stellan Desean would never had uttered it, had he any idea of its crude meaning. Stellan stood there, looking at Declan through the bars, clearly hoping for some sort of affirmation that he wasn't losing his mind. "Jaxyn was talking about the Immortal Prince, wasn't he?"

"You're asking *me*?"

"Yes, I'm asking *you*, Declan," Stellan replied, stepping up to the bars. "I want you to tell me what's going on. You've been pulling the strings in this particular puppet theatre all along. You're the one who sent Arkady to interview Kyle Lakesh. The last time you came here you told me my niece is *not* my niece. You claimed Kylia is probably dead, and the impostor's name is Diala. You also claimed she was a great deal older and a lot less innocent than she looks and that she's known Jaxyn for longer than I can imagine."

"You scoffed at any suggestion of a plot, as I recall."

"Arkady claimed Kyle Lakesh was a Tide Lord."

"You scoffed at that suggestion too."

"Prison gives a man plenty of time to think," Stellan said. "And I've had Tilly Ponting telling fortunes in my parlour long enough to know the names of her Tarot full of immortal Tide Lords. If Arkady was right; if Kyle Lakesh really was Cayal, the Immortal Prince, as he claimed—and Arkady believes—and my niece has been supplanted by a woman named Diala, then logically, the young man calling himself Jaxyn Aranville is one of them, too."

Declan said nothing, wondering what it must have cost Stellan Desean to come to such a conclusion on his own.

"It also follows, you've known about this for some time, Hawkes," he continued, "otherwise, you'd not have come here to warn me about Diala, and quite possibly it's the reason you involved Arkady in your schemes in the first place. You never wanted her help debunking Lakesh's claim that he was immortal, did you? You wanted her to prove it."

Declan studied Stellan for a moment and then shook his head. "You've picked a fine time to start believing in the cause."

"Then I'm right, aren't I? There *is* a cause?"

"The cause is to stop the rise of the Tide Lords, your grace, something you've been doing your damnedest to help along thus far."

"I'm still not sure I believe it now, Declan."

"What do you expect me to do?"

"Find a way to save Arkady."

"I may not be able to. There's more at stake here than your duchy, you know."

Stellan gripped the bars angrily. "Aren't you listening to me? Jaxyn threatened to bring Arkady here, Declan! Unless I agree to confess so he can call off the trial, he's going to make me watch. He plans to torment her in ways he thinks I can't imagine in my wildest nightmares. But he's wrong. I *can* imagine her fate. Very well indeed. I'm sure with your experience in the darker side of human nature *you* don't have to think too hard to know what is going to happen to her, either."

His promise to Tilly still fresh in his mind, Declan considered the duke, wondering how far he could be trusted. This man—for all that he represented a painful reminder of what Declan had lost—was now the heir to the Glaeban throne. He was the only reasonable rallying point should the Cabal decide to back a resistance movement once the Tide Lords took power and disposed of Glaeba's credulous and inevitably doomed young king.

"You mustn't confess, Desean. To *anything*."

Stellan shook his head. "I can't promise that. Unless you can assure me, here and now, you know of a way to save Arkady, I will have no choice."

Declan hesitated before replying. "What if you *had* a choice? What would you do then?"

"I don't see one."

"That wasn't the question."

The duke seemed a little confused. "Are you asking what I'd do if I had a chance to save Arkady? Or a chance to save myself?"

"Both."

Stellan sighed, shaking his head. "Your optimism is admirable, but I don't see any way out of this. You must do what you can to save Arkady. I will do what I can to buy you the time you need to do it."

I ought to let you rot in here, Declan thought, both irritated and impressed by this wretched nobleman's insistence on throwing everything away for the sake of someone he really wasn't in a position to help. Arkady's fate, although hastened by the actions of her husband, was out of his control now. It mattered little to Arkady's future what happened to Stellan Desean.

But Jaxyn's words chilled Declan to his core. *She knows.*

Arkady was in danger for much, much more than being Stellan Desean's wife.

"Let the trial go ahead," he advised. "Arkady's not here and I've not heard anything to indicate she's even on her way from Torlenia, as yet. If you want to buy me the time to help her, that's the best I can do at the moment."

Letting go of the bars, Stellan nodded. "Thank you."

"Don't thank me, Desean. I haven't thought of anything yet."

Declan left the prison on foot, sending his carriage back to the palace without him. He needed to think. He had a decision to make.

It was raining as he turned away from the gloomy prison walls. The storm wasn't a particularly harsh one. The lightning was sporadic, the thunder muted, the rain more of an irritant than a downpour. Declan pulled his collar up, thrust his hands into the pockets of his long coat, and headed away from the prison toward the docks where only a few months ago he'd helped Stellan Desean rescue Prince Mathu from his own folly at the Friendly Futtock.

It felt like a lifetime ago.

His promise to Tilly notwithstanding, Stellan Desean's importance had little to do with his friendship with Lady Ponting or even his marriage to Arkady. With King Enteny dead and Mathu still childless, Stellan was Glaeba's heir. It was unlikely Diala was interested in providing her husband with another heir anytime soon, and she certainly hadn't conspired with Jaxyn to take the throne just so she could hand it over to her own child.

Even if she had planned such a thing, Jaxyn would never stand for it.

No, this plan of the Tide Lords with their eye on Glaeba required the removal of all viable contenders to the Glaeban throne, one way or another.

Which means, Declan realised in a flash of inspiration, *that's all I really need to do to solve the problem.*

The answer was so elegantly simple, when he thought about it, he was surprised it had taken him this long to come up with the solution.

In order to save Stellan Desean, Declan decided, and with luck, thwart the plans Jaxyn and Diala had for Glaeba's throne, the former Duke of Lebec was going to have to die.

Chapter 56

When Arkady regained consciousness she was no longer surrounded by a terrifying vortex of swirling sand. It was dark when her eyes flickered open. From the feel of the hard stone beneath her, and the muffled, distant howling of the wind, she realised she was in some sort of cellar. She could hear the sandstorm raging beyond the thick walls, but she was safe from it.

She opened her eyes a little wider. A torch flickered fitfully in a bracket on the wall above her head, another near the entrance to the cavern, leaving the room in as much shadow as light. She was half sitting, half lying on the floor of a dark, cavernous hall, her head resting against someone's shoulder, strong arms holding her safe from the nightmare. She closed her eyes again, relishing the feeling for the moment or two it took to register the fact that someone was holding her and then she sat up in a panic. On the floor beside her lay Tiji, her shroud discarded, apparently asleep. There was a bruise on the Crasii's cheek and a trickle of blood leaking from the corner of her mouth.

"Careful!"

She scrambled free and turned to find she hadn't been hallucinating earlier.

"*Cayal*? What happened? Where are we? What's wrong with Tiji?" Arkady leaned over and shook the Crasii, to no avail. "Tiji?" The Crasii didn't respond. Worriedly, Arkady shook her a little harder. "*Tiji*? Can you hear me?"

"I had to knock her out."

The Immortal Prince was sitting with his back to the wall he'd been leaning against, holding Arkady while she slept.

"Why?" she asked, not sure if she should be thankful or afraid to discover he'd rescued them.

"She's a Scard." He pushed off the wall, climbed to his feet and walked to the corner where the luggage sacks they'd left tied to their saddle on Terailia were lying. He tossed the sacks aside and picked up the waterskin.

Arkady rubbed her gritty eyes and leaned over to feel Tiji's forehead. The Crasii's scaly skin was smooth and cool to the touch and she seemed to be breathing normally. Arkady turned to look at Cayal. "Was being a Scard reason enough for you to knock her unconscious?"

"You were the reason," he said, in a tone that made her want to squirm with the memory of him finding her in the storm. He walked back to where she knelt over Tiji and squatted down beside them. "Don't you remember? You were frantic and wouldn't move without her. Your little Scard here got hysterical when I tried to dig her out of the sand, so I had to quiet her down. How are you feeling?"

Arkady hoped he was talking about her physical condition. She certainly wasn't in the mood to discuss the conflicted emotions she had to deal with every time she confronted this man. "Like I've been scrubbed raw with a hasp file. Where are the others?"

"They're probably dead by now."

Arkady stared at him. "Dead?"

"I suppose."

"But you don't know for certain?"

Cayal shrugged. "If this storm keeps up much longer it wouldn't make any difference, even if I did know."

Cayal's calm and detached appraisal of the fate of the rest of the caravan left her breathless. She scrambled to her feet. "Can't *you* help them?"

He looked genuinely puzzled by her question. "Why would I want to?"

"Because you *can*?" she suggested, reminding herself as she did, *this is why he's so dangerous. The reason he wants to die. He doesn't feel things like a mortal. He doesn't feel some things at all.* "Because you can walk through that storm with impunity and they can't?"

He shook his head. "You're crediting me with heroic abilities I don't have, Arkady. That gale's been blowing sand over your travelling companions for the better part of a day and night. They're nothing more than featureless lumps in the sand, by now. Tides, I only found *you* because you panicked and tried to leave the only shelter you had."

"But you found the camels," she said, pointing to the sacks. The idea the rest of their caravan—Farek, with his endless "hurry-hurry," the boisterous cameleers and the nervous young acolytes heading for Brynden's abbey—might be dead already was too unbearable to contemplate.

To think she might have survived when the others didn't was more troubling. That she survived because Cayal, with his god-like powers, had decided that she could live while the others would have to die, was even worse. That notion came with a burden of guilt she wasn't equipped to deal with.

"I didn't need to find the camels," Cayal said. "They found this place on their own. Camels are smarter than humans in a storm. They have enough sense to find shelter and stay there." He thrust the water-skin at her. "That was a really stupid thing you did, by the way. If I hadn't found you, you'd be dead, too."

If you hadn't found me, I might be safer. And the others might have lived.

"I thought I was suffocating."

"You probably were. Didn't make trying to wander about in a sandstorm any less dangerous, though. We're less than a mile from where you were standing, by the way. Why didn't your guides just bring you here when they saw the storm coming?"

"I can't believe you just let them die."

Cayal didn't answer her. Clearly, he didn't feel the need to justify anything he'd done. She glanced around, only now thinking to wonder where she was. "What is this place, anyway?"

"Brynden's old palace."

Arkady understood now, why Farek and his cameleers had refused to seek shelter in the ridge so close to where they'd dug in to weather the storm. "They feared it was haunted."

"Idiots."

Arkady frowned, recalling Cayal telling her of this place when they were still in Lebec. Of his meeting here with Brynden and Kinta. With Lukys.

And of making love to Medwen in the chill darkness of Brynden's austere fortress.

She forced that image from her mind and looked around again, afraid Cayal might guess what she was thinking. "How can this be Brynden's old palace? You said it was on the edge of the Great Inland Sea. We're a hundred miles or more into the desert here."

"I emptied the sea the better part of six thousand years ago. The desert's spread, since then." He squatted down beside her, pointing at the waterskin. "Drink it slowly or you'll make yourself sick."

She lifted the waterskin, tipped her head back, letting the tepid water stream into her mouth. It was stale and faintly metallic and tasted better than the most prized wine ever served in Lebec Palace. When she was done, she lowered the skin and looked at Cayal, as another thought occurred to her. "Are you responsible for this storm?"

The Immortal Prince shook his head. "No."

"Can you stop it?"

"It'd be safer to let it run its course."

"Safer for whom, exactly?"

"Everyone living in the southern hemisphere of Amyrantha, actually. Messing with the weather's a dangerous thing, Arkady. Believe me, I know." He examined her more closely, reaching out to brush an errant strand of hair from her face. "Are you sure you're all right?"

Instinctively, she flinched from his touch. "I'm more concerned about Tiji."

He dropped his hand. "She'll come to. Eventually."

"Are you sure?"

Cayal sat back on his heels, frowning. "You think I *want* your Scard to die?" Despite his words, the contempt in his voice when he spoke of the Scards was disturbing.

"How do you even *know* she's a Scard, Cayal?"

He glanced down at the unconscious Crasii before answering. "Better than half of all the reptiles were. The behavioural compulsion to obey us never really took with them. That's why we didn't pursue them as a species. Too hard to control. I was surprised to find you had one, truth be told. They were rare, even back when we were experimenting with them. Tryan thinks he got rid of all the Scards. He'll be peeved to realise he didn't."

"She's not *mine*, Cayal. Quite the opposite. Tiji's the diplomat. *I'm* the servant."

He shook his head, as if such a circumstance was beyond his comprehension. "That's just wrong."

She smiled wanly. "How very Tide Lordish of you to think so."

Cayal ignored the jibe and pointed at the waterskin. "Drink some more."

She did as he instructed, letting the moisture work its own particular magic on her parched throat, and then glanced around the cellar, wondering how long they would have to remain in the ruin. The danger of being effectively alone in this place with Cayal notwithstanding, she felt exhausted, dirty, gritty and yet—contrarily—safe for the first time since Stellan had left Ramahn. That was a dangerous thing to allow herself to feel. Cayal wasn't her knight in shining armour. In reality, she was trapped in a long-forgotten ruin in the middle of a sandstorm in the Torlenian desert with a self-confessed mass-murderer who couldn't decide whether he loved her or hated her.

How can you possibly think you're safe here with Cayal? she asked herself sternly.

"How long can we stay here?"

As if he could read her mind, he reached out to touch her cheek in a gesture that was as tender as it was dangerous. "As long as you want to. The cisterns are full and the pack camels have most of your caravan's supplies still tied to their saddles."

As long as you want, he'd said, not *as long as you* need *to*. Arkady wondered if it was a slip of the tongue, a warning, or if she was reading more into his statement than it warranted.

Then she realised what else Cayal had said. "Cisterns?"

He nodded. "This place is fed by a hot underground spring. Always was. Brynden's one concession to luxury. His baths."

Arkady's eyes lit up, and not only because she might have found an escape from Cayal for a time. "There are baths here? And they're full?"

"Down on the next level," he said as Arkady scrambled to her feet. "Did you want me to show you?"

Arkady didn't answer him. She didn't even hear him calling her back as she snatched a torch from the wall and hurried toward the cavernous cellar entrance and the dark halls beyond.

Tides, there are baths, here. Hot baths. She didn't need directions. Arkady was so desperate for the unexpected chance to be clean again—and the excuse to get away from Cayal's disturbing presence—she reckoned she could find them with nothing more than her sense of smell.

As it turned out, her sense of smell was exactly what led Arkady to the baths. The faintly sulphuric spring bubbled out of a broken clay pipe in the wall on the lower level, into several large pools that steamed even in the desert heat. The spring tumbled down a rock face worn smooth by thousands of years of falling water. Below the fall, the water flowed over a series of man-made steps which ended in the first of the pools. The torch wasn't bright enough for her to see beyond the first pool. She sensed rather than saw the other pools stretching away in the vast, low-ceilinged vaulted cavern.

Looking around, Arkady spied a bracket on the wall to her right. She reached up and dropped the torch into it and then scrambled up the slippery steps to the cascade. In the distance, she could hear Cayal calling her, but she ignored him. Closing her eyes, still dressed in her storm-shredded clothes, Arkady pressed her face against the warm rock and let the water splash over her.

It was only a moment—barely time to enjoy this unexpected bounty—before Cayal grabbed her arm and turned her around to face him, his body pressed to hers. "Don't you run away from me like that."

Arkady was drenched. The water tumbled over her, over them both, like a warm embrace. He was too close. Too overpowering. The cavern was dark and steamy and the flickering light from the torch fractured into myriad rainbows as it beaded on Cayal's dark hair.

And in the last few hours he'd knocked Tiji unconscious for being a Scard and let a score of people die because he didn't have enough humanity left in him to save them, she reminded herself.

"Let go of me."

"I won't hurt you, Arkady."

"You can't help yourself, Cayal," she said, trying to shake free of him.

"But I *saved* you. And your wretched pet."

"Why? Because you *love* me? I don't think so."

He didn't answer her. Arkady held her breath, part of her afraid he'd try to kiss her again, another part of her afraid he wouldn't.

And then he did let her go. As if aware no sensible conversation was likely to take place under a waterfall with her so close, he stepped back from her, out of the tumbling cascade, and pushed his wet hair back off his face as she collapsed against the wall partly in relief and more than a little disappointed. "Tides, you're like a burr under my saddle blanket, woman. You irritate me. You rub me raw."

Arkady closed her eyes. *Oh great . . . we're back to "I hate you" again.* "If I'm such an irritant, Cayal, why not let me die like the others? Why don't you leave me in peace?"

"Because you remind me I'm alive, Arkady."

She opened her eyes again and looked at him, knowing much of the danger of Cayal was that she could almost empathise with his pain. But letting him know that was the short route to a place she wasn't prepared to go. "Something you're not fond of being reminded about, Cayal." She pushed herself off the wall and stepped out of the water, wrapping her arms around her body. The water had soaked her through, plastering her tangled hair to her body and making her clothes all but transparent. She was intensely aware of that and could tell it hadn't escaped Cayal's attention either. "Why did you save me and Tiji, Cayal? Really?"

"Because I need you, Arkady," he said.

"For what?"

"To be my envoy."

It took a moment for her to get what he was driving at and then Arkady recalled where they were headed and she nodded in understanding. "You need me to speak to Brynden for you. Why?"

He hesitated and then shrugged, as if it made no difference to tell her the truth. "Because Lukys thinks he's found a way to put an end to this, Arkady. But Brynden won't speak to me."

"You need Brynden's help to die?"

Cayal nodded. "I need Brynden's help to die."

Chapter 57

Tryan and Elyssa were in Herino for more than a week before Warlock finally managed to arrange time alone with the King's Spymaster. He was getting so impatient, in fact, that in the end, he took the initiative and offered—in a suitably servile tone—to visit the spymaster himself, to see if there was any information available about the progress on the search for Princess Nyah.

Elyssa agreed with his suggestion without hesitation, even going so far as to suggest Warlock should check with Master Hawkes daily, to ensure they were being fully informed. Armed with permission to visit Declan Hawkes at will, Warlock hurried to the King's Spymaster's office as soon as he received word he was back in the palace.

Hawkes was getting ready to go out again, by the time Warlock arrived. He was shrugging on his long riding coat, heading out the door, and clearly in a hurry.

"Can this wait?" the spymaster asked. "I was just on my way out."

"Lord Torfail requests an update on the progress of your search for his fiancée, Master Hawkes."

Declan sighed and motioned Warlock back into the office. "Close the door."

Warlock did as he was bid, making sure the door was shut firmly before he turned to face the spymaster. The man's scent reeked of impatience, but he didn't seem afraid. "The suzerain grow impatient, Master Hawkes," he said. "As do I."

"I know," Declan agreed. "Tell them there's no sign of her yet."

"Are you even looking?"

Hawkes smiled. "Not so's you'd notice."

"Is that because you *know* where she is, or you don't *care* where she is?"

"Either way, I've no intention of producing the heir to the Caelish throne so she can marry a Tide Lord," he said, dodging the question entirely. "Was that all you wanted, Cecil? I really do have to go."

"And what about our deal?"

"What deal?"

"You said I could return to Hidden Valley before my mate whelps. Time grows short, Master Hawkes."

"I need you here."

"My mate needs me more."

Declan studied him for a moment, neither his expression nor his scent betraying anything, and then he shook his head. "You know what's at stake here, Cecil."

"I do, Master Hawkes. I also know the futility of it. You cannot stop the rising Tide any more than you can stop the rise of the Tide Lords. You know that. And I know that. What *I* can do, however, is be there for Boots."

"You gave me your word."

"As did you, Master Hawkes. I'm not a slave any longer. I intend to hold you to your promise, even if it means walking away from this place without your permission to go."

Declan shook his head. "If you walk away, they'll know you were a Scard, Cecil. You'll endanger everyone."

Warlock refused to be cowed by the threat of what might happen. The only future event he could predict with any certainty was Boots giving birth to his pups. "That won't be *my* problem, Master Hawkes."

Hawkes studied him closely for a moment and then frowned. "You know, for someone who was terrified he'd never be able to pull this off, you've come a long way in a very short time. Tiji would be proud of you."

"You cannot flatter me into staying, Master Hawkes."

Declan seemed to know that. He smiled. "What if I arranged to have your mate brought to Herino?"

Warlock shook his head. "You can't do that, for the same reason she couldn't come with me this time. Jaxyn knows her. He knows she's a Scard."

The spymaster was silent for a moment, hopefully trying to think up a solution to this dilemma with which he was confronted. He rubbed his chin thoughtfully and looked up at the big Crasii. Tall as Hawkes was for a human, he still wasn't as tall as Warlock.

"Tell me something, Warlock. Do you want to leave Herino because you don't think you can do this anymore, or because you want to be with your mate?"

It was significant, Warlock thought, that Hawkes had stopped calling him Cecil and reverted to his real name. It was almost as if the spymaster understood he would get no meaningful cooperation from Warlock while he was addressing him by his hated "free" name. A name which he'd come to loathe even more, now it had become the pet name the suzerain knew him by.

But Warlock was not as easily seduced as that. "I want to be there for my pups."

"And if I could arrange it so we both get what we want?"

Warlock couldn't imagine how Hawkes would manage that, but it seemed a reasonable, if improbable, compromise. Truth was, despite his declaration to the contrary—and his desperate wish to get back to Boots—Warlock was beginning to enjoy the intrigue; the knowledge that he alone was privy to the secret machinations of the Tide Lords. It was seductive, this knowledge he might be doing something tangible—however unlikely that scenario might be—to bring them down.

There was another issue, too, which unsettled Warlock more than he was willing to admit. Even if he had no desire to prevent history repeating itself, he'd been forced to stand by and watch Jaxyn call up a storm which murdered a score of innocent people. That made it very personal. A part of him hungered for a chance to redress that awful deed and he wasn't going to get a chance to do that hiding up in Hidden Valley with Boots.

"If you can find a way to keep me in the service of the Tide Lords, keep my family together, and not endanger any of us, then yes, I would consider staying."

Declan nodded, apparently satisfied with Warlock's conditional agreement. "Will you give me some time to find a solution?"

"It will take the better part of two weeks to get home and I don't intend to wait until the last minute before I leave."

"Don't worry," Hawkes said with a smile. "If what I have in mind works, it won't take that long to arrange."

Warlock frowned, not seeing any reason to smile. "Then you've already got something planned."

"I'm not sure if you could call the tenuous idea I have an actual *plan*, Warlock, but there might be a way for us both to get what we want. Just give me some time, eh?"

Warlock nodded cautiously. "I will be there for my mate, Master Hawkes. Make no mistake about that."

"In your place, I'd be doing the same thing," Hawkes said, clapping him on the shoulder in a brotherly fashion. "Now I really have to go. The King's Private Secretary wants me to go riding with him this morning."

"I wasn't aware you and Lord Aranville were such good friends."

"Neither was I," Declan said with a grimace. "That's what worries me."

"What shall I tell Lord Torfail?"

"Tell him we're questioning every barge operator on the Upper and Lower Oran, to find out if Nyah was brought across the lake. Tell him I said there are hundreds of them, so it's going to take time."

"Tryan is not a patient man," Warlock warned.

"He's not a man at all," the spymaster said. "That's most of our problem."

Warlock nodded in agreement, thinking Hawkes was right. No man ever smelled as bad as an immortal to a Crasii. "I shall visit you again tomorrow, Master Hawkes. The Lady Alysa has decided I am to receive daily reports from you."

Hawkes nodded in approval. "Was that your idea?"

"I may have mentioned it in passing."

"Elyssa's really taken to you, hasn't she?"

"She is easier to please than most, I will admit. And a little more susceptible to . . . suggestion."

The spymaster smiled. "You're starting to enjoy this, aren't you?"

"Certainly not!"

"Really?" Hawkes wasn't fooled. "You're telling me you *don't* like the feeling you get from knowing something everyone else doesn't? The way your heart pounds when you're in danger? The way the hairs stand up on your back when you learn something that might make a real difference? You don't fool me, Warlock. Your tail wags just thinking about it."

To Warlock's intense embarrassment, Hawkes was right. He lowered his tail abruptly and squared his shoulders. "I am not a spy, Master Hawkes. I am a Crasii doing you a favour because you offered me and my mate freedom and shelter. That's all."

Hawkes remained unconvinced. "Whatever you say, Warlock. For my part, I shall do my best to see you get your freedom and shelter. Just you keep doing *your* best to stay in the good books of the suzerain." He opened the door and held out his arm, indicating Warlock should leave first. "And now, if you don't mind, Cecil, I really have to go. And so do you. Our masters await us."

"I have no master any longer," Warlock replied in a voice so low it was almost a growl.

"No, you have a mate and a family on the way," Hawkes replied with a smile. "And in the long run, old son, you might find that a lot more confining."

He glared at the spymaster for a moment, trying to determine if he was joking, but Declan Hawkes was already locking the door behind them, and without waiting for a response, turned and headed off down the wide palace hall to meet the King's Private Secretary.

Warlock watched him leave with a deep frown creasing his forehead, unable to decide if the spymaster was teasing him or predicting his future.

Chapter 58

Jaxyn Aranville was waiting for Declan in the stables. He was already mounted, wearing an oilskin coat and wide-brimmed hat, riding a fractious bay gelding who apparently wasn't all that enchanted with the idea of going for a ride in the rain. Declan felt the animal's pain. He wasn't all that interested in riding in the rain, either.

"You're late."

"I'm sorry, my lord," Declan said, as a groom brought his mount forward, already saddled and ready to go. "Lord Torfail sent Cecil for a report on our search for Princess Nyah."

"What did you tell him?"

"That we're questioning every barge operator on the Lower and Upper Oran," he said, swinging into the saddle. He turned his collar up against the rain and gathered up his reins, wishing he'd thought to bring a hat, too.

"That's very creative, Hawkes. You're quite good at this sort of thing, aren't you?" Jaxyn clucked at his horse, which nipped at the neck of Declan's mare before the immortal could bring him under control and get him heading in the direction he desired.

"Despite any rumours you may have heard to the contrary, my lord," Declan said, his much-better-behaved mare moving off after them without complaint, "I didn't get my job because of my impressive family connections."

Jaxyn laughed as they rode out of the shelter of the stables and into the drizzling autumn rain. He seemed in a rare mood for someone with his woes. When they'd been standing there at the palace dock watching

Tryan and Elyssa disembark, Declan had gained a great deal of malicious satisfaction from seeing the immortal's horrified look when he realised the identity of his guests. He'd been hoping it might slow the
immortals down. It wasn't an idle hope. Just when Jaxyn thought Glaeba
was in his grasp—and he was probably assuming Caelum would follow
naturally in a year or two—he'd discovered his neighbours were actually
his Tide Lord brethren with their eyes on conquest of the entire continent, just as his were.

Following him out of the stables, Declan glanced at Jaxyn, looking
for some sign as to why the suzerain was so anxious for this meeting, but
the Tide Lord was giving nothing away. Declan looked up, wondering if
the rain would stop soon. Fortunately, the downpour wasn't as bad as
he'd feared and it seemed to make little difference in any case. The rain
barely touched them. Clearly, Jaxyn was doing something to affect the
weather.

"I've heard a great many rumours about you, Hawkes," the immortal remarked as they headed out across the courtyard toward the palace
gates and into the city beyond.

"Such as?"

"That your mother was a whore."

"True."

"And the rumour you'd killed three men by the time you were fifteen?"

Declan couldn't help himself. He laughed aloud at the suggestion.
"Tides, I haven't heard that one in years."

"Is it true?"

He glanced at the Tide Lord, knowing there was a great deal more to
this casual and seemingly banal conversation than the king's new Private
Secretary taking the opportunity to better acquaint himself with the
King's Spymaster. "I make it a rule not to deny or confirm any rumour
about me that can't be substantiated by recorded fact, Lord Aranville.
Reputation is everything in this game."

Jaxyn nodded with approval. "You'll go far, Hawkes, I think, if you
play your cards right."

Declan looked at him curiously. "How much farther is there to go,
my lord? I'm already the King's Spymaster. For a common-born man
with my . . . *background* . . . that's about as high as I'm ever likely to get."

The immortal shrugged. "Go back far enough, Hawkes, and you'll find all the high-born families were low-born once, so don't let that stand in the way of your ambition. You do *have* some ambition, don't you?"

Why? Declan wondered. *Will that make me more pliable if you think I'll do anything to get where I want to be?*

"I suppose," he admitted aloud.

"Is it true your grandfather claims he's a Tidewatcher?"

To cover his alarm at the unexpected question, Declan forced a laugh, as if the very suggestion *any* man could be a Tidewatcher was ridiculous, let alone a relative of his. "Tides, Lord Aranville, who have you been talking to?"

"Is it true?"

"That he was a Tidewatcher, or that he claimed to be one?"

"You tell me," Jaxyn said.

Declan nodded, smiling in what he hoped was fond remembrance. "My grandfather used to claim it all the time. The more he had to drink, the more insistent he was about it, too."

"You speak of your grandfather in the past tense."

"He died a few weeks ago, my lord. That's why I had to return to Lebec. To settle his affairs."

"His *affairs*?" Jaxyn asked, a little sceptically. "You were gone for weeks, Hawkes. How many affairs could an old drunkard have had for you to settle?"

"Perhaps it would be more accurate to say I was settling his debts, then," Declan corrected, cursing his own stupidity for not realising Jaxyn would have checked into the spymaster's background, almost as closely as Declan had checked into the Tide Lord's.

Still, this was proving an interesting conversation. It was almost as if Jaxyn was sounding him out. Interviewing him, perhaps? Was that why he was so interested in knowing if Shalimar was a Tidewatcher? Because the grandson of a man who claimed to believe in the Tide Lords would be more accepting of the idea they had returned? Jaxyn would have power to burn once the Tide returned, but it took more than brute strength to subdue an entire nation. He needed allies—minions—to help him maintain control.

Tilly is going to love this.

"And are his debts settled?"

"Pretty much."

"Then you can give the king's business your undivided attention."

"I thought I *was* giving it my undivided attention, my lord."

Declan followed Jaxyn as he turned onto the main thoroughfare into the city, leading to the central markets. It was midmorning and even the rain couldn't stop the commerce of the city. They walked their horses in the centre of the road, over the slick paving, expecting the pedestrians to get out of their path.

"You've done well distracting our Caelish visitors, but I'm not sure how long it will last. Lord Torfail is threatening to invade if we don't produce the princess."

"We don't have the princess."

"He's threatening it, none the less."

Declan shook his head, certain—like the rest of this discussion—the question was some sort of test. Maybe Jaxyn wanted to know something of his tactical assessment abilities. "It's an empty threat he can't back up. Torfail hasn't got the authority to raise an army in Caelum, and even if he did, the Caelish are woefully undermanned. Our felines would outnumber theirs three to one, if it came to a pitched battle."

"That was my assessment, too," Jaxyn agreed, with an approving nod. "What do you suggest we do then?"

"Send them home for starters, my lord."

"Easier said than done."

"Bribe them."

Jaxyn turned to him. "Bribe them, did you say? With *what*?"

"With whatever it takes," Declan said with a shrug. "Tides, there's got to be *something* they want."

"Tryan wants the Caelish throne, Hawkes," Jaxyn retorted impatiently, forgetting himself for a moment, "something I have neither the power nor the inclination to grant him."

"What about his sister?"

"What about her?"

"What does she want?"

"A good fucking, probably," Jaxyn announced sourly.

Now, now, Jaxyn, you're getting testy.

"And if we can't arrange that?" he asked in a bland tone.

"Tides, I don't know. What do you suggest?"

Declan made a show of thinking about it for a moment, and then said, "Shower them with gifts. Send them home overburdened with tokens of Glaeba's goodwill toward her closest neighbour. You know what I mean . . . a barge full of our finest vintages, handfuls of freshwater pearls from Lebec, a few slaves, maybe even a breeding pair of canines or something like that." He glanced at Jaxyn, who seemed to be receptive, hoping he didn't destroy everything with the next part of his not-very-well-thought-out plan. "We could tell them we've got a lead on Nyah's location, too, which should get them moving. Tell them we think she was taken down the lake to Whitewater City by whoever took her out of Caelum. That we think she's been caught by Senestran slavers. We could even offer to help look for her in Senestra."

"Better yet, *they'll* go looking for her in Senestra and leave us alone," Jaxyn mused. "Suppose they don't buy it?"

"Then perhaps a show of force is in order, my lord?"

Jaxyn shook his head, but his expression was thoughtful. "I doubt even our young and inexperienced king would wish to provoke his neighbours by threatening them with his army at this point."

"No reason *you* can't, though."

"What do you mean?"

"You're the new Duke of Lebec, my lord. Nobody would think it odd if you decided to bring your felines to the city as an honour guard. The king won't mind and I'm sure Lord Torfail won't miss the hint, either."

Jaxyn smiled. "You're probably right." They had reached the vast Herino markets. He stopped his mount and leaned forward to pat its neck and then turned to look at Declan. "I hope you're putting as much care into securing the appropriate outcome in the trial of Stellan Desean as you are into misleading our neighbours."

"Never fear, my lord," Declan promised. "It won't be long before the former Duke of Lebec will bother you no more."

"You have no qualms about arranging false witnesses?"

Declan shrugged, glancing out over the marketplace. "As I told you the first time we discussed this, my lord. The man's a pervert and the crown needs to be protected from the scandal. I have no moral dilemma over what you've asked me to do."

Jaxyn smiled. "You see, that's what I like about you, Hawkes. I suspect you don't have any morals, at all."

Declan decided not to respond to such a backhanded compliment. "And what of the former Duchess of Lebec, my lord? Do you have word from Torlenia on when we can expect her home?"

Jaxyn shook his head. "Not yet. But it won't be long, I imagine."

"Did you want me to take care of her trial the same way I've taken care of her husband's?"

Jaxyn looked at him curiously for a moment, and then he smiled so cruelly it chilled Declan to his core.

"No, Hawkes," the Tide Lord said. "You needn't do a thing. When Arkady gets back to Glaeba, I'll take care of her myself."

Chapter 59

Tiji was quite sure she would never get over the shock of waking up in a cellar in the middle of a sandstorm in Brynden's old palace with a suzerain standing over her.

As best she could tell when she woke, she'd been out for several hours, which was worrying for any number of reasons, not the least of which was that on waking, she felt surprisingly well. A blow to the head hard enough to leave her unconscious for several hours shouldn't have her waking in the peak of good health, and the bruise on her cheek was tender rather than painful. She remembered the storm, she remembered someone digging her out of the swirling sand. She remembered the stench of suzerain around her, so powerful that even the savage wind couldn't whip it away.

And then she remembered nothing, until she came to in the ruined fortress.

The only conclusion she could draw—despite what he'd told Arkady—was that Cayal had done something to her, to keep her out of his way for a while.

And the only logical reason he would do something like that is so he could be alone with Arkady.

She looked up from the fire, frowning as the thought occurred to her for the hundredth time since they'd left the shelter of the old ruin and headed out into the desert again. The sandstorm was long gone, the landscape sculpted into something entirely different by the wind. There was no caravan any longer, just Arkady and Tiji and the camels who'd sought shelter in the ruins. And the Immortal Prince.

Cayal was their guide, their saviour and their enemy. He was the only one of them who knew the way to Brynden's abbey, the only one of them with any idea of how to survive in the desert. But he wasn't helping them because he was generous or noble or even particularly nice.

He was helping them because it helped him. They had something he didn't have. Something he needed, apparently.

Access to Brynden.

"Is that water boiled yet?"

Tiji looked up and nodded to Arkady, pointing to the pot sitting on the edge of the reeking, camel-dung fire. "Help yourself."

The duchess had shed her shroud, now it was just the three of them. There wasn't much point in wearing what was left of it, in any case. She wore a burnous instead, a light hooded cloak favoured by the cameleers that protected them from the sun, which they'd found in the saddlebags of one of the camels. It was just on dusk, so she had pushed the hood back, revealing her sun-freckled face and dark, windblown hair, which was braided to keep it untangled.

"Finally," Arkady said with a weary smile. "I'd kill for some tea."

Before Tiji could answer Cayal came up behind Arkady and looked over her shoulder at Tiji. "Who's killing what, and how can I help?"

Tiji frowned, not seeing the joke. Cayal stood so close behind Arkady their bodies must be touching. He did that a lot. While he kept his distance from Tiji—barely even acknowledged her presence most of the time—he was acutely aware of Arkady. If he spoke to her, he leaned in close, until his lips were all but touching her hair. If he was near her, it was always too near, as if the scent of her was so enticing he had to breathe it in as often as he could. And when he looked at her, it was with a kind of wistful longing for what might have been that both puzzled and infuriated the little Crasii.

For her part, sometimes Arkady seemed uncomfortable with his attention, but Tiji thought that was mostly for her benefit. When Arkady wasn't aware of being observed, she seemed far less discomforted by Cayal's presumptuousness than she did when she thought Tiji was watching them.

Tides, Declan, what do you see in this woman?

"Her grace was suggesting she was prepared to kill something for a cup of hot tea," Tiji informed him. And then she added, under her breath, "What a pity it can't be you."

"I heard that," Cayal said, squatting down to take the water off the fire. He put the bubbling pot down on the sand and looked at her. "I'm curious, *gemang*. What have I ever done to warrant such animosity from you?"

"You are suzerain."

"Which is not actually my fault."

"Cayal . . ." Arkady said, putting her hand on his shoulder, perhaps hoping to discourage him from getting involved in such a conversation.

"No, Arkady, let her answer," he said, brushing her off. "Why do you despise me, *gemang*?"

"Well, for one thing, my name is Tiji, not *gemang*."

"I saved your life."

"Really? For all I know you *caused* the sandstorm in the first place."

"Why would I do that?"

"To get rid of the others. So when we get to the abbey, Brynden won't be distracted."

He smiled. "You think I'd kill a score of innocent men for so trivial a reason?"

"In a heartbeat."

"Tiji, there's nothing to be gained by accusing Cayal of—"

"Actually, the *gemang* may know me better than you think, Arkady," Cayal cut in. He smiled even wider, fixing his gaze on Tiji. "But in this case, I merely took advantage of the situation. I didn't *cause* the situation in the first place."

"So you say," Tiji replied, unconvinced.

"I do say," he agreed. "And I need to be sure you're convinced of that. I'm not your enemy, Tiji. Quite the opposite—I *need* your friendship. I saved you and Arkady because—"

"You want us to negotiate with Brynden for you," Tiji finished for him. "So you've been telling us for three days now. I still don't get why. You know where he is. You know how to find him. And it's not as if he can kill you when he sees you, regardless of how pissed off he is at you."

Cayal took a deep breath. "You carry diplomatic papers and Arkady carries a letter from Kinta. You'll get to see Brynden within an hour of arriving at the abbey. If he thought I wanted to speak with him, he'd make me wait a year or two, just to teach me a lesson, assuming he'd agree to see me at all. You and Arkady, on the other hand, once you've met with him, can deliver my message without any of the histrionics likely to be involved if I arrive unannounced. *That's* why I saved you both from the sandstorm."

"You might have saved *me* for that reason, suzerain, but that's not the reason you saved Arkady." Tiji climbed to her feet and looked down at him. "You want us to set up a meeting between you and Brynden? Fine. Just don't try to make it sound as if there's anything remotely noble about what you're up to."

Tiji stalked off toward the camels without waiting for an answer, torn between her desire to run and her desire to see this play out as it would. Much as she despised being forced to travel with Cayal, the chance to report back to the Cabal about a meeting between two of the most powerful Tide Lords on Amyrantha was a rare opportunity.

She reached Terailia, patting the beast on her flank as she ducked under her neck, thinking the camels better company than the humans she had on offer. With the bulk of the dromedary between her and the others, she turned to watch them. Cayal had risen to his feet again. He was talking to Arkady, but so low even Tiji's reptilian hearing couldn't tell what he was saying. As usual, he was standing too close. Arkady listened to what he was saying and then shook her head. With the blazing sunset behind them, standing so close like that, they looked like lovers meeting for the first time.

What a pity it isn't the last time.

Terailia snorted, shaking her head. Tiji realised she'd been pulling on the lead rope so hard it was irritating the camel. She let the rope go, and on the pretence of checking the hobbles, knelt down to watch Arkady and Cayal some more. Whatever he was saying to her, the duchess didn't like it. She certainly didn't agree with it. After she shook her head again, he tried to pull her closer, but she pushed him away and bent down to fix the tea. Cayal was clearly annoyed with her intransigence, but in the end, he threw his hands up and walked over to the saddlebags, where he retrieved a small packet Tiji recognised as Torlenian tea. He walked back to Arkady, tossed the packet on the sand beside her and then stalked off in the opposite direction.

Arkady glanced over her shoulder at him, but she didn't call him back. She went back to making the tea as if she was at a wretched palace tea party.

Standing up, Tiji leaned against Terailia's shaggy side, sighing heavily, wondering what they were arguing about.

And how it would affect her.

Arkady might be distracted by the presence of the Immortal Prince, but Tiji hadn't forgotten why she was here. Or the job she had to do. The news that Cayal wanted a meeting with Brynden because he may have found a way to die was news for which the Cabal had been hoping for thousands of years.

Given the strange, tension-charged relationship between Arkady and Cayal, Tiji was fairly certain it would be up to her to deliver it.

Chapter 60

The fifth day after they left Brynden's old ruined fortress, Cayal stopped their small caravan in the lee of another large rocky outcrop that curved away into the distance so far it became lost in the heat shimmer. Arkady and Tiji climbed up to the peak of the outcrop after Cayal, where he stood gazing out over the desert. When the women reached him, he ignored Tiji, but took Arkady's hand, led her to the edge of the ledge and pointed across the sand with his arm over her shoulder, his body pressed against her back, his lips next to her ear.

"Behold the Abbey of the Way of the Tide."

Arkady valiantly ignored the shiver running down her spine as he whispered the information—quite unnecessarily—next to her ear. She could just make the abbey out, several miles away, built into the side of the same rocky outcrop on which they stood.

Constructed of the local stone, it blended so well with the surrounding landscape it was almost invisible unless you knew to look for it. The design shared a disturbing similarity to the ruined fortress they'd taken shelter in so recently, a fact which Arkady remarked upon as she squinted in the bright light, her arm raised to shield her eyes from the sun.

"Imagination was never Brynden's strong suit," Cayal said. "He'd have thought of something better than his wretched Way of the Tide by now, if it was." He slipped his arm around her and pulled her close. "Careful, now, you don't want to fall."

"You don't like his religion?" Arkady asked, shaking free of him as she stepped back from the edge.

Cayal smiled at her discomfort and let her go without resistance. He'd made his point. "It's not a religion, in the strictest sense of the word. It's part martial art, part philosophy, part mumbo jumbo, if you ask me. But it makes men feel like they've taken control of their lives, which is why it's survived so long. Thinking you have control over your own destiny is a very seductive idea, you know."

"But not quite as seductive as having control over *other* people's lives," Tiji remarked as she stared into the distance, pretending to ignore them.

She was a sharp little thing, Arkady knew, and missed nothing. Cayal's constant attempts to touch her, be near her, be with her these last few days would have been much easier to deal with had she not had those scowling, judgmental reptilian eyes glaring at her every time Cayal came close.

On the other hand, she may well have given in to the temptation, had not Tiji been here to act as her conscience. Even worse was the idea that somehow they might survive this and her every move might one day be reported back to Declan.

She didn't need his wounded looks, or judgmental censure, either.

Unaware of Arkady's inner turmoil, Cayal glared at the Crasii. "You know, there's a *reason* we tried to eradicate the Scards, Tiji, and every time you open that smart-arse mouth of yours, you remind me of it."

"You don't scare me, suzerain."

"Perhaps not," Arkady said, impatiently. This had gone on long enough. "But your bickering is really starting to irritate *me*. Could we focus on the task at hand, please, and put our personal differences aside for now?"

Neither Cayal nor Tiji answered her, but neither did they continue their sniping, which was something to be grateful for.

"What should we say when we get there?"

"*We?*" Cayal echoed, and then he shook his head. "No, I think you should go on alone from here, Arkady."

"And leave me here with you?" Tiji said. "I don't think so."

"If I'd wanted to be rid of you, *gemang*, I could have left you buried under that sandstorm and saved myself a whole world of grief."

"Cayal . . ."

"I'm suggesting your little pet lizard there shouldn't go with you, Arkady, because Brynden hates the Crasii and he *will* kill her, soon as look at her." Cayal smiled widely then, and turned to Tiji. "On second thought, off you go, reptile. Been nice knowing you."

Arkady let out a long-suffering sigh. "Stop it, Cayal." She turned to Tiji. "But he's probably right, Tiji. We don't know how Brynden will react to your presence. Maybe it would be safer for you to stay out of sight until I've spoken with him."

"Who's going to protect *you*?"

"I bear a letter of introduction from Kinta," she reminded the little Crasii. "She sent me here to keep me safe from Jaxyn. I should be fine."

"And if you're not?"

"Then you and Cayal can come rescue me."

"Assuming we haven't already killed each other," Tiji grumbled.

"If you *could* kill me, *gemang*, at least then your existence would be serving some useful purpose."

Tiji loftily ignored the remark, keeping her gaze fixed on Arkady. "I can hide. If I get inside, I can move around at will."

"But you'd have to get inside first," Arkady said, shaking her head. "You can't maintain your camouflage when you're moving, remember?" She smiled, giving the Crasii a reassuring pat on the shoulder. "I'll be all right, Tiji. Really. I'll go down to the abbey, ask to speak with Brynden, give him Kinta's letter, tell him Cayal wants to see him and that I have a Crasii servant waiting for me. After that I can arrange for you both to come to the abbey."

Tiji shook her head. "It's not going to be that simple, my lady."

"Of course it is," Cayal said. "Brynden's simple, so anything to do with him is going to be simple, too."

Arkady glared at Cayal. He really wasn't helping much at all. "No wonder Brynden doesn't like you."

"That's not the reason he doesn't like me."

"No, but if you keep this up, it may well be the reason *I* decide I don't like you."

"There's a very fine line between love and hate, Arkady," he said with a languorous smile, somehow managing to make it sound like an invitation.

"I've one foot in either camp at the moment, Cayal. You're very close to pushing me the wrong way."

Cayal was silent for a moment, perhaps debating the wisdom of arguing with her. Then he shrugged and turned to look back over the desert. "Are you going to be able to handle that camel on your own?"

"I think so."

"Then let's get this done," he said. "I'm sick of waiting."

Not surprisingly, the arrival of a lone female at the front gate of the Abbey of the Way of the Tide caused something of a stir. Arkady was bustled inside, Kinta's letter of introduction snatched from her grasp by an acolyte, and then she was taken to a room off the main hall that reminded her of nothing so much as a prison cell.

To her relief she was offered water and a platter of dried fruit, asked to remain shrouded and told the abbot would be with her shortly.

Shortly, it seemed, was a very relative term, in the Abbey of the Way of the Tide.

It was almost dark, in fact, before she saw anybody. Nervous, frightened and nauseous with the thought of all the terrible fates her long wait had given her time to imagine, Arkady jumped to her feet as the door opened. She braced herself as she turned to face the Lord of Reckoning, only to discover the man entering her cell was well into middle age.

It couldn't be the Tide Lord. Brynden, according to Cayal, had been made immortal before he turned thirty.

"The letter you bring claims you are the Duchess of Lebec," the saffron-robed man said without preamble. He spoke passable Glaeban, lifting the candle he carried a little higher to examine her more closely as he approached.

Not that there was much point, she thought, given she was still wearing the shroud she'd borrowed from Tiji.

"I am . . . was . . ."

"This is a place somewhere in Glaeba, I assume?"

She nodded. "It's about sixty miles north of Herino."

"The consort's letter to the Lord of Reckoning, while reassuringly devout, also seems to assume Lord Brynden is resident here in the abbey."

Arkady stared at him in shock. "You mean he's *not*?"

The monk smiled. "I think someone might have noticed."

"But . . . Kinta said . . ."

"Kinta?" The monk smiled. "Your faith is admirable, my lady, particularly given you are Glaeban, but you have been sadly misin-formed, she is certainly not the consort of our Imperator. If the Lady Kinta is in Torlenia, her presence is unknown to us here. And I can as-sure you, there is no immortal living here in this abbey either."

"Are you certain?"

The abbot smiled serenely. "The Way of the Tide teaches men to live with honour and frugality, my lady. This is easy enough to do in a place like this, but no true test of a warrior's strength. No man may spend longer than ten years in this place. He may use that time as he wishes, mastering the discipline of the Tide, but after that, he must return to civilisation and put his training into practice. Lord Brynden could not be hiding here, even in posing as one of us, because I can vouch for the fact that there is no man who has been here longer than a decade."

Arkady shook her head, unable to grasp the notion she had come all this way for nothing. Or that Kinta had sent her on a wild goose chase. It made no sense.

"Are you so certain one of your brothers *isn't* Brynden in disguise?"

The monk smiled even wider. "You think the Lord of Reckoning would hide among his followers? Or that we would fail to recognise him? Really, my lady, you must think us all fools."

No, she replied silently, *I think the immortals are cleverer than you know and very good at hiding when they don't want to be found.* Arkady wished she could tell if he was lying about Brynden not being here, but his occasional hesitation could just as easily be attributed to his unfa-miliarity with her language, as it could to deliberate evasiveness.

"I bring a letter from the Imperator's Consort and a message from the Immortal Prince, brother. Is that not of interest to you?"

The monk's eyebrows shot up at the mention of Cayal. "You bring a message from the Immortal Prince?"

"Would it make a difference to whether or not Lord Brynden was here, if I *did* have a message from Cayal?"

He shook his head. "Sadly, no, my lady. I cannot conjure up some-thing that does not exist. Not for the Lady Chintara and certainly not for the Immortal Prince."

"Then I have travelled all this way for nothing."

"It would seem so, my lady."

"I have two servants waiting for me out in the desert. A young man and a Crasii. I would be grateful if—"

"You will bring no Crasii to this place," he said, cutting her off, all hint of his serene smile gone in a heartbeat at the mention of the Crasii. "They are abominations. Bring it here, and it will be killed."

Arkady nodded, glad she'd listened to Cayal's warning about Tiji. "Of course not, brother. But I will need supplies for my return to Ramahn."

"If you wish, although surely, it would be faster and safer for you to travel to Elvere? The consort's letter states you are in some danger from your husband's enemies. They would be looking for you in Ramahn, would they not?"

"They would," she agreed. "Thank you for the suggestion."

The monk smiled at her, having recovered his good humour now they were off the topic of the Crasii. "It is not our way to add to the troubles of those we encounter, my lady. You will be provided with a bed and a meal tonight and supplies when you leave on the morrow. That is all we can do for you."

"Thank you."

The monk bowed and turned for the door, taking the light with him when he left, leaving Arkady alone in the darkness, wondering what sort of game Kinta was playing with her.

And wondering what—having come all this way for no reason—she was supposed to do next.

Chapter 61

It was dark by the time Declan Hawkes was finished arranging for the Lebec feline Crasii to be moved into the palace barracks when they arrived, several days after his discussion with Jaxyn Aranville. The new Duke of Lebec had lost no time in making his point to Lord Torfail. Nor had the hint been lost on the other Tide Lords.

Jaxyn bringing his Crasii to Herino was a show of force in more ways than one. Not to mention an encouraging sign. He had listened to Declan's advice and acted on it.

Tides, Declan had said to himself as he watched the felines falling into line on the palace lawns less than a week after he'd suggested they be brought to Herino, *I'm officially a flanking immortal's minion.*

It had taken an effort to ensure the task of settling them in would fall to him, so when they arrived just on sunset, Declan made a point of being there to make certain everything went smoothly and they didn't get into any fights with the felines of the royal guard. The feline quarters were clean and comfortable enough, but they were still lockable cells when all was said and done, and for these felines, used to Stellan Desean's liberal village setting, likely to be something of a contentious issue.

They were very well behaved, however, and once he'd addressed them on the lawns (quite deliberately in full view of the guest apartments on the second floor), given them their instructions and dismissed them, he pointed to a good-looking Crasii in the front rank. She was a sleek, ginger feline, whose fur was so fine it looked like tanned human skin from a distance.

He beckoned her forward. "You there! Ginger! Come here!"

The Crasii did as she was bid, standing to attention in front of him. "My lord?"

"Once you're settled, have someone show you to my office. You'll be spending the night with me."

The feline glared at him silently, the impatient twitch of her tail the only indication of her displeasure, and then picked up her bedroll and headed off toward the barracks.

"I didn't know you had a taste for feline flesh, Master Hawkes."

Declan stiffened in alarm and turned to find Diala—or Queen Kylia as he forced himself to think of her—standing on the terrace behind him. She wore a languid smile; the look on her face all too knowing for one supposedly so young and innocent. She was behaving less and less like the credulous seventeen-year-old she was posing as, he'd noticed, now her in-laws were dead.

Poor Mathu was too overwhelmed by his sudden kingship to notice.

"I'm sorry. I didn't realise you were standing there, your majesty."

"Don't apologise, Master Hawkes. How you entertain yourself when you're off duty is no concern of mine. She's a looker, though, that one. Almost human, from a distance. If you don't pay any attention to the tail." The immortal impostor smiled nastily and added, "Does the perfectly proper Arkady know her favourite friend from her desperately humble childhood likes to play with kittens?"

"It's not something I brag about, your majesty," he said, lowering his eyes.

Diala smiled even wider. "I'll bet it isn't." She pulled her shawl a little tighter and held out her hand for him to kiss. "Well, just be careful, Master Hawkes. Lord Aranville speaks highly of you, but you'll not be much use to anybody if you get yourself shredded playing with the pussies, now, will you?"

With a courtly bow, Declan kissed her proffered hand, and waited until the queen had left the terrace, and then he smiled, as it occurred to him being caught out by Diala like that was probably the most fortuitous thing that had happened to him all day.

Several hours later, just as he was finishing writing up his final orders for the gifts to be assembled for their Caelish visitors, and how to acquire them, there was a timid knock on his door. Undoubtedly, the feline he'd arranged to visit him had arrived. He glanced around. Everything was ready. The drapes were drawn, there was a pallet made up in the corner, a wineskin and some cold meat and bread on a platter on the desk.

Declan sealed the orders with the spymaster's seal and slipped the folded papers into his vest, so he could deliver them later and then rose to his feet and crossed the room to the door. He unlocked it, glanced up the hall, and then stood back to let the feline through.

She stepped into the office, waiting until he had locked the door behind him, before she turned to look at him. As soon as he was facing her, the Crasii reached up, claws bared, and swiped him across the cheek.

"Tides!" he cried, clutching his bleeding face. "What was *that* for?"

"You want to make this look believable, don't you?"

"You could have warned me!"

"You'd have flinched," she said with a shrug, glancing around. "Is this really your office?"

Collapsing against the door, Declan nodded, in too much pain to answer. *Tides, but a feline scratch stings.*

"Thought it would be bigger."

"Sorry . . . to disappoint . . . you."

The feline began to walk around, examining things as she went. "Aleki says to say hello, by the way."

Through eyes watering with pain, Declan reached for his kerchief to dab at his bleeding face, and pushed off the door. "Right after he told you to permanently maim me, was it?"

She looked over her shoulder at him, demonstrating not a shred of remorse or sympathy. "Don't be such a baby, Declan. It's only a scratch."

"A *scratch*? You've probably scarred me for life, Chikita! *Tides*, but this smarts!"

"It'll stop hurting after a while. Is this food for me?"

He nodded, flopping into the chair opposite his desk. "We were all out of freshly killed snow bears."

She grinned and began helping herself to the sliced meat on the plate. "You heard about that, did you?"

"Everyone in Glaeba knows of the Lebec feline who took down a Jelidian snow bear. How *did* you manage that, by the way?"

"Rat poison."

"*Rat* poison?" Declan said, shaking his head in disbelief. "The story

I heard was that you took him down with a single swipe to his jugular."
Wincing, he pushed the kerchief harder onto his cheek, hoping pressure would stop the bleeding. "Poor bastard. I know exactly how he
felt, too."

"Well, I did do that," she agreed, through a mouthful of meat. "But
rat poison stops blood from clotting and I'd dipped my claws in rat
poison first, you see, so . . ."

"So when you opened him up there was no chance he'd stop bleeding," Declan concluded. "Bit risky, though. And unnecessary, too. I told
Aleki we could have just sold you at auction and arranged to have someone from Lebec in attendance."

She shook her head. "I'd never have come to the attention of the
suzerain, that way. This was more effective."

"And how are you getting along as a slave?"

It was more than an idle question. Chikita was a very special Crasii.
Born unfettered by slavery in Hidden Valley to Scard parents, like her
sister Marianne, she was one of the few felines the Cabal was reason-
ably sure they could rely on to be completely free of any compulsion
to obey the Tide Lords. It had been a risk—not to mention a long and
carefully planned operation—to infiltrate the feline ranks of the Lebec
forces. They'd set the wheels in motion not long after Jaxyn Aranville
had appeared in Lebec as the new Kennel Master and Tilly began to
wonder about him.

Nobody had anticipated events would move so swiftly, though, once
the Tide began to turn.

"It's hard sometimes," she admitted. "But I'm learning to keep my
opinion to myself. I want to puke every time I smell a suzerain, though."

"Try to get a grip on that, kitten. There's four of them here at the
moment and I've suggested Jaxyn appoint you his personal bodyguard."

"Won't he think it suspicious if you single me out?"

"Not as suspicious as he might have," Declan told her. "I had a run-
in with the queen, not long after I spoke to you, which may end up
working in our favour."

"How so?"

"After I spoke with Diala, I went straight to Jaxyn and spoke to him
about you. I think he'll accept my recommendation about you being
his bodyguard. You are, after all, the feline that took down a Jelidian
snow bear."

"Kinda silly, though, don't you think? Tide Lords having body-guards? I mean, it's not as if you can kill them."

"You'll be there to run interference, Chikita. To stand between him and whoever's threatening him."

"So I can be cut down while he runs away?"

"Pretty much."

"And you're hoping Diala will assume you're asking favours for your pet?"

"If we're lucky."

"Maybe I'd better give you a few more of those," she suggested, pointing to his cheek with a suggestive leer that only a feline was capable of. "Just to make it look good." She moved closer, dropped to her knees in front of his chair and bared a single, viciously sharp claw on her index finger. Her voice dropped to a low purr as she gently ran the claw down his chest. "Take off your shirt, Declan, and I'll *really* give you something to remember me by."

He smiled and pushed her away. "I think not, kitten. You've had all the raw bleeding flesh you're going to get from me for one evening."

Chikita shrugged and glanced across at the pallet. "Is that bed for me?"

He nodded. "I need you to stay here until morning."

"Why?"

"You're my alibi."

She grinned even wider. "You're off to do something naughty, aren't you?"

"Very naughty," he agreed. "And in the morning, I'll need you to swear I was here all night with you."

"All night?" she asked with a quizzical look. "Are you *sure* you don't want me to open a few scratches on your back for you, Declan? Just to make it look plausible? I mean . . . all night with a wild little thing like me . . ."

"I'll tell them I tied you up," he said, rising to his feet.

"Do humans do that sort of thing?" she asked.

"Do they have *sex*?" he asked with wide-eyed surprise. "Tides, Chikita, I thought you were a woman of the world?"

She grinned at him, revealing her dangerously sharp little teeth. "Do they tie their mates up for it, I meant, you fool."

"You'd be surprised at some of the things humans do, Chikita." He tossed the bloody kerchief aside. His face was still stinging, but his eyes were no longer watering, and the bleeding appeared to have stopped. "Keep the lamp burning for an hour or two, and then put it out. With luck, I'll be back by dawn."

"What if you *don't* come back?"

"Then tell the truth. Tell them I ordered you to stay the night here to provide me with an alibi."

"Won't that blow your cover?"

"If I *don't* come back, Chikita, that will be the least of my problems. And your only concern will be protecting *your* cover."

The feline nodded in agreement and picked up his coat for him, where he'd tossed it over the back of a chair. "They're all going to hate me in the barracks, after this," she said, holding it out for him. "Among felines, sleeping with a human is the worst kind of perversion."

"It's not exactly the most respectable pastime among humans, either, kitten. Anyway, you despise all Crasii who aren't Scards," he reminded her, shrugging the leather coat on. "What do you care what the felines back in the barracks think?"

"I don't, I suppose. What about you, though? Aren't you worried about what other humans will think of you?"

"I wouldn't be the King's Spymaster if I cared about what people thought of me, Chikita."

She nodded and looked around the office one more time. "I'll be fine, here. You go do your naughty thing, and then come back and we can have breakfast together before I go back to the barracks where I'll be branded a shameless human-loving whore, and you a bestial pervert."

"You have such a happy way of looking at things, Chikita. Make sure you lock the door behind me."

She nodded and walked to the door with him. "Is there any point in telling you to be careful?" she asked, as he unlocked it and eased it open to check if the hall was clear.

"Not a lot."

"Then have fun."

He leaned forward and kissed the top of her sleek, furry head. "Don't touch anything. And lock the door behind me."

He didn't wait for her to answer. The hall was clear and he was on a tight timetable. As Declan slipped out of the office and down the hall, he heard the lock turning, and then he forgot all about Chikita.

Declan had other things on his mind, not the least of which was busting the former Duke of Lebec out of gaol.

Chapter 62

The abbot provided an escort for Arkady, to take her back to Cayal and Tiji, for which she was grateful. She was fairly sure both the immortal and the Crasii waiting for her across the sand on the other side of the rocky valley would be furious to learn this journey and its appallingly high cost in lives had all been in vain. At least Tiji would bemoan the loss of life.

Cayal would just be annoyed at Brynden for not being where he wanted him to be.

A third party present when she arrived would force them to contain their anger and perhaps, by the time she had to answer their questions, they'd have calmed down a bit.

Brynden's absence from the abbey still didn't make sense to Arkady, swaying to-and-fro as Terailia pushed herself to her feet in the cobbled abbey yard. The brother who was to escort her back to her servants—which is what the abbot believed Cayal and Tiji to be—was a young man with hair so closely cut, it was impossible to tell what colour it might be. He was rangy and tall, his bare arms well defined, and surprisingly pale for one who lived in the desert. Still, she supposed, when one was so fair, it would pay to stay out of the sun. This poor fellow would probably burn to a crisp if he spent more than an hour in the harsh desert sunlight, something he clearly understood, because he took the time to wrap a cameleer's burnous around his shoulders, pulling the hood up to shade his face, before taking Terailia's lead rope and heading for the abbey gate. There were few to see her off. The acolytes had chores to do and exercises to master.

The Way of the Tide left no room for idle sightseeing.

The whole trip into the desert, and the purposeless nature of it, and the lives it had cost, concerned Arkady greatly. Why would Kinta send her all this way for nothing? What was the meaning of those messages?

Who had they come from if not from Brynden?

"Am I not keeping you from your prayers, brother?" Arkady asked, as they headed down the sloped roadway that led out onto the sand.

The brother glanced over his shoulder, shaking his head. "I have chosen a different path this morning, my lady. The Way of the Tide is not always a straight line."

Arkady really wasn't sure how to answer that.

"Have you been here at the abbey long?"

"Long enough."

"For what?" she asked, finding herself filled with the sudden urge to interrogate every monk in the abbey, in the hope of finding out why she'd been sent on this merry chase by Kinta.

"Long enough to seek the meaning of the Tide."

"Does it *have* a meaning?"

"That's what we who follow its path are trying to discern."

Terailia's gait changed subtly as she stepped off the stone ramp leading to the abbey's entrance and onto the sand. With the monk leading her mount, Arkady had little to do but sit back and enjoy the ride. Although she hadn't told him specifically in which direction her people were waiting, he seemed to be heading the right way, so she didn't bother to correct him.

"And what of the immortals?"

"What of them, my lady?"

"What is their purpose?"

"That is for each of them to decide."

"Doesn't your Lord Brynden believe the Tide Lords were created to help humanity?"

"Why would they only wish to help humanity?" he asked. "Are you implying human life is the only life on Amyrantha worth helping?"

"No, of course not. I just was wondering if *you* felt that way."

"The Tide Lords have the power to make or break this world, my lady. It is incumbent upon them to care for the *whole* planet, not just those parts of it they individually care for."

"But it was Brynden who caused the last Cataclysm, wasn't it? In a fit of jealous rage?" She was surprised to find him so willing to argue with her. Perhaps this was why he was trusted with the task of escorting a lone female into the desert. He clearly had a firm grip on his beliefs and wasn't going to easily be tempted off the path of righteousness. "How do his actions fit with your pursuit of the Way of the Tide?"

"Lord Brynden's stumble along the Way of the Tide merely serves to demonstrate that even the greatest among us can fall from grace, my lady. His actions remind us that vast power is not without risk, and if Lord Brynden can falter, how much more easily must the rest of us fall? His actions give us hope. Hope that we strive as he does. Hope that if he can regain inner peace after such a setback, then we should strive to do no less."

Arkady studied the figure leading her camel, wondering if he was an intelligent man making his own observations or just a golem, indoctrinated by hour upon hour of repetitive prayers into believing the teachings of his abbey. Although she couldn't see his face, and therefore judge his words by anything other than the sincerity with which they were delivered, he seemed too alert, too responsive and far too sure of himself to be the latter.

"And what of Kinta? Does the behaviour of your lord's consort not concern you?"

"Women are frail creatures by nature, my lady," he informed her, as if the matter was common knowledge. "Both physically and morally. The fault for her misdemeanours lies with the Immortal Prince, not with her."

Kinta? she thought, glad the monk was watching the sand ahead and couldn't see her smile. *Weak? Morally frail? I don't think so.*

"So followers of the Way of the Tide blame Cayal then, for Kinta running away with him?"

"She was seduced by an immortal whose speciality is seduction, my lady. Just as Lord Brynden showed us his humanity by falling victim to his rage, so the Lady Kinta shows us that all women, no matter how low, no matter how high, will always be subject to the basic instability of their natures. She serves as a reminder to all men, that women cannot be trusted."

Arkady wanted to throw something at him. "*No* woman can be trusted?"

"Not with the important things," the monk confirmed. "They are equipped to give birth and pleasure. Unfortunately, they do not always separate the two. It is the duty of all responsible men to ensure their women are kept safe from their own feeble judgement."

"Which is why you make all women in Torlenia dress up in bedsheets, I suppose."

"A meaningful relationship is not based on physical attraction, my lady, but on mutual respect and trust."

"Respect and *trust*?" she said in disbelief. "How does *that* work when you think all women are of feeble mind and questionable moral character? Or is it only men who deserve respect and trust in this crazy theology of yours?"

He glanced over his shoulder at her. "You are getting excited, my lady. Clearly, these are new concepts to you."

"Actually, they're very old and tired concepts, brother. Concepts I'm fairly sick of hearing about."

"All the more reason for you to consider them," he said.

"I refuse to believe that I am somehow morally inferior, just because I'm a woman."

"And I apologise if I have misjudged you, my lady. Tell me, have you ever done anything you consider morally questionable?"

"Everybody's done *something* morally questionable," she said. "Even your precious Lord of Reckoning."

"True enough, but we are talking about you, my lady. Think back over the past year. Have you lied? Have you betrayed your husband, either in thought or deed? Have you consciously decided to take an action you know to be wrong, justifying it to yourself because you think only you—better than anybody else—knows the issues at stake?"

"Tides, what *are* you?" she cut in. "Did the abbot set you on to me as some sort of punishment for defiling your wretched abbey with my morally inferior presence?"

They were more than halfway across the bay of sand enclosed by the crescent-shaped rocky outcrop that encompassed both the abbey and the place where Cayal and Tiji were waiting for her. The monk's steady ground-eating pace was surprisingly efficient.

"You did not defile our abbey, my lady. Not by your presence. In fact, your sin is not a sin at all. If anything, you have answered my lord's prayers."

Arkady was left to puzzle that answer out for the better part of the next hour. The monk fell thankfully silent and Arkady was quite happy to let him stay that way, fearful any attempt at conversation might get him started on the failings of women again.

The reason for his attitude, when it did come, however, seemed so blindingly obvious, and so terrifying, she wondered at her own stupidity.

They had reached the other side of the outcrop and were less than a hundred paces from the rocky ledge where Cayal and Tiji waited when the monk stopped and pushed back his hood, uncaring of the sun beating down on him. Barely had Arkady time to register that strange fact, than she spied Cayal clambering down the rock face.

He hit the ground running, coming to a stop when he was within shouting distance.

"Let her go!" he called, still moving toward them, although now he'd slowed to a cautious walk. He was too far away to read his expression, but he didn't sound thrilled to see her arrive with a member of Brynden's order as her escort.

"Why?" the monk called back. "Does she mean something to you?"

Arkady stared at Cayal and then at the monk for a moment, and then cursed softly under her breath. *Tides, he was right. I am mentally feeble not to have seen this coming.*

"She's Kinta's plaything, not mine," Cayal said, confirming Arkady's stomach-churning suspicion as he got close enough to stop yelling. "But by all means, piss your girl off again, Bryn, by harming her little messenger. Then she'll take even less convincing the next time to leave you."

The monk—who clearly wasn't a monk—was silent for a moment and then he turned to Arkady. "You know who he is, don't you?"

Arkady nodded, seeing no point in denying it.

"And you've met Chintara? You know who she is, too?"

Again she nodded, wondering if Cayal would come to her rescue if Brynden tried to harm her.

But he wasn't, it seemed, in the slightest bit interested in her. "Get down. Tend to your animal and your Crasii, who I imagine is hiding over there in those rocks somewhere. Cayal and I have things to discuss."

———

For the next three hours, from the rocky ledge overlooking the desert, Arkady watched the meeting going on between the two Tide Lords with nervous anticipation. It was a frustratingly uneventful affair. There were no storms whipped up by their rage, no hurling lightning bolts or meteorites at each other in an attempt to settle old scores. The two of them sat cross-legged on the sand, uncaring of the heat, like two old friends, discussing the Tide alone knew what.

"What do you suppose they're talking about?" Tiji asked as she sat herself down beside Arkady with the waterskin, giving voice to the very question Arkady had been asking herself. The chameleon had been on the other side of the ledge for some time now, watching another caravan approach the abbey, this one from the north, which probably meant it had made the much shorter journey from Elvere.

Arkady accepted the waterskin and took a long swallow before she answered. "I wish I knew."

Tiji smiled. "Well, on the bright side, we haven't had a Cataclysm. Yet."

"Always something to be grateful for."

The Crasii was silent for a moment, and then she asked, "Didn't you have *any* idea it was Brynden who was leading your camel?"

Arkady shook her head. "I'm not like you, Tiji. I can't smell them. I can't sense them. Tides! I can't tell a Tide Lord from a turtle, truth be told. And yet I always imagine I'll know one when I meet them. The Tide knows why. I never suspected Jaxyn of being anything more than an ambitious opportunist. If I'd met Maralyce under any other circumstances, I'd have considered her completely unremarkable. I only learned about Diala because Declan sent you to tell me about her, and I lived in the same house as her for months. If you hadn't arrived, I'd never have learned the truth about Kinta, either. And I thought Cayal was nothing but a convicted murderer."

"That's because he *is* a convicted murderer," Tiji pointed out sourly.

"My point, Tiji," Arkady continued, ignoring the interruption, "is there's nothing about them that gives them away. At least not to humans. And not while the Tide is still on the turn. Maybe, once the Tide comes back all the way, the immortals will be considerate enough to glow in the dark or something, which might give those of us who lack your instincts the ability to sense them, but I'm not hopeful."

The little Crasii shook her head, not able to comprehend Arkady's lack of sensibility when it came to the Tide Lords. "I really don't understand how you can't tell them from a mortal human, my lady. But it does explain why they're so successful at hiding while the Tide is out."

"And why it will be such a chore to root them all out before the Tide returns," she agreed. Then she pointed to the two immortals, who were rising to their feet. "Looks like the talking's done."

"Is this where they start chucking mountains at each other?" Tiji asked, climbing to her feet.

"Tides, I hope not."

Down on the sand, Cayal waved to them, signalling they should come down from the ridge. With more than a little trepidation, the two of them did as he bid, climbing carefully down the rocky slope, before walking across the burning sand to where the Tide Lords waited.

"We've come to an agreement," Cayal announced as they approached.

"How terribly civilised of you both," Arkady replied, looking at the two of them warily. For immortals whose last encounter had all but destroyed civilisation, they were showing remarkable restraint.

"Cayal has explained to me his desire to end his life," Brynden said. "I have agreed to aid him."

"Just like that?"

The faintest hint of a smile flickered over the immortal's face. "It is a situation from which we will both benefit."

"So you've just decided to help him, have you?" she said to Brynden, deeply suspicious. Then she turned to Cayal. "And you trust this remarkable act of altruism?"

"There are conditions."

She rolled her eyes. "*There's* a shock."

"You will stay here, my lady," Brynden said, Cayal nodding in agreement. "Your presence will assure Cayal's swift return. Of course, the Crasii must leave with him and not come back. My cooperation does not extend to harbouring abominations."

Tiji opened her mouth to object, but Arkady silenced her with a look. Now was not the time to argue about the Crasii with a Tide Lord.

"And where is Cayal going, exactly?"

"To fetch Lukys," Cayal said. "He's the only one who can tell us exactly what needs to be done. I'll bring him back here and then you'll be free to go."

"Does that mean I'm a prisoner?"

"Not at all," Brynden said. "I will honour Kinta's request that I offer you sanctuary, in a way that ensures Cayal's . . . cooperation."

"I don't remember volunteering to be a bargaining chip."

Cayal looked at her askance. "Did you have someplace *better* to be?"

He had a point. Other than staying here at the abbey, Arkady's choices were to return to Ramahn, where Jaxyn's warrant was waiting for her, along with a squad of felines to escort her home, to be tried and executed—if she was lucky. Or she could head for Elvere, maybe even Acern, and take her chances on her own, with only a passing acquaintance with the language and no money or resources to speak of. "I suppose not."

"Never fear, my lady," Brynden assured her. "I have given Cayal my word you will be alive when he returns."

Alive, he said, not alive and *well*. Arkady wondered if she should demand clarification on that small but significant point.

"I won't be long," Cayal promised. "A couple of weeks at most. Lukys's place isn't that far from here."

"What about Tiji?"

"I'll see she gets to Elvere in one piece," Cayal promised. "After that, she's on her own." When Arkady opened her mouth to object, he added, "She has diplomatic papers that will see her safely home, Arkady. In fact, she's better off than you. And she speaks Torlenian far more fluently than you ever will."

Sadly, he spoke the truth, and although the Crasii clearly wasn't happy about it, Tiji knew it as well as Arkady.

"Tell Declan what's happened," she ordered, certain Tiji would understand Arkady didn't just mean she was to tell Declan where she was hiding. "Tell him everything. He'll fret otherwise."

Tiji nodded in understanding. "Don't worry, my lady. I'll make sure he knows."

That was all she could do for now, Arkady decided. Play along with this, wait for Cayal to return, and then see where the fates took her after that. Cayal might surprise everyone by doing as he promised. Just in case he didn't, she impulsively hugged the Crasii. "Thank you, Tiji. For everything."

Tiji didn't answer. But she hugged Arkady back and then stood glaring at Brynden, as Cayal went to fetch Terailia, so Arkady could return to the abbey, a virtual prisoner of the Lord of Reckoning.

When he returned, he led the camel forward and handed the rope to Brynden.

"Wait!" Arkady called, as Brynden took her arm. "When I get to El-vere, how will I find you, Tiji?"

The Crasii looked at the two Tide Lords for a moment, as if debating the wisdom of sharing such information with them and then turned to Arkady when she realised she had little choice. "There's an inn near the slave markets called The Dog and Bone, my lady. Free Crasii are allowed to stay there. I'll wait for you."

Arkady nodded and smiled with a confidence she certainly didn't feel. "I'll see you in a few weeks then."

Tiji nodded, clearly sceptical of Arkady's optimism, but she said nothing, just stood beside Cayal—who was acting as if Arkady didn't exist—watching Arkady being led away.

Chapter 63

With four immortals roaming Herino at will, Declan was forced to operate on the assumption that any and/or all of the Crasii normally on the payroll of either the Cabal or the King's Spymaster had been compromised.

Or they would be, the moment they came into contact with a Tide Lord.

He was further hampered by the fact that he couldn't do anything officially as the King's Spymaster to have Stellan Desean released, nor call on the considerable resources of the Cabal. Freeing Arkady's husband was a favour to Tilly, and something he would not have bothered with, had she not specifically requested his help.

That left Declan only one place to go for assistance.

Although the thieves and extortionists of Herino were hardly an organised force, little or no crime took place in the city without the permission of a shadowy, almost mythical figure known as the Patriarch. Whispered about in hushed, fearful tones, even among the honest citizens of Herino, he was a man who protected his identity better than most lords protected their wives' honour.

Making contact with him was no mean feat, so two days earlier, Declan had ordered a raid on an illegal gaming house not far from the Friendly Futtock, where he and Stellan Desean had rescued Prince Mathu from his own folly almost a year ago. The gaming house, which he'd known about for years, was run by Dodgy Peet, a portly, jovial man with a fulsome black moustache.

Dodgy Peet was now cooling his heels in Herino Prison in a cell one floor below Stellan Desean, awaiting his trial and a lengthy sentence for a long list of misdemeanours that up until now had never seemed to warrant the trouble of arresting him. Dodgy Peet's problem—and the problem for all criminally inclined individuals in Glaeba—was that Glaeban justice was consequential, which meant the worse the perceived consequences of a crime, the stiffer the penalty for the perpetrator.

As Dodgy had been cheating some very reputable people for quite a number of years, there was no shortage of willing witnesses prepared to testify to all manner of dire consequences his house of ill-fortune had visited upon them. The list of minor charges was likely to add up to a considerable amount of time behind bars, once Dodgy's dissatisfied customers got through with him.

Taking a gamble of his own, Declan put the word out that he wished to meet with the Patriarch, to discuss Dodgy Peet's fate.

Dodgy Peet, by no small coincidence, was the Patriarch's nephew.

The Patriarch, who remained hidden in the shadows when Declan was brought before him, even after the blindfold had been removed, had taken surprisingly little persuasion when Declan told him what he wanted. Declan had even told him the truth—up to a point—about why he wanted to free Stellan Desean. It was a favour for a friend, he'd explained, and he couldn't act officially, nor be seen to be involved.

Because he was known to a great many people in Herino and Lebec as someone who'd grown up on the fringes of society, Declan was one of those rare creatures able to straddle both the legitimate and illegitimate sides of the law with ease. He got away with it, generally, because he didn't bother harassing those whom both he and the Patriarch thought of as "honest criminals."

Declan concentrated on the real threats: threats to Glaeba's sovereignty and the occasional murderer or rapist. He didn't order random sweeps of the slums to clean them up, or try to impress the nobility with his arrest record. He left enterprising businessmen free to do their business, and it hadn't escaped the Patriarch's notice.

His forbearance had bought a meeting with the Patriarch without being beaten to a pulp first.

Under the Patriarch's sharp and probing interrogation, Declan quite openly admitted Dodgy had been arrested to get the old man's attention. He also explained that Stellan Desean would never be free if anybody thought he lived. Therefore, he had to die.

A fire at the prison which left unidentifiable remains would do the trick. Dodgy Peet would be free (Declan had arranged a pardon in advance, forging the king's signature on the document with no qualms whatsoever), and everyone would believe the former duke was no more.

The Patriarch had seemed rather taken with the idea. Not only would burning down Herino Prison free his nephew, but a great many other members of his fraternity, too, not to mention slowing down the whole process of incarcerating his colleagues in the first place.

A deal had been struck, oaths exchanged, and the details agreed upon days ago.

The Patriarch's men would start a controlled fire, they decided, the only effective way to terrify a well-trained feline into abandoning her post. With the majority of the prison guards in Herino coming from the king's own stables, they had little chance of scaring them off any other way, and no hope of surviving if they tried taking them on directly. While Declan was freeing Desean, the Patriarch's men would create a diversion by freeing as many other prisoners as possible.

It was Declan's job to get Desean out and away from the prison. He had plans—which he'd not shared with the Patriarch—to send him to Tilly's house first, and from there arrange to send him to Hidden Valley, once the fuss died down.

With Chikita taking care of his alibi, Declan hurried to the prison to find they'd started without him.

Two streets away Declan realised there was trouble. He could smell the smoke and a crowd had already begun to gather in the streets surrounding the prison. He bullied his way through the throng, only to discover the building well alight by the time he got there.

Declan had been hoping for a bit of confusion to cover his tracks. He was greeted with total chaos. The felines who'd been guarding the gaol were panicked, irrationally afraid of the flames hungrily devouring the wooden structures within the stone prison walls. There was nothing even remotely like an organised evacuation going on, nor had anybody thought to organise a bucket line.

He grabbed the arm of a feline he recognised, wearing a warder's tabard, and a belt on which she carried a truncheon and a large ring of keys. He turned her to face him. The tabby's fur was singed, her eyes wide with fear, her tail standing almost straight up.

"What happened?"

"Some . . . some of the prisoners started to riot," she said. He could feel her trembling beneath his hand. She was barely holding on. "They set . . . set . . . fire to the place."

That wasn't the plan Declan had agreed to, but now was not the time to quibble about it. "Have the prisoners been freed?"

She shook her head. "Lockdown . . ."

"*What*?" Declan demanded, afraid he'd misheard her.

"When they started to riot . . . we locked everyone in their cells . . ."

Declan swore viciously and let her go. "Give me your keys."

"But . . ."

"Give me your keys, Sharisha, or go back there and open the cells yourself."

The feline's fear of fire clearly outweighed her fear of retribution for letting the prisoners escape. She unhooked the ring of keys from her belt; her hands trembling so hard the keys rattled.

She handed them to Declan. "Our orders . . . we're not supposed to let them escape, Master Hawkes," she reminded him.

"That doesn't include letting men burn to death," he replied, snatching the keys from her paw. "Now, instead of just standing about here doing nothing, get a bucket line organised. If this fire spreads, it'll take out half the city."

The feline glanced up. "But it should rain again, soon, and—"

"Do it!" Declan yelled in her face, so close he made her jump, and then he turned and ran toward the flaming prison and the broken gate that some of the Herino residents had already battered their way through, in an attempt to free the men trapped inside.

There was even more panic in the courtyard.

Some of the prisoners had been freed and some of the others Declan recognised as the Patriarch's men. One of them, a rangy, red-headed man Declan knew only as Splinter, ran to him as soon as he saw the spymaster, his face sooty, his breathing short and raspy. Smoke trapped in the central courtyard made it hard to make out what was happening, but there were at least two dead felines Declan could see, men pawing over them to find the keys they carried.

Splinter grinned as he bounded over a burning beam from the gateway. "Some diversion, huh?"

Declan glared at him. "You'll kill every man here and burn half the city at this rate, you flanking fools."

Splinter shrugged. "Just so long as it's the high-born half, what do I care? The Patriarch said you know where they're keeping Dodgy?"

Declan nodded and coughed, squinting through the smoke. He pointed at the north tower, the one closest to the lake. The tower was already well ablaze, the flaming rooftop lighting the night.

Tides, he thought. *We may already be too late.*

"Come with me."

Declan didn't wait to see if Splinter was following him. He sprinted across the courtyard to the north tower, kicked his way through the narrow door. The fire must have spread to the tower from a stray spark setting the wooden shingles alight, he realised. It was burning from the top down. The lower floors, although choked with acrid smoke, were still relatively free of fire.

He pounded up the wooden stairs, taking them two at a time, the sound of Splinter behind him, his wheezy breath unnaturally loud in the narrow stairwell. Above them they could hear shouting, although it was hard to tell how many men remained trapped in here. It might well be only Stellan Desean and Dodgy Peet, if they were lucky. Stellan was incarcerated in the cell on the fourth floor, in the cell reserved for high-born prisoners, and Dodgy Peet was in the cell directly beneath him on the third floor on Declan's express orders.

A quick glance at the cells on the second floor had Declan cursing. There were three men locked in them and a very nervous ginger feline pacing in front of the bars, too panicked by the flames to think rationally, or do anything to save either herself or her charges.

"Get out of here!" Declan yelled.

The prisoners began yelling frantically when they spied him. Cursing, Declan shoved the feline aside and ran to the cells, unlocking each cell as he went.

"Go!" he cried, as he released the men. "Get out!"

He returned to the stairs at a run, following Splinter, who was ahead of him now, up to the next floor. Dodgy Peet was alone in the cells, standing at the bars, a torn piece of his shirt wrapped around his face.

He seemed unsurprised, by either the fire, or that one of his uncle's men had come to rescue him.

"Told you I wouldn't be here long, Hawkes," he said with a smug look, as Declan unlocked his cell.

"Yeah, you're a regular prophet, Dodgy." Declan threw the door open, stepped back to let Dodgy out, and then turned to Splinter. "You right to get him out of here?"

Splinter shrugged and then looked up at the ceiling. Smoke and the occasional lick of flame were already visible through the boards. "We'll be fine. *You'd* better hurry, though, my friend, or you won't have anything left to rescue up there."

Declan nodded, and headed back to the stairs. By now the smoke was so thick in the narrow stairwell, he could barely see. Every breath he took was painful. He thought he could hear Desean calling for help, which was a good thing. It meant he was still alive, at least.

The door to the outer room on the fourth floor was already ablaze when Declan reached it. He kicked it clear of the charred doorframe and stepped into an inferno. The floor above was burning fiercely. Like Dodgy on the floor below, Desean had had the wit to cover his face, and he was crouched on the floor to get below the smoke. The metal bars of his cell were glowing red at the top, where they were in contact with the burning ceiling.

There were no felines left guarding him. Declan wasn't surprised. This fire would have been too much for the staunchest creature.

"*Hawkes*?" Stellan coughed in surprise, when he looked up and realised rescue was at hand.

Declan didn't waste any precious breath replying. With his eyes watering from the smoke, he ran to the cell door, shoving the key in the lock, hoping the heated bars hadn't melted the locking mechanism. The floor above creaked and groaned alarmingly. His throat was burning from the stinging smoke as he turned the key, which was growing warm in his hand already. The lock was stiff, but it worked. He stepped back and kicked the door open, aware that touching that superheated metal would have taken his hands off.

"Come on!"

Desean needed no other encouragement. He crawled on his hands and knees through the cell door and then climbed to his feet, still crouching to keep below the smoke. The ceiling was making loud popping sounds now, the other side of the room and the location of the stairwell totally obscured by the smoke and the flames.

And then a crack sounded and the floor above them gave way.

Declan had the presence of mind to shove Desean back into his cell, as the ceiling caved in.

After that it was as if the world had slowed down to ensure Declan was able to register each minute detail.

He heard another series of cracks splintering the timber overhead. Looking up, the air searing his lungs, he raised his arm to shield himself from the fountain of cascading sparks as the ceiling gave way. He heard Desean yell something but couldn't make out the words; could barely make *him* out through the wall of smoke and flame. The fire had completely devoured the massive central beam supporting the upper floor. It was no longer able to support its own weight, let alone the weight of the structure above. Declan raised his other arm, too—a desperate, useless attempt to ward off the falling beam; knowing it was futile, wondering why it seemed to be taking so long to fall.

He had time, as the blazing beam crashed down, to realise his cover was blown. Too many people had seen him at the prison for his alibi to pass even the most casual scrutiny. *Finding my body here won't do much for the cause, either,* he thought, a little surprised he had the time to find humour in the prospect of his own death.

Still, Chikita's a smart little kitten. No doubt she'll be able to talk her way out of trouble.

The irony of being killed in the process of rescuing Arkady's husband—a task at which he had failed dismally—wasn't lost on him either . . .

When the blow came, it happened too fast for Declan to feel much pain. He registered the crushing weight, heard screams as the flames licked at his clothes, not sure if he was the one doing the screaming . . .

He couldn't breathe, could barely think. Acrid smoke filled his airways, blistering his lungs as surely as the roaring flames were blistering his skin. After what seemed an eternity of intense, scorching agony, the darkness reached for him.

When the end came, it was blissful by comparison. He understood now, why people referred to death as paradise.

Declan's last thought, however, wasn't peaceful. It was filled with regret.

I'm so sorry, Arkady. I've let you down again.

Chapter 64

The abbot seemed unsurprised when Arkady returned to the Abbey of the Way of the Tide later that afternoon with the young man posing as a monk. It was clear to Arkady, as they entered the abbey gates, that the abbot must have known who this man really was. And that the immortal, Brynden, the head of his order, was the one who'd been masterminding everything from behind the scenes, from the moment she first appeared with her letter from Kinta and her foolish declaration that she sought to pass on a message from Cayal.

Two of the younger acolytes had opened the gates as they approached, and left the gates open after they entered the abbey's small courtyard. Her camel turned a nervous circle in the confined yard and she noticed, through the gate, in the far distance, the caravan Tiji had been watching from the ridge making its way across the sand toward the abbey.

The older man dismissed the acolytes with a wave of his hand, leaving the three of them alone. He bowed respectfully to Brynden—who looked a good thirty years younger than the abbot—and then bowed to Arkady as Terailia knelt down to let her dismount.

"Your meeting went as planned, my lord?"

"It did."

"Welcome back, my lady."

The abbot seemed surprised neither by her return, nor the identity of the monk. She glanced at Brynden and then the abbot, shaking her head at her own foolishness. "You knew all along who he was, didn't you?"

The abbot shrugged, holding his hands out in a gesture of helplessness.

Arkady was astonished. "And you *lied?* What about your noble *Way of the Tide*, brother? Is mendacity one of the virtues your philosophy embraces?"

The abbot didn't seem insulted by the accusation. If anything, he seemed quite pleased with himself. "I follow the wishes of my lord."

"Even when your lord tells you to lie?"

He shrugged again. "What is the greater sin, my lady? A truth which starts a war or a lie which brings peace?"

"I wasn't aware my presence here was liable to start a war."

"It was a rhetorical question, my lady."

Arkady knew that, she just wasn't in the mood to cooperate. "So you teach rhetoric *and* deceit? You're not training monks here, Lord Brynden, are you? You're training politicians."

"Any person arriving here claiming to bring word from another immortal is to be viewed with deep suspicion," Brynden told her, not appreciating her attempt at wit in the slightest. "You cannot blame us for wanting to check your credentials."

She looked at Brynden curiously. "Why? Surely you're not *afraid*, are you?"

"Of you?" Brynden asked. "Not at all. But you claim acquaintance with both Kinta and Cayal, which makes you immediately suspect. And even if that proves to be nothing more than a rare coincidence, we immortals have enemies, my lady. Even mortal ones. Until the Tide has fully returned, one cannot be too careful."

"I can't imagine what you'd have to fear from mortal men."

The abbot answered for him. "The Cabal of the Tarot, for one, would give a great deal to know the location of every immortal on Amyrantha."

Arkady was glad she was still shrouded and they couldn't read her expression. According to Declan, the immortals believed the Cabal destroyed during the last Cataclysm. *How did they know it had survived?* Or was Brynden just unusually cautious? She forced a laugh, certain they must suspect the truth about her involvement with the Cabal, too. And knowing that if they knew of it for certain, given her association with Cayal, she would be doubly damned. "You mean there's actually an organisation opposed to the immortals? Tides, where do I sign up?"

Brynden didn't see the joke. "They have devoted themselves to destroying the Tide Lords, my lady."

"And you just agreed to help one kill himself," she reminded him.

"I'd say you've just signed on with the opposition, Lord Brynden, wouldn't you?"

Arkady realised her cutting repartee was having quite the opposite effect to the one she intended when Brynden looked at her with utter disdain.

"I'm not going to help Cayal kill himself," he said. "As far as I'm concerned the Immortal Prince can suffer for all eternity, and I'll enjoy watching every tormented moment of it. I've no intention of putting him out of his misery."

"But you said . . ."

"What I had to, to be rid of him for a time. Long enough for me to redress the ill done to me, at any rate."

"Ill?" Arkady asked. "You mean the affair he had with Kinta?"

He nodded. "There will come a time, very soon, my lady, when my consort will be restored to me. We cannot repair those bridges broken by her infidelity while the man who seduced her remains unpunished."

"*Unpunished*? Tides, you caused a Cataclysm, Lord Brynden. The whole *world* was punished for her infidelity, last I heard."

"Cayal barely even noticed the last Cataclysm," Brynden said. "This time, however, I believe he *will* take note."

There was an air about him that spoke of ineffable smugness which worried Arkady a great deal. "What are you going to do to him?"

"I'm not going to do anything to him," Brynden said. "There's no point, my lady. I'll be doing it to you."

"Me? Why *me*?" she asked, panic-stricken by his emotionless declaration. "He won't care what you do to me!"

Arkady didn't know if that was true or not. Cayal's fickle moods meant she could never tell if she was the great love of his eternal life or merely a passing fad that he had recovered from months ago, when they'd parted at Maralyce's mine.

"Cayal has taken an interest in you, my lady. That's enough."

"Are you *insane*?" she asked, desperation making her bold. She did wonder if insulting a Tide Lord was such a brilliant idea, given she was completely at his mercy and he was planning to take his revenge on Cayal through her. She reasoned it wouldn't make much difference.

It seemed Brynden didn't have any mercy left in him.

"There is a caravan on its way from Elvere, even as we speak," the Tide Lord informed her, glancing toward the gate and the dark speck crossing the sand in the distance. "In three days' time, when it leaves to return to the coast, *you* will return with it. When it reaches Elvere, you will be sold at general auction as a slave."

"*No!*"

Brynden continued as if she hadn't spoken. "If Cayal wants to save you, he can buy you back. If he chooses not to, then I have still kept my word. You will be alive, as I promised Cayal you would be, and safe from your husband's enemies—as Kinta requested. They will never think of searching for a Glaeban duchess in the Elvere slave markets."

Slavery? Tides, this can't be happening! "But . . . but . . . you gave Cayal your word . . ."

"That you would be alive when he returned, my lady. I did not prom- ise you would remain here or be kept in the manner to which you are clearly accustomed. Although if you're lucky," he added, his eyes raking her shrouded figure dispassionately, "being a beautiful woman, you will probably be purchased as a concubine, so you may yet get to enjoy the luxury you're so clearly used to."

"You've never seen me unshrouded," she said. "How would you know *what* I look like?"

"Cayal is a shallow and venal creature. He would not have taken the slightest interest in you if you *weren't* beautiful," Brynden replied. "So, for your sake, I hope his tastes haven't changed since I saw him last. You'll not last long as a drudge in slavery, I suspect. Still, you'll not have long to find out your fate. The caravan will be here soon."

Arkady stared at the implacable set of his shoulders and knew there was nothing she could do or say to change this obdurate immortal's mind. For all his noble posturing about the Way of the Tide, Brynden wanted revenge and Cayal had handed it to him on a plate, by using her to deliver his message.

Tides, someone pinch me and wake me from this nightmare.

"Brother Rath will show you to a cell where you may rest and recu- perate until you leave us," Brynden added, as if he was ordering the palace steward to show her to the royal guest apartments. "You will be fed, allowed to bathe, and a change of clothing will be provided. It will be a day or two before the caravan returns to Elvere. You may wish to use that time, my lady, to contemplate the error of your ways."

"The *error* of my ways?" *You arrogant, judgemental little prick. You know nothing about me.*

Brynden's eyes were cold and unrelenting. "Trust me, my lady. There is no possible way you would be allied with the Immortal Prince if you hadn't done something to entice him. That you are married would not deter Cayal. More likely it would beguile him. He prefers his women to be a little more . . . *experienced*. If I'm surprised about anything in this affair, it's that it's your husband's *enemies* hunting you and not your husband himself."

Without giving Arkady an opportunity to answer, the Tide Lord turned on his heel and headed toward the arched entrance to the abbey's main hall, leaving her alone in the sandy courtyard with Brother Rath and Terailia, who was still kneeling on the sandy cobblestones, chewing on her lead rope, as if nothing remarkable had taken place.

Arkady didn't know if it was the heat or the spectre of her fate that was making her feel faint.

"You said Cayal could buy me back," she called after him. "Does that mean you'll tell him where I've been sent?"

Brynden hesitated and then he kept walking, without looking back or saying another word.

So this is Brynden's revenge.

She would be sold into slavery. Brynden would tell Cayal that much, for certain.

But he won't tell Cayal where I am. He'll know I've been sold but he won't know where to find me. That's his punishment.

And what if it wasn't any punishment at all? What if Cayal didn't care? If the part of him that wanted to forget Arkady existed was in ascendancy the day Cayal got the news?

Well, then, for Cayal, it would mean nothing and this punishment wrought on her by a vengeful immortal would be Arkady's burden and she would have no choice but to bear it alone.

Chapter 65

Word about the fate of Stellan Desean and the King's Spymaster reached the palace long after news of the prison fire. Not that they'd needed a messenger for that, either. The fire lit the night sky like a beacon. Tryan and Elyssa were so entranced by the sight, they ordered Warlock to move chairs out onto the balcony so they could watch it burn.

He was serving them their third glass of wine when Diala let herself into the guest apartment and joined her fellow immortals on the balcony. It was rare for her to meet with the others without Jaxyn or indeed, her husband, present. She still paid lip service to protocol, but apparently the unusual sight of the Herino skyline ablaze was enough for her to break with tradition.

"Did you put this show on for us, Diala?" Elyssa asked, as the queen stepped out onto the balcony. She didn't look around as the other immortal approached. She didn't need to. Elyssa would have felt Diala's approach on the Tide.

"Do you like it?" Diala asked.

"Most impressive," Tryan said. "What is it that's burning, exactly?"

"Herino Prison, I believe," she said, and then she turned to Warlock. "Cecil, bring me wine. And something to sit on. There's a good boy."

Warlock bowed and hurried inside to find the queen a chair. As usual, the immortals made no attempt to hide their true identity from him. Their arrogance appalled him. And was probably their one great weakness. Thousands of years of survival with no lasting consequences had made them think they could do anything to anybody, and not be held accountable for it.

Sadly, Warlock realised, they'd come to that conclusion because it was pretty much the truth.

There *were* no consequences for the likes of these immortals.

Making sure none of his anger was evident in either his expression or his bearing, Warlock lifted his tail and brought out the chair, placed it on Tryan's left and then turned to pour wine for the false queen. In the distance, over the lake, lightning streaked the sky, followed by a distant rumble of thunder. Perhaps, if the rain was headed this way, it would take care of the fire and these wretched creatures could find themselves another, less ghoulish, spectator sport.

"Is Herino Prison supposed to be burning?" Elyssa asked, as Warlock handed Diala her drink.

"I don't think so. Mind you, I shan't lose any sleep over it. There's a few people incarcerated in there who would be doing us a very big favour by getting themselves roasted."

"The king's cousin and heir, for instance?" Tryan asked.

Diala glared at him. "Who told you that?"

He laughed at her expression. "Nobody *told* me, Diala. His trial is the talk of Herino."

"Tryan's right, you know," Elyssa said. "You can't go five paces in this place without someone stopping you to ask if you'd heard the latest about his trial."

"There seems to be some doubt about the veracity of the charges," Tryan added. "Apparently the crown witnesses have been less than compelling. And there's a fairly confident rumour getting about too, that the charges have been trumped up to cover an even more . . . embarrassing . . . problem."

"If you're talking about the rumour that Desean takes his pleasure from the wrong side of the blanket," Diala said, not the least bit concerned, "it's true enough. Something *I* figured out about three days after I met him, by the way. So did Jaxyn."

"Well, that explains a lot."

"Why aren't they just putting him on trial for that?" Elyssa asked, holding her glass out for a refill. Warlock hurried to her side with the decanter. "Jaxyn could stand witness himself, I don't doubt."

Diala shrugged. "These Glaebans are all so wretchedly repressed. They carry on like *any* sex is a capital crime. Think about it! These people are so embarrassed about it all that Desean *preferred* to be tried as a murderer than a sodomite. What does that tell you?"

"You should have settled in Caelum," Tryan suggested. "They're much more liberal about those sorts of things across the lake. Tides, my bride is only ten years old. They don't have a problem with that."

"Eleven," Elyssa corrected.

"What?"

"Nyah will have turned eleven by now."

Tryan shrugged. "Whatever."

"If I'd known they were going to be this piteously dull and conservative, I might have considered it," Diala said, frowning. "But you know how it is. One must play the hand one is dealt."

"Our young king not up to the job, then?" Tryan asked.

"He's enthusiastic," Diala conceded with a condescending smile. "But most of what he's learned about pleasure, he's learned in brothels, I fear. Establishments his soon-to-be-condemned cousin was fairly famous for dragging him out of, by the way. His re-education is taking time. Particularly as he's convinced I was a virgin when we married."

"How did you manage to convince him of that?" Elyssa asked with a sceptical laugh. Even Warlock thought that was funny. Fancy anybody mistaking the Minion Maker for a virgin!

"He's nineteen," Diala said with a shrug. "He believes everything I tell him."

Tryan seemed to find it very amusing, too. "You've not told him you're *older* than you look, I'm guessing."

Diala smiled. "He's not quite ready for that."

Warlock didn't hear the rest of it. Someone knocked on the door to the visitors' suite and he hurried to answer it. Somewhat to his amazement, he opened the door to find the young King of Glaeba waiting outside.

"Your majesty," he said, bowing low.

"Is my wife here, Cecil?"

"She is, your majesty," he said, holding the door open for him. "Shall I announce you?"

"Don't be ridiculous."

Mathu pushed past him and walked through the suite to the balcony.

Diala—or rather Kylia—jumped to her feet when she saw her husband. "Mathu! I thought you'd be hours, yet!"

"I've been looking everywhere for you."

"I was just reassuring our Caelish guests about the fire," she said, sliding her arm through his. "They were worried the fire might spread. Or that we might be overrun by thieves and murderers."

"My cousin is dead," he announced.

Warlock thought the young king looked upset by the news. In fact, it was probably why he'd sought out his wife. His parents had been dead little more than a month and now the man he'd considered a brother—right up until he fabricated charges against him, at least—was dead, too.

Diala was smart enough to realise now was not the time to toy with his fragile emotions. She was instantly contrite. "Oh my love, I'm so sorry. I know he betrayed you, but you were fond of him, just the same, weren't you?"

The young king was holding back his emotions by sheer force of will. "They tell me Declan Hawkes is dead too. He died trying to free Stellan."

"Tides, why would he do that?" Tryan asked. He looked at his sister with a frown. "That was really very inconsiderate of him to get himself killed. Who's going to supervise the search for my fiancée now?"

Mathu turned on the man he believed was nothing more than a nobleman with his eye on the Caelish throne. "How dare you, sir! Have you no common decency? People have died down in that fire tonight, and all you can think of is your own troubles?" He turned to Kylia. "Come, my dear. Jaxyn thinks it would be a good idea for us to visit the hall where they're laying out the bodies and treating the injured."

"Of course," she agreed. "I'll join you in a moment, dear."

The young king nodded to his wife, glared at the Caelish visitors for a moment and then left the balcony. Once they heard the door slamming behind him, Diala turned to the other immortals. "Don't worry about your child bride. Hawkes was efficient enough and our intelligence service isn't reliant on just one man. We'll find your little princess for you and send her home when we do." Without waiting for them to answer, she left the balcony to join her husband on his tour of the fire-damaged part of the city.

"Cecil!" she snapped on the way past. "Come."

Warlock followed the queen outside into the corridor. Diala stopped and turned to look up at him. "Lord Jaxyn says you're very loyal, Cecil."

"To serve you and Lord Jaxyn is the reason I breathe, my lady."

"Will that loyalty withstand a test, I wonder?"

"I'm not sure I understand what you mean, my lady."

"If you were commanded by another . . . of our kind . . . whose orders would take precedence?"

Warlock had often wondered the same thing about true Crasii. If they were ordered to do conflicting things by two different Tide Lords, whose orders would be obeyed? The most recent orders? Or the first orders the Crasii received?

For the sake of this discussion, Warlock guessed the answer Diala wanted to hear. "The orders of my first master would be those I felt most compelled to follow, my lady."

She smiled, patting his arm. "There's a good boy, Cecil. I was hoping you would say that. Now go back and take care of our guests. I'll call for you when I need you."

Warlock bowed respectfully. "As you wish, my lady."

She turned to leave, but halted as Warlock was turning to the door. "And Cecil?"

"Yes, my lady?

"You were a gift to me from Lady Ponting. I want you to remember that. You're mine, which means you must follow my orders first, even before Lord Jaxyn. Do you understand?"

"I understand, my lady."

She beamed at him. "Good boy. Off you go then."

This time, Warlock waited until he was sure she wasn't coming back, before returning to the visiting Caelish Tide Lords, wondering why she thought it was so important that he follow her orders first.

And what would happen to the plans of the Cabal of the Tarot now that Declan Hawkes was dead.

Because Boots's time was drawing nearer every day, and unless the Cabal contacted him soon, and provided him with a compelling reason to stay, the first chance he had to escape, now that Hawkes wasn't here to order him to do otherwise, Warlock was heading home.

Chapter 66

The trip from the Abbey of the Way of the Tide to Elvere was short, only three days compared to the fifteen-day trek the same trip had taken from Ramahn. Arkady spent most of it in a state of frantic despair, and trying to find a way to escape her fate. She debated fleeing the caravan, but knew she'd not survive in the desert long without food or water, even this close to a city. She made plans to flee as soon as they reached the outskirts of Elvere. To find the inn Tiji spoke of. If she unexpectedly jumped off Terailia (didn't break an ankle as she landed) and fled into the slums, before they had time to find her, then maybe they wouldn't pursue her . . .

Arkady's planning usually stopped at that point. She had no idea where The Dog and Bone was, or the slave markets it was near, either. And she knew, better than anyone, how hard it was for a stranger to find sanctuary in the slums of a foreign city. She'd grown up in the Lebec slums and knew how they treated outsiders there. Her poor grasp of Torlenian, her lack of money, her lack of anything but her own body to offer in trade meant hiding in the slums would, more than likely, produce the same result as being sold into slavery. The only difference was, in slavery she would be fed regularly and quite possibly treated well if she was lucky enough to be purchased by a slaver with even a shred of humanity in him.

Brynden's prediction she would be sold as a concubine was probably correct. Arkady knew, without vanity, that she was healthy, considered beautiful, and in the Elvere slave markets, would be thought of as exotically foreign. The only thing likely to go against her was her age.

She was twenty-eight. If the slavers of Torlenia liked their meat young and tender, she may well be sold as a drudge, doomed to a life of hard labour on a date farm or olive plantation, or worse. Sold off before Tiji could find her and be sent . . . where?

Somewhere Jaxyn would never find her.

For a time, the idea almost seemed attractive. To disappear; to put her entire life behind her. To start afresh as someone else, someone with no ambition, no expectations, no desire to do anything but get through the day, and survive the night, only to repeat the whole process again on the morrow . . .

Somewhere Declan could never find her, either.

Arkady caught herself daydreaming like that once too often. She recognised the symptoms of despair and forced herself not to give in to them. She was alive, in one piece, and while ever she drew breath, she could fight. If she was sold as a concubine, so be it. It might not even be that bad. Many Torlenian men filled their seraglium with beautiful slaves just to impress their neighbours. Some were so large it wasn't physically possible to sleep with every woman they owned and get any other work done. Then there were the other women in a seraglium to contend with, too. If she was bought by a man who already had several wives, the chances were good the current favourites would bend over backward to ensure Arkady never got the opportunity to take their place. Perhaps she'd never be allowed near the master of the house. On the other hand, she'd heard of women scarred with acid by their rivals in a seraglium for that very reason, but dismissed the rumours as nonsense.

No, if she was to be sold, unless she was bought by someone who took a particular fancy to her, the chances were good that after as little as one night in a stranger's bed, she would be left alone.

Arkady could survive one night in a stranger's bed. If she had to, she could survive much longer than that. She'd survived six years of Fillion Rybank, after all.

And maybe, if she was extraordinarily lucky, she would be purchased by a man with enough wealth and power—and perhaps the will—to help her. There was a chance, however slender, that she would be bought by someone prepared to offer the former Duchess of Lebec sanctuary, and maybe even freedom.

The latter was a pipedream, Arkady knew that, but as Elvere resolved out of the heat mirage on the horizon late on the third day after the caravan had left the abbey, it was all she had to cling to.

Arkady was delivered to the city slave markets almost as soon as they reached Elvere. Her grandiose plans to flee the moment they reached the edge of town proved worthless. There were no slums. The vast slave markets took up most of the city outskirts. If there were slum-dwellers anywhere in Elvere, they were nowhere Arkady Desean was likely to see.

As for the location of The Dog and Bone, it might as well be back in the desert at the abbey for all the chance Arkady had of finding it.

She was delivered to a slaver who was wealthy enough to have his own compound on the western edge of the city. The cameleers, acting under strict instructions from Brynden, had taken little interest in her on the journey from the abbey, and seemed well rid of her when they finally handed her over to the slavers, taking Terailia with them when they left as payment for their services.

Still shrouded, trembling with anticipation and more than a little afraid of what the future might hold, Arkady was taken through a series of passageways, every one of which had bars along the sides and barred gates at each end. She was escorted by a large, intimidating bare-chested man with a Torlenian slave brand—the image of two joined links of a chain burned into his flesh—just below his breastbone. The man said nothing, just grunted at her, pointing in the direction he wanted her to go, every time they came to an intersection in the labyrinthine corridors of the slaver's compound.

Finally, they reached a chamber with a wooden door, rather than a barred gate. Her escort knocked twice, opened the door without waiting for an answer, pushed her through, and then closed it behind her.

Arkady stumbled forward and then looked around. The candle-lit room was quite well furnished, with imported carpets and a polished rosewood desk against the far wall that looked suspiciously Glaeban in its design and craftsmanship.

There was a thin, well-dressed man sitting at the desk, writing in a ledger. He glanced up when he heard the door close. His face was pinched with worry and he seemed irritated by her arrival.

"Take it off," he said.

Arkady guessed he meant the shroud. She pulled it over her head and dropped it on the floor beside her, glad to be rid of it.

The slaver looked up and studied her for a moment and then rose to his feet and walked closer, peering at her myopically. "You're foreign. Caelish, are you?"

For no reason she could readily name, Arkady nodded. "Yes. I'm Caelish."

He studied her for a time, walking a full circle to examine her from every angle. Then he stopped in front of her, rubbing his chin. "Take off your clothes."

"I beg your pardon?"

The slaver backhanded her soundly across the face. "Take off your clothes."

Arkady wasn't fool enough to argue about it twice. Her cheek stinging from the blow, she slipped her shift from her shoulders and let it fall to the floor. The slaver did another full circle of her with a thoughtful expression before he stopped in front of her, poking her in the belly with a sharp fingernail. "You've had a baby?"

"No."

"You a virgin?"

"No."

He frowned. "How old?"

"Twenty-four," she lied.

He shook his head. "Pity."

"A *pity*?" Even Arkady's poor Torlenian was good enough to know that word.

The slaver shrugged. "The big money's in virgins, these days. *Young* virgins. You're pretty enough, woman, but too old and you're used goods. You got a name?"

"Ah . . . Kady."

"I'll put you with the Senestran batch," he said, returning to his ledger. "They're not as fussy as the Torlenian buyers."

"I have a friend here in the city," she said, hoping her Torlenian was good enough to convince the slaver she was worth listening to. "If I can get a message to her, she'll pay whatever you want for me."

The man smiled. "They've all got someone."

Arkady wasn't sure she understood what he was saying. "Pardon?"

"Every third slave who walks through that door," the slaver told her, "reckons there's someone on the outside waiting to rescue them. The debtor slaves are the worst. All think there's someone going to pay their debts for them, they do." He shook his head. "There's nobody out there for you, woman. Don't go pining away imagining there is."

Arkady opened her mouth to speak and then shut it abruptly. This man traded in human flesh for a living. It occurred to her that to give him any idea she might be valuable to her enemies could be a death sentence. Suppose she told him who she really was, and instead of looking for Tiji, the man found one of Jaxyn's agents instead?

She shrugged. "I can dream, can't I?"

The slaver shook his head. "Not around here you can't. Not if you plan to survive."

With that dire prediction, the slaver returned his attention to his ledger, after ringing a bell on his desk, presumably to summon another guard to take her away. Without waiting to be asked, Arkady bent down and picked up her shift, slipping her arms through the sleeves as she rose to her feet. The slaver seemed neither to notice, nor care, so completely inured to the spectre of naked human flesh that he no longer associated the lives in which he traded with anything more than his wretched ledger.

It was dark by the time Arkady was escorted from the slaver's office to her cell, via a detour she didn't anticipate. A different guard had come for her this time, and he led her through the torch-lit compound to another enclosure that looked like a smithy as much as anything. At almost the same time as she realised what was going on, the guard grabbed her arm and dragged her forward toward the forge.

The farrier was working on a set of shackles, but he put them aside when he spied the guard and his prisoner. Arkady began to struggle violently as they approached the stifling fires, truly afraid for the first time since embarking on this journey.

"New one?" the farrier asked, spitting uninterestedly onto the floor as he picked up a rag, wrapped it around his hand and then turned to the forge, where he withdrew a long metal handle that had been resting in the flames.

"*No!*" Arkady screamed, when she saw the brand. "Tides! You can't be *serious!*"

But they were serious. Even the farrier wore the interlinked chain brand of slavery on his chest. They'd all suffered this and weren't planning to let her off.

He turned toward her with the brand, as the guard grabbed Arkady from behind, pinning her arms back so she couldn't escape. The glowing metal left a trail of sparks in the air as the farrier turned it toward her.

The farrier pulled aside her shift, exposing her right breast. Arkady struggled harder. The guard wrenched her arms back. She screamed, but it seemed he wasn't trying to hurt her. Quite the reverse.

"Stop it!" he ordered impatiently. "If you move, he'll miss and you'll wind up wearing the brand on your face."

He was right, of course, and if he'd done this before, probably speaking from experience. Sobbing uncontrollably, Arkady forced herself to stop struggling, forced her panic under control. Through eyes filled with tears, she watched the farrier come closer. So close she could count every pore on his sweaty brow, so close she could smell the stench of his unwashed body.

At the last minute, she turned her face away, terrified, unable to watch.

Arkady's scream split the night as the brand bored into her. The stench of burning flesh made her stomach retch. Pain shot through her whole body like a lightning bolt. The guard held her tight, strangely sympathetic, whispering useless reassurances in her ear that did nothing to dull the pain.

After a moment—although it felt like a tormented lifetime—the farrier withdrew the brand, and then smeared a thick greasy paste over the burn, which seemed to sting even more than the burning metal, if that was possible.

Arkady collapsed into the arms of the guard, the pain stealing her will to fight.

With a gruff command to stand, the guard pulled her to her feet and half-dragged, half-carried the newly branded slave from the forge.

Chapter 67

Warlock's fears about his future were not occupying only *his* thoughts, it seemed. Several days after it was confirmed that the former Duke of Lebec and the King's Spymaster had been killed in the prison fire, Warlock was summoned to the office of the King's Private Secretary.

The news of their deaths was the talk of the city. Bodies had been found in the tower which were assumed to be the duke and the spymaster, but they were so badly burned nobody was sure which body belonged to whom. Rumour had it they were to be buried in a mass grave, along with all the other victims from the fire, a stone put over the top to commemorate the event, and then the whole thing would quietly be forgotten.

When Warlock arrived at the King's Private Secretary's office, somewhat to his amazement he discovered Tilly Ponting enjoying afternoon tea with Jaxyn Aranville. Clearly the immortal had no inkling the woman he was entertaining was the Guardian of the Lore, head of the Pentangle of the Cabal of the Tarot, the organisation devoted to his eradication.

Hoping he didn't look too surprised, Warlock bowed, first to Jaxyn and then to Lady Ponting.

"I can come back later if you're busy, my lord," he said, after greeting Lady Ponting.

"Not at all, Cecil," Tilly said. "We were just talking about you, in fact, weren't we, Jaxyn?"

"Yes, we were."

"I trust I have done nothing to displease my lord? Or her highness?"

Tilly smiled at him encouragingly. "On the contrary, Cecil. Jaxyn was just saying he was surprised at how well you were working out."

"To serve her majesty is the reason I breathe," Warlock replied, certain Tilly would hear the irony in his tone, even if Jaxyn didn't.

"Well, yes, I can see that. Which is why I was so concerned when I heard she was planning to send you away."

This was news to Warlock. "I am not aware of any such plan, my lady."

"That's because we haven't shared it with you," Jaxyn said. "Hawkes gave us the idea, actually."

"I'm still not aware of what the idea is, my lord."

"Lord Jaxyn wants to recruit you as a spy, Cecil."

It was impossible to tell if Tilly Ponting was joking. In this room where nobody was really who or what they were claiming to be, it was hard to be sure of anything.

"A spy?" he echoed stupidly, the question buying him time, if nothing else.

"He wants to send you back to Caelum with Lord Torfail and his sister. He seems to think you've won their confidence and that if we gifted you to them as a parting present, you'd be well placed to infiltrate their household for us."

But who is "us"? Warlock wanted to demand. Was Tilly talking about his being sent to Caelum to spy for the Cabal? Was she merely repeating Jaxyn's wish to send him to Caelum to spy for Glaeba? *And does anybody care that my mate is about to whelp and I want to be gone from this place?*

The uncertainty of it was driving him mad.

"To serve you is the reason I breathe," Warlock replied mechanically, unable to think of anything else to say.

"The problem is that the Caelish are expecting a breeding pair," Jaxyn said.

"But I have no mate," Warlock said, determined to give this immortal monster no leverage over him.

"I know," Jaxyn said. "Lady Ponting was suggesting she might have a solution to that problem."

"I have a pregnant female in my kennels," Tilly explained, after taking another sip of tea. "No idea who fathered her pups. One of the males got over the fence, I suppose. Anyway, I was just suggesting to Lord Jaxyn that he send Tabitha Belle along as your mate."

Behind that guileless smile was the sharp mind of a woman who commanded an organisation whose roots went back several thousand years. Tilly affected a daft exterior, but it was no more real than the facade of the Tide Lord sitting across the desk from her posing as Lord Aranville. Warlock stared at her, not sure whether to thank her, or tear her throat out. To involve his family in such a fashion was monstrous.

But he knew what she was telling him. *This is your only choice, Warlock. You work for the Cabal now, and if you want our protection for your family, you will do as we bid.*

But what sort of protection could he offer Boots if she was sent to Caelum with him? His mate, posing as his mate? How was he supposed to treat her? How would he be *expected* to treat her? For the Caelish to believe she was his mate, he would have to act as if she was. But if he did, then would Jaxyn realise Tabitha Belle was someone he cared for? Someone he'd die for?

That was something he would never risk any immortal learning about him.

Which brought up a compelling reason to refuse this ludicrous plan outright—Jaxyn knew who Boots was. She'd grown up in the Lebec Kennels. Worse, because she'd clashed with him in the past, he knew she was a Scard. If he so much as lay eyes on Tilly's "Tabitha Belle" the whole tottering house of cards this subterfuge was built on would come tumbling down.

And if I refuse?

Then Jaxyn would know he was a Scard and the even shakier foundation underpinning this raft of lies would be exposed.

Tides, just thinking about it is enough to make your head explode.

"To serve you is the reason I breathe," he repeated, certain any other response would betray his true feelings. "When would I . . . where would I meet up with this . . . female? My understanding is that Lord Torfail and his sister are planning to leave in the next few days. Will that be time to bring this . . . female . . . to Herino?"

Tilly smiled broadly and looked at Jaxyn. "You see, he's a clever one, this boy. Uses his head. But you've no need to fear on that score, Cecil. I'll have Aleki ship her straight across the lake from Lebec. There's no need for her to come anywhere near Herino."

It was a shaky reassurance at best, but he was relieved to discover Tilly realised the danger if Jaxyn saw Boots and recognised her for the escaped Lebec canine who'd killed a feline guard during her escape.

"Just try to look happy when you meet up with her in Caelum," Jaxyn advised. "We don't want the Caelish getting the idea you're there for any other reason than to serve them."

"They'll be suspicious, anyway, won't they, my lord?" Warlock asked.

"Lord Torfail might be, but the queen is making a gift of you to the Lady Alysa. She's much less . . . discerning."

Gullible is what he really meant, Warlock knew, but it was some small comfort, nonetheless. Of the two immortals visiting from Caelum, Elyssa was by far the lesser evil.

"Then I look forward to serving Glaeba and Queen Kylia, my lord, in whatever capacity you deem most effective."

Jaxyn nodded, his belief in the infallibility of the Crasii magical compulsion to obey the Tide Lords making every compliant word Warlock uttered sound plausible.

"It's settled then!" Tilly declared happily, placing her empty cup and saucer on the cart beside Jaxyn's desk. I'll send a message to Aleki and have him arrange to ship Tabitha direct to Cycrane."

"And what's this breeding female going to cost?" Jaxyn asked.

"You just keep me on the guest list at Lebec Palace, dearest, and it won't cost you very much at all."

"Really?" The Tide Lord studied her suspiciously. "And all this time, I thought you were Stellan's friend."

"I am the friend of whoever is in power, Jaxyn," the old woman said, rising to her feet. "That used to be Stellan. Now it's you. I do not intend my estates, or my son's future, to go the way of the Deseans out of some misguided notion of loyalty. I am loyal to Glaeba and to those who support her king. Last I heard, Stellan was on trial for high treason just before he so fortuitously perished. Seems to me the sensible thing to do, in a case like this, is to ally oneself with the faction doing the prosecuting, not the faction imprisoned and on trial. I wouldn't like to fortuitously perish, either."

Tides, Warlock thought. *These people lie so smoothly, you're never sure when they're telling the truth.*

"You're a very pragmatic woman, Tilly," Jaxyn said. "How do you think Arkady is going to take your change of allegiance when she gets back?"

"Unless she's on the guest list at the palace, Jaxyn, I don't really care."

Jaxyn smiled. Tilly's cold-blooded willingness to drop friends under a cloud for those who were in favour didn't disturb him in the slightest. He seemed to accept it without question, probably because it was precisely what he would have done, had he been in her shoes.

Where there is no difference, Warlock asked himself with some concern, as he watched the head of the Cabal verbally fencing with the Tide Lord, *between the actions of two opposing forces, how does one ever really tell who is good and who is evil?*

Chapter 68

The "Senestran batch" turned out to be a group of five Torlenian women of varying ages, waiting in a holding cell on the other side of the compound. Arkady could just make them out in the fitful light from the torch across the hall. Two of the women were younger than Arkady, one seemed about the same age, the other two were well into their thirties.

Still faint from the pain of her branding, Arkady staggered as she was shoved into the cell with the other women. None of them showed much interest in her. The two older women returned to the game of stones they had improvised on the sandy cell floor, the younger pair seemed completely disinterested, and the woman who seemed about Arkady's age glared at her with such venom, she recoiled from her in shock.

She turned, instead, to the guard who was locking the gate, forcing back the tears of pain that choked her. The man had seemed almost sympathetic as he held her down while she was branded. Perhaps there was something left in him. Some shred of decency she could appeal to. "Please! Can you get a message to someone for me?"

The guard looked at her for a moment without answering. He took so long to answer, in fact, that Arkady was starting to wonder if he understood what she'd said to him.

"How much?"

"I'm sorry?"

"How much to deliver your message?"

Tides! He wants to get paid. But he hadn't said no. That was a start. "My friend will pay you when you tell her where I am. Anything you ask."

He shook his head. "I don't work on promises. You want me to deliver a message? You pay up front."

"With what?"

"Tides, you silly bitch," one of the women behind her remarked. "You have to *ask*?"

Arkady glanced over her shoulder. It was one of the older women who had spoken. "What does he want?"

"You *are* new, aren't you?" the other woman remarked with a shake of her head.

The woman who had spoken first laughed. "Get down on your knees, stick your face through the bars, and open your mouth, lass," she suggested, not taking her eyes off the game she was playing in the sand. "You'll find out what Strakam accepts as payment, quick enough."

Arkady turned to look at the guard. Strakam—presumably that was his name—grinned at her, and thrust his groin forward until it was up against the bars. Disgusted, Arkady stepped back, not sure she was quite that desperate.

The guard shrugged, a little disappointed perhaps, but not surprised. "You got three days to change your mind, sweet thing," he told her. "After that it won't make a difference."

He turned and headed back down the corridor, leaving Arkady staring after him. After a moment, she turned to the other women, wincing as the fabric of her shift rubbed against her injured breast, which had settled down to a dull throbbing pain. Whatever was in the paste the farrier had slathered on the wound, it seemed to be numbing the agony somewhat. "What did he mean?"

"What did who mean?" the older woman asked.

"The guard. Strakam? He said I had three days to change my mind, didn't he? What did he mean?"

"He meant you've only got three days to change your mind," the woman replied. She smiled at her companion. "Not real bright, this one, is she?"

"Are we to be auctioned off, then?"

The woman shook her head. "We ain't up for auction. They only auction off something a person's likely to want to bid on. You, me, the rest of us here . . . we ain't worth the worry." She looked up, squinting a little at Arkady in the gloom. "You might have been all right if you'd been a bit younger, I reckon. You're probably a looker when you're cleaned up, but not enough to tempt the men of Elvere."

"Then what's going to happen to us?"

"We've been batch sold to the Senestrans."

"*Batch* sold?" she asked, unfamiliar with the phrase.

"Means we've been bought in a bulk lot," her companion explained. "The Senestrans just put in an order for slaves . . . you know, certain sex, certain height . . . weight . . . colouring . . . whatever—I don't know exactly how it works—and the slavers fill the order. We ship out in three days' time."

Three days. Three days for Tiji to find her, assuming she had any idea Arkady was now a slave waiting to be shipped off to Senestra. Three days for Arkady to decide if she was desperate enough to give Strakam what he wanted, with no guarantee he'd even attempt to deliver her message, and she was willing to risk catching something disgusting from him in the process.

Three days for Cayal to learn of her fate and come looking for her. Assuming he *cared* enough to come looking for her.

There was no guarantee of that, either.

In pain, filled with despair and lost in a world full of people she didn't understand—either their language or their customs—Arkady sank to the floor, her back against the bars. She gave in to her tears for a time, telling herself it was the pain of her burn, but knowing it was much more than that.

There had never been a time in Arkady's life when she'd felt as desperate as this. Not the night they arrested her father, not even the first time she knocked on Fillion Rybank's door when she was fourteen years old. Then she had been younger, more easily persuaded to hope. Less able to see the consequences; less harsh in her judgement of the reality of her situation.

The truth was, Arkady had now been enslaved. Worse, she'd been *branded* as a slave—which meant nobody in Torlenia would believe she had ever been anything else—and the only four people on Amyrantha who might care enough about her to come to her aid were completely out of her reach.

Stellan was imprisoned, possibly even executed by now, falsely accused of killing the Glaeban king and queen. The Tides alone knew where Declan was, with the frightening spectre of him being the one responsible for fabricating the charges against Stellan a real possibility. Cayal was off looking for another Tide Lord in the mistaken belief his old enemy had agreed to help him.

And Tiji . . . the clever, resourceful little Scard might only be several streets away, but to get a message to her, Arkady would have to give Strakam what he wanted, and then hope the guard would keep his word. And hope his offer wasn't just a ploy to get himself pleasured at the expense of a desperate slave.

The older woman glanced up, noticing Arkady's shuddering despair. "If you're that desperate to get out of here, lass, give Strakam what he wants."

Arkady wiped away her tears, sniffing loudly, and turned her head to look at the woman who had spoken, wincing as the movement once again made the fabric of her shift brush against her burn. "I don't think I'm that far gone, just yet."

"See how you feel three days from now," the other woman advised. "Strakam's cock may start to look a mite tastier than spending the rest of your life underground in a Senestran copper mine."

Three days. Tides, this can't be happening to me.

Arkady didn't sleep much that night, nor the next night, either. The pain from her branding would have kept her awake, even if the dire nature of her circumstances didn't make her afraid to close her eyes. The other women in the cell showed little interest in befriending her, except for the older woman who'd advised her so pragmatically to give Strakam what he wanted to get a message out to her friend.

Her name, it turned out, was Saxtyn. She was a debtor slave, sold into servitude when she couldn't pay her late husband's debts. She'd been a slave for more than a decade, she informed Arkady, and was resigned to whatever the fates might bring.

When Arkady asked her how far she'd be willing to go to escape this place, Saxtyn smiled sadly and shook her head. "Not that far, Kady. But then, I ain't as desperate as you, neither."

"You'd do it, then? If you were me?"

The older woman laughed harshly. "Puttin' Strakam's cock in my mouth on purpose is way past the point I'd be willing to go, I'd reckon, even if it meant a pardon. Tides. Who knows where it's been?"

In the end, the decision was taken from her. The guard changed the following morning and the new man showed no interest in any of the women. He did bring them news, however. Their departure had been moved up and they were to be loaded onto the Senestran ship later that morning.

With her burn still throbbing in time with her heartbeat, Arkady began making plans, this time to flee as soon as they were out of the compound. Her plans were dashed once again, however, when later that morning, the guards returned with shackles for the women. Arkady was chained between Saxtyn and the youngest girl in the cell, a dark-haired young woman of about twenty, with a lazy eye and drooping eyelid that distorted her face and made her seem quite vapid. She was not, however, Arkady decided, judging by the stream of invective she unleashed on the guards who tried to shackle her. They slapped her for her temerity and after that she quieted down and allowed them to chain her.

The women were marched from the cell, through the compound, and then loaded onto an ox-drawn wagon for the journey to the docks. Every movement caused Arkady pain and the bright sunlight beat down on her like a relentless weight as they rocked along the crowded, pot-holed streets of Elvere. Adding to Arkady's surreal feeling was the realisation that this journey was the first time since arriving in Torlenia she had appeared in the streets unshrouded. To be able to see everything, and not just the small view of the world afforded by the narrow eye-slit of a shroud, was a strange and unsettling experience. And she didn't like what she saw, through her tear-misted eyes. The place was crowded and dirty and smelled like raw sewage.

"*Your grace!*" she imagined someone calling, wondering if the heat and the pain were making her delirious. "*Over here!*"

Arkady closed her eyes, wishing the pain was bad enough to make her pass out, rather than this agony that bordered on intolerable.

"*Arkady!*"

Her eyes snapped open. She hadn't imagined *that*. Arkady twisted around, trying to determine where the call had come from.

"Tiji?" she called out, certain the little Crasii was the only person in Torlenia who would recognise her. Certainly the only female in Torlenia likely to seek her out. And the call had *definitely* been a woman's voice. "Tiji!" she cried again, trying to climb to her feet, but Saxtyn pulled her down.

"Tides, woman, do you want to get us all beaten?"

"But I heard my friend! She called to me!"

Saxtyn rolled her eyes impatiently. "Then she's seen you and she can follow you to the ship and try to buy you back from the Senestran captain. Now sit down and shut up, you silly bitch, before you get us all into trouble."

Saxtyn probably had the right of it, and in the crowded streets, Arkady had no hope of finding Tiji. She could be looking at her right now, camouflaged against a wall somewhere, watching as the wagon inched past, and she'd never know it.

Arkady turned and settled herself down again, filled with hope. Tiji was somewhere out there. Tiji had seen her. Tiji would follow them to the docks as Saxtyn suggested and with the resources she had at her disposal—provided she hadn't lost her diplomatic papers—she would be able to buy Arkady back and set her free.

Arkady dared not think beyond that moment, afraid she would jinx her imminent release if she allowed her excitement to run away with her.

But she had hope now. A future.

Arkady clung to that hope for the next few hours. She clung to it as they were marched aboard the Senestran freighter. Clung to it even as she was led below decks, freed from her shackles, and then shoved into a narrow, foul-smelling compartment in the hold with the other female slaves.

It wasn't until she felt the ship lurching beneath them, and she realised they were pulling away from the dock as the amphibians towed the freighter out into open water, that Arkady was forced to let the hope go.

Only then was she willing to admit that she was on her way to Senestra as a branded slave and nobody was going to save her.

Chapter 69

The Dog and Bone was, for an inn that catered almost exclusively to Crasii, quite a salubrious establishment. Like much of Torlenian architecture, the inn was really more a set of separate buildings contained within a high, enclosing wall, than the traditional definition of a house. It offered separate taprooms for canine and feline patrons, and a smaller room with a shallow pool out the back for the many amphibious sailors who frequented this busy seaport. Tiji, with her diplomatic papers and guarantee of Glaeban funds to settle her bill, was able to secure the best room in the house.

Cayal and Tiji had parted ways on the outskirts of the city. The Tide Lord kept his promise to Arkady to see Tiji safely back to civilisation, but had no interest in prolonging their acquaintanceship. Even so, he'd been in a strangely buoyant mood on the way from the abbey, as if the prospect of Brynden's assistance had lifted a heavy weight off him. Tiji had been unable to glean any useful details from him—she'd begun to suspect Cayal had no idea *how* this miraculous cure for immortality was supposed to work—but she was certain of one thing.

Cayal believed he'd found a way to die.

And if you could kill one Tide Lord, you could kill all of them.

All Tiji had to do now was find a way to get a message to someone in the Cabal, and let them know about it.

This is where her plans fell apart. She had no reliable way of sending a message back to Declan without delivering it herself. That was something she was reluctant to do, until she was sure Arkady was safe. It wasn't all affection for the duchess that made her worry for Arkady's fate. Tiji had a suspicion that if Declan had to choose between finding a way to kill a Tide Lord and finding Arkady, the immortals would run a poor second.

Even if that wasn't the case, the truth was Arkady's situation was more immediate, and something Tiji could do something to affect. The Tide Lords had been around for thousands of years, and if Cayal were to be believed, any method for disposing of them was dependent on the Tide peaking.

That was years away.

She had time, she figured, to wait here in Elvere for a couple of weeks, meet up with Arkady again, and then find a way to get a message back to the Cabal that didn't involve either of them being arrested and tried for anything. If she could find somewhere safe for Arkady to hide, then she could head back to Glaeba herself, deliver her news about the Tide Lords, and tell Declan where Arkady was stashed.

Then it would be up to him to decide which was more important.

It took her several days to come to this conclusion, by which time she'd also decided something else. Back when she'd first been rescued from the travelling carnival by Declan and Markun Far Jisa—the only Senestran member of the Pentangle—she'd heard another name mentioned in connection with the Cabal of the Tarot.

Ryda Tarek.

He was mixed up with the Cabal, somehow, which meant she could probably count on his help. And he lived near Elvere. Markun had told her that much about him the last time she'd visited Senestra on business for the King's Spymaster. On her way home from Senestra, she'd shipped through Elvere, and stayed at The Dog and Bone before boarding another ship bound for Glaeba.

If she could find the gem merchant Ryda Tarek, and prevail upon him to hide Arkady, then she'd have nothing more to worry about. Arkady would be safe, Declan would be happy, and Tiji could stop worrying about both of them and get on with the more important job, which was finding out about this potential weapon they could use against the Tide Lords.

After enquiring of the innkeeper where the gem merchants of Elvere were likely to be found, and getting directions from him, Tiji left the inn, heading in the direction of the merchant quarter, which would take her away from the slave markets and further into the city near the wharves. As was the case in most Torlenian cities, all the women were shrouded unless they were slaves, Crasii or prostitutes. The double standard always intrigued her about Torlenians. They insisted "respectable women" be shrouded, but prostitutes seemed to be unconcerned by the law and many Crasii, from a distance, looked human enough to tempt any man easily led off the path of righteousness. Not being human, Tiji wasn't required to wear a shroud, but she still had the burnous she'd worn in the desert and chose that to conceal—and protect—her silver-scaled skin. She wouldn't pass close inspection, but she wouldn't cause idle comment, either.

The alternative—to go naked and have the ability to blend in against any wall she stopped against—was only useful if she was playing a watching game. And bordering on dangerous in such a hot place, where the sun was likely to burn her to a crisp if she stayed out in it for too long.

It was quite a walk to the merchant quarter and by midday, when the heat of the day prompted the shop owners the city over to close for a few hours, Tiji was hungry. She stopped for a drink at the community well in the centre of one of the small markets dotting the city. Spying a cart-owner selling skewers of cooked meat, about to pack up for the midday break, she hurried over to him, offering him five copper fenets for the last two skewers he had on his grill. The man happily sold her the somewhat dry and overcooked meat, grabbing her hand as she proffered the coins.

He looked at her silver-scaled skin for a moment and then studied her curiously. "Don't see your type in the city too often."

Tiji snatched her hand out of his grasp. "That's probably because you're so damned rude here in the city, we'd rather stay at home."

The food-seller smiled. "Too afraid of us big, scary, hairy humans, be more like it. Still, I ain't the sort to pick on a person just because they're different. Takes all kinds, I say. Where're you headed?"

She glared at him. "What's it to you?"

He shrugged. "Nothin', I suppose. You enjoy your meal, now, won't you?"

Tiji turned from the cart, frowning, not sure why the cart-owner had taken such an interest in her. She bit into the meat on the skewer, pleased to discover it was quite spicy and much more edible than it looked. She ate as she walked, tossing the skewers aside once she'd finished. Because the city was about to close for the midday break, there was a last-minute frenzy of activity, and for a time the streets seemed to fill to overflowing.

She rounded the corner of the next street and turned onto the main thoroughfare leading to the city centre and the wharves. It was then she spied the ox-drawn wagon full of slaves, heading toward the docks. At first she paid it little attention, just another wagon in a crowded street, but then she glanced at the wagon again, mostly because of the rare sight of its unshrouded human female passengers.

Her first thought was the strangeness of the sight, her next an overwhelming feeling of pity for such wretched creatures. It was then that she noticed the woman in the centre, taller than her companions, paler, and definitely not Torlenian.

Tides, she looks so much like Arkady . . .

Only it couldn't be Arkady, Tiji knew, because Arkady was back at Brynden's abbey, safe and sound for the time being, until Cayal returned with Lukys.

Safe in the care of an immortal bent on vengeance against the man who had escorted her to him . . .

Oh Tides . . . Tiji thought, shouldering her way through the crowd to catch up. *Would Brynden do something so awful to Arkady?* she asked herself, as the wagon plodded forward.

Of course he would, she replied to herself. *There's no limit to what he'd do to get back at Cayal.*

"*Your grace!*" she called, wondering if Arkady would even hear her over the noise of the market, the crowd and the unexpectedness of anybody finding her here. "*Over here!*"

She watched in despair as Arkady closed her eyes, perhaps thinking she imagined the call, maybe not hearing it at all.

"*Arkady!*" she yelled, as loud as she could, drawing curious looks from the people around her.

This time Arkady heard her. She sat up, looking around, searching the crowded street for a familiar face. Tiji raised her arm to signal her, but before she could do more than wave once, someone grabbed her from behind.

A gloved hand was clamped over her mouth to prevent her screaming and she was dragged backward through a doorway, into a dark room beyond. Struggling frantically, she sensed another person waiting inside.

"Help me keep her still," the man holding her said, as she tried to wriggle out of his grasp. "Tides, it's like trying to hold down a swamp eel."

Tiji was glad they were having trouble holding on to her, but it didn't seem to make much difference. A dark bag was forced over her head, shutting out all the light, which made her struggle even harder. She kicked the man who'd grabbed her in the shin as hard as she could, gratified to hear him grunt in pain, and then tried to bite his gloved hand, when she felt the ropes around her ankles. It made little difference in the end. With the speed that comes only with true expertise, she was bound and immobile within seconds, after which, she was laid—with surprising care—onto the floor.

She felt, rather than saw one of the men come closer. She could tell he'd squatted down beside her, because his voice sounded just near her ear when he spoke.

"Take it easy, little lizard," the man advised gently. "Be still and you won't be hurt."

Tiji thought of any number of crude and rebellious responses, but she never got to voice any of them. No sooner had he spoken than a damp cloth was pressed over her mouth and nose through the dark bag covering her head. It smelled faintly sweet and damp and she had no choice but to breathe it in, after which Tiji saw and felt nothing more.

When Tiji came to, it happened abruptly. One moment she was out cold, the next she realised she was lying on the ground surrounded by a circle of torch-bearing strangers. In a panic, she struggled to sit up, glaring at the circle of faceless bodies surrounding her. In the darkness she could only make out their eyes, which reflected like small, lidless mirrors in the firelight.

"Don't be afraid," a voice whispered gently. "We're not going to hurt you."

"Yeah, I got that when you jumped me in broad daylight, knocked me unconscious and kidnapped me."

"It was necessary," another disembodied voice told her. "You might not have come willingly."

"You've got that much right," she said, climbing warily to her feet, figuring she had a much better chance of running from that position than sitting on the ground. Nobody tried to stop her from standing. If anything, they moved back a little to give her room. "Who are you people, anyway? Slavers?"

Someone laughed. "Actually, we're quite the opposite. We're . . . *un*-slavers . . . I suppose you could call us."

"I don't think that's a word."

"Probably not. What's your name?"

"Tiji," she told them warily, wishing she could see beyond the circle of torches. "What's yours?"

Finally, one of her captors stepped into the light to reveal himself. A little taller than her and completely hairless, he wore not a stitch of clothing. It was immediately apparent why Tiji had such trouble making out her kidnappers. It wasn't the light.

They were camouflaged.

The young male stepped forward—and he was most definitely male—allowing his skin to assume its natural silver sheen. He smiled at her, amused—it seemed—by Tiji's slack-jawed shock.

"My name is Azquil and we haven't come to enslave you, Tiji," the chameleon Crasii said. "We've come to take you home."

Chapter 70

Lukys was not at home. Cayal didn't even need to reach the villa to re-alise this, but he stopped there, just the same, hoping the Tide Lord had left some hint about his location with his wife, Oritha. He was greeted by the young woman like an honoured guest. Pathetically grateful for some company, she arranged a lavish feast for her husband's old friend, and then told Cayal of the message Lukys had left for him.

"He's gone to Jelidia, my lord," Oritha announced later that evening, as she cleared away the supper dishes. She had served him herself, never leaving him alone for more than a moment or two, as if afraid he would vanish if she took her eyes off him for too long.

"Jelidia?"

"My Ryda travels a lot," the young woman explained with a smile. "He's a very important man."

Cayal frowned for a moment at the name, and then remembered that was the identity Lukys was using these days. Ryda Tarek, wealthy gem merchant from Stevania.

"Why Jelidia?"

"He said something about checking on something valuable he'd left in storage, down there." She smiled coyly. "Will you be staying the night, my lord?"

Cayal nodded, wondering what possible reason Lukys could have for checking on Kentravyon now. Unless he feared the returning Tide was weakening the bonds that held the frozen Tide Lord, there was no reason for him to go there.

"Has he been gone long?" he asked, thinking if Lukys didn't have too big a head start on him, it might be worth catching up with his old friend to enquire why he felt the need to head for the southern continent. Kentravyon had been trapped for thousands of years. It seemed an odd time to think about him now.

"Several months now, my lord," Oritha said. "Of course, he wasn't going straight to Jelidia. He had business in Glaeba first, that he had to take care of."

"Lu— Ryda had business in Glaeba? What sort of business?"

The young woman shrugged. "Gem business, I suppose. Lebec is the source of most of the world's freshwater pearls, isn't it? I imagine his business in Glaeba had something to do with that. And he'd probably wanted to visit his son."

Cayal stared at her. "His *son*?"

She nodded. "I've never met him, of course, and he's probably a grown man by now. His mother was Ryda's first wife."

"Ryda Tarek has a son in Glaeba?" Cayal said, very slowly and precisely, just to make certain he was hearing this right. He was afraid to ask too closely about the "first" wife, either, in case he gave the game away by laughing out loud. Whoever he was referring to, it certainly *wasn't* Lukys's first wife. Tides, Lukys's first wife had probably been dead ten thousand years. Oritha—assuming Lukys even bothered to keep count any longer—might well be his fiftieth bride.

What lies has that old swindler spun this poor girl to keep her from asking too many awkward questions about his past?

"It pains him so much, not having been there to watch his son grow up," Oritha sighed, oblivious to Cayal's cynicism. "And it's one of the reasons he's so reluctant to bring another child into the world, I'm sure. He refuses to admit it, but I can tell how much he fears dying unexpectedly and leaving another child to grow up fatherless, just as his son was forced to grow up without a father after his mother died."

"And why, exactly, wasn't Ryda there to raise his son?"

"He was away buying gems when the boy's mother died," she explained. "By the time Ryda had returned, the boy had been taken back to Glaeba by his mother's family, and by the time he discovered where they were, the boy was almost grown and it didn't seem fair to take him away from everything he knew and loved. It pained him greatly, to accept it, but in the end, everyone agreed it was better to let the child stay with his mother's family in Glaeba."

Cayal took a good long swallow of wine to hide his amusement. *You sly old bastard*, he thought, watching Oritha's credulous sympathy for her husband's loss and the plight of his undoubtedly imaginary son. *How long did it take you to come up with that pathetic sob story to stop her pressuring you for a child of her own?*

He took a good swallow and put the wine cup down once he was sure he was in no danger of smiling. "So, after buying up his gems in Glaeba and dropping in on his boy, Ryda was heading for Jelidia, you say?"

"That's what he told me."

"Wasn't he worried about arriving in Jelidia just as winter will be setting in?"

"He didn't seem to be," Oritha said. "Would you like more wine, my lord?"

Cayal nodded and held out his cup for a refill. "Did he leave any other messages for me?"

She filled his wine, put down the decanter and then turned away, going to the sideboard where she opened a drawer and took out a small roll of parchment, sealed with a dollop of red wax. She walked back to the table and handed it to Cayal.

"Ryda said you'd probably be back, and that when you arrived, I was to give you this."

Cayal took the small scroll, broke the seal and opened it curiously. There was one short paragraph written in ancient Magrethan, a language so old only another immortal was likely to understand it.

When you're done fooling around with Brynden, the note said, *get your sorry royal arse to Caelum and start wooing Elyssa. Brynden has no interest in aiding you and will screw you any way he can, but I fear he's going to have to prove that to you in person before you listen to me. We need quite a few of us to do this, Cayal, and we're going to have to do it when the Tide peaks. I can convince the others, but you are the only one on Amyrantha who can convince Elyssa to join us.*

Underneath was a postscript.

And while you're a guest in my house, I would consider it a personal favour if you refrained from sleeping with my wife.

"The message is good news?" Oritha asked.

Cayal rolled the letter up, and studied her closely for a moment. *Tides, Lukys . . . "I'd appreciate it if you refrained from sleeping with my wife"?* That bordered on a dare.

And Oritha really was *very* pretty.

"It's . . . mixed news. Did you say something about staying the night?"

She nodded, lowering her eyes. "It's too late for you to head back into the city now, my lord. I'll make up a pallet for you in the guest room, if you like."

"Haven't you got servants to do that for you?"

She shook her head. "Ryda doesn't like servants. They distract him, he says."

"That must make it very lonely out here for you, my lady," he said, wondering what he was doing, even as he said it. He even spared Arkady a momentary thought, which actually hardened his resolve. Cayal was determined not to let that woman get under his skin any more than she already was.

How better to forget one woman than to entertain oneself with another? "You must get very lonely on your own for months at a time."

Oritha shook her head. "My love for my husband is all the company I need, my lord."

You lucky bastard, Lukys, Cayal thought. *She really loves you.* But he was glad in a way, that Oritha had no interest in him. Despite the open challenge Lukys had left him in his letter, despite his desire to put Arkady out of his mind, his heart wasn't in the chase.

That was probably Arkady's fault, too, curse her.

Cayal wasted another two days at Lukys's house agonising over this strange turn of events that meant he would rather honour Oritha's marriage vows than go to the bother of seducing her. In that at least, Cayal had learned his lesson about running off with other immortals' wives.

When he finally rode away with enough supplies to see him through a month in the desert, rather than the few days it would take to reach Brynden's abbey, Cayal was still pondering this alarming tendency he had for complicating his life more than was absolutely necessary by finding himself attracted to the wrong women, when he finally reached the abbey. The thought of seeing Arkady again shoved any lingering desire for Oritha from his mind. His resolve not to let her get to him was weakening in direct proportion to his proximity to her.

The gates of the abbey opened for him as he approached, an acolyte met him in the courtyard, helped him dismount and took his camel away to be cared for. The abbot himself came out to greet him after that, bowing low, clearly having been briefed about the identity of this new arrival.

"My lord will see you now, your highness," the saffron-robed monk announced, holding out his arm to indicate that Cayal should go first.

Pleased with this show of respect, Cayal headed in the direction the abbot was pointing, which was the entrance to the main hall of the abbey.

It was a long time since Cayal had been here. The last time was before he and Kinta had had their fling. He'd been welcome in Brynden's hall in those days. Or at least more welcome than he was now.

Brynden was waiting for him at the end of the hall, standing on the dais that, to Cayal's mind, always seemed to be missing an altar. The sun streamed in through the high windows behind him, shadowing the Tide Lord and making it impossible to see the expression on his face.

"I expected you back days ago," Brynden said, as he approached. The immortal had shed his monkish robes and was dressed as a warrior once more. The time of Brynden's hiding was at an end, Cayal guessed.

"I was delayed."

"Is Lukys not with you?"

Cayal shook his head. "He's off gathering the others together. He'll be back soon, though. And then we can get things moving." He glanced around the hall curiously. "Where's Arkady?"

"Somewhere safe."

There was a note in Brynden's tone that hinted at some hidden meaning in his innocuous statement.

"What does 'somewhere safe' mean, *precisely*?"

"The letter your friend brought me from Kinta spoke of the dire trouble that might befall her, should her husband's enemies locate her. She tells me both Jaxyn and Diala are involved in Glaeban politics, these days, too."

"All the more reason for me to get Arkady to safety, Brynden. Where is she?"

"Somewhere her enemies will never think to look for her."

Cayal frowned, certain now something was amiss.

Brynden has no interest in aiding you and will screw you any way he can, Lukys's note had warned.

When will I ever learn to listen to you, Lukys?

"You wouldn't be this cryptic unless you knew I wasn't going to like it."

Brynden smiled, which was a rare and frightening thing to behold. "I'm enjoying the moment, Cayal. Don't spoil it for me by making me rush."

By now, Cayal knew something was horribly wrong. *Tides, Arkady, what have I done? I handed you over to him without thinking . . . What has he done to you?*

"Where is she, Brynden?"

"Elvere."

Cayal breathed a sigh of relief.

"I sold her into slavery," the Tide Lord added with an openly malicious smile. "If you want her back, your immortal highness, you can buy her at auction like any other bidder. Of course, that's assuming someone else hasn't already purchased her. And you may not want her at all, once she's been branded a slave, but then . . . there never was any accounting for your taste in women."

Cayal didn't answer, too angry to speak.

Brynden seemed inordinately pleased with himself. "It's not the same, I know, as being able to make you suffer for the wrong you did me, Cayal, but it will have to do."

Cayal could feel the Tide welling up in him, fuelled by his rage. This was what it had felt like the day he extinguished the Eternal Flame. Then it had been High Tide. Now, with the Tide on its way back, but still far from peaking, there was little he could do that Brynden couldn't counter with ease.

This was the constant state of stand-off in which the Tide Lords lived.

"Don't even think about attacking me, Cayal," Brynden added, feeling Cayal's rage and the magical power he was gathering with it. "You are in *my* abbey, surrounded by *my* people. They cannot kill you, granted, but oh . . . by the Tides, they could make you suffer until the Tide had turned enough for you to free yourself."

It was a fair warning, and a well-timed one. Cayal could already feel himself wanting to level this place. Unfortunately he didn't have the power yet for anything quite as ambitious as that.

Fists clenched by his sides, Cayal held his temper in check by sheer force of will. "You don't want to start a war with me, Brynden."

"*You* started the war, Cayal, when you took Kinta from me. It's too late to complain now, when the boot is on the other foot."

Helpless, filled with impotent rage and feeling more than a little guilty that his hesitation may have given Brynden all the time he needed to rid himself of Arkady, Cayal pointed at Brynden, filled with the overwhelming need to destroy something.

"This thing between us isn't finished, Brynden."

"Then you'd best pray Lukys really has found a way to end your life for you, Cayal, because it never will be finished any other way, if I have any say in the matter."

There was no point in arguing. No point in any of this. Cayal turned on his heel and strode the length of the hall. He raised his hand, blowing the heavy double doors off their hinges as he approached them, for no other reason than it felt good to vent some of his frustration.

"Go to her, Cayal!" Brynden called after him, as he stepped through the remains of the entrance to Brynden's hall, the air filled with dust from the settling masonry. "Find her if you can! Consider this a favour! Until you find her, at least, I've given you something to live for!"

Chapter 71

When Declan Hawkes regained consciousness, he didn't know where he was at first. It was still dark and the last thing he remembered was looking up to find the top floor of the north tower of Herino Prison crashing down on top of him. He risked moving his head and discovered that other than being chilled, he seemed to be in one piece and, inexplicably, lying naked in the bottom of a small boat being rowed at a slow but steady pace by a shadowy figure he could not, at first, identify.

"You're awake," the rower observed, without breaking his rhythm.

"*Desean?*" Declan pushed himself up onto his elbows and looked around. The city of Herino was nowhere in sight. "Where are we?"

"About twenty miles north of Herino, near as I can tell. How are you feeling?"

Declan took a moment to take stock before answering. "A bit sore, a bit stiff, but surprisingly healthy. How did I get here?"

Desean smiled. "A small miracle, I suspect."

"Not so small," Declan said, frowning. "The last I remember was the roof caving in."

The duke nodded. "You pushed me clear as it fell, and to be honest, I thought you were done for. And then I heard you cry out and discovered that somehow you'd survived being crushed, although your clothes were alight. I dragged you clear, back into my cell, actually, and was on the verge of accepting that saving you was probably the most heroic, stupid and undoubtedly *last* thing I would ever do, when the cell window shattered from the heat. You were stunned, but able to move. I dragged you to the window, shoved you out of it and then jumped out after you. I figured the fall to the water might kill us both, but it was going to be marginally less painful than burning to death. You lost consciousness when you hit the water, I suppose, but on the upside, it put out the flames and saved you from being badly burned. I towed you to the shore, stole a boat and started rowing like there's no tomorrow, which I reason could well be the case if I'm recaptured." He shipped the oars and rested his elbows on them. "There's some rags stuffed in the stern that look like they might once have been clothes. Sorry I couldn't find you anything else on such short notice. I fear what the flames didn't take of your clothing, the water did. You must be chilled to the bone."

"I'll survive," he said, surprised to discover he wasn't as cold as he might have been, given he'd been lying naked in a puddle of stagnant water for half the night. He gingerly felt the scratches on his face but they seemed to have healed already, which was something to be grateful for.

"How do you know we're twenty miles north of Herino?"

"We passed the oyster farms just before you woke."

Declan nodded. Desean was probably right. He pushed himself up and turned to examine the pile of rags Stellan had indicated in the stern, finding a shirt with the sleeves ripped off and a pair of rough, motheaten trousers among them. With some difficulty he managed to get dressed without capsizing the rocking dinghy and then sat on the seat facing Stellan Desean.

"Did you want me to row for a bit?"

Desean nodded. "If you think you're up to it. My blisters are starting to get blisters of their own."

"It'll warm me up." Declan stood up and carefully changed places with Stellan, picked up the oars and began to pull on them, pleasantly surprised to find the task much less painful than expected.

Stellan Desean watched him from the other seat in silence for a time before asking, "Why did you come for me?"

"Tilly asked me to. Why did you risk your neck to help me?"

"I wasn't sure I would ever be able to face Arkady again if I didn't." When Declan didn't answer, the duke fell silent again for a while.

"Do you know what's happened to her?" he asked, some time later.

Declan shook his head. "All I know is that Jaxyn doesn't have her. She may have given him the slip in Ramahn. I have one of my people there with orders to help her if they can."

"You love her, don't you?"

Declan didn't break the rhythm of his rowing. "She's my oldest friend."

"That's not what I mean, Declan. And you know it."

"It's all the answer I'm going to give you, though," he replied. "Were you heading for Lebec?"

"I have friends there," he said.

"You have no friends, Desean. Not anywhere. If you show your face in Lebec you'll be back in custody within the hour."

"I believe my staff is loyal to me, Declan, despite the fact I'm no longer officially their duke."

"Your *staff*, as you so delicately refer to them, your grace, are for the most part Crasii slaves. Every one of them will be under orders to report so much as a rumour of your survival to Jaxyn."

He shook his head. "I don't believe they'd betray me."

"They won't even think of it as betraying you. They are compelled to obey the Tide Lords. Didn't you ever wonder why Jaxyn was so damned good at getting the Crasii to obey him?"

Desean shrugged. "I just thought he was good with animals."

"There's no Lebec for you anymore, Desean."

"Where *were* you going to take me?" he asked. "I mean, you came to get me out. Were you planning to hand me back into custody, or did you have some sort of escape route in mind?"

"I was planning to hide you in Tilly's house until I could get you out of Herino."

"Well, that plan is rather moot. What now?"

Declan thought about it for a moment, realising that along with everyone thinking Desean was dead, they probably thought he was dead, too. He tried to decide if it mattered any longer and was a little disturbed to realise it probably didn't. Chikita was well placed to become Jaxyn's bodyguard, which meant the Cabal would have a pair of eyes and ears in his inner sanctum. The orders he'd delivered on the way to the prison would ensure Warlock and Boots were on their way to Caelum within a few days, firmly ensconced in Syrolee's court.

Other than Jaxyn losing a cooperative minion, who was really going to suffer if he was no longer the King's Spymaster?

"We'll go north, for now. Past Lebec and into the Shevron Mountains," he said, thinking there was at least one safe place he could hide Desean.

"What's in the mountains?" the duke asked.

Declan began to pull a little harder on the oars now he had a destination in mind. "Family," he said.

"Whose family?"

"My family." The former spymaster smiled at the former duke in the darkness. "I'm going to take you to meet my Pop."

It was nearly two weeks later when Declan and Stellan arrived at Maralyce's mine. It was late afternoon, the wind-driven snows of the past few days relenting for a time as autumn tried, one last time, to make its presence felt in the mountains. When they arrived they found Shalimar sitting on a chair by the cabin door, taking advantage of the last of the autumn sunlight while he watched Nyah tossing horseshoes at a stick poking up out of the ground by the entrance to the forge.

Nyah squealed when she saw them, dropping the horseshoes and running to Declan. She threw her arms around him gleefully. "You're back!"

Declan glanced at his grandfather with a questioning look. The old man smiled, but made no attempt to move from his chair. "She's bored with the company of two old fogies, I suspect," he called. "Welcome back."

Declan untangled Nyah, pushing her away firmly. "Your highness."

She bobbed a quick curtsey, grinning broadly. "Master Hawkes. Who's this?"

"Princess Nyah of Caelum, allow me to introduce his grace, the Duke of Lebec, Stellan Desean."

Nyah curtsied much more formally to Stellan when she realised he was high-born. The duke stared at him, aghast. "*You're* the one who kidnapped Princess Nyah?"

"I did some people in Caelum a favour," Declan said with a shrug.

"But . . . everyone in two nations is looking for her. Tides, even I heard about it in prison. And you had her here all this time?"

"So arrest me," Declan said, a little puzzled by Stellan's reaction. Perhaps the duke in him couldn't let go. The idea that he was consorting with criminals was going to be a hard adjustment to make. Perhaps even harder than accepting the Tide Lords were real. That just took enough evidence to make him see the truth.

Putting aside generations of inborn prejudice might well prove the insurmountable task.

Declan pushed past Nyah and crossed the yard to where his grandfather was sitting. On closer inspection, he had aged even more since Declan had seen him last. His eyes were rheumy and he was trembling faintly. Declan squatted down beside him. "How are you doing, Pop?"

"I'm still alive."

"That's a start."

"You been traipsing around the mountains dressed like that?" he asked, taking in Declan's fagged sailor's garb. They'd been too afraid to go anywhere near civilisation, and Declan still wore the clothes he'd found in the stolen dinghy. Oddly enough, until Shalimar pointed it out to him, he hadn't really noticed the chill breeze that swirled around the small yard.

"It's not that cold, Pop."

"That's young bones talking." He smiled weakly, jerking his head in Nyah's direction. "It's been nice to have some company while you were gone."

"Is Maralyce not here?"

Shalimar shrugged. "She comes and goes. It pains her to see me weakening."

"So she just abandons you here to die?"

"You judge her too harshly, Declan."

"Maybe."

The old man stared at Stellan for a moment and then turned to look at Declan. "What's Desean doing here?"

Declan glanced at the duke, who was talking to Nyah, still in a state of shock over finding the Crown Princess of Caelum hiding out in a miner's camp in the Shevron Mountains. "Tilly wanted me to save him from Jaxyn."

"I'm guessing she didn't instruct you to bring him here?"

Declan shook his head. "No, it wasn't part of the plan. Do you know when Maralyce will be back?"

"You in such a hurry to see her?"

"I need to ask her something."

"Haven't seen her for a few days. I couldn't really say. Are you hungry?"

"Not particularly. But I'm guessing Desean is. We've been living off what we could forage on the way here."

"Well, you must have been living the high life in Herino, lad, because you look none the worse for it. Help me inside, eh? There's a stew on the fire, and I wouldn't mind some tea. It's getting a bit too chilly out here, anyway."

Declan helped his grandfather to his feet, appalled at how frail he was. It was as if the Tide was eating him away from the inside out. Soon there would be nothing left of him but a dried-up, hollow old shell.

Nyah saw them heading indoors, and with Stellan Desean following, they all retired to Maralyce's tiny cabin so Declan could bring his grandfather up to date on what was happening in the outside world.

It was after dark before Maralyce arrived, and although he couldn't say how, Declan knew she was coming even before the cabin door burst open. She stared at this sudden and unwelcome influx of visitors in her small sanctuary and then glowered at Declan.

"It's you."

"Last time I looked," Declan replied warily. "We weren't expecting you for days. This is Stellan Desean, by the way. Arkady's husband."

Maralyce glared at the man with ill grace. "So we're to be honoured by the whole wretched royal family, now, are we?"

Stellan rose to his feet and bowed with court-bred grace. "It's an honour to meet you, my lady."

Maralyce ignored him. Her gaze was fixed firmly on Declan.

"Outside," she ordered. "I want to talk to you."

Declan rose to his feet and followed her to the forge where she turned on him, studying him in the darkness for a time before asking, "How?"

"How what?" he asked, afraid he knew the answer. More afraid of that answer than anything he had ever faced in his entire life.

"Don't play games with me, boy."

He looked at her closely, hoping for some sign his fears were groundless. "You can tell, can't you?"

She nodded. "Felt you before I even reached the surface. What happened?"

"There was a fire . . ." he said, not sure where to begin. Then he threw his hands up helplessly. "Tides, Maralyce, I don't *know* what happened."

"It's pretty flankin' obvious what's happened, boy."

Declan shook his head. "It can't be. The Eternal Flame is gone. The Immortal Prince extinguished it five thousand years ago."

"Bah! Eternal Flame, my arse. It wasn't that special."

He stared at her in shock. "*What?*"

Maralyce shrugged uncomfortably. "We thought it was better if people believed there was only one way to make an immortal. Kept the numbers down, you see . . ."

"We? Who is *we?*"

"Me . . . and a few of the others . . ."

"Other immortals?"

"Well . . . of course . . . who else would I be talking about?"

"But . . . but Cayal told Arkady it took him a whole damned ocean to put the Eternal Flame out."

Maralyce shrugged. "Well, he would, wouldn't he? Makes him sound much more heroic, that way. Truth is, Cayal wouldn't have had a clue when the flames actually died. He was so lost to his rage he didn't know which way was up until it was all over."

"Why didn't you say something sooner?"

"Didn't know you were gonna get yourself toasted, otherwise I might have." When she saw he wasn't amused, she shook her head. "Look . . . you don't understand, Declan . . ."

"I understand, Maralyce, *believe* me, I understand." He closed his eyes for a moment, unable to accept what was happening, and then opened them and looked at her bleakly. "Is there any chance this is . . . I don't know . . ."

"What?" she asked. "A mistake? Temporary? A big mix-up?" Impatiently, Maralyce grabbed his wrist and pulled the knife from her belt. Before he had a chance to object, she sliced across his forearm with it, cutting so deep he felt the blade grazing bone on its way through.

He cried out in pain, as the blood sprayed from his severed veins, but Maralyce refused to let him go. "Look!" she commanded. "You tell me, boy."

Declan forced himself to look, forced himself to watch the bleeding stop and the muscles begin to knit together. The pain was unbelievable, almost as unbelievable as what he was seeing.

Declan fell to his knees, Maralyce still gripping his arm, as his flesh repaired itself with alarming speed.

"No," he whispered through the pain. "Tides . . . not this . . ."

It wasn't Maralyce who said it aloud, however. It was Nyah who put Declan's greatest fear into words, making it so horribly final. It was as if somehow, by giving voice to the suspicion he'd been living with since waking up in the bottom of Stellan Desean's stolen dinghy without a mark, not a burn, even the wound Chikita had inflicted on his face a few hours earlier healed without a trace, she had made it real.

He glanced up and saw the little princess through his tears of despair and desolation, standing at the entrance to the forge, her eyes wide. She must have followed them from the cabin.

"Tides, Declan!" Nyah exclaimed. "You're an immortal."

EPILOGUE

Even through the ice, he could feel the Tide returning.

It was a subtle feeling at first, but then everything was subtle these days. His ability to feel anything, to even frame a coherent thought, was so painfully slow that the mere act of forming a sentence meant the first words were lost before the last words were thought of.

He lived on instinct now. And even then he wasn't sure if you could call this living. Maybe it was. If living was defined by awareness, then he was alive.

That was one thought he could form. The shortest sentence of all.

I am.

Beyond that, he was lost. Somewhere, he suspected, there must be an explanation. Logically, he did not come into being in this state. Somewhere in the frozen recesses of his mind were the reasons for his imprisonment. Somewhere the identities of those responsible for his stasis must be buried.

Should he ever find them, he'd decided—in a process that had taken centuries—should he ever escape this frozen prison, he would devote his time to repaying the favour.

It wasn't as if he didn't have the time. That was all he had, in fact.

He dreamed occasionally, immobile in his solid prison of ice. The dreams were sometimes pleasant, more often tormented. In them, he had an identity that seemed real and *right*.

Because in his dreams, more often than not, he was *God*.

And the Tide was turning.

He'd felt it come back before, several times. And then he felt it leave again. Each time it peaked, he seemed a little more aware of it. A little more able to understand that it *was* the Tide and that if he could only grasp it fully, he could be free.

He dreamed more often when the Tide was turning. Sometimes he saw faces. Faces he couldn't name. Faces whose names must be important, or why else would he dream of them?

Sometimes, too, he heard music. The music of cracking ice. The symphony of the shifting tectonic plates, something he felt through the very core of the planet, as much as heard, as if the music vibrated through him to compensate for his frozen ears.

He had no concept of time here. He couldn't imagine how long he'd been in this state. The memories of how he got here were frozen and beyond his reach.

But the music had changed subtly since the Tide had begun to turn. There was a different tenor to it now, a shift in the vibrations that heralded something out of the ordinary.

He tried to listen for it, to lean forward for a better chance to hear, but any movement he made existed only in his frozen imagination, so it was impossible to tell if this change was something new, or something he'd created in his own mind to alleviate the boredom.

The answer was too hard.

And it took so long to frame the thought that by the time he'd posed the question, he'd forgotten why he wanted to know.

He slept. And he dreamed of being God again.

And then the tenor of the Tide changed and he felt it.

He *felt* it.

The Tide swelled on the edge of his frozen awareness. It surged against the ice, surged against his ice-bound mind. Little by little he became aware, and with awareness came the pain.

He'd always understood he was frozen, but until now, the meaning of that was something he didn't have the awareness to appreciate.

He appreciated it now.

He was frozen. Worse, he was bone-chillingly *cold*, and it seeped through every frozen fibre of his being until it reached for his very soul. The ice around him crackled and split, but this wasn't the slow symphony of time, it was sharp and immediate and it hurt and he was *cold* . . .

The Tide swelled again as the realisation began to seep through his mind. The ice was melting. Cracking. Disintegrating around him.

His concept of time was still awry, so he had no idea how long the thawing took. The sound of dripping and then running water as the ice surrendered filled ears that had began to ache as they softened. The cracking of the walls that bound him, the pain and the bitter, blood-freezing cold were all he had the ability to focus on.

If there were memories, or any other thoughts in his mind, the pain overwhelmed them all . . .

And then a pain split his chest that left all the other agony a pale imitation of torment. He felt his heart force a beat, and then another, and he cried out, surprised to discover he *could* cry out, that his jaw moved and there was something left in his lungs to force past his vocal cords.

Another loud crack sounded, and the ice let him go. It was almost as if he was being spat out, an irritating seed being spat from the mouth of the ice monster. He crashed to the floor and would have screamed had he had the strength to do so. His limbs cried out in agony as joints immobilised for an unthinkable time were forced to move again. His heart laboured as blood so sluggish it felt like syrup moved through his veins.

He opened his eyes, squinting in the harsh torchlight reflecting off the icy cavern into which he had fallen. After a long moment, his eyes adjusted to the light, muscles unused for so long finding their purpose once more.

A face appeared in front of him, familiar, hated and yet welcome . . .

"Lukys?" he managed to gasp through his parched and frozen throat.

"Kentravyon!" his saviour replied with a smile more chilling than the icy cavern in which they were enclosed. "Welcome back."